MW01178117

T

BRIAN HILDEBRAND

THE NEVERMIND OF BRIAN HILDEBRAND

A NOVEL

MARTIN MYERS

CROWSNEST BOOKS
TORONTO · CHICAGO

Crowsnest Books
www.crowsnestbooks.com
Distributed by the University of Toronto Press

Cataloguing data available from Library and Archives Canada
ISBN 978-1-895131-27-7 (paperback)
ISBN 978-1-895131-28-4 (ebook)

Cover design by Kevin Cockburn
Printed and bound in Canada

THE NEVERMIND OF BRIAN HILDEBRAND

1

BACK IN A FLASH

ALL AROUND ME, there is a clamor of alarmed voices. I am having another one of those sudden, startling, personal flashbacks to an earlier time. Since I am the star of these mini-movies, the leading man, so to speak, in these brief, reflective, retrospective, film-like experiences, I've come to expect to see myself in one form or another, but on this occasion, all I'm able to see is the road surface, literally, smack in my mug, extremely close-up, and not at all friendly. I conclude from this that, in this particular retrospective recall, I'm lying face down on the road with my nose pressed into the pavement and, basically, what I'm looking at is a layer of asphalt. That would explain why I can't see myself, or anything else, for that matter. But I can hear what's happening and, as I've already said, all around me, there is a clamor of alarmed voices. A clamor. It has a classical ring to it, doesn't it? Right up there with hue and cry.

"Jeeziz!"

"Oh, man."

"Somebody call an ambulance."

3

"I already called. It's on the way."

"I can hear the siren."

"Anybody see what happened?"

"It was like slow motion in a movie. He parked, got out of his car. And then the car rolled and knocked him down and ran over him."

"What? His own car?"

"That's really weird."

"He walked in front of it. He was texting."

"It's this crazy street. We're on a hill. The car started rolling, knocked him flat on his face, and then rolled right over him."

"We have to help him."

"It may be too late."

"Doesn't look good. His head is under one of the back wheels."

"Is he alive?"

"How do you tell with him pinned under the car like that?"

"We can't just stand here talking till the ambulance shows up. We've got to do something."

"But what?"

"Let's at least try to lift the car off him."

"I'm parked just across the street. I'll get a jack from my trunk."

"No time. There are six of us. Maybe four of us can lift the back end enough so the other two can pull him out."

"All right. Let's try. All together guys. Ready? On the count of three. One. Two. Three. Lift. Up. Up. Now hold it there. Hold it. Quick. Move. Get him out."

"Okay. He's out."

"All right. Let the car down slowly."

"Good work, guys. We did it."

"But look at him. He's a mess."

"Is he breathing?"

"Barely. But there's a pulse."

"Anybody know the guy?"

"Yeah. He lives two doors over from me in the duplex. Brian something. I don't know his last name."

"He'll be in shock. We should put a blanket around him."

"Never mind. Here's the ambulance, now."

"And a fire truck right behind it."

"And two police cars."

"Well, at least, we did what we could."

"Poor bastard. I hope he makes it."

And on that dark note, the flashback comes to an abrupt end, leaving me with the realization that six of my neighbours got me out from under my car after it ran over me. I never knew that before. It was all blanked out until now. No one ever mentioned their help. Those guys, those neighbours, may have saved my life by lifting the car off me. I don't even know who they were. I wonder if I'll ever get a chance to find out and thank them.

NOW THAT I THINK ABOUT IT, five years on, maybe, I have no reason to thank them.

2

MORE ROPE

GIVE THE SUSPECT enough rope, the old saw goes, and he'll hang himself. Well, I'm not the suspect; I'm the protagonist, the put-upon protagonist as bad luck would have it. And besides, I don't have enough rope. And I'm almost at the end of the little rope I do have and hanging on to it for dear life and fear of death. All the while, all around me, the dying are doing what the dying do. Daily. Sometimes, twice daily. But so far, the dear departing have not included in their numbing number yours truly, your comatose but comprehending correspondent. Unlike my expiring fellow sufferers, I, the longer suffering I, the obsessively stubborn I, struggle on, hanging on, holding out, and as of this moment, holding forth, despite the coma I'm imprisoned in, despite the unmoving blob that I've become, despite the odds, the long odds. I am not a fan of long odds.

All right, let's be clear. I'm not supposed to be able to do what I'm doing. So say all the medical mavens, the neuro connoisseurs, the coma cognoscenti. But unbeknownst to the know-alls, to medicine, to science, to family, to friends, unbeknownst to the world, I'm actually conscious. Minimally conscious, some of those who used to call me a vegetable now say. But never mind. Quibble away. It doesn't matter what they say. I don't give a flying whatever for what they say. All that matters is that I'm fully conscious, fully cognitive, fully aware, but fully locked in, fully trapped in my own inert body. But my brain, the organ that reference books so blithely describe as "the control centre of the nervous system in vertebrates," though no longer in control in this vertebrate, is nonetheless not only fully employed, but over-employed, hyper-employed and frantically working away twenty-four seven, three sixty-five.

And ranting, ranting, ranting, as you may have noticed, as we move not so merrily along. But bear with me. I'll settle down in a minute.

3

NO PICTURES

"I'D PREFER no pictures," my mother says to Vince, the photographer who has come with Globe and Mail columnist, Heather Walker. Heather is doing a fifth anniversary follow-up story on the young executive who'd been left in a persistent vegetative state by a bizarre accident that the Globe had covered five years earlier. The young executive, that would be me, is still young but not looking very executive.

"I agreed to the interview," Bessie says to Heather, "because I enjoy your column and also because I'm hoping that press coverage may alert someone in the medical or scientific community with advanced knowledge or breakthrough technology that could somehow help Brian. But please, no pictures. I don't want my son turning into a sideshow."

"I understand. Well, then, how about just a casual shot of you?" asks Heather. "Nothing formal."

"Fine," says my mother. Then, deadpan, she turns to me and says, "Brian, you stay put while I talk to this helpful journalist, okay?"

"It's nice to see that you haven't lost your sense of humour through this long ordeal," says Heather.

"I try to do my best; it's not always easy," Bessie says. "But I'm programmed to be optimistic. Life must go on and in humour there is hope. I believe that."

"How much hope is there?" asks Heather. "It's been five years since Brian's accident. Where is the medical community on Brian's condition? Is any progress being made?"

"Progress, that's the key word. So far, there hasn't been much progress. Still, brain research is ongoing. There are new findings every day as neuroscience moves forward. And good news could conceivably be out there at any time. In the meantime, the medical profession still cautiously insists that Brian is in a persistent vegetative state. I still feel strongly that he's conscious but locked in. While continuing to cling to their original diagnosis, the medical community is now more respectful of my opinion and treat it as an option, however unlikely, but I had to make a lot of noise to get their attention."

"That has to be very tough," says Heather.

"Tough for me. Hell for Brian, I'm sure. And total incomprehension for everybody else. It's a daily struggle to stay positive. But that's the assignment on this project. The challenge is to keep Brian going until we have the science to unlock him. I'm sure he comprehends what's going on around him. I keep hoping that with enough outside encouragement and data input, maybe Brian can somehow figure out how to unlock himself from within. I know it sounds far-fetched but there are a lot of backup systems in the brain and if we can somehow trigger one or more of them maybe we can make some headway. The pun is intentional. We're working on it."

It's pretty much a given that with the passage of time the social networks of patients in long-term care facilities diminish. Not surprisingly, therefore, over several years my already short roster of visitors largely dwindles away. But then, for a couple of months after Heather Walker's article appears in the Globe and Mail, there is an upsurge of sympathetic strangers making the pilgrimage into my room, bearing gifts: flowers, religious icons, good luck tokens, as well as not very thoughtful but well-intentioned chocolates, wine, and whiskey. A farmer in Oxford County just outside Woodstock sends a bushel of apples that the Woodgreen staff, at Bessie's repeated invitation, gnash on for months. Of course, I am grateful for the kindness of strangers. But only the flowers really work for me. Camera-like, I record whatever is in my line of vision. Flowers are a favorite.

Thanks to the Globe article, there is also an outpouring of mail and email and cards, as well as a flurry of queries from medical researchers in Europe and in South America. One of the most promising comes from a deep coma researcher in Budapest. This sounds like it has good possibilities at first, looks hopeful for awhile, but after a spirited exchange of emails and phone calls, it becomes clear that the Hungarian's research is still at a very early stage and is not yet ready for prime time. Ultimately, it goes nowhere.

Just like me.

Disappointment, of course, abounds. Bessie tries to hide hers but I can tell. I don't have to hide my disappointment because no one else can tell. In any case, I force myself to get over my disappointment so I can get on with my life and my normal daily activities like not moving, not speaking, and talking to myself inside my head.

4

UTTERINGS AND MUTTERINGS

I don't look like I know what's happening. But don't be fooled by the look of me. Trust me, I know what's what. I know who's who. I'm clued in big-time. Hey, I not only know where it's at, I know where it's been. But, obviously, I can't tell anybody because I can't speak. My lips might as well be sealed. If it wasn't for what you're reading here, right now, I'd be unable to share my improbable story with you.

Lucky me. Baffled you. I'm confusing you, right? Wait. I'll spell it out for you. I can't speak. Okay? I have no outer voice. What you're reading, what's set down here, what you're probably picking at and puzzling over, are the utterings and mutterings of my inner voice, my hyper, non-stop, hippety-hop, inner voice rattling around inside the cage that my damaged head has become, nattering on and on, gibbering like a bloody marmoset, indulging in alliterative allusions and dim-witted delusions and firing off volleys of vile verse, limp-dick limericks and piss sonnets, for which you wouldn't pay a penny, even if you were henny and the sky was falling. How galling. It's appalling. I'm not just stalled. I'm stalling. Enough. Let's wrap up, rap off, rant less, and rock on. Am I waxing poetic or what? Or maybe it's just bile.

Now, here's an irony for you. Although there's no rousing me, my story is a rousing saga, an at times intemperate tale of a thousand and one sentences, beginning with the life sentence that I'm serving as a prisoner in my own mind. From that shaky launch pad, this convulsive and compulsive chronicle of mine blasts off daringly and unsparingly in all directions with at least a thousand other sentences that it will likely take to tell my unlikely story. Word by word, line by line, page by page, you will read here what my inner voice has somehow managed to convey. The core question is, how have I, the comatose I, the insufficient I, the limp lump on life support, been able to accomplish this remarkable feat?

Plunging in remarkable feat first, I'll do my best to answer that question, but to do so, I have to invite you into the chaotic, disordered, anarchic prison of my mind, my overtaxed, overloaded, overflowing mind. Please, come in and watch your step. It's a god-awful mess in here. I'm the biggest liability. And I don't have liability insurance. The insurance company took one look at me, packed up their actuarial tables, and left the room.

I know what you're thinking. What the hell is this all about? What's going on here? Who is this guy?

Well, let's start with a name. My name is Brian Hildebrand. Whatever you do, please, don't dismiss me as some sort of flaky metaphor. To be blunt upfront, I abhor the metaphor. That may sound like a jolly little jingle or a smartass bumper sticker, but the fact is metaphors fake me out and make me furious. Metaphors muck up meaning. And the verb is a euphemism and not a spelling error. Besides, even if I were to grumblingly agree to be thought of as a metaphor, what would I be a metaphor for? A metaphor, by definition, has to stand for something. And I don't stand for anything.

When you get right down to it, I don't stand, period. I can't stand. I can't move. I can't walk. I can't talk. As already repeatedly reported, I'm in a coma, on hold, long-term hold. So to the casual observer on the outside, not much seems to be happening in my comatose, life-supported life. But – big but, huge but - inside this hectic head of mine, between my ears, behind my eyes, inside my lobes, the whole world is happening, the whole wacky world. And what makes it even more distressing, more disconcerting, is that I'm constantly beset by simultaneity. It's happening all at once. In other words, it's not just a zoo in here but a circus, a circus of endless rings and dingalings and far too many other things.

All right. Given that I'm my own worst problem and, worst of all, that I'm a problem of my own making as I am about to make achingly clear, I try to take comfort in the fact that, despite a surplus of shortcomings, this mangled, manic mind of mine is not encumbered by any of the hard drive drivel or cyber electro burble that have become the hallmarks of the digital age. And best of all, frantic though it is, frenzied though it is, fraught though it is, my raging, ranting, roaring brain never crashes, never quits, never confronts with perplexingly numbered error messages, and never has to be restarted.

This surely warrants a whoop-dee-doo or two! But certainly not three. Three whoop-dee-doos would be pushing it. I never push my whoop-dee-doos. Truth to tell, I never push anything. I'm the one that needs pushing. But make no mistake, I'm no pushover.

I worry that I'm being too internal. I can't deny that, of necessity, I've become infernally internal. But you have to understand that thinking is all I'm able to do. I can't do anything else, nothing at all. Thinking has become my all, the awl with which I tediously struggle to stitch my torn and troubled being back together. In my singularly strained and straitened circumstances, this is easier said than done. That's worrisome enough but what's even more worrisome is that there are distressing moments when my brain, my overburdened brain, suddenly elects to have a mind of its own and proceeds to dredge up the dreary dregs of times past, the detritus of a squandered youth, bitter memories, acutely painful recollections, like the three devastating unpleasantries that befell me in my pre-coma days, back when I deluded myself that I had a life, when what I really had was a mess, a dozen or so years ago, over three hateful, fateful days in the decidedly unmerry month of May. That's why, for me at least May, not April, is the cruelest month. Sorry, Tom.

5

Three Unpleasantries in May

Three unpleasantries in May, cruel, cruel May. One, two, three, just like that. They stand out in retrospect because they were acutely, achingly painful. It's very strange, now, to recall how all three began with "I'm sorry, Brian" followed by an almost identical expression of regret from the person with whom I was pleading not only for my life but also for my wasteful, self-indulgent, self-defeating life style. In each case, my plea fell on deaf ears and was followed in quick succession by my being soundly lectured for my failings and then told in no uncertain terms to go away, to get lost, to fuck off. Please, forgive the Anglo-Saxon monosyllable. I get incensed when I recall the three-day débacle. That, incidentally, is an Anglo-Norman duosyllable. No forgiveness needed on that one.

"I'm sorry, Brian," said the dean on day one. "As you are well aware, your hockey scholarship must be renewed annually and is conditional on maintaining your grades. You performed well last year. But this year you dropped below the required grade level. As a consequence, your scholarship will not be renewed. I understand that without the scholarship, you can't afford to stay in school. You have two options. One is to ask for consideration on the grounds of stress. If stress problems are confirmed by the health services, bursary provisions may be possible. The other option is your hockey coach. If he feels strongly that losing you will hurt the team, he may be able to make a plea on your behalf to the alumni representative on the board of governors for special case financial assistance. Otherwise, failing the foregoing, you will be dropping out."

"I'm sorry, Brian," said the coach on day two. "You're wasting your time. Look, I don't need to hear your side of it. I already know your side of it. Everybody on the team knows your side of it. You're not going to get my support on this. Last year, you looked like a pro hockey prospect. But this year, you look like a bum. You're not playing like you used to, not scoring like you used to. You're just going through the motions, trying to stay out of the way. You're off your game. And consequently, off the team. It's a shame. But you've done it to yourself. Forget about hockey as a career. It's not going to happen for you. You're too into that playboy thing of yours to ever be a serious athlete. Stop and take a good hard look at yourself and make some decisions about what you want to do with your life when you grow up."

"I'm sorry, Brian," said Rivalda Santiago on day three. She didn't sound sorry. The oh so lovely Rivalda, a psychology major from Phoenix, Arizona, with whom I'd consorted at length and in depth, was furious and taking me apart.

"It's over," she intoned with vitriolic vehemence. "I've loved loving you but I can't go on like this. You're not just screwing me, you're screwing up my life. You don't see that, do you? Something is happening to you. I don't know what it is. But I can't deal with it. There's got to be more to my life than just crawling into the sack with you. I have plans, goals, dreams. I need to succeed in school, in a career, in my life. But if I stick with you, I'm trapped. Your life is falling apart, becoming a series of failures and starting to drag me down with you. I'm not going to let it happen. I can't do this anymore. It's over, finished. We're through."

But the tirade wasn't over. There was a final bravura outpouring before the curtain came down for the last time. "Farewell, dear, dear Brian. I'll always love you. And I'll never forget you. But Brian, I beg you, get your shit together and get your life sorted out. No, please, don't touch me. And don't come to the door with me. My bag is packed and at the door. I'll let myself out." Curtain.

One. Two. Three. Just like that. Three strikes and I'm out. And my game was hockey, not baseball. But with those three unpleasantries, it was game over. That was it. There would be no more fun and games. Still, nowadays, I sometimes foolishly try to reassure myself with yet another superficial cliché that that was then and this is now. The trouble is that as things have turned out now is not fun and games either. Now is more of a cross between intensive care and a detention center.

6

MILLIE

ONCE in a while I get fed up with the non-stop nattering of my relentless inner voice, going on and on, filling my head with thoughts and ideas that I can't share with anyone or do anything about. And when I've had enough, I will it to shut the fuck up, in effect, tuning out, turning my head off while I try to trance out and escape into inner silence and nothingness. Not that anyone would notice. In my circumstances, I always look tranced out. It comes with the territory, the extremely limited territory.

On one such occasion, while focused on inner silence, I am startled to have my silent reverie abruptly interrupted by a voice, a voice other than my own inner voice.

"Hi," says the voice, somewhat tentatively, it seems to me. "Are you here?"

It's the voice of a young girl, ten or eleven years old, I would guess. It's hard to tell for sure. Having been startled and trying, unsuccessfully to cling to the fleeting remains of my precious time-out, I realize with some alarm there is no one else in my room. I am alone. The voice, the girl's voice, is coming not from without but from within. The voice is in my head.

In my head! Wait a minute! How can this be? Has the gated community between my ears been breached, broken into, invaded, infiltrated? Where the hell is security? Where is the concierge? As if I didn't have enough going on in my head! Would I now have to put up with two voices yammering at each other in my already overloaded noggin? Just what the doctor ordered. Jeezis!

"Hi," says the visiting voice again, less tentatively this time. "Are you here?"

My briefly snoozing inner voice snarls back to wakefulness.

"Of course, I'm here. Where else would I be? I'm not out there, am I? And neither are you. You're in my head. How did you get into my head?"

"I don't really know. I was in my room, doing my homework. And suddenly, here I am."

"How did you manage to do that?"

"It just happens. I sometimes have these episodes."

"What episodes? What are you talking about?"

"I may be autistic."

"That's no explanation. You don't sound autistic."

"I may be a high functioning autistic, they say."

"They? Who are they?"

"The doctors."

"The doctors? Don't talk to me about doctors. What do they know?"

"I'm normal, they say, except for these episodes."

"Is that what this is? An episode?"

"I guess so. That's what they call it. Once in awhile, I just drift off and pop into somebody's head for a few minutes. I don't know why. Nobody knows why. I can't control it. And then, next thing I know, I drift back and I'm in my room again doing my homework. It only happens when I'm doing my homework."

"That doesn't sound like autism. Let's try a little experiment. What's my name?

"Your name? Your name is Brian."

"Okay. Now, how did you know that?"

"I don't know. It just came to me."

"Well, there you are. You're not autistic. Maybe you're psychic. What's your name?"

"Don't you know?"

"No. I'm not psychic. I wish I were."

"Well, then, I guess I better tell you. My name is Millie."

"How old are you, Millie?"

"Twelve."

"Where are you when you're not popping into other people's heads?"

"In Sedona."

"Never heard of it."

"I guess you don't get out much, do you?"

"I don't get out at all, Millie. Where exactly is Sedona?"

"It's in Arizona."

"Sedona, Arizona? That rhymes. You're a long way from home. This is Toronto. Not much rhymes with Toronto."

"What about Tonto and pronto?"

"I never thought of those. They might be fine in Arizona, I suppose, but they wouldn't do much good in Toronto."

"I haven't come this far before. Mostly this happens to me right in Sedona."

"And you go to school in Sedona?"

"Yes. I'm in junior high."

"What does your dad do?"

"I don't know. He split with my mom before I was born."

"I'm sorry."

"Me, too. Oh. Oh. I have to be going. I'm starting to drift back."

"Wait."

"There's nothing I can do. I'd better say goodbye."

"We need to talk some more. Can you come back?"

"I don't know. These episodes just happen and…"

There is a sound like a sigh and then, silence.

"Try to come back," my inner voice says.

But there's no response. And despite my earlier antagonism, I'm overcome with a feeling of sadness and disappointment. Still, I can't help but wonder if this is really happening to me. Maybe I'm coming unglued. Maybe I'm not only in my mind but also out of my mind. Maybe I'm a nut case. Maybe I'm hallucinating. Maybe it's all a dream. Maybe I'll soon wake up and find that I don't exist.

7

IN THE CLEAR

HAVE I mentioned the window washer who's been hanging around, dangling at the end of a rope outside my window? Maybe I should. He's a wiry little guy in a faded blue windbreaker with a scraggly black beard, one raised eyebrow, and squinty gray eyes. His presence on a rope outside my window is very strange because my room is on the ground floor of Woodgreen and my window should be washable from the ground ropelessly.

Ropelessly? Now, there's a word you don't see too often, if at all. I'm happy to include it for your entertainment and edification at this time.

In any case, it appears that I'm alone in my concerns about what's going on just outside my window. No one else seems to be aware of either the redundant rope or the persistent window washer. The nurses never acknowledge the dangling man's presence in any way. Nor does anyone else. Not Bessie. Not any of the physiotherapists who come in daily to work on my muscles to keep them from turning into mush. Not even the cleaning staff who in cleaning my room also clean the inside of the window. It certainly appears as if the window washer hanging outside my window is apparent only to me. I assume that his presence is a sign of some sort, but is it a good sign or a bad sign? Or maybe it's an omen. But good? Or bad? How do you assess these things? Ropelessly which rhymes with hopelessly is all I can come up with.

All this is odd enough. But what makes it even odder is that often the window washer is out there day after day, much more frequently than any normal window washer should be. Despite the old adage dating back to the ancient Greeks that you can't wash your windows too often, maybe you can. How do you quantify window washing? How much is too often?

Seated on a tiny plywood seat, my little washer guy dangles daily outside my window at the end of a rope. Is there a message here? Is the end of the rope meant to be the end of his rope or mine? Which of us is at the end of his rope? Since my room is on the ground floor, what the dangling man is doing makes no sense whatsoever unless he's deliberately trying to either send me a message of some sort or keep me under close surveillance. I can't imagine why he would want to do either of those. Still, he seems to be dedicated to the location and committed to his task, whatever it is. His sponge and squeegee glide smoothly over the glass without ever appearing to touch it. Yet he thoroughly cleans the panes. My window is always spotless. How many of us can say that about our windows or about ourselves, for that matter? We all have a spot or two.

As he goes about his business, he never smiles, my window washer, and never takes his eyes off me. From a hook attached to his seat hangs a pail of sudsy window washer water. From a backpack he extracts the expected tools of his trade. But once in a while, he extracts the unexpected; on one occasion, a cellphone on which he checks his email and then makes a call. At precisely the same time, my room phone rings. Is it a coincidence? I wonder. Or can he be trying to phone me? When I'm unable to answer either the phone or the question, he puts his phone back into his backpack and extracts a small chalkboard and a piece of chalk. He writes on the chalkboard and then holds it up to show me what he has written.

It says, "All clear."

I assume he's talking about the window. But how can I be sure? "All clear" does have a kind of official ring to it. Does it mean it's safe to emerge from the bombshelters? Then, again, it could mean the plunger worked and it's safe to flush the toilet. I'd love to flush the toilet. It's been years since I flushed a toilet.

On other days, my window washer chalkboards me an ongoing series of ever changing "clear" messages. A few examples: "Do I make myself clear?" "I can see clearly now." "Let's be clear." "Is that clear?" "Let's clear this up." "Clear enough for you?" "You're in the clear."

Clearly, this guy's a joker and he's got a million of them.

One sunny afternoon, when his windbreaker is not done up, I'm able to read the inscription on his T-shirt. Hanging over a desert scene of red rock formations, are the words, Sedona, Arizona. This gives me pause. Is this another coincidence or is this part of the conspiracy that Amos's mother keeps going on about? Bear with me. I'll get to Amos in a minute.

There's something almost mythical about my window washer, almost as mythical maybe as the long-forgotten window washers of ancient Greek mythology who never get a mention in our history books. Don't believe me? Check it out for yourself.

The window washer's backpack also has an inscription on it, a much smaller one that I finally make out. It says, "Clear out." And below it the word "Millie."

Could my persistent window washer be an angel-sent messenger? If so, I don't care for the angel's message. There's no way that I can clear out.

8

GOOD MORNING, JEFFERSON

THIS MORNING, just as he has five mornings a week for the last five years, Jefferson strides briskly into the inky dinky darkness of my silent room, slashes open the vertical blinds to let the daylight sidle through the slats, taps the remote control that cranks my motorized bed – and my silent, staring, unmoving form along with it – into an approximation of the sitting position. Look, mom, I'm sitting! Oh, how my mother would like to hear me say that. Or anything else, for that matter. But there's no way. And all the while, Jefferson smiles at me. Every morning, without fail, he smiles at me. And he talks to me. I can't tell you how much this means to me. I can't tell Jefferson either. Jefferson has no idea how much it means to me because I'm unable to react, unable to communicate, unable to tell him. Jefferson's consistent and amiable communicative behavior may be partly in response to my mother's frequently declared theory that some of whatever is said or done in my presence ("not just the mindless TV," she repeatedly insists) will get through to me and maybe help me climb out of the nothingness in which, the neurologists insist, I am forever hopelessly suspended.

"Nothingness? Bullshit!" rails my mother. She's not buying it. She has lectured – hectored would be more accurate – the specialists and the nursing staff endlessly on the subject of her hopes for my ultimate recovery. She's relentless. She never lets up. And make no mistake, I'm grateful for it.

Good old mom. Where would I be without her? The next question in this hopeless self-quiz is: Where am I with her? The answer to both questions is, for the moment the same. Nowhere. That's where I am. Nowhere. Welcome to nowhere! Thanks for coming by.

"How you doing today, dude?" Jefferson says, giving me a little pat on the head.

I don't react. I would if I could. I wish I could. But I can't. Not waiting for the response he knows he won't get, Jefferson gently sponges my face with a warm facecloth. Then he cleans up the rest of me. He's very thorough. It's a tedious routine that he's become used to, removing all the night's wastes, replacing soaked pads, soiled linens, tidying as he goes, straightening blankets, fluffing up pillows, turning me to prevent bedsores, adjusting my feeding tube, checking that my mechanical ventilator is running smoothly, making sure that all my shunts and hook-ups and connections are in place and intact and finally, that all my meds bags are topped up and working. On his way out, he stops for a moment, lingers briefly in the doorway, surveying the room one more time, to make sure all the bells and whistles – all my bells and whistles – are in order and delivers a closing statement.

"Now, you stay cool, dude," he says, grinning and wagging a finger at me in mock admonishment. "And call if you need anything," he adds as he departs.

Call if I need anything? Give me a break. I need everything. Jefferson's joking, of course. But he's not making fun of me. He knows that I couldn't call if my life depended on it. I hope it never will. It's just Jefferson's way of showing respect for me not merely as a hapless patient dangling at the end of his rope but as a living being, as a life upended and then, suspended, a life with little hope. Out of rope and out of hope but not giving in or giving up, that's the quintessential Brian Hildebrand. Not an ideal arrangement, I grant you. But when you're nowhere, somewhere is anywhere you want to go but can't get to. That's either profound or obscure. Or maybe, it's profoundly obscure.

Jefferson Baines is my daytime nurse and he comes on duty every morning at seven a.m. Jefferson – no one ever calls him Jeff – is thirty-eight, a big black bruiser, built like a tank, six foot four maybe, about two hundred and twenty-five pounds. And he still looks like the lineman he was when he played college football for Tuskegee U in Alabama. That was maybe fifteen years ago before moving to Toronto after graduation with his Canadian bride. And though Jefferson believes, like the rest of the nursing staff, that I'm right out of it and that there's no way that I can communicate or be communicated with, he talks to me much more than the other nurses.

I sense it's not just because my mother encourages him to, but because he feels great compassion for my plight and believes talk is comforting, if not healing. Every morning, without fail, he tries to chat me back to my old self. He jokes with me. And we chuckle together except that he does all the audible chuckling. I chuckle to myself, internally. He often interviews me, asks me questions. And then he answers them himself. Sometimes, his answers are even better than mine.

He tells me all sorts of things. I know all about his life and his wife, Inez—she's an x-ray technician at Mount Sinai Hospital and one of the world's great cookie bakers—and his kids: twin boys, Adam and Aaron, and a girl, Rose, all in high school at Harbord Collegiate—and his interests: he's a conscientious conservationist and rides to work on a ten-speed bicycle, writes poetry and has written a novel that he's trying to get published. He has told me all this and more. But, of course, he has no idea that it's getting through to me, no idea that I understand what he's telling me, and that I'm retaining it all in the soft hard drive of my frenetic, hyperactive mind. If only my soft hard drive could send wireless email. If only. Where's the bloody router when you need it?

Jefferson. That's pretty much how the day starts, every day, in the life support unit at Woodgreen House. Woodgreen is a long-term care facility, a sort of specialty hospital for patients who, after treatment, have been released from regular hospitals but who can't go home because there is no home to go to or because their ongoing medical conditions or disabilities won't permit them to function at home, if they function at all. Woodgreen, however, functions very well and is an excellent facility of its kind. I don't know what I would do without it. But it's not a fun place.

I can sum it up for you in a sound bite. Woodgreen is a haven, a hospice, a holding station, for patients where there's still a little bit of life but not a hell of a lot of hope. Sound bite, sound bit, sound bitten, sound awful, sound off, sound mind. Never mind. I'd like to hope there's hope. Surely, the fact that you're reading my words here has to mean there is at least some hope. But how can that be? I'm supposed to be in a coma and unable to communicate. It's ironic. As you'll discover, if you bear with me, the point here is how I'm somehow able to communicate. It's an unbelievable tale. I'm not sure I believe it myself, and I often wonder if it's really happening. Maybe I'm making the whole thing up. I wouldn't put it past me. I can be a tricky bastard. Thank you, for believing in me.

And while you're believing in me, let's start by getting some of the believable but depressing stuff out of the way. I think we can agree that being kept alive on life support for five years is not much of a life. Still, that life, such as it is, is mine and it's the only one I've got. And I cling to it, grimly at times, desperately at others, but resolutely, always resolutely. I'm not ready to give up and pack it in. Again, I hope I don't sound bitter. Believe me, I'm not. I know I'm repeating myself. But I'm just trying to emphasize that although I may whine a teeny bit from time to time or toss off a rant or two, it's mostly out of impatience rather than bitterness. The fact is, I'm beyond the bitterness, now. After all, I could, when all is done and said, have been undone and dead. Which, in the minds of some – though not in mine – might have been preferable. If my medical advisors had had their say and their way, I'd have been unplugged, unhooked, and unceremoniously carted off to the boneyard long ago. Or boothill. No future in either of those. This here ain't no cowboy movie. Westward no!

This protracted medical misadventure of mine began with a traumatic brain injury or TBI as it's called in the brain trade. I'd been run over by my own car and was unconscious. Imaging showed hemorrhaging in the skull. It was not a pretty picture. Nobody was asking for reprints. Nobody was betting on my making it.

"He may or may not wake up," the attending physician told my mother. "And if he does, he may or may not be your son."

He didn't say whose son I might be, if I wasn't hers. And, at that point, my mother was too freaked out to ask.

9

HOW I BECAME AN ACRONYM

AFTER THE ACCIDENT, a team of critical care specialists did their professional damnedest to maintain blood flow to all parts of my brain in order to relieve intercranial pressure and also to cool my body hoping to prevent further damage and promote healing. Still, it was all the flip of a coin. I lost the toss and didn't wake up. At least, as far as any one could tell. And no one knows what became of the coin. It seems to have gotten lost, too.

Platoons of medicine's finest, brigades of brain surgeons and troops of neurologists, experts all, and good, decent, caring guys of all genders marched in and repeatedly confirmed that I was brain dead. Brain dead, brain dead, brain dead, became the medical mantra when, in fact, albeit unrecognized by all of the no-way-naysayers, my brain was still on active duty. But I was the only one who knew it. And I, of course, silent and prone, was in no position to point this out, was I? Talk about still life.

As far as they were concerned—all those learned experts, all those white-coated, well-intentioned, medspeak, jargon-heads—I had regressed from traumatic brain injury to persistent vegetative state. And they insisted that if I existed at all, it was in a persistent vegetative state. PVS, they call it. I'd gone from one acronym to another, from TBI to PVS. And I'd done it PDQ. Pretty damn quick, that's life in the big city.

I'm not a big fan of acronyms. I'm not even a small fan. PVS especially gets up my nose. Is that a confusing acronym or what? PVS. It could be plastic pipe or a television network or pretty vucking stupid or a lifetime sentence. Go ahead. Pick one. Persistent vegetative state? If they'd been right, you'd be reading the utterances of a cabbage or a rutabaga. Do I sound like a cabbage or a rutabaga? But I must get off my rant and get on with my tale which, I promise, is about to get a little less dreary.

10

THE WOODGREEN WANDERER

ONE DAY, something oddly hopeful happens. The Woodgreen wanderer shuffles into my room. The wanderer is a longtime patient called Amos who keeps leaving his own room and erratically wandering about the hospital getting lost. Woodgreen personnel are used to this. Amos wears a tag saying: Please return Amos to Room 203.

Amos is very tall, very thin, gaunt almost, very gray, both hair and skin, and he wears a dreary chenille dressing gown also gray and badly worn once-blue velvet slippers. He carries with him a plastic shopping bag filled with torn up paper scraps. He never goes anywhere without it. Amos has come into my room a few times before but he has never said much, and the little he has said has not made much sense.

What I know about Amos I have overheard in conversations of hospital staff. Apparently, as a young law student, Amos repeatedly fails the bar exams and after three or four failures, he goes into long-term clinical depression. At the time, one of the treatments of choice for this unhappy condition is a prefrontal lobotomy, a surgical procedure, now long discredited. This surgery is recommended by the leading brain surgeons of the day to Amos's distraught mother who, not well versed in these matters, nor well balanced herself—she thinks everything is a conspiracy—agrees, without seeking a second opinion.

For a week after the operation, Amos appears to be back to his normal self and there is much rejoicing. Then, he grows silent, withdrawn, incoherent and fades away into a ghost of his former self. And now, thirty years later, he is a shambling fifty something, brains permanently scrambled, body permanently institutionalized, and given to bouts of wandering about the hospital corridors getting lost. A sad and lonely gray figure and not particularly good company, he now stands at the foot of my bed looking intently at me.

Expecting little that is meaningful from him, I am startled when he says, "Maybe we should talk."

My inner voice reflexively says, "I'd like to but I can't."

"What do you mean you can't?" Amos says.

I am stunned even more speechless than my usual silent self but still manage to say in my inner voice, "You can hear me?"

"Sure. What's the big deal?"

I desperately don't want this unlikely conversation to stop. I frantically try to figure out how to respond. Finally, I say, "How are things going?"

"Not so great. My mother died last year. No one visits. There's no one to talk to. I'm having these headaches. And every time I go for a walk they tell me I'm lost and take me back to room 203. It's a real drag. How about you?"

"Same old. Same old. Not much changes. They still think I'm a vegetable, but actually I'm locked in. You're the first person here that I've been able to talk to."

"Maybe we could talk some more."

"Good idea. You want to sit down for a while?"

"I can't. I have to keep moving or I get antsy. I could come back tomorrow."

A light goes on. Suddenly, I have a plan.

"Tomorrow would be fine. Can you come about lunchtime? My mother will be here then. I'd like her to meet you. You could talk to her, too."

"Tomorrow lunchtime? Okay."

I grow excited by the possibilities of Amos facilitating a communications breakthrough with Bessie.

"Maybe you could tell my mother what I tell you."

"Can't you tell her yourself?"

"No, I can't. She can't hear me. But you can. You could be my intermediary, sort of like my translator."

"I've never done that before. That would be interesting. Okay. I'll come back tomorrow."

"Lunchtime. Brian's room. Will you remember how to find me? Don't get lost."

"Brian's room. Don't worry. I'll find you. Inside my mind, I'm not nearly as screwed up as they think I am."

"Me, either," I add in solidarity with my newly acquired colleague.

"Okay. I'm going now."

Even as Amos shuffles out, clutching the plastic shopping bag with the torn-up paper scraps in it, I realize with falling heart that my exciting breakthrough plan is already in dire jeopardy. At the very moment of his departure, my mind takes what appears to be a diagnostic turn, and I somehow detect in Amos a life-threatening brain aneurism. His condition is critical. He is at death's door and running out of time. I try unsuccessfully to reject this dire foretelling.

The next day at noon, Bessie, the indefatigable mother of mine, arrives but Amos, the lost, shuffling wanderer, doesn't. I learn later, to my extreme distress, that Amos is lost again, this time for good. He has died that morning.

I am overcome with grief. I would cry if I could. A lamentation is the best I can manage. Oh, Amos, poor Amos, I am so sorry. I had such high hopes for you. Farewell to the Woodgreen wanderer. And to my brilliant breakthrough communications plan.

11

BESSIE

As YOUR doubting Thomas eyes drift in disbelief and perhaps even dismay, over these high flown, possibly overblown statements, I, the supposed source of what you are reading, and deemed by the experts to be in a persistent vegetative state, am entrapped in the tentacles of a state-of-the-art life support system and kept alive largely at the stubborn insistence of my mother, Bessie Hildebrand. But I've already told you that.

Now, let me tell you a little more about my mother. Bessie Hildebrand is the head librarian at the Law Society of Upper Canada. If I appear to have more facility with language than you'd expect of a jock drop-out, I can thank my mother for that. Born in Manchester in the UK, she had to battle her way out of the north country dialect of her family and learn, as she put it, to "talk posh." She passed some of that onto me. I can't talk posh these days, but when it suits me I can think posh, as you may have noticed.

But even posh-talking librarians are not generally known for their influence on medical professionals, some of whom are more likely to be swayed by the blandishments of pharmaceutical detail people. And Bessie, the librarian, might easily have been dismissed by the neurological experts as a just another deeply concerned mother or an obsessive crank but for the fact that she's an accredited telepath and somewhat of an expert herself. In addition to a doctorate in library science, she is a widely recognized forensic clairvoyant and sometime consultant to the law enforcement community. She has helped solve many a case, including some famous ones. The RCMP swears by her. And so do the FBI, Scotland Yard, and Interpol. Presented by the constabulary with the problem and the pertinent data, she just goes very still, looks off into the distance and then tells them where to look for the body or the loot or the killer, and she's right on the mark about ninety percent of the time.

On one particularly memorable occasion, she pinpointed the precise location of a thirty-million-dollar drug stash in the Nevada desert. I don't know how she does it. I don't think she knows. But in any case, thanks to her credentials as a frequently consulted clairvoyant, Bessie was able to convince the medical skeptics that, despite my apparently comatose state, she was picking up emanations from the otherwise inert me very strongly indicating to her that I was not brain dead.

So here I am, five years on, still thinking posh and still clinging to the edge of the ledge. If I'd had a standard mom, I'd have been gone with the wind long ago. Clearly, Bessie is not your run-of-the-mill mom or your run-of-the-stacks librarian either. In addition to her forensic telepathic talents, she has also been known, from time to time, to peer into the future and make profound sounding prophetic pronouncements, mostly ambiguous, frequently jocular. I don't mean to make Bessie sound like an oddball, but she's a character and has always had—how shall I put this—her idiosyncratic moments.

In the north country of Great Britain, where Bessie was born and where idiosyncrasy is not only cherished but also cultivated as a cultural credential, she'd have been affectionately called an eccentric, and they would have loved her. In any case, I love her and she loves me and I owe her, not only for giving me my first life when as a single mother she bore me full term and delivered me under straitened circumstances, but also for my second life, as a born again vegetable—well, alleged vegetable. Without my beloved Bessie's insistent resolve and intervention, the white-coated ward healers would have pulled the plug on me years ago. And, then, of course, you wouldn't be reading this, would you? But miraculously—and thankfully—you are. But I've already told you that. There I go, repeating myself again. I have a tendency to repeat myself. There is, after all, a certain repetitive quality to my circumstances. Or maybe I'm trying too hard to be the reliable narrator. So I'd better get on with it.

I must have inherited my sense of humour from my mother. Bessie Hildebrand, in addition to her many other unusual qualities, can be outrageously funny. When I was growing up, without a father to talk to, Bessie would make up for it, by talking to me for two, usually over the dinner table. We'd have long discussions on all sorts of subjects that would suddenly veer off the wall into comic dialogues, sometimes to the point of inanity and forgetting to eat. Here's my memory of one such. I was about ten at the time.

"Are we gonna eat soon, Bessie?"

"That depends on what you mean by soon, Brian."

"What I mean by soon is right away."

"In that case, we're not going to eat soon. We're going to eat in a little while."

"Aren't soon and a little while the same?"

"Not if soon means right away."

"What's the hold up?"

"There's no holdup. Do you see a gun anywhere?"

"No. But why can't we eat now, Bessie?"

"We have to cook first. I'm your mother, Brian. How come you never call me Mom?"

"I'm your son, Bessie. How come you never call me Son?"

"Would you like me to call you Son?"

"No way."

"You don't like to be called Son. How about I call you Moon?"

"Moon? Come on, Bessie."

"Don't you like the name Moon, Brian?"

"No."

"And you don't like Mom either? Is that it?"

"No. I call you Bessie because I like the name Bessie. Don't you?"

"Of course, I do. That's why I chose it."

"How could you choose your own name? Didn't your parents give you a name?"

"They did. They named me Beth. But it made me sound like I lisp. And I hated the jokes when I was introduced to anybody. Have you met Beth? And they'd answer, Yeth."

"That's not true. You're kidding me, aren't you, Bessie?"

"If you can't kid your own kid, who can you kid?"

"Your kid is starved, Bessie. Can we eat now?"

"I just told you. Dinner's not cooked yet."

"In that case, can we cook now?"

"Yeth."

"Don't you mean Yessie, Bessie?"

At the time, I simply assumed that all kids had this kind of jocular relationship with their moms. Later, of course, I learned otherwise. But Bessie and I continued our comedic exchanges into my adulthood, face to face, by phone, by mail, by e-mail, right up to the time of my accident. And then, when the trading of quips suddenly stopped, she was left with the stage all to herself, carrying on in what in effect was a monologue, and it was a sad one. Still, over time, some of the humour of old crept back into what had become one-woman performances.

Bessie comes to visit me daily, generally dropping in at noon, clutching her lunch, usually a sandwich and a cup of black coffee. After the hug contrived between all my life supporting paraphernalia and the kiss and the pat on the arm, she sits in a chair near the foot of the bed, so she can look directly into my face. Nibbling away reflectively at her sandwich – on dark rye, always on dark rye – and carefully sipping away at her too hot coffee, she is still and thoughtful for a few minutes and then she starts.

"You're in there, aren't you, Brian? You can't fool me. I know you're in there. Come on. There has to be some way you can tell me. I'm your mother. We never had secrets from each other. You can fool all those other guys, but I know you're in there. Work with me on this. Give me a sign, a signal, that you hear me. Try. Anything, a wink, a blink, a tear. Hell, even a fart will do."

Then she looks at me sternly for a minute and adds, "Just don't overdo it."

Overdo it? I couldn't do it at all without help. Still, my mind never stops working, never stops churning out thoughts, never stops sending out messages. But I might as well be talking to myself. The fact is I am talking to myself. Despite Bessie's talents as a clairvoyant, beyond picking up faint emanations of brain activity, she is unable to receive my thoughts, unable to read my mind. Oh, she tries and tries and keeps trying but it just doesn't happen. It's frustrating to her and to me. If any two people should be able to communicate telepathically, it should be Bessie and Brian. But no such luck. No such link.

12

RESTORATION

As MENTIONED earlier, my name is Brian Hildebrand. Only in my present tightly constricted circumstances did it occur to me that the name Brian was an anagram for the word brain, which was not much help since all the aforementioned experts kept insisting that I no longer had one that worked. Even less help, if such a thing is possible, was the fact that the word brain rhymes with bird brain, which I confess, I, in clear retrospect was, in my callous, incautious, devil-may-care youth. As luck would have it, however, I was also a promising young hockey player. That's how I managed to get accepted into Cornell University in Ithaca, N.Y., on a hockey scholarship. Cornell has had a long love affair with promising young Canadian hockey players.

Unfortunately, the promising young hockey player didn't keep his promise. The hockey didn't stick. Surrounded by a surfeit of comely coeds, I tried to stick handle my way around as many as possible, a playboy, in effect, playing the field instead of the rink and the lecture hall, all to the detriment of both my game and my studies. On this unwise, ill-advised extra-curriculum of my own rutting, alpha male design, I became especially enamored of Rivalda Santiago whose angry departure I lamented earlier. A big man on campus but flailing on the ice and failing in the classroom, I was, as testified in my rambling preamble, unable to maintain my grades, lost my scholarship, got cut from the team, got dumped by Rivalda, and was dropped out of Cornell at the end of second year. Farewell, Cornell. Farewell, hockey. Farewell, Rivalda. Hello, uncertainty.

Though saddened by all of this and distraught at losing Rivalda, whom I loved madly, I somehow sensed that I would make my way. Still, it was tough on my mother. Bessie had had such high hopes for me. She had never married. I was her life, an only child. And she was an only parent. I had no other and never knew my father. Neither, I learned early, did my mother, except in the biblical sense, of course. As lust would have it, Bessie was a free spirit in her girlhood and there was a short list of biblical paternal possibilities, but it would have taken DNA testing to sort out the lusty listees, if they could be found, to establish fatherhood. Bessie never tried. I never pushed it. Neither of us really wanted to deal with it. Husbandless, fatherless, feckless, it didn't seem to matter to us, somehow. We supported each other, relied on each other, and that was enough. Though mom was distressed by my fall from academic and athletic grace, I hastened to assure her that she needn't worry. I would, I promised, buckle down, sort myself out, and make her proud of me. And much to everyone's surprise, including my own, I soon did. And she was. Albeit only briefly.

13

THE BIG CRUNCH

CASTING ABOUT for a career path (corporate jargon for looking for a job with prospects), I was able to trade on my hockey background to talk myself into a job as a management trainee with Health House, a large health food chain founded by fitness guru and former Maple Leaf hockey star, Mitt Shlage. As luck would have it, as a body building gym rat, working out three times a week, I was a good fit for fitness. I took to the work, applied myself and quickly moved up in the marketing department and into the upper corporate ranks.

It's laughable in retrospect that one of my claims to fame should have been the vitamin enriched mini-bagel. Though never acknowledged, I was one of the first to recognize the enriched mini-bagel as the next big thing that was a little thing with a hole in it. Early in my corporate career, I suggested to Health House senior management that the vitamin enriched mini-bagel should be added to the Health House product list. But this suggestion was, sad to say, resisted for years out of concern about possible confusion due to the similarity in product shape to the nutritionally deficient deadly donut and, also, out of unwarranted fear that the mini-bagel was somehow too exotic for the company's cautious customer base. By the time senior management finally embraced the enriched mini-bagel as if they had invented it, I was long out of the Health House picture. In fact, I was out of everybody's picture by then, including my own. Let me tell you how that happened.

Five years ago, at twenty-four, I was promoted to vice president of marketing of Health House. This was accompanied by the customary appointment notice in the Globe and Mail's Report On Business, the smiling, slightly tilted, head shot, the neatly knotted power tie, the congratulatory cliché copy, the whole much ado about not too much. I was delighted, of course, and so was my mother. I had only held the position for four weeks when suddenly my life was changed forever by a car. This led to a write-up in the news section of The Globe and Mail headlined:

YOUNG EXECUTIVE CRITICALLY INJURED IN BIZARRE ACCIDENT

I'm repeating myself but bear with me. There will be a modicum of new information. I was run over by my own car. And guess what? I was at fault. I did it to myself. Does it sound unlikely? It was. And I was as sober as a justice of the supreme court. The accident was the result of stupidity, compounded stupidity. And whose stupidity, do you suppose it was? Mine, of course, who else? The stupidity was mine, mine, all mine, mine alone. Debit where debit is due.

One snowy Sunday in late January, after brunch with Carey Shumaker, a visiting former team-mate of mine from Cornell, I had parked my car, a brand-new BMW 328i, facing downhill on steeply sloping Churchill Street where I was living at the time in a rented duplex. I had bought the car a few weeks earlier, to celebrate my promotion, and at the dealer's suggestion, put a hundred-pound bag of sand in the trunk to overcome the tendency of the car's light rear end to fishtail on wintry roads. After parking, I had unthinkingly left the vehicle in neutral, failed to set the handbrake, neglected to turn the wheels into the curb. And then, to cap it all off, texting, I had walked unconcernedly, unthinkingly, in front of the car which had meanwhile, unbeknownst to me, started slowly rolling downhill and which, as it picked up speed, knocked me to the ground where I lay stunned as it rolled over me. One of the rear wheels ran over my head. The car was equipped with snow tires with deep treads. The extra hundred pounds of sand in the trunk may have added to the trauma and helped to make a good impression. I still bear the distinctive Michelin tread marks as head marks.

As far as future parking on hills was concerned, this should have been a wake-up call. But I never woke up, never regained consciousness, at least as far as anyone knew. And as I pointed out, I was repeatedly declared brain dead by some of the brainiest brains in medicine. No one was in the control tower, the brainiacs insisted, as I lay there like a corpse, unmoving, staring fixedly ahead, yet taking it all in, hearing every word, unable to speak, unable to utter a sound, unable to rebut the wrong diagnosis of my would-be healers. To this day, I don't know why the electroencephalograms showed no brain activity. Maybe my electrical circuitry is inherently faulty. Maybe there was a short circuit. Or maybe, I'm just not electrical. Maybe, I run on natural gas. Lord knows, I have enough of it. In the interest of decorum, I will resist the temptation to regale you with flatulence jokes and get on with my tale.

Poor Brian will be a vegetable for life and that's no life, even for a vegetable, those monitoring me continued to report. No brain activity, no hope, no point in prolonging this sad state, they insisted, recommending I be taken off life support. But as always, that wonderfully stubborn mother of mine came to the rescue. Bessie wasn't having any of it. She had her own sources—they could have been extraterrestrial, for all I know—and she insisted—quite rightly, as it turned out—that I was not brain dead, made a fuss, got the media involved, turned my unhappy circumstances into a cause célèbre, and wouldn't let the medicos pull the plug on me.

So here I am, five years later, still on life support, sustained by my mother's insistence, by the constant care of dedicated attendants, and by cutting edge biomedical technology and all its aids, adjuncts and attachments, the whole gritty, grotty, life-saving lot, without which I would have gone bye-bye and long ago been landfill instead of bed fill. Of late, I look like an experiment in somebody's lab, and I wonder, if that's the case, when the results of the experiment will be published. Not until there are some, I would suppose. So far, at least, there is a decided lack of results. And I'm not the one who decided.

While I'm grateful for my continued existence, constricted though it is, I have to say that even though my sharply attenuated lifestyle marginally beats being dead, it's a kind of purgatory. Where the hell would I be without the concept of purgatory? It's a very useful concept for a person in my unimproving state of disrepair and despair. I try, of course, to take comfort in my private knowledge—and the frustrating reality—that my brain isn't dead as alleged. Still, there's no escaping the fact that I'm a prisoner not only in my head but also in my body, unable to move a muscle. Not a one. Nothing. Nada. I can't shrug a shoulder, wiggle a finger, blink an eye. I'm unable to speak, unable to burp, unable to break wind unaided, unable to break the news to anybody that the building is, in fact, not empty as reported, that I'm still up there in the control tower, though not in control. And most important, that I'm still aware, very much aware, painfully aware, maddeningly aware.

Being unable to communicate my awareness makes me want to scream with frustration but, of course, I can't. And the thing is, I'm not in a permanent vegetative state as first diagnosed or minimally conscious as later decided. The bloody diagnosis is still wrong, dead wrong. The correct diagnosis should have been that I was "locked-in", that is to say, that I was conscious but unable to respond. And I should know, shouldn't I? After all, I'm the one locked in here. As if this purgatory isn't bad enough, the hell of it is that despite all the expert opinions about my lack of brain activity, I have all my marbles. My mind is intact. My senses are intact. My sense of feel is intact. I can feel when I'm touched. I hurt when I'm injected. My sense of smell is not only intact, it's acute at times to the point of overkill. I smell the mess all around me, the urine, the fecal matter, the medicine, the isopropyl alcohol, the rubber tubing, the electric wiring, the disinfectant, the cleaning and laundry supplies, and most maddeningly, I smell the vapours rising from all the caregiving lives swirling around me, sustaining mine. The sweat, the deodorants, the aftershave, the cologne. The fragrance, the heady scent of the women when they come close, attending to me, drives me up the wall. Talk about an unlikely image.

14

I Am a Camera

Unbeknownst to my redolent caregivers who hover over me, tenderly tending to my every need, I am fully cognitive and I stress fully. I see. I hear. I comprehend. The irony is that I do so more capably now than before the accident that did this to me. It's almost as if these functions have been enhanced by the trauma. Though I'm eerily silent, and scarily still, I'm acutely watchful. In effect, I've become a sort of surveillance camera. And as already noted after my last discussion with Amos before he died, as a bonus, an almost perverse bonus, since being locked in, I've developed diagnostic insights that enable me to look at people who come into my line of vision and tell who suffers from what. In fact, I may be better at it than the diagnostic professionals all around me. In the recent past, as I've indicated, I haven't been able to tell Jefferson or anyone else about any of this. Jefferson, for example, has a stress fracture in one of the bones in the metatarsal arch of his right foot. I can't point this out to him. You must be wondering how I am managing to tell it to you now. Well, that's the story that I want to tell and, if you're patient, I'll tell here. And I hope you'll find it compelling. You may also find it amusing. Despite my unenviable circumstances, I haven't lost my sense of humor. And I like to exercise it as much as I can. It is, after all, the only exercise I get.

When I first came to Woodgreen House, on life support, the traffic of neurologists and neurosurgeons in and out of my room was incessant. But as the specialists grew more and more convinced that I was at a dead end and there was no hope, they started to give up on me and write me off. As they did so and as I settled into what they believed to be nothingness, the visits of brain specialists and neurologists diminished and then, became infrequent and perhaps, even, irrelevant. Still, a few look in on me daily.

What you've read to this point is a much-condensed version of what actually goes on in critical care life support. It really takes many other lives to keep one damaged life like mine going. I continue to be seen daily by a whole squad of dedicated critical care people without whose ministrations I would no longer be around to tell you about all this.

Ironically, talking about the minutiae of life support is pretty deadly stuff. Instead, I'll give you a quick rundown of what's happening all around me and then I'll edit most of the bodies involved out of my room and out of my tale, except for my own inert body, of course, and a few key players.

To stay alive, a life support patient like me in critical care commands the attention of a platoon of professional care-givers. The roster includes three or four specialists, a supervising physician or two, all sorts of around-the-clock nurses, at least one, maybe two physiotherapists, an occupational therapist, a pharmacist and various technicians, as needed. All these concerned folks convene around my bed and body early each day to compare notes about patient problems. Patients like me with severe problems may have to be checked hourly by specially trained nurses, working through the standard list: vital signs, blood pressure, respiratory rate, neurological state, sputum content, and urine output. From inside this project and as its object, I can tell you, it's a rotten, lousy, awful job. And the old cliché applies in spades. Somebody has to do it. If not, the patient goes bye-bye.

And that isn't the whole story. There's the ongoing patient clean up, the catheter bag to empty, the sponging of the patient, the shifting of the inert body to avoid bedsores. And of course, nurses are saddled with all that, too. In addition, a critical care specialist physician comes by and studies the patient closely looking for signs of hope or nope. A respiratory technician keeps a constant check on the ventilator. A pharmacist monitors meds dosage, adjusting where necessary to fight off infection. Later in the day the troop of intent interveners reconvenes to plan how to help me make it through the night. Without all of the dedicated attention and care of all of the above, I could wake up in the morning only to discover that I'd shuffled off during the night. And not to Buffalo, either. We're talking mortal coil, here.

15

NOT ANYWHERE

ONCE in a long while, two resident wheelchairioteers meet in my presence having inadvertently rolled in for a visit at the same time. After the obligatory sympathetic look and the friendly hand wave in my direction often accompanied by a "God bless you, Brian" or a "Good luck, buddy," they sometimes sit awhile and chat quietly as if I'm not there because as far as hospital lore is concerned, I'm not there. I'm not anywhere. As a consequence, I am a secret surveillance camera privy to some offbeat conversations. On one such occasion, two men in their nineties, after dutifully acknowledging my presence, greet each other.

"How goes the battle?"

"Which one? There's fighting all over the world."

"I'm having trouble hearing you. Can you speak up?

"It's hard for me to talk louder. Can you come a little closer?"

"Okay. Better?"

"Better."

"Good. There's something I have to tell you."

"I'm listening."

"I'm not sure how to put this ..."

"You don't have to put it. Just tell it."

'It's hard to find the words."

"Words are all we have left. Give it your best shot."

"Well, the long and short of it is …"

"Forget the long. Just give me the short."

"All right. All right."

"Well?"

"Well… Just between us, not a word to anyone."

"No problem. I won't remember a word you say."

"Well, the fact is, I'm dying."

"You're dying?"

"That's what I said. I'm dying."

"Hold on a minute. How old are you?"

"Ninety-six and a half. How old are you?"

"Ninety-eight and three quarters."

"You don't look ninety-eight and three quarters."

"You don't look ninety-six and a half. Does it matter how we look? At our age, we're all dying."

"You're not dying. Did your doctor tell you you're dying?"

"Not in so many words. But I know I am. We all are."

"That's not true."

"Yes, it is. We're dying, all of us."

"You're just saying that to try and make me feel better."

"I'm not. We're all dying. It's a question of when. Each of us has his own when."

"Well, I'm dying now."

"Then, this is your when."

"You're saying my when is now?"

"Your when is now. My when could be whenever. Who knows? Who cares?"

"You don't care?"

"We all care. But care won't help. Care is not a cure."

"I'm not looking for a cure. There is no cure."

"Maybe dying is the cure."

"Dying? The cure? For what?"

"The cure for being disabled, the cure for living too long."

I don't care much for that last comment. It hits too close to home. But before I can give it more thought or hear the response, in comes Elissa, my afternoon nurse, Elissa Hargit. She directs her silent gaze at these two wizened wiseguys in their wheelchairs and they just look at her and then at each other and without another word to each other or to her, they slowly take off and roll out of the room.

And then, Elissa turns her attention to me.

16

ELISSA

As USUAL, Elissa says nothing. She hardly talks to me. Well, the fact of it is, she hardly talks to anybody, except Bessie. But she is a conscientious caregiver and performs her duties diligently, humming softly and constantly to herself. My hearing is acute, as I explained, and I can hear that she is humming some sort of a gypsy air. It sounds like the Russian song 'Dorogoi dlinnoyu'. "Those were the days, my friend. I thought they'd never end." But I can't be sure because she never sings the words. She just hums.

Elissa, whom Bessie was instrumental in getting hired at Woodgreen, is a short, taciturn, middle-aged woman of Eastern European extraction with a mole on her chin and a laboured walk. I confess this did not make the best first impression. But she keeps close watch over me, doing her job silently but well.

There is something unusual about Elissa's eyes, I discover early on. When Elissa looks at me, her eyes dart about strangely. Despite my own limited view of the world outside my head, it is clear that she is struggling to see me. I quickly recognize that

Elissa is suffering from macular degeneration and may, in fact, be legally blind. This doesn't interfere with the performance of her duties. And no one else seems to be aware of her visual impairment. Or of her humming.

There is much more to Elissa than my first impressions. Over time, from overheard conversations between Bessie and Jefferson and other Woodgreen worthies, I manage to piece together some of Elissa's story. She is Russian born, speaks five languages, has a medical degree and a doctorate in neurology. She was a highly regarded brain researcher in Moscow but was at political odds with the Russian administration for reasons she never discusses. Her husband was a high-level apparatchik in the central government but she had split with him after a long, often unharmonious marriage, leaving behind two grown and married sons and three young grandchildren.

When she talks at all, Elissa talks mostly to Bessie, her advocate and sponsor, but she rarely speaks of home. If she misses home or family, she never lets on. She is tough, capable, self-assured, and protects herself with silence. She came to Canada at the invitation of a Canadian agency seeking to help overcome Canada's shortage of medical practitioners. But upon arrival, she discovers there is little acceptance of her offshore credentials. With limited funds and no income, she cannot afford to re-qualify here due to the expensive and time-consuming requirements placed in the path of immigrant medical practitioners by an overzealous Canadian government in cahoots with the Canadian medical establishment. This must surely have been further complicated when she begins losing her eyesight, about which she tells no one, not even Bessie. Instead, she opts for private nursing as a quicker route to an earning credential. But behind the mask of silence it is clear to me, the silent patient, that Elissa is a trove of untapped, invaluable medical knowledge and experience.

As I already mentioned, since being locked in by my accident, I have developed uncanny insights that I cannot explain. Ironically, somehow through observation only, I seem to have acquired diagnostic skills, skills equal to or superior to those of the medical professionals around me who continue to diagnose me incorrectly. I know it's implausible, but I can tell, just by looking, who suffers from what. Of course, up till now, there's been no way to communicate this to anybody, no way to alert people and perhaps help save lives. This, I suppose, makes me not simply a surveillance camera, but a frustrated surveillance camera with diagnostic capabilities that I cannot share. Being a camera, it occurs to me, is a metaphor. Unexpectedly, I seem to be wallowing in the metaphors I prefer to avoid. Maybe I was too hasty in my earlier expressed reluctance to be a metaphor. For someone who can't speak, I shoot my mouth off too often.

17

THE KIWI

Inevitably, after my first few months at Woodgreen, the stream of outside visitors diminishes to a trickle and then dries up. But then one morning just before noon, a well-dressed, middle-aged man rolls himself into my unmoving presence in a wheelchair. Wheelchair visits aren't all that unusual. There are a handful of Woodgreen residents who, if not bedridden or about to leave us, are able to get about in wheelchairs. Some of these chairpersons have to be trundled about by nursing staff, but a few can roll their own and every so often wheel and deal themselves into my hideaway for a brief visit, a sympathetic look at me, a sad shake of the head, and a quick departure. Sometimes, they mumble something to me or maybe it's to themselves. One, a former fire fighter whose legs had been badly crushed in the collapse of a burning warehouse, never fails to raise a clenched fist in solidarity with me, I suppose, and say, "You poor, poor bastard," in a hoarse, teary voice. It's fair to say that I get to know these visitors, although they aren't aware that I know them. Or if they are, they never let on. But then, neither do I. The incommunicado kid, that's me.

Today's visitor, however, is not one of my Woodgreen familiars. He's new to me. And unlike the in-house visitors, he doesn't just wheel in, visit briefly, and then wheel out. Instead, he slowly wheels himself over close to the bed and then, stays put, sitting silently in his parked vehicle studying me intently. At the same time, of course, without his being aware of it, I am studying him, too.

He'd be about fifty, I guess. A handsome man, deep blue eyes, a full head of very black hair parted in the centre and long at the back. A stylish sort, attired in a well-cut suit of navy blue wool with an almost imperceptible red stripe in it, a neatly knotted silk tie in an attractive floral pattern, matching silk puff in the breast pocket of his jacket, highly polished black oxfords. Unlike the rumpled in-house wheelcharioteers in their hospital gowns, my well-dressed mystery guest is clearly not an inmate of the institution. He is an outsider, in all likelihood, a captain of industry by the look of him, perhaps a corporate type, a lawyer, accountant, stockbroker, who knows? But why is he visiting me? I wonder. Who is he, sitting there silently, somberly, eyes fixed contemplatively on me? At one point, he clears his throat, leans in my direction, and makes as if about to speak, but then appears to change his mind and remains silent.

At that very moment, as he does at regular intervals, in strides Jefferson Baines to check on me. "Hey, dude," he says. "Oh. You have a visitor. Sorry. Didn't mean to interrupt."

"No worries, mate," says the man in the wheelchair. "We're just having a quiet little visit."

He has an Australian accent. No. It's a Kiwi accent. He's from New Zealand. There's a subtle difference. But I can tell. In my carefree youth I used to do a little routine where I mimicked all sorts of accents. I was quite good at it. He's a Kiwi, for sure, a New Zealander. Maybe that's a clue to his identity. Now, if only Jefferson would engage him in conversation and draw him out, maybe I'd find out who he is.

"It's almost lunchtime," says Jefferson. "Why don't you let me get you a cup of coffee while you're keeping Brian company. He can't join you but I'm sure he'd want you to have a little refreshment."

"That's very kind of you. Thank you, doctor."

"Nurse. I'm Brian's nurse."

"Oh. Sorry."

"No problem. How do you take your coffee?"

"Black with double sugar."

Jefferson goes out the door and a moment later is back carrying a little tray with a mug of coffee on it accompanied by a very large cookie. It's the size of a small pizza. "Here you go," he says.

"Thank you. That's quite a cookie."

"Pecan, orange, and oatmeal. My wife made a batch for me to try out on the unsuspecting. You're my first victim."

"I'm honoured. It's delicious. Shame Brian can't join me."

"Yeah. It really is. But I'm sure Brian appreciates your visit. Don't you, dude? He hasn't been getting too many visitors the last little while. Are you a family friend?"

"Not exactly. More of a long-ago acquaintance, actually. I'm over here on business from Auckland, New Zealand."

"Well, Brian's mom will be here soon. She comes in every day about this time. I'm sure she'll be glad to see you."

"Unfortunately, I can't stay longer today. But I'll be in Toronto for a bit and I'll come by for another visit. At the moment, I have to rush off to a meeting with your managing director. My company is going to be building a new wing on Woodgreen House. Woodgreen West."

"Good one. Woodgreen can use the extra space. It's getting more crowded in here all the time. I'll tell Mrs. Hildebrand that you came by, Mr. …."

"Triggs. Raymond Triggs. But I doubt she'll remember the name." He looks at me silently for a moment as if trying to think of something to say in farewell. Finally, with a little wave of his hand, actually, sort of a cross between a wave and a salute, he says, "You take care, now, Brian. See you soon."

And then, he vigorously swings his wheelchair about in an arc and rolls himself out the door. He's doing amazingly well, mending brilliantly, my inner diagnostic surveillance camera tells me, for someone who has only recently had a hip replacement.

Who is this guy? I wonder. What brought him in to see me?

18

DREAM ON

EVEN IN this limbo, I have my ups and downs. Sometimes, in my more desperate moments, I try to tell myself that none of this is really happening to me, that it's just a dream. The truth is, I don't really know if it's a dream or not, although it sometimes feels like one, especially when I contemplate the suspended state that I'm in, which I do a lot of the time. Like the state of Texas, this state of suspension just goes on and on, frustratingly on. That's the way it is here in limbo. There's no end to it. I definitely do not recommend limbo. I adjure you to eschew limbo. But it's okay to enjoy funny words.

While I'm going on about dreams, let me say that it's not clear to me, or to my caregivers, for that matter, if I ever actually sleep or dream. My eyes are always wide open. Nonetheless, once in a while, at night with the blinds drawn, my room is pitch black and my inner voice trails off into noisy breathing that's not quite a snore, and I find myself in strange situations in distant places. I'm not sure what to make of this except that maybe it's possible that I do sleep and dream from time to time. What's unusual about this is that when this, whatever it is, does happen, it's like a dream within a dream that isn't a dream but a sort of suspended state. If you find that confusing, you're not alone. Thank you for joining me. I find it confusing for me, too.

At other times, I use my suspended condition to question god's motives. I'm not sure there is a god or if there is, that he has motives, but I question them anyhow. There's no original thinking here. I indulge myself in all the standard whining that you hear from the godless, the people of little faith, the ye people. Why would a caring, compassionate god let this happen to me? Why isn't he helping me? Before long, I'm questioning the very existence of god. If he exists, where is he? And what about all my prayers? Why aren't they being answered? Isn't god listening? Isn't god there? Was he ever there? Have I been talking to myself? Never mind. I'm used to talking to myself.

These days, most people who seem to be talking to themselves and aren't locked up, are actually talking on cellphones. I don't have a cellphone any more. I just have a cell and I'm locked up in it. I am my own cell. I hope that's not a metaphor. If it is, it's a convoluted one. I tend to be convoluted.

It's odd about god. Before my accident, I never gave god much thought. I could take him or leave him. And mostly, I left him. I didn't believe or disbelieve. I wasn't religious or irreligious. I just didn't care. It didn't seem to matter. Bessie, on the other hand, is a militant atheist, and if you so much as mention the G-word to her, she launches into a diatribe about the persistence of superstition in countless generations of frightened minds through the ages from time immemorial. The passing on of paranoia through the perpetuation of myths, she calls it. She loves alliteration. I get my alliterative predilection from Bessie.

And if you happen to be of a religious bent and take issue with her, heaven help you. She can out-chapter and out-verse you in any religion you profess to adhere to. She has studied all the holy books, all the scriptures, all the testaments, old, new, and just emerging, and she remembers them all in excruciatingly precise detail and can cite accurately and at length to counter the arguments of even the most learned of clergy who soon learn to avoid debating with her. Making theologians crazy is one of Bessie's specialties. Making doctors crazy is another one of her specialties, especially brain surgeons and neurologists.

Hey! It must be noon. Here's Bessie now, sandwich and coffee in hand.

"Hi, big guy. How are you doing today?" she says from the doorway.

There are cliché responses I ache to utter like, "Can't complain" or "Same old. Same old." But of course, I can't. So I just say them in my head and hope in vain that Bessie will divine something and react with delight. But there's no way. The now familiar hug, the pat on the arm, the kiss on the cheek, all cautiously threaded through the tangle of tubes ands wires sprouting out of me. Then, moving the chair to her favorite place. Sitting down. A little nibble on the sandwich. It looks like egg salad today. I can't be sure. A careful sip of the black, always black, coffee. A large, preparatory sigh. She is about to launch into her daily dissertation of positivity and encouragement but before she can get started, Jefferson enters with a plate bearing one of his wife's giant cookies.

"Hi, Mrs. Hildebrand. I brought you one of Inez's new pecan, orange, and oatmeal cookies to try out. I'm conducting an informal survey."

"Thank you, Jefferson. It looks delicious. I'll demolish it as soon as I finish my sandwich. How's my kid doing today?"

"He's his usual well-behaved self. No breakthroughs. The only news is he had a new visitor this morning. A dapper gent in a wheelchair. Just left a little while ago. Gave his name as Raymond Triggs."

"Name doesn't ring a bell," Bessie says.

"Said he was a long-ago friend of the family. He didn't think you'd remember."

"He was right. I don't. What did he look like?"

"Pin stripe, corporate type. Business suit. Power tie. His construction company is going to be building an extension to Woodgreen. Oh. Almost forgot. Said he had come over from Auckland, New Zealand, for the project and expected to be here for awhile and would come visit Brian again."

"Auckland, New Zealand? Strange. I don't know anyone from New Zealand."

Then, having finished her sandwich, Bessie takes a bite of the cookie and her face lights up.

"This is some cookie, Jefferson. Inez gets a ten for this one."

19

ANOTHER FLASHBACK

I'M HAVING another one of those sudden, startling flashbacks that I've been experiencing lately. It takes me back about six years to my early days in Woodgreen just after going on life support. I'm not starring in the film-like event this time. I'm just a prop in the scene, the coma patient in PVS, a mute, unmoving figure in the background whose cognitive powers have yet to be recognized.

The principal performer in this brief retrospective drama is Jefferson Baines, who is being interviewed by Bessie for the job as one of my caregivers. I look on and listen, unbeknownst to the other cast members, as Bessie introduces Jefferson to the patient he will be looking after. She wants him to see what he's letting himself in for.

"That's my kid," Bessie says, stifling a snuffle. "That's Brian."

Pale as the sheets I lie on and with all manner of unprepossessing but life supporting apparatus sprouting from me in every direction, I'm a site to behold, many sites, in fact, but not a pretty sight. Jefferson studies me, nodding his head thoughtfully and

69

not at all daunted by my off-putting appearance or my unhappy circumstances.

"Hey, Brian," he says. "I'm Jefferson Baines. How you doing?" He reaches out and gives me a gentle pat on the head.

"I'm sorry for him, Mrs. Hildebrand. He must've been quite the dude."

"Oh, yes. My baby boy was quite the dude. Weren't you, Brian?" This is followed by another stifled snuffle.

"I'm up for the assignment. I'd like to work with Brian. He'll need someone who won't just care for him but who will care about him. I'm a very conscientious nurse."

"Your references are excellent and they make it clear that you're not only conscientious, you're also compassionate and that's important to me."

"It's important to me, too, Mrs. Hildebrand. Life matters, all life. I've always believed that we're not here to exploit one another but to help one other. I hope I don't sound too righteous. A little may have rubbed off from my father. He was a Baptist preacher. I'm a long ago lapsed Baptist. Now, the golden rule takes care of it all for me."

"So you've given up on god?"

"It would probably be more accurate to say he's given up on me. But I know right from wrong and fair from unfair and live my life accordingly."

''I suppose everybody asks you this question, Jefferson. Your pre-meds grades were excellent. Why did you decide to become a nurse, rather than a doctor?"

"The answer is that I started writing poetry in high school and decided I was going to be a writer, no matter what. At the same time, I wanted to be able to support my writing habit and a family without taking years and years before I could make a living. Nursing made that possible and it also left me time to write."

"And you're still writing?"

"Absolutely. Every day. I keep a notebook. No matter what's going on, I manage to jot down a few lines of a poem or an essay, and I'm also working on a novel."

"I hope you and Brian can make time for each other. You're going to be busy. Keeping Brian going will be demanding."

"That won't be a problem. Writing is demanding, too. But I'm very determined."

And then, just like that, the flashback ends, having reminded me that's when Jefferson first called me dude. How lucky I am to have Jefferson's support all these years. Without him I might have been called dud instead of dude.

20

BLAINE

AT THE TIME of my self-inflicted accident, as I mentioned, I was living in a rented duplex on Churchill Street. My girlfriend, at the time, Blaine Cooper, had moved in with me. Blaine Cooper was a dietician by profession and a physical fitness buff by inclination. And I, as already noted, was a rink rat turned gym rat and no slouch myself in the physical fitness department.

Still, I have to admit Blaine outpaced me and outraced me every which way. She not only worked out regularly but also did so with uncompromising intensity. She ran. She swam. She skied. She hiked. She biked. She played all the racquet sports: squash, tennis, and badminton, as well as table tennis and ping pong, somehow, indulging also in golf and soccer and basketball and beach volleyball. Oh, and I mustn't forget hockey. How could I forget hockey? Even among the overzealous sweat set, Blaine was a standout, an unflagging dynamo, gung ho for almost any sport, game for almost any game. Yet this jock was the most charming and delightful of creatures, tall and good looking and good fun and given to giggling when amused.

We'd met a year earlier at a health food convention in Las Vegas, of all places. Blaine was employed as a research director by one of our competitors, Nutrients for Life, and as competitors, we were a little wary of each other at first, keeping our distance and trading jolly little health food jokes only when encountering each other by chance. As the encounters grew more frequent, and chance grew less frequent, we soon became fast friends and indispensible to each other. We seemed to be well matched in many ways and inclined to agree on a lot of things, including Las Vegas which both of us concurred was an unlikely place for a health foods convention.

Nonetheless, the five-day meeting was a huge success. Participation in the rousing get-together was substantial. To begin with, some four thousand remarkably hale and wholesome health food conventioneers from around the globe descended on Las Vegas. They came from thirty-one countries and set up and supervised more than two thousand booths in the North Hall of the Las Vegas Convention Center to display and demonstrate their products, introduce new ones, and offer endless flyers and catalogues and coupons, as well as tastings and samplings. All the while, hourly speeches and seminars and meetings ran non-stop in the adjoining South Hall.

But that wasn't all of it. In addition, there was an impressive response from the general public. More than a hundred thousand paying visitors joined us over the five days of the event. It was full up, a lively experience bustling with energetic crowds and brimming with eager faces. Many of the ticket holders were locals, full time residents of Las Vegas who we learned, to our surprise, almost never frequent the casinos. As far as they were concerned, all that gambling stuff was for tourists. The residents were more inclined to the laid-back life style of the southwest and health was part of it. They flocked to the Health Food Convention in large numbers.

By contrast, a mere stone's throw away from the Convention Center, the tourists, the weary, rumpled, sleep deprived tourists, who at infrequent intervals came up for air from the casinos where they had come to gamble, were the unhealthiest looking lot you could possibly imagine, out of place out of doors, recognizable by the gambling palace pallor of their gray, sagging faces, thick necks, multiple chins, bloated bellies, swollen feet, and bad posture. Obsessed with beating the system and hoping to enrich themselves at the tables or the wheels or the slots, this bedeviled and bedraggled bunch had zero interest in the health food activities next door. And of course, we, the health food floggers and bloggers of the world, were too taken up with our monster health food bash to even peek into, let alone enter, the casinos that, in any case, we deemed unworthy, unhealthy venues. We were too busy showing off our wares and making the case for the benefits of our various health food products and breakthroughs. And in addition, Blaine and I were extra busy since we were also among the keynote speakers holding forth in the South Hall.

My talk was titled, "You Are What You Eat So Don't Swallow the Cutlery". Nuff said. Blaine's talk was titled, "Run For Your Life". Subtitled, "Get Moving or Die", it counseled activity, frequent, regular activity, no matter what it was.

What else can I say about Blaine? Curly red hair and freckles, always well turned out even in her most casual moments, bright, articulate, well organized, fun to be with, and never without a smile. We got along, respected each other's space, and enjoyed many of the same things, books, films, theatre. Was this a mad love affair? Well, maybe not mad. But it was certainly a warm, loving one. Both of us were in busy careers eagerly chasing after success and had no plans to marry or have children. Until the accident, our lives together were going along swimmingly. Then suddenly, it was everybody out of the pool. Sad to say, I was not the only victim of that unhappy event. The other victim was Blaine. From the very moment of my abrupt lifestyle change, Blaine was constantly by my side, caring, attentive, concerned. But when I was repeatedly labeled as being in a persistent vegetative state, the high-energy dynamo slowly ran down, fell apart, and had to be hospitalized, medicated, and counseled. Six months later after getting herself put back together, pale and looking twenty pounds lighter, she came in to see me late one afternoon. Somberly, silently, she held my hand for the longest time and then, finally succumbing to tears, she said, "Good luck, baby. I'm rooting for you."

And then, she got up and left and I never saw her again. I couldn't help thinking that history was repeating itself. And in my internal voice in the echoing cathedral of my head, I roundly cursed history.

21

DARK THOUGHTS AND DREAMS

AMOS'S DEATH, of course, was a blow to my momentary enthusiasm about the possibility of being able to enlist the Woodgreen wanderer as an intermediary to communicate to Bessie and to the world. Only later, after I have gone through a period of what I would have to describe as mourning or depression or both, during which my mind was filled with thoughts of death and dying, did it occur to me that even if Amos hadn't died, there might still have been a disconnect. Maybe only he and I in our somehow shared, internalized mental state were able to communicate. Maybe what I would have told him to tell Bessie might have emerged from him as meaningless gibberish to her. Maybe there would have been no communications breakthrough. Maybe. Maybe. Maybe, it's all maybe. Maybe, I'll never know.

In my darker moments, I sometimes have dark dreams, if dreams are, in fact, what they are. I'm really not sure they are dreams. I'm not even sure that I am actually sleeping. I may even be awake and what I think are dreams may be hallucinations or visions of some sort. Whatever they are, the real and surreal run into each other and over each other, overlapping, often taking me with them into another dimension.

I'm walking west along College Street in Toronto's west end. It's late afternoon and the sun hangs low in the sky and burns into my eyes making me squint uncomfortably. I fish in my jacket pockets for my sunglasses. No luck. Damn. I must've left them somewhere. I'm on my way to Bar None, a tiny neighbourhood bistro just west of Dovercourt Avenue. The woman I'm meeting I haven't met before. I know her only by her name and her fearsome reputation. She is Death. And she has invited me to meet her for a drink to discuss my current situation and my future prospects. Needless to say, I'm somewhat apprehensive.

Outside the bar, I hesitate, trying to compose myself. Reluctant to enter, I stall for time, looking in the window, and I see her sitting at the bar. At first glance, she is just another patron in a little hole-in-the-wall Portuguese cafe, perched on a bar stool, nursing a bloody Mary, and nibbling away on a few tired looking tapas laid out on a plate in front of her. But on closer study, it is clear that she is not your average bar habitué. In her modish, all-black ensemble, stylishly cut jet black hair, striking scarlet lipstick, slate grey eyes, and startlingly blue eye makeup, she is somehow too well turned out, too attractive, too assured, too self-contained, to be merely average. She is merely magnificent. There is about her an awesome aura of authority. An executive aura, some might call it. She could, for example, be the CEO of a Fortune 500 company or a highly placed honcho in government, a mandarin, or a civic leader, a woman accustomed to running things, having her way, being in charge. Certainly, her no-nonsense mien, her determined demeanor, make it clear that she is not there to strike up a casual conversation with any of the regulars who out of curiosity look her way from time to time. She does not look back. She is not about to be chatted up. She is there with purpose.

And soon, the purpose is made manifest, when plucking up my courage, I enter the establishment and approach the bar as if called to it. Though we have never met before, there is a sort of immediate recognition. We nod to each other. She waits silently as I seat myself on the stool next to her, order a Tuborg and slowly and expertly pour the beer down one side of the tall glass producing a precise head of foam. For a brief moment, I hold the glass with the amber liquid and the perfect head up to the light and admiringly contemplate the product of my precision. Then, I lower the glass to my lips, slowly take a sip, swallow, savour, sigh appreciatively, set the glass down on the counter, and sit waiting. I do not wait long.

The woman on the stool beside me swivels about in my direction and smiles. And when she smiles, her wonderfully white teeth emerge from between the striking scarlet of her lips, and light up her face, while her eyes, which are the colour of slate, flash fiercely, almost menacingly. She is alarmingly – dangerously – handsome, so handsome that it hurts to look at her. I experience an oppressive weight on my chest and a shortness of breath. My eyes smart and I am forced to look away.

"Permit me to introduce myself," she says.

"Oh, that's not necessary," I manage to reply. "Though, thanks to my mother's persistence, I've managed to avoid you till now, I'm quite aware of who you are. And I must say that it's—how shall I put this?—fascinating to meet you finally. But I'm happy to say, I haven't given up, haven't lost hope, and I don't think we're going to be doing any business together. Not today, in any case."

If she is surprised by my rejoinder, she doesn't let on but carries on talking to me as if to an old friend, in an amiable and intimate manner.

"I was sorry to learn that you've been incapacitated ever since your accident," she says sympathetically. "Five years is a long time. And I thought I'd have a little visit with you to see for myself first hand how you were getting along."

This is not rote sympathy. It is the real thing. For a moment, the unexpectedness of it leaves me without words.

"That's very kind of you," I say finally. "Thank you for your concern."

"Not at all. You can't engage in a calling like mine without caring about people in pain. Transitions, after all, can be very painful for all of us. And disability, of course, is a hell all its own, isn't it?"

"It certainly is. It's one hell of a hell," I agree.

"That's quite understandable. PVS can be devastating."

"PVS? Let me correct that. PVS is the wrong diagnosis. I'm not in a permanent vegetative state. I'm locked in. And yes, it's devastating, as you say. But I'm sentient and I've been able to focus on my struggle to try to get unlocked."

"And how goes the struggle?"

"The struggle? It sounds like class war. It was rough there for a while. But my mother has been very supportive and I've become very determined and now, I sense a breakthrough is just ahead."

"How brave of you, Brian. And how gratifying it will be for you when you find your breakthrough. You're very lucky to have a mother like Bessie on your side. She's always been a dogged fighter. Keep up the good fight and chances are, we won't have to talk again for a long, long while."

"Oh, I may whine about it from time to time, but I'm hanging in for as long as it takes," I say smiling.

She smiles back at me. The teeth come out from behind the scarlet lips, and briefly the bar lights up.

"Well, I must be off. More calls to make." She puts down an absolutely pristine twenty-dollar bill on the bar. "The beer is on me." She shakes my hand and sheathes her dangerously radiant smile. "All the best," she says. "Have a good day."

And with that she is off the stool and, attaché case in hand, out of the bar and on about her grim business, while I sit and slowly finish my Tuborg.

I put down the empty glass with a sigh of contentment and Elissa comes into my room humming quietly as usual and begins checking my feeding tube and my respirator and making adjustments.

22

DR. ROOPA

THOUGH YOU'D never know to look at me, I am excited by the news that a new doctor is coming all the way from Baltimore, Maryland, to see me today. His name is Victor Roopa. A week ago, he phoned Bessie offering to come to Toronto to assess me in order to determine my suitability as a candidate for the clinical trials he is conducting on an experimental procedure, a procedure that might help me escape my prison, using an electronic device that he and his team have developed.

Victor Roopa is something of a medical whirlwind. The boy wonder, as he has been labeled by his medical colleagues, is a professor at the Johns Hopkins University Medical School. At 19, right out of high school and with no undergraduate degree, he earned a PhD in biomechanical engineering. By the age of 22, he had collected a medical degree, two more PhDs, and an assortment of advanced neurosurgical credentials. Now, at 34, Roopa is a leading brain and spinal cord surgeon with a global reputation for innovative life-saving and life-changing techniques. He has explained to my mother that if I am deemed a suitable candidate for his trials project, all costs will be funded by a major research grant from the Johns Hopkins Medical Foundation.

Funding is vitally important since bottom line American medical treatment is disastrously expensive and the Ontario medical plan that pays all my medical expenses at home does not cover the cost of out of country medical aid. In any case, Bessie has agreed to Roopa's visit and is telling all this to Jefferson. Unbeknownst to them, I am excitedly taking it all in.

Having endured a series of my treatment disappointments before, Bessie is cautiously trying to suppress her own excitement. Nonetheless, she turns to me and says, "This guy with the funny accent may be the one who has the key to unlock you. Keep your fingers crossed, kiddo."

I certainly hope so. I've been keeping my fingers crossed for five years. I'm ready for good news from this doctor with the funny accent. Besides, I love funny accents. I used to be able to imitate them so well when I was young that I could have been a standup. Now, I'm not even a situp. I'm a fuckup.

Dr. Roopa arrives as scheduled. He is a little guy, small and brown and has tribal tattoos on his face. And yes, he does have a funny accent, a very funny accent. Victor Roopa is a Maori, a New Zealand aboriginal. And his uniquely accented English is a Maori dialectal overlay of the Kiwi accent of New Zealand.

As I look at him with delight I am unable to express, it occurs to me that Raymond Triggs, my wheelchair visitor of a few weeks earlier, is also a Kiwi. I can't help but wonder if there is a connection between Triggs and Roopa. Could Triggs have put Dr. Roopa onto me? More important, is Roopa going to be able to help me?

"G'day, mate," he says to me. "I'm Dr. Roopa. I'm going to see if I can help you."

"I'm sure Brian appreciates your efforts to help him as much as I do," Bessie says on our joint behalf.

Roopa scrutinizes me with a practiced eye as I scrutinize him in return through the surveillance camera with diagnostic capabilities that I have somehow become. I detect that he suffers from varicose veins, unusual for someone so young. Still, since they are not life threatening, his varicosities should be no impediment to his treating me, if he decides to do so. I wait expectantly to find out. I would hold my breath if I could, but thinking about holding it is the best I can do.

"Brian is in remarkably good physical shape for over five years on life support," Roopa says to my mother, nodding his head as he continues to examine me.

"They've taken very good care of him here. The physiotherapists work with him constantly. They have to. I nag them constantly," says my mom with a straight face. She's testing Dr. Roopa's sense of humour.

Roopa smiles broadly. "Thanks for the tip. I'll nag the buggers too."

Bessie smiles back at this rejoinder. She and Roopa are on the same wavelength. Now, if only I pass muster and get accepted into his clinical trials program.

23

Measure for Measure

Dr. Roopa extracts what look like large, stainless steel calipers from his bag and clamps them tightly onto my head at the temples. The device is controlled wirelessly from a hand-held, guitar-shaped apparatus with a screen, keyboard, and dials on it. Roopa puts on wireless headphones, presses a key, turns a dial. And I hear Leonard Cohen's 'Bird on the Wire' in a tongue I don't recognize. Can it be Te Reo, the language of the Maori? What's going on?

"Oops," says Dr. Roopa. "Wrong key. Sorry about that. My people love Leonard. Everybody loves Leonard."

So do I. But Leonard Cohen's bird flies off. Roopa presses another key and studies the screen on the control unit, while talking to me and rhyming off a list of unconnected words.

"Tennis. Hockey. Leonard Cohen. Michelin. Donuts. Erection. Recovery. Dereliction. Renewal. Misdemeanor. Trustworthy.

"Brian is in there, no doubt about it," he says to Bessie. "Locked in as you have correctly recognized and hearing all this.

According to my read-out, Brian loves Leonard, too. We're kindred spirits, Brian and I. I can work with him. Listen carefully, mate," he says to me. "I'm going to explain your situation and the procedure to your mother.

"Once in a long while, Mrs. Hildebrand, mental activity shows up in a brain that has been gravely injured. Though Brian is severely brain-damaged and in what functional M.R.I. diagnosis calls an unresponsive, vegetative state, on our own recently developed, more advanced brain imaging device, he is showing clear signs that he is aware of himself and his surroundings. In response to my word cues, Brian's brain changes in activity, spiking up the same language areas in the brain that respond to word cues in healthy people.

"These results contradict Brian's condition as determined by standard diagnosis and show me that there is much more going on in terms of Brian's' self-awareness than previously understood. Though it was assumed Brian was not aware, I think, Mrs. Hildebrand, you were absolutely on the right track in insisting that his caregivers should always talk to him, always explain what's going on, always keep him comfortable, because, no question about it, he is there, inside, aware of everything. He knows what's happening.

"This suggests that somewhere along the line, Brian has undergone a transition from an unresponsive, vegetative state to a minimally conscious state. Traumatic injuries to the head, while they tend to sever brain cell connections, often leave many neurons intact, and because of this, I am hopeful that Brian can be helped to eventually regain full awareness and with things going our way, perhaps, even rehabilitation.

"My team has developed a corrective high-beam microwave device that we'll use on Brian. It very slowly warms up various areas of the brain beginning with the four lobes of the cerebral cortex and then moves on to the corpus callosum and the two hemispheres of the cerebellum. At a certain critical temperature, different in every patient, the brain tries to escape the heat by, in effect, making a run for it and regressing to its pre-trauma state. When it works, it's brilliant. The patient makes a startling recovery. And Bob's your uncle. But, let me be frank with you, Mrs. Hildebrand, and with you, mate, there's no guarantee. It doesn't always work. To date, we've used the device on ten similar cases with a sixty percent success rate. And please note that none were on life support as long as Brian."

"What if the procedure fails?" Bessie asks. "Does the heating do more harm to the brain? What if cooking the brain makes the patient worse?"

What could be worse than being locked in? I ask myself. Come on, Bessie. Let's go for it.

"To tell you the truth, Mrs. Hildebrand, we don't know and our failed patients can't tell us. Our research is ongoing and we expect to improve our success rate. And hopefully, if we can help Brian, it will be another positive step in that direction."

"I'm sure Brian would want us to go for it," says Bessie. "Just don't overcook him. Well done, is what we're after."

"Well done is rare, Mrs. Hildebrand," Roopa replies with a grin. "But I promise we'll do our best to get there without overcooking him."

24

THE PLAN

IN ORDER to participate in Dr. Roopa's experimental program, it will be necessary for me to be treated in his research clinic at the Johns Hopkins Hospital in Baltimore, Maryland. This necessitates travel. Not having been anywhere but in my room (and in my head) for five years, I find the idea of travel not only exciting but also intimidating. Clearly, with my lack of mobility and my loyal and unwavering attachment to life sustaining devices, this is not going to be an uncomplicated move for me.

Still, Roopa, ever the problem solver, is not easily daunted, and with my mother urging him on, a travel plan takes shape. A specially equipped ambulance van will carry me out to Pearson airport. There, I will be transferred to a medical transport jet specifically set up for infrequent flyers like me. My mother and Jefferson and Elissa and two paramedics will accompany me. And all this is slated to happen in exactly one week's time.

That decided and organized, Roopa gives me an encouraging thumbs-up, says, "Good on you, mate. See you at Hopkins in a week." And away he goes, back to Baltimore, leaving me with a week to impatiently wait and ponder my prospects.

While I wait, the world goes on. The day after Roopa's departure, two things happen. First, who should reappear at noon hour but the other Kiwi, Raymond Triggs. Well turned out and dapper as before, he is not in a wheelchair this time. This time, he is walking, albeit slowly and with the help of a cane. Clearly, he is on the mend from his hip replacement operation. As before, he sits and looks at me thoughtfully, pensively almost, and says nothing. At intervals he looks at his watch.

Jefferson enters with a mug of coffee that he bestows on Triggs. "I took the liberty of bringing you a coffee, Mr. Triggs. Black with double sugar. Sorry, there's no cookie this time. Maybe next time."

"That's very thoughtful of you, Jefferson. Thank you."

"You know my name. That's very thoughtful of you."

"Oh, not really. Just a little research. Are we expecting Mrs. Hildebrand?"

"We are, but she seems to be running late today."

"Shame. I was hoping to meet her. I must be off. Meetings. More bloody meetings."

"Well, maybe on another visit. I'll tell Mrs. H. you asked about her."

'That will be great."

As he gets ready to leave, Triggs turns to me. "No worries, Brian. My mate, Roopa is brilliant. He'll get you fixed up. You wait and see."

I was right. The two Kiwis know each other. There is a connection between Triggs and Roopa. Assisting himself with his cane, Triggs rises slowly, walks carefully to the door, gives me a little farewell wave with his free hand, and is gone.

Following Triggs' departure, there is an upsetting glitch when Bessie, having missed her noontime visit, doesn't show up at all. This is not like her. Something has gone wrong. But if anyone knows the reason for her absence they're not sharing it with me. Thinking they can't, they never share anything with me, except unintentionally. Jefferson looks puzzled at first, then concerned. At that point, I begin to worry about what might have happened to Bessie and about how this might affect my forthcoming trip to Baltimore. If something is wrong with Bessie, my trip could be in jeopardy. Only later in the day, do I find out what happened to Bessie when I overhear Jefferson telling Elissa about it.

Out of the blue, that morning, the normally healthy Bessie has woken up suffering from unusual dizziness. Fearing she might be having a stroke, she calls 911 and an ambulance comes and takes her to the emergency ward of St. Michael's Hospital where she spends the rest of the day being examined and undergoing various tests and then waiting some more for the results. Finally, she is diagnosed with labyrinthitis, an easily treated inflammation of the inner ear and is sent home with Gravol and head exercises to do.

The next day she is as good as old or gold and back on her regular noontime visit schedule, coffee, sandwich, and all. Needless to say, I am greatly relieved. Since the accident, Bessie has been my lifeline. And she's the best mother I ever had.

25

GO FIGURE

As the departure date for my Baltimore trip and what could turn out to be a life changing opportunity for me approaches, I try to stay calm, but I am not succeeding. The truth is, I am a nervous wreck. If I could twitch, I would. And then, two days before I am due to leave, while I am trying to empty my clattering head for a brief respite in quiet nothingness, a voice I recognize breaks in.

"Brian? Hi. It's Millie. I'm back."

"Oh, Millie. Hi. I'm so glad. How did you manage it?"

"I was doing my homework, but I couldn't help thinking about you. Suddenly, I felt something important was going to happen in your life but that you might be disappointed by it. And I knew that I had to talk to you about it right away. So I focused on you and here I am."

"Do you know what's going to happen?"

"Not really. All I know is that you have a problem and that you're about to take a trip hoping to solve it. But I also know that you may not solve your problem on this trip. I felt I had to warn you. I didn't want you to make the trip and be disappointed."

"I'm disappointed right now, by what you're telling me, Millie. Are you saying I shouldn't make the trip?"

"No. I think you have to go. But you mustn't be disappointed if you fail. There may be another opportunity." What she's telling me has the ambiguity of a horoscope.

"Anything else you can tell me, Millie?"

"I wish I could. But so far, that's all I know."

"Thank you for worrying about me. You're an angel. I think I love you, Millie."

"I think I love you, too, Brian. I have to go now."

"I hope you'll come back."

"I will if I can."

There is a sound like a sigh and then silence, and I'm left worrying about what might turn out to be a disappointing trip. Hope is so fragile and worry is so sturdy. But maybe I'm just imagining all this and there's nothing to hope for or to worry about. But that would be limbo, again, wouldn't it?

26

Baltimore or Less

EMERGING FROM Brian's room for the first time in five years is a dreamlike experience. Or maybe, I should call it a surreal experience. As I have said and keep saying, I can't tell them apart any more. Suddenly, though completely immobile, I am moving, moving, moving. Or to be more accurate, I am being moved. In fact, I am being moved both physically and emotionally as I am slowly and cautiously wheeled out to the ambulance van, capturing everything that passes before my lens as merrily, though warily, we roll along. Briefly, I am a movie camera, Brian the movie camera, on a dolly in a long tracking shot down a hospital corridor in a movie of my own making inside my head. For a few fleeting and ecstatic minutes, I am engulfed in an exhilarating sense of something akin to freedom, yet not quite. And then, as I am hoisted up into the ambulance van, the movie ends, and I am back once more in an enclosed space. It's Brian's room all over again but this time it's on wheels. Bessie and Jefferson and Elissa and a couple of paramedics all of whom are accompanying me to Baltimore climb in and we are off to the airport.

Pearson Airport is maybe twenty miles from Woodgreen House and the roads are choked with slow moving traffic that grows thicker and thicker as we get closer to the airport. Our progress, if it can be called that, is infuriatingly sluggish. I am aware of this only because Bessie and Jefferson hover around me and Bessie shares her impatience with Jefferson who agrees with her but does his best to be philosophical.

"When it comes to the movement of traffic," Bessie says, "this city is constipated. It could use a good enema."

"Maybe," says Jefferson grinning. "But where would we insert it?"

"Well, we could start with City Hall. It's full of assholes."

"That may be true, Mrs. Hildebrand. But remember, we put them there with our votes. What does that make us?"

"Accomplices," Bessie deadpans. "And guilty as charged. At our next meeting, at a place and time to be announced, we will debate how to repair the dysfunctional municipal electoral system and simultaneously unclog traffic."

Jefferson grins some more. Elissa permits herself a slight smile. And the two nameless paramedics look at each other and chortle.

It feels oddly like watching a scene of a play from the wings. Still, I lose interest, grow increasingly tense and stop paying attention to what's happening around me and instead go back to agonizing about what's going to happen to me in Baltimore. What if Millie's prediction, if that's what it was, is right? What if Roopa's treatment doesn't work and fails to help me? What if the microwaves turn my brain into lasagna or a stir-fry? What will I do then? Bessie is doing her damnedest to help me. There must be something I can do to help myself. But what? As we inch our way out to the airport, my restive brain tries to assemble and review everything I can think of that might somehow be helpful.

Coma. I learned a lot about coma listening to the various medical teams trying to help me. Where a coma results from a brain injury, the patient is supposed to be unconscious, insensitive to pain, unable to move and unable to remember. That's what all the textbooks say. That's what the coma specialists who worked on me cited again and again. Reinforcing this and making my situation even more difficult, when the titans of neuroscience imaged my brain in functional MRI scanners and measured my brain activities with electroencephalography monitors, the high-tech hardware agreed with the textbooks totally, failing somehow to detect that my brain was, in fact, not entirely shut down. Obviously, some parts of my brain were turned off. I can't move and I can't speak. But other parts must be active. After all, I'm conscious, sensitive to pain, sensitive to touch, and able to remember vast amounts of information in minute detail going back decades. And to top it all off, I'm newly endowed with enhanced powers of cognition and medical insight. Technology let me down once before. I can't explain why. The question is, will technology let me down once again? If, as Millie suggests, Roopa's clinical trial fails me and technology lets me down again, how can I make my true condition known to neuroscience, to my mother, to the world? Who can I talk to that can hear me?

Despite Bessie's credentials as a clairvoyant, no matter how hard I tried, I've been unable to convey my thoughts to her. Surprisingly, I was able to talk with Amos, the wanderer, and hoped to communicate through him as an intermediary but tragically he died, dammit. At the moment, I'm able to talk, but only in a limited way, and only to Millie, a twelve-year-old who may be psychic. But I'm not really sure. Her brief visits are puzzling and uncertain and too ephemeral to permit us to exchange much information. And there's always the possibility that she may be an illusion, a fantasy, and exist only in my harried mind. Besides, if, in fact, Millie actually exists, she's a child in school in Arizona, more than two thousand miles away and thus unlikely to be able to act as my communications intermediary.

My head is racing and I am frenetically stringing ideas together into idea chains, trying to come up with a backup plan in the event that my Baltimore trip is a bust. Supposing Dr. Roopa can't help me and supposing my marbles haven't been cooked into compote, and supposing Millie is not just a voice in my head but really exists, and supposing there is some way that I can persuade Millie to come from Arizona to Toronto and supposing she is able to talk to me in person, not just head to head but face to face, and supposing that Millie can then tell Bessie what I tell her. Then, Bessie, in turn, can tell everybody what I desperately need to be known. Brilliant. But how likely is all of that supposing? If Millie doesn't unpredictably pop into my head, I don't even know how to contact her. I'm getting nowhere with this line of thinking. But I'm already nowhere. That's not progress. That's nogress .

Finally, the coma kid (c'est moi) and his entourage arrive at the airport where on a tarmac distant from the main terminal, I am to be downloaded from the ambulance and uploaded onto a Gulfstream medical transport jet. Everybody on the flight has been pre-cleared by the security people of both Canada and the US, assuring both countries that there are no terrorists among us. I may not be a terrorist but I'm feeling terror. Flying time to Baltimore/Washington Airport located eight miles from the Johns Hopkins Hospital is about forty minutes, forty very worrisome minutes during which I grow more and more tense. My head is buzzing.

About thirty minutes into the flight, an unexpected but welcome visitor pops into my head. My head stops buzzing.

"Hi, Brian. It's Millie. Are you okay?"

"Hi, Millie. I'm not sure, yet. I'm just on my way."

"Well, maybe you can stop worrying. I know a little more. Your trip may not be disappointing, after all. Oh, I'm going. Sorry I can't…"

"Millie, wait. I need to…"

There is a sound like a sigh and then silence, and she is gone before I can learn more. What is this on again off again business? I will be disappointed. I won't be disappointed. What the hell is going on?

At the Baltimore/Washington airport, an ambulance van is waiting to meet us. But before my traveling troupe can download me from the hospital jet, a surly security officer comes on board with a huge police dog. Despite our pre-clearance before our takeoff, he insists on checking us out, taking a particular fancy to me. I'm the suspicious one. Maybe I'm a bad guy in bedclothes. Maybe there's a terrorist bomb between my sheets. He pokes around while my mother glares at him. Maybe one of the fluids keeping me alive is really an explosive. And drugs. Let's not forget drugs. If I'm not a terrorist, maybe I'm a drug smuggler? Why not? Everybody is hiding something. Right? There are no innocents any more.

The obstinate official addresses his dog. "Dirk, drugs, Dirk. Sniff drugs."

Dirk gives a couple of unenthusiastic sniffs in my general direction, looks at his commanding officer with puzzlement, and pees on the cabin floor. That does it for Bessie. She blows a gasket.

"Get the fuck off this aircraft, you inconsiderate idiot, and take that poor enslaved animal with you. If you give us any more trouble, I'll report you." And then, in an awesome display of her psychic ability, she recites the stunned man's entire resumé in chronological order with dates and places, ending with the name of his superior officer.

"Sorry about that," says the now chastened, inconsiderate idiot. "I'll clean up the mess." He quickly gets out of the plane.

Treading carefully to avoid the puddle, my tour group eases me off the plane and over and into the waiting ambulance van. Bessie looks back at the plane just in time to see the security guy coming back with a mop and pail.

"Mop and pail," she says. "The perfect job fit for that that turkey."

"How did you know all that stuff about that guy," asks Jefferson.

"I'm a clairvoyant," Bessie says.

Jefferson looks at me and then at Bessie questioningly. "Then why can't you…?"

"I know what you're going to ask," says Bessie.

"Of course, you do," says Jefferson. "You are a clairvoyant, after all."

Bessie smiles. "I ask myself the same question all the time. Why can't I? I don't know why. I don't have an answer to that one."

They both look at me. Jefferson gives me a smile and a thumbs-up. Bessie shakes her head sadly. Elissa pats my shoulder reassuringly but says nothing. The anonymous paramedics look at each other in puzzlement, wondering what the hell my two traveling companions are talking about

27

CLINIC

DR. ROOPA greets me effusively on my arrival at his clinic. "Ah, Brian. Here you are. Good on you, mate. Welcome to Baltimore and Johns Hopkins. Now, let's see if we can make a new man of you. Or better still, let's see if we can turn you back into the man you once were."

Yes, please. Either would be fine. Whatever works works for me.

Roopa announces that the whitecoats are coming to commence preparations for the procedure. His enthusiastic white-coated team of four men and two women gather around me and begin readying me for the exciting yet uncertain adventure that lies just ahead. Having been briefed before my arrival and having already performed ten similar procedures, the teamsters know precisely what needs doing, with Bessie and Jefferson and Elissa standing by to be consulted, if required, which seems highly unlikely to me, at least. They begin by shaving my head exposing the tread marks on my skull, a hurtful memento of my ill-advised, self-inflicted encounter with my own car over five years earlier. The simple act of shaving the site of the damage brings back a deluge of painful memories. The wheel rolling over my head, the deep tread of the winter tire and then, for some bizarre reason, the hundred-pound bag of sand in the trunk of the car. I am deeply distressed by all this, drowning in despair and desperately wanting to cry for help, or even just cry, but I don't have an app for either of those.

"I'd know those deep tread marks anywhere," says one of the Roopa team. "That's a Michelin Primacy Alpin PA3 winter tire. No question about it."

The others all nod sagely, scratch themselves thoughtfully in various favorite places and mumble incoherent agreement. Maybe they're just trying to be easy to get along with. But more likely, they're car buffs. It's hard to know for sure. But Jefferson thinks he knows. In the background, thanks to my heightened acuteness of hearing, I overhear Jefferson, ever the cycling (and recycling) environmentalist, whispering to Bessie, "Can you believe it, Mrs. Hildebrand. We're surrounded by auto polluters, eco-terrorists. Maybe we should call for help."

"Never mind," says Bessie. "We're safe as long as they don't start offroad driving in here."

Two of the possible polluters admire the shape of my skull.

"Not too flattened out, considering the nature of the trauma," says one, running his fingers over my newly shaved head.

"Mighty like a melon," says another.

"A melon with treadmarks," says a third.

Through the veil of tears I am unable to shed, I contemplate the emptiness that awaits me at both ends of my silent, unmoving being. I, the silent vessel, am about to become an empty vessel, foregoing nourishment for twenty-four hours before the procedure and having my bowels purged of all fecal matter. The prospect does not please me but, what the hell, shit happens. And what's a little more unhappiness when I'm already unhappy. Besides, I'm not a free agent, am I? Actually, I'm not any kind of agent. And not much of a principal, either.

The white-coated group of six untether me from my various cables and cords and tubes and lifelines, leaving in place only those that if removed would shut me down completely, something that I have managed with Bessie's help to avoid for over five years. Hey, let's not do it now, team. During the concerted untethering, I uneasily envision myself as an astronaut out in space inadvertently untethered from his orbiting space station and drifting off in the great unknown to who knows where.

Who knows where is clearly a popular destination. I will, in fact, be drifting off to who knows where during the actual microwaving session for which I will have been sedated with purpua resca, a fine purple dust extracted from a smelly rare mushroom of the same name growing only in the rainforests of Tasmania. The purple dust will be blown into my nostrils by a specially designed two-outlet airpump. But before all that, I will be lulled into a state of pre-procedural tranquility by carefully selected music that will be played to me through headphones starting immediately. The phones go on my newly shaved head. They feel cold. And once again, I hear the resonant rumble of Leonard Cohen but this time he's singing in English.

"I've heard there was a secret chord that David played and it pleased the Lord, but you don't really care for music, do you?"

Hallelujah!

During the inner great emptiness, the twenty-four hour no-nourishment waiting period, the Roopa sextet has given me a complete surface makeover. I've been transformed head to toe into a smoothie. My fingernails and my toenails have been trimmed and buffed to keep me from inadvertently scratching myself in case I twitch, which seems highly unlikely, while under sedation. Apparently, purpua resca makes some patients itch and twitch and as a result scratch themselves. With a name like purpua resca, I'm not surprised. Just thinking of the name makes me want to scratch. But, of course, I can't. Maybe later. If I win this lottery.

The clinic has assembled eighteen different shapes of electric shavers and hair clippers, large, medium, small, mighty small, and teeny-weeny. They can thrust and cut anywhere there's hair, even in the very tightest, most unlikely places. And all eighteen of them were used in the depilatory assault on my hairy body. In addition to removing the hair on my head, the members of the team have also shaved off all my facial hair, beard, mustache, eyebrows, eyelashes, nostrils, ears, and also all my body hair, armpits, chest, back, arms, legs, pubic hair. I feel like the Pillsbury doughboy. The team has explained to Bessie that sometimes, during the high beam microwaving procedure, the patient's hair may smolder and smoke and could possibly burn the patient and perhaps even interfere with his breathing. So, away with the hair, all of it. No smoking.

Well, here I am, a clinical test subject on neuroscience's threshold. Or maybe it's on neuroscience's kitchen table since microwave cooking of the brain is involved. I'm shaven and shorn and washed and scrubbed and shined and polished and unfed for twenty-four hours and emptied of waste and filled instead with dread and hope and being trundled on a gurney into the heart of Dr. Roopa's stainless steel microwave cave where a gleaming array of tubular microwave units hangs from the roof like stalactites. I try to distract myself by counting the stalactites. Twenty-four.

The Roopa six and all my devoted fans and followers are being ushered into a large glass control booth from which they will watch the proceedings without exposure to the microwaves. And I can't help but think of how very like a Texas death-row execution chamber the place is. Not a heartening thought. And all the while, Leonard continues to sing his aching, breaking heart out into my earphones.

"There's a crack, a crack in everything. That's how the light gets in. That's how the light gets in."

But before the light gets in, the purpua resca gets in and then Leonard's singing fades into purple silence.

Dr. Roopa is the last to leave the microwave cave and has the last word. Before going, he bends over me and smiles reassuringly. "Not to worry, mate. You won't feel a thing. You may dream a bit. But it will be mostly talk, nothing unpleasant. I'll be at the controls just behind that glass microwaving at you and monitoring your progress. And I'll be back with you as soon as it's over."

Then, as the purple dust continues to be blown into my nostrils, Roopa's microwave cave fills with the aroma of eggplant. Or maybe it's my head that is filled with it. This is strange. It never occurred to me before that eggplant had an aroma. As I am lulled lazily into unawareness in the intoxicating vapors of aromatic eggplant, the stalactites overhead begin to pulse worryingly and then methodically and menacingly descend from the roof of Roopa's cave and station themselves in a halo around my shaved head. For a moment, I stop feeling secular. But only for a moment. As the stalactites encircle me, they address me in unison, singing in the style of an opera recitative. It must be contagious. I find I am replying in the same fashion, tra la la.

"Hello, Brian. Hello, Brian."

"Hello, yourself."

"Are you ready, are you ready, for the questionnaire?"

"I was not aware there would be a questionnaire."

"There's always a questionnaire. That's how the light gets in. There is no crack."

"Leonard wouldn't agree with that. I'm not sure I do either."

"You didn't think you were simply going to sleep through this, did you?"

"Isn't that what the purpua resca is supposed to do?"

"We don't know what the purpua resca is supposed to do but we do know that we are supposed to ask the questions, not you."

"No problem. If you'll just ask me what the purpua resca is supposed to do, I'll tell you."

"Sorry. That's not one of our questions. We can only ask our questions."

"All right. Why don't you go ahead and ask your questions?"

"That's a question. We're supposed to ask …"

"Let's not go through that again. Please, just ask your questions."

"Very well. If a penny saved is a penny earned, why doesn't saving replace earning?"

"You can't save what you don't earn. And I should know. I haven't earned or saved a penny in over five years. Next question."

"If cheaters never prosper, why are big business and government so full of them?"

"Maybe it's because that's where cheaters do, in fact, prosper."

"If the grass is always greener on the other side of the street, why don't we stop whining and cross the street?"

"There's too much traffic and we're afraid to jaywalk. And besides the grass isn't always greener over there. Sometimes, it's browner and covered in dog poo."

"If you can't take it with you, why don't we refuse to leave?"

"That's precisely what I've been doing with a lot of help, even though I have nothing I want to take with me."

"If too many cooks spoil the broth, why don't we skip the soup course?"

"Fine with me. With the exception of the last twenty-four hours, I'm exclusively on nutritionally supplemented clear fluids."

"If God doesn't show up soon, why don't we leave without him?"

"I haven't been expecting God any time soon for a long time. So maybe I have already left without him."

"If we can subsidize other countries to buy from us, why can't we subsidize the needy?"

"Because we're selfish and uncaring and think that the poor are needy by choice. We seem to look on poverty as a conspiracy of the poor, when, in fact, the opposite may be true. Wealth may actually be a conspiracy of the rich."

"If the poor are always with us, how come they look so forlorn and lonely?"

"Maybe the poor are always with us but we're not always with them. That can make them look forlorn and lonely."

"If a fool and his money are soon parted, how did the fool get his money in the first place?"

"Maybe he was a cheater who prospered while working for big business or the government."

"If a stitch in time saves nine, how come thread makers are still in business?"

"No matter how much it saves, a stitch in time still requires thread."

"If God is omnipresent, where is she when you need her?"

"I'm not sure that God is either omnipresent or a woman, but I agree with the rest of the question."

"If you can't find a needle in the haystack, why don't you buy another needle?"

"Because the point here is not the sewing but the searching."

"If it's a small world, how come it's such a big mess?"

"It's not a small world. It's a big world. What's small are the minds of its inhabitants. That's why it's such a big mess."

"If we don't have children, who will hit us up for money in our old age?"

"There will still be the taxman and telephone solicitations."

"If the early bird gets the worm, what does the early worm get?"

"The early worm gets harvested by the early bait collector."

"If money is the root of all evil, how are poorly financed, would-be evil-doers to manage?"

"Credit cards."

"If you neither a borrower nor a lender be, what be you?"

"I be a Martian."

"If all religions claim to be chosen, how are we to choose among them?"

"Maybe we could have a plebiscite every four years. Or maybe they could take turns."

"Would you describe yourself as a socialist?"

"Only if tortured. Otherwise, I'd say I was a pragmatist."

"Thank you for your responses to our questionnaire. Rest assured that we respect your privacy and will never share your confidential information with anyone."

"Hallelujah."

Dr. Roopa is back at my side. "How do you feel, mate?"

I feel like my head has just been run over by my own car again. I try to convey this to Roopa, but I hear my words echoing inside the new and strange emptiness in my head. Above my head, the microwave stalactites are back hanging from the cave roof and no longer pulsing. Dr. Roopa is busy assessing me with a cartful of electronic devices that he is applying to my head, to my chest, and to my big toes.

"I know you can hear me, mate. I want you to concentrate and try to move parts of your body as I direct you. We'll start with your toes. I'll help you."

He takes hold of my big toes and wiggles them.

"Now, you wiggle them."

I try. I do my best. I focus. I concentrate. I will my toes to wiggle. I order them to wiggle. I command them to wiggle. Wiggle, dammit. Wiggle, you little buggers. Wiggle. My toes remain oblivious to my imprecations. Nothing happens.

I hear Bessie from somewhere over Roopa's shoulder. "It's not working, is it, Doctor?"

"It's too soon to know, Mrs. Hildebrand. We have to be patient. It sometimes takes a while to kick in."

"Let's try your legs, mate." He bends my right leg. "Now, you bend it."

I try to bend my leg, but nothing happens. We repeat the exercise with the left leg. Again, nothing happens.

We try again with both arms and again without success.

"Fingers. Let's try your fingers. Like this." One at a time, Roopa bends each of the fingers of my right hand. "Now, you bend them."

Again, I concentrate on my right hand and one at a time, order my fingers to respond. Thumb. No response. Index finger. No response. Middle finger. No re… Wait. In the middle finger there is a slight tingling. I get excited. But my excitement is short-lived. The tingling stops. The finger does not move. There is nothing for Roopa to see and I'm unable to tell him about the tingling. I press on. Ring finger. No response. Little finger. No response.

I try the fingers of my left hand all without any response. As I finish with the left hand, the middle finger of my right hand tingles slightly again and I go back to it and concentrate. And then, it quivers slightly. I get excited again. Watching for the slightest movement, Roopa sees the finger quiver and lets out a delighted whoop and his team and mine descend on us and start hugging and applauding.

"Does that mean it's working now?" asks Bessie amidst the uproar.

"It's a good sign. But it's too soon to be sure," Roopa says. "We have to wait and see if it will last."

The middle finger of my right hand continues to quiver as Roopa continues to watch it. He tries to bend it, but it refuses to be bent.

"Can you bend that finger, mate?"

I try but the finger will not bend. Instead, it stiffens and stands out from the other fingers like the well-known Italian hand signal. I can't help thinking that if I could just move my arm, I could flip the bird to the group around me. But I can't move the arm.

Everybody is so busy watching the middle finger of my right hand that no one is watching the rest of me except Elissa who has been constantly scanning all of me for any promising signs of recovery. Suddenly, she spots something, nudges Bessie and points. Bessie looks, reacts, emits a cry of discovery.

"Look. Brian's lips. He's trying to move his lips."

And indeed, I am. Without realizing it, I have been making fumbling attempts to move my lips.

All eyes now turn to my lips, watching, waiting, hoping. Am I trying to talk?

Bessie thinks so. "He's trying to talk. Brian is trying to talk."

Roopa is not so sure. "We'll have to wait and see, Mrs. Hildebrand. He may just be trying to move his lips."

But, in fact, I am trying to do more than move my lips. I am trying to talk but finding it hard going. Nothing wants to come out. Still, I persist and finally, with the greatest of difficulty I manage to get a word out, one word, one solitary word.

"Hallelujah!" I say.

Bessie lights up. She is ecstatic. "He can talk. Brian can talk. Brian, sweetheart, talk to me."

"Hallelujah!" I repeat, unable to say more. "Hallelujah!"

And that's it. That's all I am able to say. "Hallelujah!" Nothing more.

"Good on you, Brian. That's a start," says Roopa. "We'll have to build on that."

"Hallelujah!" I say again. That's all I can manage. Between the one word that I'm able to utter and the erect and unbending middle finger of my right hand, I seem to be stuck. And not in a very good place. Several days pass and I stay stuck. So far, at least, the microwave procedure isn't working as hoped for and now it's time for me to be shipped back to Woodgreen House in Toronto.

"Hang in there, mate. Be patient," Roopa advises."

"Hallelujah!" I reply.

"Give it a few weeks," Roopa tells Bessie. "Every case is different. It might yet come to pass. Only time will tell. Don't give up."

A string of clichés, none promising. I am pissed off but persist in one-word utterances at inappropriate times. It's always the same word. "Hallelujah!"

Bessie descends into unhappy silence. Jefferson tries to keep our morale up with encouraging remarks but can't hide the disappointment in his eyes. Elissa stops her humming. Disappointment reigns. Disappointment pours.

"Hallelujah!"

28

HOMECOMING

MARK ME D plus. Disappointed, dispirited, dejected, I'm back in my room, my private preserve at Woodgreen, where I hang out or maybe I should say where I hang in. It's been a bleak homecoming. Somehow, it's the same old less, only there's more of it. The days hang on me like wet laundry. The weeks drag drearily by scraping at my already scarred psyche but nothing changes, nothing moves or improves. I may be imagining it but the status is not just quo but even more quo than ever, hyper-quo. It's a bloody bore. If I should suddenly expire without known cause, it will be because I will have been bored to death which, I suppose, beats death by having been punched, reamed, or drilled which would be death by cliché.

Bessie and Jefferson and even the usually silent Elissa try at every opportunity to encourage more words out of me and to get me to bend the unbending middle finger that stands out like a mini-erection from my right hand. "Hallelujah!" I continue to proclaim at inappropriate times and for no reason that they or I can discern. But I am utterly unable to utter another word.

111

No matter how hard I try, all that comes out is "Hallelujah!" and maybe a little bit of spit. At the end of my limp right arm, the middle finger of my right hand remains extended, unbendable, immobile, and implausibly menacing. Implicit in the fixed stance of the middle finger of my right hand is a sort of threatening aspect. Were I to recover the use of my right arm, the rigid digit could have weapons capability. I could, for example, poke someone in the eye, or in some other vulnerable area, for that matter. There are several such areas of vulnerability. Of course, I would have to think about it and decide among them which, if any, to attack.

I am jangled this morning, jingle-jangled. My thoughts are dancing around all over the place. It's March, the tedious TV tells me. The Ides of March spring to mind. The ideas of March would suit me better. I could use some ideas right now to help me shift out of Park. I've been in Park far too long. I need desperately to shift into Drive. Maybe I need a new transmission. Maybe that's my problem. Maybe I've become a car, a stalled car. There I go with the maybe, maybe, maybe, again. Maybe I'll stop.

All right. So it's March. So what? Do I really care what month it is? All months seem to be the same from my disadvantage point. It's mid-morning on what is starting out to be another one of those dismal, dull Fridays. Rain has been falling during the night and stopped only a little while ago. I envision the grass out there sopping wet and remind myself how as a young boy I loved to romp barefoot through the wet grass, stomping in the puddles to make them splash. That stopped when I stomped on a piece of broken glass and bled all over the good green grass of home, earning three stitches in the sole of my foot and a limp for a week or so. If there's a point to this rambling reminiscence, it's that anytime you're stuck in Park and can't shift into Drive, you can always Reverse into yesteryear. But don't stomp on the gas or on broken glass. And don't mangle metaphors unless absolutely necessary. Steer clear of metaphors.

Why am I doing this? Can it be because I am simultaneously in my mind and out of my mind? I must clear my head of this past pluperfect subjunctive retrogressive nonsense and try somehow to make the present tense relax and work for me. But I'm ticked off by the gray light seeping through my window this morning. If there's one thing I don't need it's more gray. Gray means it's cloudy out there in the free world. I don't care much for cloudy. I am already in a cloud. My life is a cloud and it's not cloud nine; it's cloud zero.

It may be my imagination, but there seems to be more stuff than ever ricocheting around in my head since my Baltimore medical misadventure. I wonder if my brain was broiled by Roopa's state of the art microwave device. Or poached. Or maybe, I'm just experiencing old fashioned data overload. My circumscribed circumstances seem not only to disproportionately magnify the value of incoming information but also to expand my eagerness to receive input, most of which comes from my eavesdropping on staff conversation. But not all. I pick up the odd thing from TV. I learned, for example, what month it was from TV. But, other than that, there is not much on TV that is useful in my unenviable circumstances. I may be easy to inform but I'm impossible to instruct and difficult to amuse. Besides, nobody but me knows the difference. Following Bessie's admonitions not to expose me to too much "mindless TV," Jefferson tries to ration what I watch. Mostly, I look at newscasts and documentaries with an occasional sitcom thrown in as a special indulgence. Fortunately, the sitcoms aren't always mindless but often they're not a treat either. The canned laughter on sitcoms drives me even crazier than I may already be. If the show is really funny, I don't understand why they don't trust us to recognize the humour without the canned laughter. What if they were to broadcast the canned laughter on its own, without the sitcom? Would that come off as funny? If it didn't, they could always insert the actors' lines to help us recognize that the canned laughter is funny. I'm starting to whinge and whine. Today is a downer, dammit. Maybe, I need a personal laugh track. A little canned haha couldn't hurt.

29

AMOS REDUX

THAT NIGHT, in the middle of the night, Amos, the Woodgreen wanderer, shuffles into Brian's room as if he had never died and is still alive. In his hand, as always, he carries the plastic bag filled with torn up paper scraps. Clearly, he never goes anywhere without it. Despite the darkness in my chamber of faint hopes, I can see quite clearly and it feels real, but I tell myself it must be a dream. The only thing is, I'm awake. Well, let me put it this way: I think I'm awake. It's gotten so I just don't know anymore. What with my old run-over head and my more recently microwaved brain, I may be working with equipment that's even more damaged than ever. Then again, maybe it's just a normal abnormal hallucination.

"Brian's room," Amos says. "Right?"

"Right."

"See. I told you I could find it."

"To tell you the truth, I wasn't expecting you Amos," I say lamely.

"No one expects me any more, since I died. I guess you heard I died."

"I heard, Amos. I'm really sorry."

"It's okay. That's life."

"So what have you been doing with yourself?"

"Not a lot. Waiting mostly. I came back three, four times to see you. But you weren't here."

"I was away."

"I figured."

"Sorry about that. I was in Baltimore."

"Baltimore? Clinical trial, right?"

"Right."

"Didn't work, right?"

"Not really."

"They took me to one of those in Rochester once. Didn't work for me either."

"It can be very disappointing."

"Yeah. Maybe, we can talk about what you want to tell me to tell your mother."

"Look, Amos, let me be honest with you. Now, that you've died, you're not going to be able to talk to my mother. She's not going to be able to hear you."

"I never thought of that. Too bad. I really would have liked to be an intermediary and tell her what you tell me to tell her."

"Sorry to disappoint you. I'm disappointed, too."

"That's okay. Maybe we can talk about other stuff."

"Like what?"

"Like no one out there really knows what's going on in here, in our minds."

"Nobody but us. And that's not much help."

"It's the out there versus the in here. They think we're out of it. But, really, we're into it. They just can't read us. So they treat us like dummies."

"Maybe, they're the dummies."

"My mother says…"

"Wait a minute. Didn't you tell me that your mother had died?"

"Oh yeah. Last year. But we keep in touch. Since I died, we talk almost every day."

"Really? I had no idea."

"She was not an educated person, my mother, or she never would have okayed my lobotomy. But it's amazing how smart she gets as time passes."

"And it's amazing how smartly time passes, isn't it?"

"Seems that way. But my mother says there's no hope."

"No hope? Why not?"

"Because it's all a conspiracy."

"All of it?"

"That's what my mother says."

"What about my problem, Amos? Could that could be a conspiracy, too?"

"I don't know. My mother hasn't mentioned it. I could talk to her and see what she says."

"Can I ask you a personal question, Amos?"

"I don't see why not."

"Where are you, now?"

"I'm in Brian's room with you."

"No. No. I mean where have you been since you died?"

"That's a good question."

"Are you in heaven?"

"I'm not sure. I keep asking. But no one seems to know."

"Are you with God?"

"He gets mentioned all the time. But he's never around."

"Are you a religious person, Amos?"

"Religious? I'm not sure. Spiritual, maybe. Let's say spiritual."

"Do you believe in God?"

"Seeing is believing and, so far, I haven't laid eyes on him."

"That must piss you off."

"I don't know. Nobody can tell God what to do. He's self-employed. He does his own thing."

"But you would like to see him and talk to him, wouldn't you?"

"Oh, absolutely. My mother says if I'm talking to God to be sure to ask him for a new dressing gown and slippers. These are pretty worn out. It's the least God can do, my mother says."

'The very least. What are you going to do when you leave here?"

"I've already left here."

"I mean when you leave my room."

"Oh. Right. I'll go back and wait and see if God shows up."

"If he does, after you talk to him about your dressing gown and slippers maybe you could do me a favor and talk to him for me."

"I could be your intermediary. Great. What do you want me to tell God? "

"Ask him what he's going to do about me?"

"Okay. I'll do that. Tell me, holy sir, what are you going to do about Brian?"

"Might as well ask your mother, too. Maybe she can come up with some ideas for me. But no lobotomy."

"Right. No lobotomy. I'll make a point of it. I'd better be going."

"Before you go, Amos, would you mind if I ask you one more question?"

"I don't mind. It feels like an interview."

"Why do you always carry that plastic bag with you?"

"Oh, that. It's the manuscript of my novel. I never let it out of my sight. It's my only copy. I don't want to lose it. Gotta go. It's getting late."

"Early. It's getting early."

"Good point. See you."

"Take care."

"I should have done that years ago."

30

REUNION

THE NEXT DAY things brighten up when Raymond Triggs, my visitor from New Zealand, walks briskly into my room unaided by a cane this time, clearly well on the mend from his hip surgery. The physiotherapy and the exercise program must be doing a good job. Mind you, Triggs has to be a big help in healing himself. He's a gung-ho, non-stop sort of guy. A moment later, almost immediately behind Triggs, Jefferson comes tripping in, bearing a little tray with a mug of coffee on it and this time not one but four cookies.

"Morning, Mr. Triggs. Good timing. You've lucked into more of Inez's famous cookies this visit and your usual black coffee, double sugar."

"If this keeps up, I'll have to visit more often. I don't get this kind of service anywhere, Jefferson. Thank you. And four cookies. You trying to fatten me up, mate?"

"No, not really. Inez made coconut macaroon chocolate chip cookies this time out. These are not the monster cookies of the recent past. These are little bitty guys, hardly any calories in them."

"I'll bet," says Triggs, smilingly tucking into the cookies.

Jefferson smiles back but doesn't leave. He just stands there silently. He appears to be waiting for Triggs to say something. Triggs, working away at the coffee and the cookies, says nothing. Finally, just as Jefferson seems as if he is about to take the initiative, Triggs looks up from the macaroons, catches on, and addresses himself to Jefferson.

"Great shame Brian's Baltimore trip didn't work out. I had high hopes that my mate, Roopa, could turn Brian around."

"Mrs. Hildebrand was very disappointed. All of us were."

"Brian must be very disappointed, too. Roopa tells me that Brian is in there, hears us and knows what's going on." He turns to Brian. "Is that right, Brian?"

"Hallelujah!"

Jefferson turns off the TV and turns to go. "I'll leave you two to have a quiet visit."

"Just one more thing, Jefferson. Are we expecting Mrs. Hildebrand today?"

"We are. And she should be here any time now."

"Great. At last, we get to meet."

Jefferson departs and Triggs, looking very earnest, turns to me. "I want you to know, Brian, how sorry I am that Roopa's treatment didn't work out for you. But hang in there, Brian my lad. Don't give up hope. We're going to keep working on it. We're not giving up on this. Don't you give up, either."

Needless to say, I am very touched by this heartfelt pep talk and the promise that accompanies it, but my inadvertent and inappropriate response is, "Hallelujah!"

Triggs finishes the last cookie and drains his coffee cup but before he can say more, in comes Bessie, coffee and sandwich in hand. She sees Triggs and stops just inside the doorway, looking startled, puzzled, confused, uncertain, all at once. I have never seen her quite that way before. Ever.

"I know you," she says in a small voice. "Aren't you...?" But she can't come up with the name.

Triggs, who has been sitting close to me, gets up, takes a step towards Bessie, and for a silent movie moment, they stand and simply look at each other. And then, she comes up with the name and can't let go of it.

"Ray? It is you, isn't it, Ray? After all these years, Ray. I don't believe it, Ray. You're Ray."

"Right on. Ray Triggs. It's been a long time. But you still remember me, don't you, Beth?"

"Yeth," she says. "Old joke. I call myself Bessie, now."

"Bessie, it is, then. Let me take those, Bessie."

Triggs reaches out and takes the coffee cup and the sandwich from her hands, deposits them on the windowsill and then comes back to where Bessie stands frozen, takes her now empty hands and holds them in his.

"I'm delighted you remember me, Bessie."

"I recognized your face right off. The Queen Mary, right?"

"Right. The old Queen Mary on an Atlantic crossing. We were en route from London to New York. They seated us together at lunch and we hit it off instantly and talked and talked and talked. All day long we talked and then, we spent that night together and…"

"And the next morning, Ray, we had breakfast together. And then, right after breakfast, you went to the loo and never came back. You disappeared. That was the last I saw of you. I was only nineteen." Bessie gets all teary-eyed and for a moment forgets she is an atheist. "Oh, my God!"

"I was just a young kid myself, just turned twenty. The reason I disappeared was that I had an acute appendicitis attack in the loo that morning and they took me off the ship in an emergency helicopter and flew me to New York for surgery."

"I remember I was heart broken at not seeing you again."

"So was I. After they took out my appendix, I tried to track you down in New York, but I was never able to find you."

"I had gone on to Montreal and then to Toronto. I had no idea you were looking for me. And now, more than thirty years later, you've found me. What a surprise."

"You can thank Brian for that. I found him first."

"That's incredible. How did you find him?"

"We have to thank my mate Roopa for that. He put me onto Brian."

"Dr. Roopa? Our Dr. Roopa?"

"That's the one. I should explain. I'm an architect and builder back home in New Zealand. My company designs a lot of medical facilities and we did a clinic for Roopa in Auckland, a few years back, and my research for the building got me interested in Roopa's research. After he went over to Johns Hopkins in Baltimore, I continued to do work for him. On more than one occasion, when I was in Baltimore, Roopa and I talked about the microwave device that he'd developed that he hoped might unlock locked-in coma victims. Turns out Roopa was searching all over the U.S. and Canada to find candidates for clinical trials of his invention. He'd come across Brian's case in a medical journal and thought Brian might be a good candidate for the clinical trials of the device. When he gave me a printout of the article and I read the name Hildebrand, I wondered if Brian could somehow be related to you. It was a long shot but I hoped he might lead me to you. It never occurred to me that he was your son. I assumed you had long ago married and had a new name."

"Only a new first name. Bessie. But the old surname Hildebrand lives on. People insist on calling me Mrs. Hildebrand, but I never married."

"I've been married three times. Either I made three bad choices or I'm just not very good at it."

"Three times unlucky. Still, you must have some nice kids."

"Only one, a son."

"Just like me."

"Right on. Just like you, Bessie."

As I listen to this exchange, a light comes on. It's as if I'm watching a movie, suddenly foresee the surprise ending and know what's coming. These two long-ago lovers each have one son. And in a moment it will turn out that each son is named Brian. And finally, it will emerge that both Brians are me, Brian Hildebrand. Raymond Triggs, the architect from New Zealand, is my father.

Except for one word, I'm speechless.

"Hallelujah!"

It's a hallelujah moment for me but it takes a moment longer for Bessie to get it. "What's your son's name?"

My newly discovered dad keeps her in suspense as long as he can.

"Same as your son's."

"Brian? Just a minute. Are you saying what I think you're saying?"

"What do you think I'm saying?"

"That Brian is your...." Bessie's eyes widen in disbelief... "son?"

"Yes, that's exactly what I'm saying, Bessie. Brian is my son."

Bessie isn't buying it.

"How can you possibly know that? You weren't the only one in my life back then."

"I'm not surprised. You were a knockout. Anyhow, that thought had occurred to me. And I didn't want to spring this on you until I was sure. So I had my mate Roopa organize some DNA testing. And guess what? Brian and I are a perfect match. And just in case, you're wondering, the risk of a coincidental match is one in a hundred billion. And so are you, Bessie. You're still a knockout."

"You cheeky bugger," Bessie says. "You got me pregnant and took off. You abandoned a pregnant woman, Ray."

There are tears in her eyes. But she is smiling.

"Well, I'm here, now, for both of you."

All of a sudden, just like that, I have two parents. And both of them are here, not just for each other, but also for me, and they're talking to me, and at me, and in front of me, and beside me, and around me. I am surrounded, encircled, enveloped, in fervent assurances of unending love, care, support, all times two, and it's coming at me every which way. Need I say, this blows my already busy – make that dizzy – mind.

And then, while I struggle to get my head around this outburst of input, my freshly reconnected parents hug me, kiss me, promise to be back in a little while and then, arm in arm, go marching off for "a long catch-up lunch in some nice quiet little place," leaving behind on the bed, their much moved but totally unmoving son and heir, yours truly, Brian Hildebrand, and on the windowsill, Bessie's untouched sandwich and coffee.

31

WHAT NEXT?

MILLIE'S VOICE hasn't popped into my head for some time. I keep wondering if I'm ever going to hear from her again. There's not much I can do to make it happen. All I can do is wait and hope that if she suddenly drops in on me that I'll somehow be able to convince her to come to Toronto and be my intermediary, so I can communicate through her and get my message out.

In the meantime, I have lots of other things to think about. Dr. Roopa is still on my case. He hasn't given up on me and talks to Bessie weekly and also to his mate, Ray Triggs. At Triggs' behest, Roopa is trying to come up with some alternative ways to help me. Bessie comes to see me daily just as before, but she seems much happier than usual. Ray Triggs, my newfound dad, also visits regularly, though less frequently, since he is facing tight deadlines on his architectural work for Woodgreen West, the new hospital wing. Sometimes, Ray visits with Bessie, and sometimes he comes on his own. When they're both here, they talk mostly to me about me and how they hope to help me.

From their body language, when they're together I am pretty certain that Bessie and Ray are in some sort of ongoing relationship, but they don't discuss it when they visit. And Bessie isn't talking about it to me or to anyone else in my presence, so I have no way of knowing precisely what is going on between my mother and father, but whatever it is it seems to be a happy arrangement and I am happy for them and for myself. Hey! Two parents! After all these years with only one parent, suddenly having two should be a shock, I suppose, except that I'm already in shock and besides, they're different kinds of shock. Father, good. Accident, not so good.

I doubt that Jefferson has any idea that Ray Triggs is anything other than a sort of long-ago friend of the family as he had earlier described himself. Bessie and Jefferson never talk about it when I'm around and I'm always around, now that I'm back from my less than life changing travel break. Jefferson continues to be his usual cheerful, witty, supportive self, and now that he knows that I can hear what he says, he talks to me at even greater length than in the past. Lately, he tells me about his writing and his dream of being a poet and novelist. He even reads me a couple of his long poems, blank verse with lots of striking images. I was never that much into poetry, so I don't really know how to judge his poems, but he reads them with great passion and I must say I enjoy the reading. But I was always a fiction fancier and I'm eager to know more about his novel, but he doesn't give me any details. All he will say is that it's experimental. Sometimes, he describes it as metafiction. I'm familiar with the term, but I'm not entirely sure I know what it means. Mind you, writers of metafiction don't always know what it means themselves.

Jefferson doesn't tell me the title of his novel or talk about the story, so I have no idea what it's about. But he describes at some length the difficulty he's having in getting it published. Though she hasn't read the manuscript, Bessie is trying to help by putting Jefferson onto a few people she knows in the publishing business, so far without any luck. One by one, perhaps out of deference to Bessie, they agree to read the first ten pages of the manuscript, but its anxious author often has to wait months for a response and then, one by one he's told "Sorry, but ..." The submission process is tedious, takes forever, and seems to lead to nothing but rejection. Still, Jefferson doesn't lose heart. He is very determined. He's not giving up. He continues to chase his dream.

Bessie must have talked to Ray about Jefferson's failed attempts to get his novel published because one day when Triggs is visiting, I overhear them talking about it.

"If you want to get your novel published, you need an agent, mate," Ray Triggs is telling Jefferson. "A literary agent, that's what you need. Mark my words."

Jefferson looks uncertain. He has been submitting his manuscript directly to publishers. The idea of a literary agent is a totally foreign notion for Jefferson.

"An agent? That never occurred to me. How do I get an agent?"

"Well, it ain't easy, mate. But you might want to try the strategy that helped me get published."

"You're a writer? I had no idea."

"Well, I'm no novelist, I can tell you that. Wish I was. I'm an architect and now and again, I write about architecture. I've published three books so far. But getting my first book published was a tough slog. None of the publishers in New Zealand or Australia was interested. And back then, I knew bloody little about agents because there were so few of them in that part of the world.

"Then, I ran across an article in The Economist about the publishing industry in Great Britain and discovered that London was not only a hotbed of British publishers, but also of hundreds of literary agents, hundreds. So I decided to try to get myself an agent in London. I found a list of British agents on the internet. Many still prefer to be contacted by snail mail. They're a stodgy lot. But because overseas post takes forever, I decided to take my chances and query them by email.

"I learned a hell of a lot about agents. Some don't accept queries of any kind. Some don't accept email queries. Some don't open their email. Some don't reply. Some reply and simply say, no thanks or not interested. And they're all wary as hell of first-time writers. They favor published authors with track records. Chasing after agents can be frustrating. And time consuming. But I'm a stubborn bugger and I stuck to my plan and just kept sending out my email queries.

Dear sir: Can I interest you in representing my book about architecture of the future? It deals with blah, blah, blah. And after about thirty queries with no luck, an agent who handled non-fiction exclusively agreed to read the first fifty pages of the manuscript and asked me to email it to him as an attachment along with a synopsis of the book, a chapter outline, and my biography. So that's what I did. And a few days later, he requested the complete manuscript and again suggested it be sent by email as an attachment. He warned me that it might take a couple of months to make a decision before he got back to me and advised me to be patient. A week later, he emailed back saying that he and his colleagues liked the book and were prepared to represent me. We signed a contract, and to my disbelief and great delight, he sold the book the next day."

"Wow!" says Jefferson. "That's a very encouraging story."

"It tells well but it's a hell of a lot of work, mate. Remember, this is non-fiction I'm talking about. I understand that it's even harder with fiction. Still, my marketing strategy should work for you. Just do what I did. You'll need a list of agents who represent fiction, a good query letter, and persistence."

"That's very helpful," Jefferson says. "Thank you for the advice. I'll get on it right away."

And so, Jefferson does his internet research, compiles a list of British literary agents who represent fiction, composes what he describes as a "dynamite" query letter and turns himself into a serial emailer, sending out query after query after query. And time passes and passes and passes. And nothing much happens. But Jefferson is undaunted and determined. He doesn't despair, doesn't let up. He persists. And so do we all.

32

G-O-D Almighty

Even though Amos stays in touch with me after his death, my plan to use him as my communications intermediary dies when Amos dies. It is clear to me that though they may somehow manage to talk to the dead or disabled, dead men tell no tales to the living and able. My best bet, then, is to get on with plan B. This depends on the return of Millie who, at the moment, is the only hope I have of being able to communicate with the outside world. But the plan is fraught with if's and maybe's. As time goes by and I don't hear from Millie, I begin to lose hope of her ever visiting me again. Besides, I worry about being able to make the plan work even if she does come back. But unless the good Dr. Roopa comes up with some breakthrough for me – and he's doing his damnedest, according to Bessie and Ray – Millie is all I have to hang my hopes on and she's an outside chance at best. Still, I wait and, still, there's no word from her. This telepathic dropping into other minds, these episodes of hers, as Millie calls them, only happen, she says, when she's doing homework.

Has she stopped doing homework? Is that it? What's going on? Where is she?

Then, one morning without warning, there's another voice in my head besides my own. But to my annoyance and great disappointment, it's not Millie's voice, dammit. It's an adult voice. Now, what? Is someone else doing homework?

"Am I in Brian's room?"

"Actually, you're in Brian's head which is in Brian's room."

"Then, you would be Brian?"

"I would."

"You wanted to talk to me."

"Did I? What about?" I try not to sound hostile but I'm irritated.

"No idea. I'm just going by what Amos told me. After our discussion about his dressing gown and slippers, he said you wanted to talk to me. It was a little garbled."

"Poor old Amos. He can get a little garbled. Still, he was able to get through to you about getting him a new dressing grown and slippers."

"Well, yeah, sort of. But I don't do wardrobe. I'm not a clothing store. His mother was after me on that, too. And all that conspiracy crap of hers. That woman is a wacko. But never mind them. What do you want to talk to me about?"

"I assume you're aware of my situation."

"Not a clue. What situation is that?"

"I'm on life support after an accident, having been wrongly diagnosed as being in a persistent vegetative state but, in fact, I'm not vegetative. I'm conscious, cognitive, all my senses work but I can't move and I can't talk. I'm locked in."

"Yeah, well, shit happens. Why are you telling me all this?"

"I need your help. I want out. I want to get unlocked. Can you help me?"

"Afraid not. That's not what I do."

"What exactly do you do?"

"Nothing."

"Nothing?"

"Well, nothing that I can share with you."

"Why not?"

"Because it's classified information."

"That's not very helpful."

"I don't do helpful."

"After all I'd heard about you, that's a let down."

"Face it. Life is a start up followed by a let down."

"If you can't help, if you don't care, what's the point?"

"There is no point."

"If there is no point, why are you here?"

"You don't get it do you, Brian?"

"What is there to get?"

"I'm not what you think I am."

"All right. I give up. What are you?"

"I'm a metaphor."

"But metaphors muck up meaning."

"Right on. So you do get it, after all."

"How long have you been a metaphor?"

"Since day one."

"I can't believe what I'm hearing. Bessie would love this."

"Who is Bessie?"

"Never mind. It doesn't matter."

33

ANOTHER PROVINCE HEARD FROM

JEFFERSON KEEPS a hand mirror on hand so that every so often, after he shaves me or cuts my hair, he can let me have a look at myself. This is usually accompanied by a running commentary, always encouraging, often amusing.

"Short on the sides, long on the top. Have I made you look good, dude, or what? Hey! Maybe I'll become a hair stylist, with my own chain of shops all over the place, my own line of shampoos, conditioners, cream rinses. I could be a hair somebody. Guten tag, hair somebody. What do you think, dude?"

I'm unable to say so to Jefferson, but I think he'd hate being a hair somebody. Besides, at the moment, I'm the hair somebody. All my body hair, depilated to prepare me for Dr. Roopa's microwave procedure, is growing back at speeds that vary by location. Via his nimbly moving mirror, Jefferson gives me a guided tour of the various sites, so I can see for myself the varying degrees of returning hirsuteness. The Pillsbury doughboy of the clinical trial is slowly morphing into a furry critter. I'm not sure I care one way or the other. How will hair help me?

"Hey, dude, you're turning into a fuzzball," Jefferson says. "Keep this up and you'll be a hairy beast again before you know it."

With or without hair, it's always a shock to look at myself in the mirror and be confronted with how my appearance has changed since the accident. There is an almost haunting gauntness about me. Due to my weight loss during my long immobility and my reduced caloric intake, I have become all skinny and bony. It's hard to bulk up on a feeding tube. And the change in my eyes, the fixed stare, is really scary. My face is frozen and expressionless except for those rare, random moments when my lips move suddenly in the desperate delivery of my newly acquired mantra, my one-word soliloquy. "Hallelujah!"

On those infrequent occasions when this inexplicable and convulsive word birthing coincides with my looking at myself in the mirror, I am riveted by the brief but fierce struggle of my lips to emit the word, one lousy word, from within the inert, inner depths of my frozen face.

But above all, what I see in the mirror now is a far cry from how I looked before the accident. I took it for granted back then, but I was a handsome rascal. I can say this now in retrospect without being accused of vanity. Six feet tall, blond, blue-eyed, buff, I worked out three times a week. In days gone by, I was a hunk. Today, I'm a clunk. And a monk.

What else is new? Not much. Mind you, the usually silent Elissa has been talking a lot to Bessie the last little while. Bessie has always been Elissa's advocate and Elissa has always related to her and talked to her while talking little, or not at all, to anyone else. And lately, there has been much more talk between Elissa and Bessie than ever before. But Elissa, when she speaks, is soft spoken and hard to hear so even with my acute hearing I am not always able to get enough out of the conversation to make sense of it. Something is going on but I don't know what it is.

Still, I sense that this is about to change. And as it turns out, I am right. In my presence, Bessie soon fills Ray Triggs in on her discussions with Elissa and so I become privy to what all the talk with Elissa is about.

Elissa has told Bessie that she thinks she may be able to help me get unlocked. Now, here's the funny part. Despite Elissa's extensive, professional though uncertified, Russian credentials in neurology, she is suggesting trying a folk remedy on me passed down by her peasant grandmother who was a midwife and backwoods healer in the Ukraine. Elissa hasn't spelled out to Bessie what the remedy entails and because she doesn't wish to be perceived as an interloper in the affairs of her certified professional betters, she would like to talk to Dr. Roopa and get his blessings before she asks Bessie for her formal approval to proceed.

"Dr. Roopa is an aboriginal," Elissa tells Bessie. "He will understand the type of healing I am proposing."

Bessie and Ray decide that there's nothing to be lost by looking into this further and agree to arrange for Elissa to talk to Roopa about it, perhaps in an exchange of emails under the editorial eye of Bessie with Ray Triggs assisting. As usual, I don't get a vote, but what the hell, right now, I'm game to try anything that might unlock me, even folk remedies.

34

Barcelona

On the button as always, Jefferson is on my case this morning, giving me my start-of-the-day pep talk as he works around me, cleaning me up and checking me out for any possible post-microwave progress. But there has been no magical overnight success and so nothing new for Jefferson to report. My forward pointing finger is still poised as if for combat but as things stand, it couldn't fight a marshmallow if it had to. And I, of course, am still personally poised for pretty much nothing whatsoever and couldn't eat a marshmallow, if I wanted to, although I don't know why I would want to eat a marshmallow, except, maybe, as a sign of recovery. Unlike the rest of the civilized world, I was never mad for marshmallows. But peanut butter—that was another story.

I'm not sure why but Jefferson isn't getting a single "Hallelujah!" out of me today, not a one. My "Hallelujah!" delivery system seems to have taken the day off without my permission. Mind you, it's nice to have a break from the unpredictability of "Hallelujah!", even though Dr. Roopa still hopes it may be the first step in recovering my ability to talk. It's a small step, granted, and a faint hope, looking fainter day by day. But I must admit that it's a bit of a hoot when, occasionally, by chance, "Hallelujah!" pops out as a perfectly timed payoff line in response to some outside comment.

"I'm going to change your diaper, dude."

"Hallelujah!"

I can take no credit for the timing. Like everything else, at the moment, it's beyond my control. I can't summon it up. It's random, ridiculously random. In the realm of one-word utterances, nobody can quoth like Poe's raven and its "Nevermore." That bird of Poe's, of course, was in charge. This bird is definitely not.

Cranked up into as much of a seating arrangement as all my life-supporting hardware will permit, I command the room, Brian's room, with my intense but narrow gauge gaze, doing my thing—nothing—while contemplating how many unresolved story threads I have managed to weave through my meandering account of the many misadventures of my over-boggled mind and how many loose, and perhaps frayed, ends this obliges me to deal with. Too many, I'm afraid. But suddenly, the question of which loose or frayed end to attend to next is answered by a visiting voice in my head. What luck! It's Millie, back at last. And now, maybe, we can move on with my plan B. Maybe. Big maybe. Jumbo maybe.

"Brian? Are you here?"

"Millie. Hi. Where have you been? I missed you."

"I missed you, too. Summer holidays. No homework."

"I should have known."

"I'm sorry your trip to Baltimore was a disappointment. Mom and I took a trip, too, to Barcelona."

"How would you and your mom like to take another trip?"

"Where to?"

"Toronto. To visit me. I need your help, but you would have to be here."

"I'd like to but I'm back in school. And mom is back at work."

"Maybe you could come for a weekend."

"I don't know. It might be difficult. I haven't told mom about you."

"Why not?"

"She worries that I'm imagining things."

"Maybe, I'm the one who's imagining things."

"I don't think so."

"Maybe, I'm imagining you."

"You're not. I'm real. Oh. Oh. I'm drifting. I have to go."

"Wait. Will you talk to your mom?"

"I'm not sure. I'll see."

"Please, try and come back and let me know."

"I'll try. I can't promise. Bye."

There is a sound like a sigh and then, silence. She is gone. Nothing is resolved. Plan B is up in the air. Just like me.

35

FOLK MEDICINE

MY EAVES DROP me the information that there has now been an exchange of emails between Elissa and Dr. Roopa. I know that much but no more. I have yet to learn what was said in the emails and still don't know if Roopa has blessed Elissa's plan to practice her granny's folk medicine on me or not. I am waiting expectantly, hoping to be brought into the loop by Bessie or Ray. Until then, I'm in the dark about what Elissa plans to do to—or for—me. Jefferson who is usually a helpful source of useful information is of little help this time out. He hasn't been party to what's been going on and so isn't able to tell me much. Mostly he makes jokes about the little he has picked up which is very little.

"You're going to be getting a tasty treatment from Elissa. She's planning to cover your entire body in guacamole, amigo," he says with a straight face.

Wait a minute. What's with this amigo stuff? He should have said, "Elissa is planning to baste you in borscht, comrade." What happened to dude? Jefferson is putting me on with a straight face. And he doesn't stop.

"And then, she's going to sprinkle you with chipotle sauce, amigo." He tries not to smile but can't help himself. He's having a good time. He enjoys pulling my leg. I don't mind. My leg isn't doing anything anyway.

Actually, if I'm going to be an amigo instead of a dude, hold the chipotle sauce. Given a choice, I'd prefer to be sprinkled with stardust, but the only stars I know are brightly burning balls in outer space light years away and as far as I can tell, they're all dust free. This line of reasoning will take astronomical research and get me nowhere, which is where I already am. Maybe I won't bother.

When I finally find out from Bessie what Elissa has in mind for my treatment, I must confess it's a bit of a let-down. Elissa's folk medicine involves no medications, no surgery, no devices, no science of any kind. It consists of the laying on of hands, the healing hands that Elissa claims to have inherited from her Ukrainian grandmother healer. And what does Roopa think of the idea? Elissa was right. Roopa gets it.

"No problem," Roopa says. "My people have been healing with healing hands for thousands of years. Does it work? It works if you think it works, the placebo effect, maybe. Let's give it a go. Even if it doesn't work, there's no harm done."

Right on. No travel required. No baked, cooked, or poached brain to worry about this time. And no master chef needed.

So Elissa's treatment program is a go. And while I'm initially skeptical about this type of healing, I have nothing to lose. Besides, if as Roopa says, it works if you think it works, and I think it works, it will work. And maybe, I'll get lucky. The odds are long, but an attenuated life is short, so I'll tell myself I think it works and let's get on with it.

But Elissa is not ready to rush into immediate action. There are preparations she must first make. She must gird herself to do battle with the forces that hold me prisoner. She must concentrate. She must focus her powers to move energy into her hands in order to heal. She must meditate. She must contemplate. She must consolidate all the energy in her mind and in every cell of her being and slowly push it, pull it, drive it, shift it, move it, through the innumerable energy channels of her body and into her healing hands right to the very vibrating fingertips. And when her hands are abuzz with energy, only then, will she will be ready.

To do all this, she must be even more silent, if such a thing is possible, than she already is, and she must be still and breathe slowly and deeply while seated in a dark room, ideally, close to the patient for however many hours it takes, until her hands are fully energized and ready to go to work.

As I may have related earlier, at night with the lights out and the blinds closed, there is no darker room than Brian's room. And that's where my support groupies have decided that Elissa's preparatory energy marshalling vigil will take place. The next evening, a reclining lounge chair is brought in and positioned in a corner outside my range of vision. Then Elissa comes in, makes herself comfortable in the chair. The slats in the blinds are closed. The lights are turned off. And with darkness and silence, part one of Elissa's folk healing ritual begins.

I see nothing. I hear only Elissa's slow, deep breathing. And then it fades away and there is silence and I am either asleep and dreaming or in another dimension. On a bitter, cold winter night, holding my right hand tentatively in front of me, I am walking into the emergency ward waiting room of a downtown hospital.

The middle finger of my right hand is a strange colour and throbs with pain. That must be why I am here. I don't remember what happened to my finger. Maybe I drove over it. That seems unlikely. Besides, there are no tread marks on it. Still, I show it to the triage nurse. The nurse is black, maybe fifty and a nifty, no-nonsense dispenser of care and not one to be messed with. She has been and seen it all. Nothing fazes her. She is warm and wise and droll, very droll. She looks at my aching finger appraisingly.

"That's quite a mess of finger you've got yourself there, boyo. But you're in luck. A shipment of fresh fingers just came in. We can replace your finger with a new one in a jiffy. Have a seat," she says. "We'll call you. It will hurt less if you keep your hand raised but don't point that finger of yours at anybody. They might take offense."

I wait for her to wink or grin, but she doesn't. So I take a seat and look around. It is 3:00 a.m., and the waiting room is crowded with dejected people in various states of despair and disrepair, the bashed, the bloodied, the worried, the harried, all waiting, waiting, waiting. There seems to be no end to the waiting, nor to the impatience of those who wait, some of whom look around and mutter complainingly to themselves every so often. A few even whimper a bit.

A man enters the waiting room from the innards of the hospital, a beaten down old guy, grizzled, bearded, seventy some-

144

thing, in bedroom slippers and wearing a thin windbreaker. He stops, looks around. All the seats are taken, except the one next to me. He shuffles over and wearily plunks himself down. Sighing deeply, he looks me over and addresses me.

"That's some sore looking finger you got yourself there."

"Yeah. It hurts like hell."

"How did you manage to do that?"

"I'm not sure. I think I must've driven over it."

"Couldn't have been easy to do."

"Guess not. If it was easy, more people would be doing it."

"Emergency's not a happy place, is it?"

"Never is. No one smiles."

The old guy rubs his arms. "Cold out there tonight."

"Sure is."

He indicates his slippers and windbreaker. "I was in a rush and didn't dress warm enough. Came in from Newmarket."

"Long way to come."

"Came in the ambulance with my wife. She had open-heart surgery about a month ago and suddenly started having trouble breathing."

"Isn't there a hospital in Newmarket?

"Her surgery was done here. It seemed wisest to come here. Didn't help though. We lost her. Died about twenty minutes ago."

"Oh, I'm terribly sorry."

"Yeah. It's tough. She had health problems for years. Now, it's all over but the memories. I'm on my own."

"Not easy losing someone you love. You have my sympathy."

The triage nurse catches my eye, shakes her head and wags a finger at me. She's trying to tell me something, but I fail to comprehend.

"And now I got to get back to Newmarket, but I left in a rush without my wallet and I have no money for bus fare."

"How much is bus fare? Maybe I can help you out."

The triage nurse rolls her eyes, shakes her head, and gives up.

"Eight dollars. I could send you the money when I get home."

"That's fine."

I reach into my pocket with my good hand and bring out a twenty-dollar bill.

"A twenty is all I have." I hesitate and for a moment, there is silence. "I guess you better take the twenty."

"Give me your card. I'll mail the twenty back to you as soon as I get home."

I give him my card and the twenty. "Good luck."

"You, too. Thanks for your help, And good luck with your finger."

The old guy gets up and shuffles off back into the hospital.

The nurse beckons to me. I go over to her desk.

"Twenty dollars. That's a big score for him. He's a panhandler, you know. I tried to warn you. Comes in here about once a month. Tells a good story. Dresses right. The bedroom slippers, the thin windbreaker, the whole bit."

"At first, I couldn't figure out your signals. But just before I handed over the twenty, it dawned on me."

"But still, you gave him the money. Why?"

"Maybe for the same reason you let him come in here. Or maybe it was as a reward for his performance. Mind you, I'd have preferred the eight-dollar performance to the twenty. But twenty was all I had. Even panhandlers are needy. Somebody has to help the needy. I guess it was my turn."

"You wouldn't like a job here, would you?"

I'm contemplating that employment opportunity when, just as he has five mornings a week for the last five years, Jefferson comes into the inky dinky darkness of my room, slashes open the vertical blinds to let the daylight sidle through the slats, taps the remote control that cranks my motorized bed – and my silent, staring, unmoving form along with it – into the sitting position. He turns on the overhead lights. And at this point, Elissa gets up from the lounge chair that she has spent the night in and looking a little sleep deprived, silently walks through my area of vision and out the door. Jefferson grins at her as she goes by and looks at me impishly.

"Hey, dude. What's going on? You sleeping with the help?"

Now, he's pulling my other leg. Well, at least, he didn't call me amigo this time.

36

HANDS ON

HAVING BEEN adequately prepared, Elissa's hands are now fully primed and not only ready, but also willing and eager, to proceed with the hands-on treatment. No change of venue necessary, I'm being treated in situ, so to speak, right here where I live, in Brian's room, my hang-in hangout, and in my very own state-of-the-art, motorized, not so rosy bed of roses that has been maneuvered electronically into a sort of reclining position. Elissa's healing hands will be traveling principally over the surface of my head, neck, and spine with excursions over my upper and lower limbs.

Not surprisingly, Bessie is present for the procedure along with Ray Triggs and my loyal laugh-a-minute amigo, Jefferson Baines, all of whom cluster together to bear hopeful witness during the procedure – silently, at Elissa's insistence – just inside the door of my room closed to keep stray visitors from unexpectedly walking or propelling their wheelchairs in during the festivities. Elissa has impressed on Bessie that for her healing powers to be effective, there must be an ambience free of interruptions. While I can't speak for my support group, or for myself for that matter, I'll certainly expect to be silent and not interrupt, unless I get lucky and win the healing hands lottery. Then, of course, I will make a lot of noise, scream with delight, dance a jig. I should get so lucky.

Standing at my bedside with her slightly cupped hands out in front of her as if holding an imaginary basketball, Elissa gives me the once over, twice, surveying me with that strange flickering gaze of hers. She is silent as always but paler than usual and still humming her theme song almost imperceptibly except to my hyper hearing. Her mien is thoughtful, focused, and somehow filled with hope. It's hard to explain, but what I read in her expression is that she really cares and is eager for her ministrations to help me. This is very reassuring and, insofar as I am able, I try to loosen up, at least in my mind. Elissa's hands holding the imaginary basketball flutter briefly, freeing the imaginary sphere that I hope will be an actual rather than imaginary slam-dunk. And the laying on of hands begins.

Hovering like hummingbirds about an inch above my body, Elissa's hands never stop moving yet never touch me. They fly over me, gliding and dipping, swooping and looping, churning the air, slowly tracing the shape of my head, of my neck, of my back. Though at first I feel nothing, the effect is strangely calming, perhaps even relaxing, as if my body in its present state ever actually relaxes. Maybe it's all in my head along with everything else that's in there. And then, as Elissa's hands continue to knead the air about the contours of my head and face in intricate patterns that shift and change and flow into one another, I begin to feel a slight sensation of warmth in my head and neck and down my arms.

The healing hands float languidly from my right shoulder over my right arm and drift slowly along to my right hand where they circumnavigate the erect and menacing middle finger. Again, there is a slight sensation of warmth but nothing to break a sweat over. Then the hands, propelling the warmth before them, swirl about my left shoulder and cascade over my left arm and flow along its length to my left hand where the warmth turns into a sudden sharp jab of heat, whereupon the middle finger in an abrupt and convulsive twitch, springs into high attack mode and stays that way. Now I have two erect and menacing middle fingers. Since a long-gone childhood limp from a broken glass cut in the sole of my foot that made me temporarily asymmetrical, bodily symmetry has always been important to me. Now, with a fighting finger standing guard not just on one but on both hands, I am, once again, symmetrical. I am not certain that symmetry will help in my special circumstances. Still, I can hope and it can't hurt.

Elissa does not react to this redressing of the asymmetrical, but I hear a gasp from Bessie over by the door and I sense she is struggling to stay silent as the healing hands wing their way through the air with the greatest of ease back to my head where they trace the ups and downs of my physiognomy, tracking over the landscape of my face and circling the hollows of my eyes and the curves of my ears and sliding down the ski slope of my nose and finally focusing on my unmovimg mouth where they circle and circle in a concerted manner until my lips quiver and my mouth once again contorts in a tortured attempt to speak.

After several attempts a word emerges, but it is the word I already know and own. "Hallelujah!" I am about to give in to disappointment. But then, there are more contortions of my mouth. Will I beget yet another "Hallelujah!" or will additional words be forthcoming? After an agony of contorting and waiting, in an explosive ejaculation, the word "Hallelujah!" is again expelled, but this time it is conjoined with the word "brother." The two words emerge together. "Hallelujah, brother!"

With this, Elissa intensifies her efforts. But another concentrated hour of Elissa's healing hands elicits nothing more from me, no more physical changes, no additional words, save only another sudden and unexpected "Hallelujah, brother!"

I feel strongly that the two words should have been "Oh shit!" because in my head that's what I'm saying. Like it or not, take it or leave it, I have been endowed with a new mantra. It is "Hallelujah, brother!" Oh, shit!

37

AFTER EFFECTS

So HERE I AM again, trying to make the most of another failed attempt to unlock me from my unrelenting limbo. As far as the restoration of the original Brian goes, I'm on a losing streak, batting zero, and cavalierly tossing about and injudiciously mixing the metaphors I disdained so vehemently at the outset. The laying on of Elissa's healing hands has succeeded only in pointlessly raising a second erect middle finger and painfully extracting a second unhelpful word from my reluctant mouth. These are not the results I was hoping for. Uncontrollably and usually at the most inappropriate times, I now blurt out, "Hallelujah, brother!" All right. So I've just doubled my verbal output. This might make me a big kahuna at a prayer meeting. But how it can possibly help me with my escape project escapes me. Everything escapes me. Except myself. I am unable to escape myself.

Once again Brian's room is so clogged with frustration, it would take a big plunger to clear it. Elissa, having done her best and drained herself in the doing of it, looks thoroughly exhausted, but otherwise shows no outward emotion. Implacable on the surface and silent as usual, she says nothing. Still, behind her mask of silence, she must be deeply disappointed with the failure of her family folk remedy. I can say this with some certainty because once again, for only the second time since I have known her, she is not humming that Russian theme song of hers. "Those were the days, my friend. I thought they'd never end." But they did end, dammit.

Unlike the impassive appearing Elissa, Jefferson, wears his gloom on his face and for the moment at least takes a turn for the glum and stops making jokes. Bessie and Ray, their heads together in earnest conversation, are talking in low voices. And then Bessie is on the phone reporting to Dr. Roopa the results of Elissa's efforts.

"Elissa worked her heart out, gave it her best shot. It didn't really do much and what it did isn't all that helpful," she tells Roopa, as she informs him of the appearance of the second stiff middle finger and the vocal emergence of the conjoined "Hallelujah, brother!"

We can't hear Roopa's response, but it goes on at some length. My guess is that he's delivering a message of hope, a pep talk, a rallying cry to the troops, all that kind of thing. What can I say? Nothing, as usual.

"Dr. Roopa has just reminded me," Bessie repeats to the assembled after she hangs up, "that there are no guarantees that any treatment of Brian will work. It's a matter of trial and error and persistence. We all agree with Dr. Roopa that we must continue to hope and try. Dr. Roopa advises patience and assures me that he hasn't abandoned Brian. He's still working to come up with some answers and a new plan of attack."

That's all very well. But his microwave device didn't work. What's he going to try on me next time, a toaster or a convection oven? Will there be a next time? I don't mean to be ungrateful or carping. But inside myself, I am beside myself. That gets more crowded than ever. I could use a rottten rant about now or a rancid poem, something really mean-spirited and nasty. I try to dream up something in my own angry and internal way, but I just can't seem to string the words together in my head as I've done so often in the past. I manage a line or two, but then I seize up and can go no further. Take this line, for example: Nothing is more trying than trying harder. Trying harder, in fact, is so trying, I can't go on. Where do I go, when I can't go on?

With despair, old doubts come flooding back. I'm inundated in my own personal, private tsunami, thrashing frantically about, clinging to the wreckage, trying to stay afloat. The biggest of all doubts, a whale of a doubt, surfaces and spouts more worrisome questions. What if none of this is really happening? What if reality doesn't exist except in the minds of those who believe it exists. What if this leaves doubters like me abandoned? Does this mean that I don't exist, that I'm imaginary, that I'm nothing more than a figment? And if so, whose fucking figment am I? What's going on? Where is reality when I need it? Nowhere. Which is where I was and still am. Nowhere. Never mind the postal code. It won't help.

After a while, the doubts recede, the disappointment abates, and life support, life in limbo, life in the no lane whatsoever, life in Brian's room, goes on in its tenuous and constricted way just as before. Jefferson is calling me dude, again, and letting loose his encouraging jokes. Once in a while, he gets off a really funny zinger, and I find myself wishing that I could laugh out loud not just for myself but also for him. Elissa is her usual silent self but starts humming again. Bessie visits unfailingly every day at noon and Ray also comes to see me frequently and lend fatherly encouragement.

"Hang in there, Brian, my lad. We're going to beat this bugger."

But this bugger hangs in too, and hangs on and on. Nothing happens. There's no progress, no news from Roopa, not a peep out of Millie. Maybe I should give up on plan B and try to come up with plan C or D or X. But I don't know where to start. I'm at a loss. I've run out of options. I think I'll scream. No, I won't.

One day, while Bessie and Ray are both here, a very excited Jefferson comes into the room with black coffee, double sugar, for Ray and some of Inez's lemon shortbread cookies.

"I'm glad you're both here," Jefferson says." I want to share my good news."

"Don't tell me," says Bessie, unable to resist the opportunity. "You're pregnant."

There is much laughter all around.

"You don't look pregnant to me, mate," says Ray, joining in the joke.

"In a manner of speaking, I am pregnant and about to deliver my novel, that is, to the agent I just got by following your advice, Mr. Triggs."

"Good on you, mate. Well done. I knew you could do it."

"I can't thank you enough, Mr. Triggs."

"If you'll stop calling me Mr. Triggs and call me Ray, that'll be thanks enough."

"And you can call me Bessie and tell us all about your agent."

"Well, her name is Adele Plumley of Plumley & Associates Literary Agents, London, England. She's an Oxford Ph.D and taught Modern Literature at the University of London for ten years before becoming an agent. She's been an agent for twenty years and has eighty clients on her roster, a dozen major writers among them. After ninety-two queries and ninety-two turn-downs, Adele Plumley was my ninety-third query and the first to ask to read the whole manuscript. And she loved it and agreed to represent me. She works with co-agents and plans to market my novel to English language publishers worldwide."

"How exciting, Jefferson," Bessie says. "We're thrilled for you. I guess this means we're going to lose you. You've been such a help. Brian will miss you. We all will."

"Well, you won't lose me for a while, I don't think. Certainly, not before the book is sold to a publisher and published which Adele says could take some time. Besides, we may have Brian all put back together by then. What do you say to that, dude?"

"Hallelujah, brother!" Coincidence. Word of honour.

"You haven't told us the title of your novel," says Ray.

"I'm making a point of not telling anybody the title until it's sold to a publisher."

"Well, what about giving us a little hint of what it's about?" suggests Bessie.

"Sorry. As soon as Adele gets me a publisher, I will tell all. Till then, it's a secret. I hope you're not offended by my stubbornness."

"Of course, we are," says Bessie. "But since you're pregnant, we have to make allowances for you. So we forgive you."

38

OVERLOOKED

BETWEEN BOUTS of doubt and sporadic surges of self-concern about the lack of progress being made in springing me from this unending prison of mine, I tend, for a while at least, to forget about my problems and think instead of other things, many of them retrospective. This includes many of the things that I have yet to mention, such as my occasional one-sided encounters with visiting clergy. I'm talking about peripatetic ecclesiastics of all stripes and types, priests, ministers, rabbis, imams, preachers, pastors, parsons, and only god-knows-who, in a vertiginous variety of shapes, sizes, and colours. These caring and dedicated religionists surf the web of halls of Woodgreen House, not just trolling for late-life conversions or eleventh-hour confessions but also dispensing god-given, near-the-end comfort and counsel. And every once in a while, they sail bravely into my particular port of last resort to appraise me as a possible prospect for their allocation of any or all of the foregoing.

Sometimes, when I'm alone in my room with no intermediary to speak on my behalf and explain me to outsiders, god's messengers enter and undaunted by my unprepossessing appearance and the formidable array of life supporting gear sprouting multi-directionally from me, they stand at my bedside and gaze upon me with moist, compassionate eyes and try, often fervently, to engage me in conversation, only to finally accept that I am unable to communicate or, as far as they are able to tell, to be communicated with. Whereupon, they nod sadly, raise their eyes to the ceiling since the heavens are not immediately at hand and resort to prayer, often accompanied by various repetitive tics or ritual motions of the head, the hands, the arms, or the body. These activities may also, at the discretion of the cleric in question, include kneeling, touching of the forehead to the ground, bobbing of the head, rocking of the upper body, putting of the palms together, making a steeple of the fingers, raising up of the open hands, and assorted overall shaking, bouncing, and jiggling of the entire person. It can be a busy time and is always fascinating to watch.

Among the many in this dedicated visitor category, a few stand out. One who springs to mind, a street preacher of uncertain religious affiliation, no black cloth, no collar, wearing a stetson, a star-spangled shirt, and western boots, takes me completely by surprise when he breaks into a little clog dance accompanied by his falsetto singing of what is clearly a homemade hymn.

"When Jesus was a rabbi and a rabid rabble rouser, the temple was a shambles and the goyim, as we now know them, had not yet been invented, J.C. was filled with holy outrage. The holy water came only later when belief turned into theater and true believers lined up see the show. Oh, oh, oh. Oh, oh, oh."

He repeats this several times. And when he finishes, he does a little spin and then bows again and again to the unspeakably silent me and to imaginary applause.

"Thank you. Thank you. Thank you very much."

For all I know, in his mind, he is receiving a standing ovation and maybe three curtain calls. I'm not really sure. It's hard to keep track of somebody else's virtual stuff.

I may be over-generalizing, but I find the clergy as a social class interesting to observe in their ministrations, even if not especially helpful to me in my difficult circumstances. Mind you, the clergymen themselves almost always look as if all this impassioned activity of theirs is helping them. And perhaps, it is. I hope so because, let's face it, I'm not much help to them. All right, make that no help.

I recall on one occasion, two robed priests cautiously entering my room. The tall, thin one, the advance man, so to speak, comes in first, surveys the room and nods his approval to a short, older priest wearing a hood that obscures his face who then enters. Speaking in German, he asks his colleague to wait in the hallway and close the door. Then, he turns to me, removes his hood and in German-accented English says, "Don't worry, I will talk to you in English."

I recognize him instantly. He's an A-level celebrity, a major religious figure, probably the best known church leader in the world. On TV, earlier in the day, I witness his triumphant arrival at Toronto's Pearson airport for a mass meeting in Downsview Park expected to attract hundreds of thousands of the faithful. And here he is in Brian's room talking to me, the unmoving, unresponsive me. What did I do to deserve this kind of top-level attention? I try to think of something, but nothing comes to mind.

My august visitor carefully takes my right hand, holds it, examines my erect middle finger without comment, looks over at the erect finger of the left hand and shakes his head in puzzlement.

"Brian, my good friend Dr. Roopa has asked me, as a special favour, to look in on you and to intercede on your behalf and I am trying to do so but it has been difficult. All I am getting by way of response is 'I don't do helpful. And I'm a metaphor.' This is perplexing to me. But I will try again and hope for a more supportive response. In the meantime, rest assured, remain calm. And not a word to anyone."

I can't tell him so, but he has nothing to worry about. He releases my hand and places his hand on my forehead, one of the few places on my body free of intervention or encumbrance.

"Blessings be upon you, Brian."

This would be the absolutely perfect time for me to shout out, "Hallelujah, brother!" I'd like to, but as I've already noted, I'm not Poe's raven and not in control here. I just can't summon it up.

My distinguished visitor replaces his hood and with it, his anonymity, goes to the door, opens it, looks back at me, says, "Remember. Not a word," and goes out.

And only then, dammit, does my mouth explode into not a word but two words. "Hallelujah, brother!" But it's too late. He's gone.

Timing is everything. And I have none.

On another occasion, a rabbi bearing a large beribboned gift box under his arm walks into my room during noon hour while Bessie is visiting. A lean man with an eccentric skipping gait, a flowing red beard and long side curls, he wears a black hat with an overly wide brim and a shiny, black frock coat, vintage Warsaw, 1850. The fringes of a prayer shawl peek from beneath his vest. And I think, oh, oh, Bessie will spar with him. But I'm wrong.

"Good day," he says smiling. "May I come in?" Surprise! Surprise! He has an Oxford accent.

Of course, English-born Bessie recognizes it immediately and out of unshakeable, deeply ingrained British habit defers to it and to him respectfully and respectively.

"Good day, Rabbi. Please, come in. Why are you here?" Bessie asks pleasantly.

"Indeed. Why am I here? Man's first question. What better way to initiate a discussion than with an existential query? Why am I here? Truth to tell, I don't know why I am here. In fact, I don't know why any of us is here. Only the messiah knows why we are here and he has yet to share this with us. We must be patient. One does not rush the messiah. I hesitate to rashly speculate on why we are here. It might put me at odds with my maker and possibly add further uncertainty to an already uncertain world. May the messiah preserve us from ourselves and grant us the patience to endure uncertainty."

"I didn't intend to raise an existential question, Rabbi. By here, I didn't mean here existentially. I meant here in Brian's room."

"Brian's room? Is that where I am? May the messiah help me. I don't know why I am here in Brian's room, either. I was looking for Amos's room."

"That would have been room 203. But Amos, sad to say, died a few months ago."

"I am sorry to hear of his passing. May he rest in peace. Clearly, my database is delinquent and needs upgrading or downloading, I'm not sure which, possibly both. I came to visit Amos at the behest of his mother who was a member of my congregation. She died last year, poor woman. A troubled soul, given to conspiracy theories and obsessively concerned about Amos's worn out dressing gown and slippers. Unaware of his passing, I went shopping for a gift for Amos and bought him a nice new dressing gown and slippers to present to him along with what counsel I could, none of which, sadly, will he any longer need. Having, alas, arrived too late, I can be of no help to Amos now. Still, since I find myself here in Brian's room, perhaps, I can be of some help to Brian."

Bessie tackles this head on. "How?"

"I'm not sure. It would depend on the nature of his problem. I presume you are Brian's mother. Perhaps, you would like to tell me about Brian's problem?"

"He's in a coma as a result of an accident. I really don't think you can help, Rabbi. But thank you. Besides, we are not of your persuasion."

"Please, don't be fooled by my traditional garb. It's become a habit over time. Behind the hard-to-shake old habit, I am the most ecumenical of religionists. There is only one god and he belongs to all persuasions."

"But we have not been persuaded by any of those persuasions. We are of no persuasion."

"Ah! How I envy you. It's an onerous burden to have to constantly bear the weight of thousands of years of history with no escape and to be expected to enjoy it and defend it, come what may."

"Yet, you put up with it."

"I do, indeed. And I'm about to defend it, again, at this very moment. You see, it's not just a calling. I have a fractious flock much in need of my counsel and a young and growing family dependent on my support. Besides, what else am I equipped to do? My only other credential is a humanities doctorate that in these hi-tech times renders me virtually unemployable. But I mustn't take up any more of your time. Still, since I can be of no help to Brian, permit me, at the very least, before I go, to wish him recovery and wellness. May you overcome the barriers around you, Brian. Be well."

He starts to leave, stops, and holds up the gift box.

"Perhaps, I can leave the new dressing gown and slippers for Brian?"

"I don't think so."

"Armani design."

"I think not. Thank you."

"One size fits all."

"He never gets out of bed."

"Oh. I'm so sorry."

"Shalom, Rabbi,"

"Quite right. Shalom."

39

NEWS

BEING CUT OFF from the outer world as I am, I often feel data deprived and I'm always eager to receive whatever information I can, when I can. I'm hungry for news and grateful for it. Having said that, one of my daily data sources, television, even as carefully rationed out to me by the loyal and conscientious Jefferson, is unfortunately, deeply flawed, and only helpful in a limited way. The flaw of television, at least for someone in my circumstances, is that, despite McLuhan's assertion to the contrary, the medium is not the message. The medium is the monster, an insatiable beast, constantly devouring and excreting massive amounts of programming. As a result, it is always starved for content and finds it both expedient and profitable to repeat itself and repeat itself and repeat itself. In its repetitiousness, it has become, to me at least, heartless, mindless, and useless. And, making matters worse, the commercials that pay for all this are regurgitated ad nauseam. How many advances in the thinness of the sanitary pad do I want to know about? How many walk-in bathtubs do I want to see shaky seniors walking into? How many alarm systems do I want to buy with no contract for only twenty-eight dollars a month? How many simulated gold coins do I want to buy from a mint I never heard of commemorating an event I don't care about? But wait! If you call right now, they will cut the price in half, double your order, or offer free shipping and handling, providing you have a fixed address. And if you don't survive the five-year limited warranty period, they will come to your funeral as long as it is in the continental USA. Unable to turn the TV on or off, I watch it warily when it is turned on for me, not only seeing what comes up on the screen but seeing through it. It's either a sham or a scam. Or maybe I'm just being an unreasonable crank. I think it's the last option.

As I've already said, information of a personal nature can only come to me through the handful of people with whom I have direct but limited interaction within the confines of my room. They speak to me or to each other and I listen and pick up what I can. Eavesdropping is not the quickest way to get information. So news slowly trickles down to me. But once in a while, a torrent of information comes down the pipe from Bessie, from Jefferson, from Ray, and almost swamps me even as it excites me. Right now, the data deluge is about Raymond Triggs, my recently revealed and much revered father, whom I have come to love dearly. You won't believe what I've just learned about Ray.

Bessie confirms what I had sensed from the start. She and Ray are much enamored of each other. And now, they're talking about getting married but not rushing into it. They're taking their time to decide. They don't want a marriage that will be short lived. Ray has already made that mistake three times. He has given up his rental pied-a-terre in the King Edward Hotel and moved into Bessie's condo in the Colonnade on Bloor Street. It's a lovely place that Bessie bought years ago with her earnings from her lucrative sideline as a forensic clairvoyant to various police forces.

The biggest surprise of all is finding out that Ray is a multi-billionaire, having made a fortune in his own right as an architect and builder and also having inherited even more money from his inventor father who was responsible for, among other things, those funny looking scissors sold all over the world that can cut through anything without cutting the cutter. Implausibly, in a world of arrogant, ultra-rich egomaniacs, Ray Triggs chooses not to flaunt his wealth and is a major but covert philanthropist, determined to give his money away anonymously. Despite this, he's not at all personally reclusive, nor especially private. On the contrary, he's outgoing, even-keeled, matter-of-fact, and totally without presumption. Determined not to be described as a philanthropist or perceived as a public benefactor, he prefers no publicity, no public recognition. His attitude is: here's the money, just take it, don't make a fuss, keep your mouth shut, and get on with it. Although he funds many of them, his name will not appear on any opera houses or museums or university buildings or the research wings of hospitals. He finds public displays of philanthropy self-aggrandizing and pretentious and calls it the commercialization of what should be an act of caring and generosity. In an example close to home, it turns out that unbeknownst to anyone, he is not only building but also funding the new wing at Woodgreen House. And, of course, he has been a longtime major source of support for Roopa's research.

As a result of his no-strings generosity, Ray has an impressive network of good friends all over the world.

For me, all this is mind-bending. Being confronted with the startling fact of Ray's immense wealth gives me an insight into myself that I never had before. I'm surprised, of course, by how rich Ray is and impressed by it. He is my father, after all. But somehow, his money doesn't matter to me. And I realize that my circumstances have made money irrelevant, meaningless, to me personally. Before my accident, I was very interested in money, in earning it, in saving it, in investing it, in getting more of it, but now, none of that matters.

It's a strange feeling, a feeling of relief, somehow, a feeling of freedom, even though my condition is one of no freedom whatsoever.

40

ENCORE MILLIE

EXCEPT FOR the cast of my internal drama series, which may exist only in my head – I'm not really sure anymore – no one listens to me but me. That means I talk to myself a hell of a lot. Just this morning, I was lamenting to myself yet again my failure to make headway in my attempts to organize my Plan B, when suddenly the renewed possibility of Plan B popped into my head in the voice of Millie, whom I was beginning to think I might never hear from again. As luck would have it, she sounded even brighter and more energized than usual.

"Brian, hi. It's Millie. I'm back."

"Hi, Millie. Glad you're back. I'm anxious to find out if you told your mother about me. I was beginning to worry I might not hear from you."

"Sorry it took so long. A lot has been going on since I last talked to you."

"Is that good news or bad?"

"Some of both. When I told my mom about you and how I visited you in your mind, she started worrying again that I was going over the edge and made me see a psychologist she works with. Lucky for me, mom's colleague convinced her I was perfectly okay and that what was happening was not autism as originally believed but maybe some sort of psychic thing just like you said the first time I dropped in on you."

"Well, that's good news, isn't it?"

"I thought it was. But then, when I asked mom if we could go visit you, she got all worried again, started asking me questions about you I couldn't answer."

"You don't know anything about this psychic buddy of yours," she said. "You don't know who he is or what his problem is or what kind of help he wants from you. You're only twelve years old. He sounds a little creepy."

"I tried to argue with her, but she wouldn't listen."

"There's no way that I'm going to take time off work and you're going to miss school to go all the way to Toronto to meet some spooky guy we know nothing about," mom said. "Besides, we can't afford a trip right now. We're still paying off Barcelona."

"That sounds like bad news to me."

"But I have some good news, too."

"Good. I can use some."

"Well, the good news is that I think I've figured out how to have longer visits with you like I'm doing now without having to leave suddenly. Maybe it will give us time to work out how to answer mom's questions and try to change her mind, so we can help you with your problem."

"That's great. But how are you managing to have longer visits?"

"These episodes of mine, like I told you, only happen when I'm doing homework. And up until now, I haven't been able to control the length of time before I suddenly drift back. But I discovered by accident that if this happened to me when I was doing my algebra, I could somehow make the episode last longer. I don't know why it works. But it only works with algebra. So far, in trying it out, I got it to last about half an hour."

"Half an hour? Wow! We could talk through a lot of stuff in half an hour."

"Why don't we start right now?"

"Do we have time? We've been talking for almost half an hour."

"Let's try and see what happens. The first thing we have to do is deal with mom's questions about you that I couldn't answer. I'm supposed to be psychic maybe, but all I know about you is that your name is Brian, you're in Toronto and you've got some kind of problem. Other than that, you're a mystery to me. Who are you? What is this all about? Why do you need me there to help you? Gee, Brian. I'm sorry. I sound just like my mother."

"That's okay, Millie. Your mother is absolutely right. To do what I'm asking you to do, you should know what this is all about. So here goes. Millie, you are my Plan B."

"I don't understand."

"Don't worry. I'll explain. I'll try to be brief. But I'd better start at the beginning. I was parking my car ..."

"Oh. Oh. I'm starting to drift."

"The half hour must be up. Damn."

"Sorry. Gotta go."

"Try to come back as soon as you can. I'll explain everything about me and Plan B."

"I'll do my best …"

There is a sound like a sigh and then, silence. She is gone. And I am still here in Brian's room and Plan B is still out there, somewhere, anywhere, who knows where, and still eludes me. Maybe, Amos's mother is right. Maybe it's all a conspiracy.

41

ON STAGE

MILLIE isn't alone in experiencing what she calls episodes. I may be having episodes of my own. Or maybe they're the dreams I'm not sure I'm dreaming or the hallucinations I'm not sure I'm hallucinating or the surreal whatever the hell they are that I'm not sure I'm experiencing. In the latest of these, I witness what appears to be an interview of some sort somewhere in Britain. In a bare box of a room with nothing in it except a small table and two chairs, two nondescript men with English accents are talking. I have absolutely no idea what they're talking about or what it means or what I'm doing there.

"You're the chap from the agency?"

"That's right."

"Please, take a seat."

"Thank you."

"I didn't get your name. You are …?"

"Downtrodden."

"Beg pardon?"

"Downtrodden. I'm Downtrodden."

"Oh. Sorry to hear that. And your name is …?"

"Downtrodden. That's my name."

"Ah. And your father, was he Downtrodden, as well?"

"As a matter of fact, he was. But it wasn't his name."

"It wasn't?"

"No. His name was Browbeaten."

"Then, how did you come by the name of Downtrodden?"

"I picked it from a list when I was legally changing my name from Browbeaten."

"So Downtrodden is not your original name?"

"That's right."

"And Browbeaten was your original name?"

"Correct."

"Why did you change it?"

"Browbeaten is lower class and subject to frivolous comment."

"What made you choose Downtrodden?"

"Downtrodden is posh and gets very little comment."

"Did you change your first name, as well?"

"No. I kept my original first name."

"Which is ….?"

"Deplorably."

"That would make you Deplorably Downtrodden, then."

"That's correct."

"Deplorably. That's quite a mouthful. I suppose your friends call you Deep, do they?"

"No. Actually, they call me Plorably."

"I see. What do you do, Mr. Downtrodden?"

"Please, call me Plorably."

"What do you do, Plorably?"

"Interviews. I do interviews."

"You're an interviewer, then?"

"Actually, I'm an interviewee."

"Is that what brought you here?"

"No. I came by bus, actually."

"And why are you here?"

"I'm here to be interviewed."

"And you have been, Mr. Downtrodden. Thank you for coming by."

Both men stand up. The interviewer turns and stands silently looking at the wall behind him. Downtrodden goes to the door and leaves. A curtain descends. And from somewhere unseen, there is applause. It dawns on me that what I am looking at is not a room at all but a stage set. I don't see an audience and wonder if the applause is canned. The curtain continues to descend, leaving me in the dark of Brian's room in the middle of the night.

Oh, one more thing. Towards the end of the interview, Downtrodden puts his hands on the table and the middle finger of each hand is erect and menacing. In fact, the two middle fingers point threateningly at each other. I didn't realize it at first, but it dawns on me that the actor playing the role of Downtrodden is me. It's a pretty good performance, if I say so myself. The English accent is flawless. Hallelujah, brother!

But what is this all about? What does it mean? It has to mean something. I don't know what I'll do if it turns out to be a metaphor. I can't imagine for what. I seem to keep tripping over unwanted metaphors. I'm going to have to start watching my step. How am I going to manage that? How can I watch where I walk when I can't walk?

42

OF TWO MINDS

IF THERE is a kind of repetitious prayer-like quality to my tale telling, it may be because my constricted, clinging-to-life life style is by its very nature repetitious. That may be why I tend to tell my tale with a kind of non-linear abandon, flinging about fragments as they occur to me, and then moving the fragments into new configurations and telling my tale all over again. It's almost as if I'm uncertain that what I've already told you has gotten through to you, so I tell you again. And again. I could be accused, I suppose, of liking to listen to my voice but for the fact that I have no voice but the inner voice that I am magically sharing with you. It must be magical. How else would I be able to communicate with you? But as I have repeatedly promised, we'll get to that.

Some people like to say they regret nothing. I am not one of them. I regret everything. But I don't let go of anything. I am my own archive.

As I've made clear repeatedly and perhaps overly, in no way, am I in control of my circumstances. Ever since my accident, if

I am able to control anything at all, it's the ideas, the words, the phrases, the sentences, buzzing around in my brain as I talk to myself. All right, maybe control is not the right word to describe how I connect with what's happening in my mind, but, at the very least, I feel that I have sole ownership of what's going on in my head. Whatever is in there is mine, all mine. No one is putting words in my mouth, or, to be more accurate, no one is putting ideas into my head. If there's one area where, albeit unbeknownst to anyone, I'm in charge, that's it. And yet, the last little while, I've begun to feel that in my mind, another mind is gradually, inexorably, sneaking up on me, hovering behind me, in effect, looking over my shoulder. It's a strange sensation that I find difficult to describe. But what's really odd is that it may be my own mind sneaking up on itself. How can that be? Not only is this unimaginable, but like everything else about me, this feeling is fraught with uncertainty. I'm going on about this because, recently, I sense a kind of duality, of joint ownership, of the mind that I used to think of as mine exclusively. I can't really explain it. I don't know where it's coming from or why. There's been no sign, no signal, no triggering event. It's as if there is a second mind in my head. I'm of two minds, if I may put it that way, except they don't differ. It's like double-vision but, in this case, it's mental rather than visual. It feels as if there are two of me in my head, overlapping but identical. Could it, I wonder, be an after-effect of Roopa's microwave treatment or of Elissa's healing hands? Or is it possible that someone, some wandering psychic, has moved into my head, is camping in there with me, anticipating my every thought and toying with me, playing me back to myself just slightly out-of-synch? But who would that be? The only psychic people I know are Bessie and Millie, and Bessie, much to my disappointment, hasn't been able to get through to me at all, and Millie, though she's been able to get into my head, has only been able to divine my name. Anything else from Millie has been like a horoscope reading, ambiguous, vague, tentative, and uncertain. Besides, I worry more and more that Millie may be a figment of my troubled mind. That would make me the one who's ambiguous, vague, tentative, and uncertain, which already seems to be an accurate description of the essential me.

In any case, I don't know what to make of this latest, puzzling, two-minds-in-one feeling. It's as if I'm looking over my own shoulder and repeating myself. Still, it's not troublesome or threatening in any way and doesn't interfere with either my mental hyperactivity or my physical inactivity. And, as always, it's possible that I'm imagining the whole thing. It may be yet another figment of my troubled mind which itself may be a figment.

Can this be a figment of a figment? If a figment is a creation of the imagination, what is a figment of a figment? Do two figments cancel each other out and make a reality? If only I could Google.

43

HERSELF, HERSELF

BESSIE AND RAY both arrive here today just a little before noon. It's always a treat to see them together. There's an aura of happiness about them that gives me a boost. Bessie is not carrying her usual sandwich and coffee. This has been happening lately when they arrive together. It usually means they're going to lunch after visiting me. How I wish I could join them. It's been years since I had a decent meal. They come into my room looking thoughtful, engaged in an animated discussion they've been having on route in which they now include me as a listener.

"How's my lad?" asks Ray, contriving to hug me through all the paraphernalia. "We have a new plan, we're going to try to make work for you, Brian. Your brilliant mother has come up with an idea that we hope may help you communicate with us. You tell him, Bessie."

"Well, Brian, as you know, it's been a great disappointment to me that despite being a card-carrying psychic I haven't been able to read your mind and pick up what you're thinking. I can read the minds of others, no problem. Mostly they're people

I don't care about. You'd think I'd be able to do the same with someone who matters so much to me. But I can't and I can't explain why. I don't know why. Anyhow, I got to thinking about it and wondering if maybe another psychic could connect with you, read your mind, and tell us what you're thinking. Then, at least, we'd have two-way communication. And maybe, you could help us help you get unlocked. It's possible that the key may be in your mind. You may have some answers for us. Or maybe, some questions that we should be asking."

"So that's the plan, Brian," says Ray. "Now, the job is to find the right psychic."

"Psychics don't grow on trees," Bessie adds. "If they did, we could just go out and pick a few. But psychics are rare birds. We'll have to do an intensive search, find a few promising prospects, and then try them out on you. It will be like a casting session and you get to be the director."

Right on! This plan rings so right with me, it warrants an excited "Hallelujah, brother!" But once again, I can't manage it in a timely manner. Bessie's idea is not only brilliant, it gives me a Plan C, if things don't work out with my Plan B. So little is happening that I need as many irons in the golf bag as possible.

Wait. Let me think. I have it. Why couldn't Plan B become part of Plan C? Why couldn't Ray and Bessie talk to Millie and her mother and arrange to bring both of them to Toronto for a psychic casting session? This would reassure Millie's mom that I'm not some sort of weirdo, and then Ray and Bessie could pay for their trip here, so they wouldn't have to worry about the expense. All this assumes, of course, that Millie will come back and drop in on me again and, most important, that she exists, that she is for real, and not just wishful imagining on my part, not just a bi-product of my messed-up mind.

All right, assuming Millie is real, how am I going to make this happen? How will I get Bessie and Ray to add Millie to their casting list of psychics? I'm unable to tell them about her. But what if Millie were to tell them about herself, herself? Herself, herself. I like that. That's it. Next time I hear from Millie, I tell her about this psychic casting plan and get her to contact Ray and Bessie and ask to be included. Herself, herself.

"Hallelujah, brother!"

44

SERIOUS PSYCHIC SOUGHT

"SERIOUS PSYCHIC SOUGHT." That's the headline, Bessie explains, for a Google ad that she and Ray plan to run, hoping to find a bona fide psychic who will be able to telepathically plumb the deepest recesses of my unspeakably unruly mind in order to convey what's going on in the gray area between my ears not only to Bessie and Ray but also to my vast legions of fans and supporters as well as to the worlds of medicine, science, and academe. In so doing, the psychic, it is hoped, will delve into and report on my innermost thoughts, thoughts that to this point I have been unable to share, talking instead to myself, not an especially productive pursuit. Still, it has kept me from going further off the rails than I may already be. Either that's a metaphor or I'm a train. Being a train may not be as far-fetched as it sounds. There may be an inherited propensity to transportation devices. Bessie's family lore has it that if her grandmother had had wheels she'd have been a streetcar. Sic transit etc.

"Serious Psychic Sought" is a seriously alliterative headline. That will be Bessie's doing. She loves alliteration. And as you may have noticed, so do I. As I've already said, I guess I caught the alliterative bug from Bessie. Can the love of alliteration be hereditary? Or maybe it's cultural, something I learned from years of listening to Bessie hold forth as I was growing up.

It's strange, I find myself thinking, that it requires an ad to find psychics. Shouldn't psychics know better than the rest of us? Shouldn't they know when someone is looking for them and come forward? I mean, they are psychics, after all. But Bessie is ahead of me on this. She has already thought of it, I soon discover, as she reads me the rest of the ad that says, "If you're the psychic we're looking for, you will contact us right now."

That's it. That's all the ad says. No explanation. No name. No phone number. No email address. And when it runs, no response. This is more consistency than Bessie had expected. She is disappointed. But Ray, as always, remains philosophical and upbeat.

"You know more about psychics than I do, Bessie," says Ray. "But looking at it from a marketing point of view, maybe we're trying too hard and expecting too much of our psychic target group. Maybe their psychic powers only kick in when they focus on something. Why don't we give them a little more information to focus on and see what happens?"

Bessie is hesitant. "I worry that revealing too much information up front may inundate us with a flood of responses from wanna-be psychics who don't have the genuine psychic powers required to find us. We don't want to have to wade through a deluge of useless replies."

"Fair enough," Ray says. "Let's keep the headline, Serious Psychic Sought, but include just a little key information for readers to focus on but again no name, no phone number, no email address, so responders are forced to prove their psychic powers by using them to find us."

"Makes sense," Bessie agrees. "We'll give it a try."

It makes sense, to me, too, but as usual, I don't get to vote. I get to wait. Never mind. Waiting is my strong suit. Actually, it's my only suit. And I don't have to wear a tie.

Next day, on her visit, Bessie reads me the revised ad. "Serious Psychic Sought. Psychic wanted to telepathically read the mind of a locked-in accident victim currently on life support and unable to move or talk but conscious and cognitive. If you're the psychic we're looking for, you will contact us right now."

Shortly after Bessie places the revised ad but before receiving any responses, an unlikely interaction of psychics occurs in an unlikely setting, just outside Bessie's place of work. Coming out of the law library late in the afternoon, Bessie is hailed by a middle-aged woman of her acquaintance. A down-on-her-luck, transplanted Newfoundlander with a leathery face and bad teeth, she is one of the street people who frequent the park around the law library, sleeping on or under the benches. Bessie encounters her from time to time and occasionally stops to chat and give her coffee money. Today, however, the woman is not asking for money.

"Hey, Bessie. I need to talk to you."

"How did you know my name, Aurora?"

"Same way you know mine. From looking at you."

Bessie knows more about Aurora than her name. Aurora is from Lobster Cove, a Newfoundland fishing village. Many years earlier, after three miscarriages and endless abuse by a violent, alcoholic husband, she had run off to Toronto and as it turned out, to less hope than ever. Still, this day, she sounds more hopeful than usual.

"You looking for a mind reader, Bessie?"

"Don't tell me you saw the Google ad."

"Google? You joshing me? I got no cell phone, no computer, none of that stuff."

"How did you know I was looking for a mind reader?"

"Same way I know your name. Some days, I just look at you coming out of the building and I know what you're thinking."

"Go on. Are you trying to tell me that you're a mind reader, Aurora?"

"Like I say. Some days, maybe. Some days, maybe not. I ain't really sure. Didn't help me any when I hooked up with that rotten prick of a husband, may his crotch rot."

"How long since you left Jimmy?"

"It's been fifteen years since I last laid eyes on that shit-head."

"That's a long time to be angry."

"I guess my heart is too filled with hate. And I haven't exactly made a success of my life, here in the big city, have I? That might've helped. I don't drink no more. Liver's shot. It was quit or die. I ain't in no rush to die. I'd like to be of use to somebody, you know, lend a hand, while I still can, while I still got all my marbles. Bessie… I… I…"

"What? Tell me."

"Can I see your boy?"

"You can, if you know my boy's name."

"Brian. Can I see Brian? Maybe, I could …"

"Sure, Aurora, you can see Brian. I'll meet you right here tomorrow at noon and take you to visit him."

"Oh, Bessie. Thank you so much. I can't promise nothing. But I'd like to give it a go. I don't know what else to say."

"You don't have to say anything else. Just show up here tomorrow a little before noon."

The next day at noon, Bessie comes in to see me as usual, but this time she is accompanied by Aurora. Each carries coffee and a sandwich. Bessie has bought them both lunch.

"Ray is en route but running late," Bessie tells Jefferson and me. "He should be here soon. Why don't we wait till he arrives, before we start?"

Jefferson brings in another chair and announces with a flourish that, "A new batch of Inez's shortbread cookies is on today's menu and will be served momentarily."

"Momentarily is good," says Bessie. "I always liked momentarily. Immediately is also a favorite."

Jefferson grins. Aurora looks puzzled. I do my usual.

"Aurora, today's visiting psychic, is a neighbour near the library. She is not here in response to the second Google ad," Bessie explains while we wait. "As yet, there are no responses to the second Google ad. We'll just have to be patient."

Okay, I think. I'll give it a try. Hi, I'm Brian, the patient patient.

The talk peters out. Nobody is saying much. Bessie and Aurora nibble on their sandwiches and gingerly sip their too-hot coffee. Sensing that he is about to be part of what might be a momentous occasion, the usually ebullient Jefferson is somewhat subdued when he delivers the promised cookies and also a black coffee, double sugar, for Ray who has just arrived.

Everybody waits expectantly for something to happen. But nothing seems to be happening. Aurora just looks at me and looks at me and looks at me. Her eyes grow large and moist. I try to do my best to connect with her in order to somehow convey some information of value that she can repeat, but my thinking is so scattered, my thoughts fly off in all directions. How do I pass on useful information to Aurora? I worry that I might suddenly emit an unintended "Hallelujah, brother!" Audibly or telepathically, it would be inappropriate and no help at all. I focus as much as I am able and try to concentrate. I need to contrive a meaningful sound bite in my head that I can relay to Aurora. But my head rings and clatters like a noisy diner at lunch. I don't know where to begin. There's too much on my plate, too much going on, too much to choose from. What should it be? Desperately, I seize on a mix of my recent thoughts. It's not quite what it should be. It's a mash-up. It may cause confusion. But I'm uptight and it's all I can manage under pressure. Will it get through to Aurora? The room is thick with silence. It feels as if no one is breathing. No one moves. Everyone is frozen as if in concert with the unmoving me. Suddenly, Aurora jerks to her feet, startled, spilling her coffee and looking distraught as she speaks.

"Ray has to bring Millie. That's what I'm picking up. Brian's head is all over the place. It's really hard to know what he's thinking. Ray has to bring Millie. That's all I make out. Ray has to bring Millie. He says it over and over. Ray has to bring Millie. I'm not getting anything else. Sorry, Bessie."

Still clutching her half-eaten sandwich, she sits down again. A disappointed looking Jefferson cleans up the spilled coffee with a paper towel.

"Let me get you another coffee," he says to Aurora." How do you like it?"

"Black will be great. Thank you."

Bessie pats Aurora on the arm. "It's okay, Aurora. You made a start. You want to try again in a few minutes?"

"I'm not sure it'll work. But I can give it a try."

"That's fine. Whenever it feels right to you."

The room goes silent again. Aurora demolishes the rest of her sandwich. It looks like bacon, lettuce, and tomato on brown, but it's been too squished to be sure. Then, she goes to work on the coffee that Jefferson has brought her. No one is saying anything.

Finally, Ray breaks the silence. "Ray has to bring Millie. What does that mean? How can Ray bring Millie when he doesn't know who Millie is? Who is Millie? Bessie, do you know who Millie is?"

"Not a clue. I don't think I've ever known a Millie. Isn't that puzzling? But Aurora will give it another try when she's ready. You okay with that, Aurora?"

"Sure. I'm ready now. I'll take another crack at it."

Aurora stands and stares at me out of that leathery face of hers. I see the pain, the angst, in her eyes. In my head, I hear her pleading inner voice: Come on, Brian. Help me out. Talk to me. This means a lot to both of us. But I'm having trouble thinking coherently. Maybe, I can, somehow, add meaning to what Aurora picked up earlier. Ray has to bring Millie. I try to deliver a scattering of thoughts that might help but I can't be sure that Aurora is getting any of it.

"I'm getting something," Aurora says.

"What is it?" asks Bessie.

"I'm not sure. Just a word," replies Aurora. "Sedona. That's all I'm getting from Brian. He keeps saying, Sedona. I don't know what it means."

"Anybody know what Sedona means?" asks Ray.

"It's a town in Arizona," says Jefferson. "About a hundred and fifty miles north of Phoenix. The area is all red sandstone. Long vistas. Incredible sunsets. That's where they used to shoot all those old Hollywood westerns. It's an arts centre. Lots of writers and artists hang out there. Neat place but way too hot."

"How come you know all this, Jefferson?" Ray asks.

"I attended a writer's summer workshop there years ago when I was still in school."

"Do you suppose there's a connection between Millie and Sedona?" Bessie wonders. "Another puzzle. Just what we need."

Another puzzle. Right. Well, now, at least, everybody's in on the puzzle and wants to know who Millie is and is wondering about her connection with Sedona. And here I am, still not even sure if Millie's for real, or if she is, if she's really in Sedona. Still, that's a start, I suppose. But of what?

45

MIND THE MIND READERS

HAVING SHAKEN things up but not having solved any of the puzzles that have fallen out of the shake-up, Aurora moves on, disappearing from my limited view but not from Bessie's much broader outlook. Grateful for Aurora's efforts and concerned about her well-being, Bessie decides to try to help Aurora get off the street. Bessie and Ray discuss with Aurora her dicey prospects if she does not escape from her present circumstances. Aurora is eager to escape and explains that she never finished high school and that her unfulfilled dream has always been to go back to school but once entrapped in life on the street, she has never been able to do so.

Ray and Bessie offer to help make it happen by setting up a scholarship fund for Aurora that will give her a place to live and pay for her schooling. After finishing school, Aurora wants to train to be a chef. And the fund will also enable that.

I feel a pang of envy. All right, I'll be frank. Maybe, it's jealousy. Maybe, I'm jealous of my parents' generosity, jealous of Aurora's sudden good fortune, jealous of her opportunity to

189

change her life. Maybe I'm feeling sorry for myself, even while denying it. Where's my good luck? Where's my opportunity for change, for a better life? Why isn't this happening to me? For a while, I whine to myself like an infant. It's petty of me, I know. I can be petty when peeved. I'm only human, after all, though I may not look it. But then, I grow pissed off with my pettiness. I order myself to stop whining and grow up. Stop your whining asshole, and grow up. It works. I stop whining almost immediately. Growing up, however, takes a little longer. I'm working on it.

In the meantime, while all this helpful activity and my unhelpful jealousy have been going on, the second psychic-seeking Google ad has been running for a week with no response. Bessie and Ray discuss pulling the ad and trying to come up with a new idea when, lo and behold, six email responses arrive all at once. At first, there is great flurry of excitement in the Bessie/Ray ménage at what appears to be a plethora of psychics, but this abates somewhat when it quickly becomes apparent that all the emails say the same thing and come from the same – perhaps over-enthusiastic, perhaps error prone – source, a psychic in Latvia named Andris Lapsa. The email says:

"My name is Andris Lapsa. I live in Riga, Latvia. I am 38 years old, married, no children. I am fluent in English as it is taught in all our schools and is the second language in Latvia. I am a graduate of the Riga Institute of Technology in Engineering Technology and sub-contract as a master crane operator on major high-rise projects in the construction industry.

I am the sixth generation in a family of hereditary telepaths and psychics who for two hundred years have correctly forewarned imperceptive world leaders of imminent disasters but much to the leaders' loss, have never been listened to or acknowledged. For reference, I invite you to Google my name and the Lapsa family history.

If I can be of service, I will be pleased to come and see Brian and communicate with him telepathically. It is a family tradition not to charge fees for our services. You need pay only travel expenses for me and my wife, Lina, who accompanies me wherever I go because she is blind and cannot be left alone for long periods.

I am between commitments for the next three weeks and available to make the trip to Toronto to see Brian in that period before I start work on a new construction project. If my credentials are to your satisfaction and my timetable is agreeable, please suggest a suitable date and I will be there. No other information is necessary. I know who you are and where to find you.

You should also be aware that because of my long deceased, maternal grandfather's long-ago radical writings, I am, pointlessly, on a no-fly list, and so cannot enter the United States. Although it is hard to be certain from this distance, I do not expect I will have to fly into the United States. But if for any reason, it becomes necessary for me to see Millie and she turns out to be in Sedona, Arizona, I will not be able to go there. I thought you should know. And I hope this will not be a problem.

Sincerely, Andris Lapsa."

"Sounds like Andris Lapsa is our guy," Bessie says. "He hasn't started on the assignment yet and he already seems to know as much as we do. Maybe more. He gets my vote."

"Mine, too," agrees Ray. "The sooner we get him here, the better. You Google him as suggested, and I'll get my travel agent to organize everything in Riga. We need to put Andris and his wife in a decent hotel handy to Woodgreen. Where do you think, Bessie?"

"How about the Four Seasons?"

"Perfect."

"What about a car?"

"I'll book them a car and a driver for while they're here. The driver can meet them at the airport, take them to the hotel, and chauffeur them around so they don't get lost or screwed up in traffic. It's a zoo driving here."

"You seem to manage."

"True. But that's how I know it's a zoo."

46

ANDRIS

Two DAYS later, Andris is at my bedside, in Brian's room, and Lina is with him. They are a charming storybook couple in their early forties, blond, blue eyed, both of them, well turned out and very attached to each other. Lina behaves as if she were normally sighted. She has a white cane but keeps it folded up in her purse and rarely uses it. And she doesn't cling cautiously to Andris, either. You'd never know she was blind except for the fact that they hold hands like lovers when walking about. And they talk endlessly and animatedly to each other in both English and Latvian.

Andris announces that he plans to simply hang out in my room for a couple of days just to be near me and, I suppose, to expose his powers of extrasensory perception to whatever vibes I might give off, before he gets down to the serious business of focused telepathy and actual mind reading. Familiarization, he calls this phase of his work. It turns out to be familiarization for me and for my caregivers, as well, giving all of us the opportunity to familiarize ourselves with him.

Jefferson is very taken with the Latvian visitors, pronounces Andris and Lina amazing and plies them with endless coffee, plates of Inez's cookies, and much Brian lore. Only Bessie knows more about me than Jefferson does, and he's quickly catching up. Watching Andris and Jefferson talk, it seems clear to me that the warm, effusive Jefferson is an easy read for the precise, thoughtful Andris who immediately perceives my premier caregiver as a not-yet but soon-to-be published author of a novel and simultaneously intuits Jefferson's reluctance to talk about it. Andris discreetly says nothing to anyone else about what he has learned of Jefferson's literary endeavours or reservations.

As always, Elissa is quiet and reserved but friendly, nonetheless. Her linguistic arsenal of five languages enables her to speak to the visiting couple in something akin to their own tongue. She doesn't say too much but just enough to let them know that she welcomes them warmly.

Andris immediately comprehends Elissa's background and is sympathetic to her circumstances. He also divines that, though she functions normally, unbeknownst to her colleagues, she is legally blind, and he shares this information with his beloved Lina. With little or no conversation, whenever they are in the room at the same time, the two women reach out to each other. The bond between them is palpable. I feel it.

Bessie and Ray are in and out of Brian's room more frequently than usual during Andris's preliminary familiarization period and their presence usually initiates lively discussion, mostly about me. This is no way to build a fan club, but I'm used to it. But mostly Andris just wants to be quietly close to me without any talk, not always directly observing me yet always appearing to pick up something from me. Vibes, I called it earlier but I'm not really sure what he's picking up. My whining, maybe, but having ordered myself to grow up, I'm trying my best not to be infantile. It's not easy.

During Andris's quiet times, Lina tucks herself away in a corner of the room in a comfortable chair that Jefferson has brought in for her and silently listens through an earbud to a digital player that delivers music or readings of books. In any case, she has a way of being engrossed and awesomely still for long periods. She never interrupts, staying silent until Andris addresses her directly.

Something interesting has happened since the Latvian pair started spending time in my room. It slowly dawns on me that when they speak Latvian to each other, I understand what they're saying, even though I have never learned Latvian. The fact is, I have no language skills, no language training. English is my only tongue and I'm still learning it. Yet, somehow, my mind translates the Latvian into English. Although Andris doesn't comment on it, I sense he knows that this is happening. Not surprisingly, he is a very knowing person and has a way of smiling knowingly when this occurs. It's just a little smile but I get it.

On day three, while I'm zenned out or dozing or in a state of grace or off in the land of who knows where, Andris's voice unexpectedly pops into my head and talks to me in Latvian. I'm not sure if this is really happening or if I'm making it up. This is one of those times when all I am certain about is my uncertainty. Still, Andris and I appear to be having a conversation.

"Hello, Brian. I am Andris and today, we are going to be talking to each other without anyone else knowing that we are talking. Is that okay?"

"I guess so," I surprise myself by replying in the Latvian that I don't speak. "But what about the mind reading? What about the telepathy?"

"Don't worry. This is all included."

It sounds like one of those holiday travel packages. I'm tempted to ask if this includes meals. But I want to be helpful, so I agree.

"All right. Let's talk."

"Would you prefer to talk in English or Latvian?"

I figure since I already seem to be talking Latvian, what the hell, why not stick with it?

"Latvian might be fun," I reply.

"I never thought of Latvian as fun. For me, English is fun. But since you are the client, you get to choose."

I never thought of myself as a client. I was always the patient. Maybe this is a promotion for good behaviour. Or maybe, it's for no behaviour, my area of expertise.

"Latvian, then," the newly promoted client chooses. "What shall we talk about?"

"What do you most want to communicate to your parents?"

"I'd like them to know that I love them, that I'm awake and aware, and that I want desperately to somehow be freed from this prison I'm locked in."

"They know all this, Brian. And they are trying very hard to free you. Is there anything you can tell them that they don't already know that might help them do so?"

"I'm not really sure. I've been thinking about it. But I haven't been able to come up with any answers. Mind you, since being in this suspended state, I've developed superior powers of observation and understanding, diagnostic powers, in fact, that could help others if only I could communicate with them."

"But these diagnostic powers of yours are no help to you, yourself? Is that correct?"

"That's correct. Unfortunately, these diagnostic powers of mine have been no help to me whatsoever. In fact, they haven't been of help to anyone else either, since I can't pass on what I find out."

I don't let on to Andris, but I have just diagnosed Lina. Her blindness is the result of an inoperable brain tumor that, even if discovered, will be the death of her within a year. Her tumor is terminal. Her case is hopeless. Andris's face suddenly looks strained. He may already know the deadly diagnosis. But there's no way for me to be sure. So taking no chances of passing on this upsetting information which in any case will not help, I immediately banish Lina from my mind and from my conscience, by quickly jumping to thoughts of Millie.

"Maybe Millie can help," I blurt out.

"Tell me, Brian, who is this Millie?"

"I really don't know. I've never seen her. I'm not even sure Millie exists. She may be nothing more than a voice in my head just like you are right now. I'm not sure voices in my head, including yours, are for real. The only difference is that you're here. I can see you. I know you exist. I've never laid eyes on Millie. Her voice just pops into my head from time to time. I don't know why and she can't explain why. This happens only, she says, when she's doing her homework. If she's for real, my guess is that she might be a psychic. But I don't know for certain. She says she's twelve years old and lives with her mother in Sedona, Arizona. That's all I can tell you."

"You said maybe Millie can help. How can she help?"

"I thought that she could come here, talk to me in my head and help me to communicate with my parents by telling them what I say to her."

"But that's exactly what I am going to do, Brian. That should help."

"Yes, but you're real. And Millie may not be. She may be a figment of my mind, a fiction, or…"

"Or what, Brian?"

"She may have special powers. She may be magical."

"Believing in magic is not rational."

"I know. I'm not sure I'm rational. And my circumstances are not rational. But I'm running out of options and magic may be my only hope. And the closest thing to magic right now is Millie. And she may not even exist. Not even in Sedona."

"What can you tell me about Sedona?"

"I'd never heard of Sedona before Millie told me she lives there. I don't know anything about the place. Maybe, you should talk to Jefferson. He's actually been there. He knows all about Sedona."

"What else can you tell me that might be helpful?"

"Only that lately, I have the feeling that, somehow, the solution to my various problems may be right here, under my nose, so to speak, in Woodgreen. I can't explain this feeling. This may not be rational, either. Or helpful."

"Your parents are trying very hard to help you find the solution you are hoping for. And I am trying to help them help you. That will be all for today. Thank you for your assistance. Your Latvian, by the way, is excellent. I couldn't tell you from a native speaker. I have to leave now but we'll meet again tomorrow."

Andris leaves my head but doesn't leave my room. He just sits there looking at me, saying nothing. I'm left wondering if we really just had a conversation or if I was dreaming or making it up and it was all a product of my agitated mind. I'm already apologizing to myself for some of my ludicrous ideas. Magic? Where did that come from? What the hell is the matter with me?

Maybe, my mind isn't just agitated. Maybe, it's gone. Maybe, I've lost it, misplaced it, left it somewhere. Maybe I'm whacko, bonkers, a nutbar. What if I'm a mental case? What if they manage to unlock me from my present prison, only to have to lock me up again in a prison of concrete and steel? That would be trading prisons.

This is not my idea of getting ahead.

47

AND I HAVE KNOWN
CONFUSION, BABY

ANDRIS AND I don't meet again the next day, as promised. Instead, on day four, much to my disappointment, I endure a holiday from mind reading matters. It's not only a psychic holiday, but also a civic holiday, the Monday of a long weekend. There are no psychic activities this day, no telepathy. No minds get read, mine or anybody else's. Not because of the holiday but because Bessie and Ray have decided that Andris and Lina need a break and are taking them to a matinee performance of a revival of the Broadway musical, Fiddler on a Hot Tin Roof, at the Smart Alex Theatre. As a special friend for Lina, Elissa has also been invited to attend, and Jefferson has agreed to work Elissa's shift in order to keep an eye on me and make sure I behave. You never know. I might wander off. It worked for Amos.

Though he has never seen Fiddler on a Hot Tin Roof, Andris recites it in detail to Bessie and Ray, whistles the overture, sings all the songs, and then expresses faux reluctance to actually go to the theatre and sit through it all again. He's joking, of course. But in any case, in the face of Bessie's persistence in playing along with his joke, he permits himself to be coaxed into going for Lina's sake.

Jefferson, whose cooperation has helped make the theatre outing possible begins to feel guilty about my abandonment and the sudden cessation of telepathic research in Brian's room. After fretting about it for a while, he looks at me ruefully and makes me an offer I can't refuse.

"Tell you what, dude. As compensation for putting up with Andris's absence, today, I'm going to give you a special treat and do something I haven't done for anybody else. I'm going to read you the first chapter of my novel. What do you say to that, dude?"

Well, what can I say? It's a given, if you ask me. It's a given, even if you don't ask me. Besides, hearing some of Jefferson's novel may give me an inkling into what his book is about. I spend so much of my life with this guy that he's become my buddy and, frankly, I'm very curious about what my buddy's written. You never can tell. Behind the devoted caregiver may lurk a literary genius. My buddy, a good lurking, literary genius. Wow!

If so, my buddy doesn't let on. He remains his self-effacing self, determined to amuse me with jolly little jokes, mostly at my expense. But no expense is too great. I don't mind. He's a decent guy. I know he really cares about me.

"What I'm going to read to you has to stay between us until my agent gets me a publisher. You have to promise me you won't talk to anyone about it," Jefferson tells me straight-faced and straight-laced. "You've never given away any of my secrets before, dude. So I know I can trust you on this one. Ready? Here goes. Chapter one."

Jefferson begins to read. He's an excellent reader. His voice is deep and well modulated. His diction is precise and he instinctively dramatizes what he reads. It's a bravura performance. The characters come to vibrant life. I identify with the protagonist and fall in love with the supporting players. It seems to be a fiction that examines itself and the author while telling the story. I guess this is what Jefferson meant when he once offhandedly described his writing as metafiction. Anyhow, I'm totally captivated by the story but at the same time, totally puzzled by it. That's a lot of totallys, I know. The fact is, I didn't think I was capable of being so puzzled and captivated at the same time. But clearly, I can be and I am. Actually, it's a puzzle in a puzzle wrapped in an enigma. Or maybe it's wrapped in a conundrum. I briefly consider doing something wildly enthusiastic like applauding, cheering, shouting out bravo, jumping up and down, maybe. But, of course, I'm on my best behaviour. Actually, it's my only behaviour.

Page after page, Jefferson doesn't let up. For the next twenty minutes, he reads on and on, spinning his narrative web around me. And then, the chapter ends, leaving me loving it, grasping for understanding and so puzzled, that, if I could talk, I wouldn't know what to say. If I could talk, I'd be speechless. I've said that before, haven't I? Sorry, but I have to say it again.

"Well, that's it, dude. That's our little secret, the first chapter of my novel. I hope you like it."

Like it? Of course, I like it. I'm puzzled by it. I'm confused by it. But I like it. How could I not like it? The writing is something else. Jefferson's not just chopped liver. Jefferson's a real writer.

Still, my puzzlement persists, and I continue to be confusedly bemused by it and to search for meaning.

Day five, the mind-reading assignment is back at full-bore. Now, somber and silent, Andris is in full telepathic mode all morning, intently focusing on me, drilling, drilling, drilling, into the clutter in my brain, reducing it to rubble, leaving me exhausted in the process and more confused than ever. All I can communicate to Andris is my confusion. Confused. I'm confused. I'm very confused. I've never been this confused before. And I have known confusion, baby. Trust me. He resignedly accepts what little I have to give and the session concludes. He's gotten as much out of me as he can. Our work is over. And I'm a wreck. Not that anyone would notice.

In the afternoon, all the usual suspects are on hand, intent as Andris shares with my parents and my care giving team what he has learned from his final encounter with the worn out and intransigent me.

"The day before we took the theatre break, my session with Brian went very well. I was able to determine from Brian that what he most wanted to communicate to you, his parents, was largely what you already know: that he loves you, that he's awake and aware and that he desperately wants to be freed from the prison he's in.

"Brian was unable to help with ideas of how to free himself or to help you free him. Mind you, he thinks he may have acquired special diagnostic powers, but there is no way to prove or disprove this and, in any case, even if proven, such powers would not help him, personally. One interesting thing that came out was Brian's feeling that, somehow, the solution to his various problems might lie right here, under his nose, under all our noses, I suppose, in this very institution, in Woodgreen House. There is no basis for this. He has no explanation for this feeling.

"In his mind, Brian is visited sporadically by the voice of a young girl named Millie with whom, in his mind, he talks. He has never seen her and doesn't know if she really exists. She pops into his head unexpectedly at intervals, but she is unable to explain why. She doesn't know why. This only happens, she says, when she is doing her homework. If she actually exists, Brian thinks she may be a psychic of some sort. She seems to intuit some things but not others. Millie says she's twelve years old and lives with her mother in Sedona, Arizona. Brian had never heard of Sedona before and knows nothing about the place. But he thinks maybe Millie can help by coming here, talking to him in his head and repeating to you what he tells her. She may not exist in reality, but he thinks she may be magical and able to help him magically. He admits that belief in magic may not be rational. But he says that everything about him may not be rational, and he feels that he is running out of options. That was a good day with Brian. I learned a lot from him that day.

"But it was more difficult this morning. In the day we were away at the theatre, something had changed. Brian was blocked and hard to read, not because he was being stubborn, but because he was confused. All I could pick up from him was confusion, massive confusion, repeated and repeated: Confused. I'm confused. I'm very confused. I've never been this confused before. And then, puzzlingly, he added: And I have known confusion, baby. Trust me.

"So that's it. I think I've done all I can with Brian. I hope this will be of some help. Are there any questions?"

There is a long silence in Brian's room, a sad, disappointed silence.

And then, Ray says, "Piecing together all the bits of information we've collected so far, we now know that Millie, if she really exists, lives in Sedona, Arizona, and that's where I, Ray, have to bring Millie from. But even if she really exists, we don't know who she is, what her last name is, or how to find her. Andris can you be any help with this?"

"Unfortunately not. I can only tell you what Brian knows and has passed on to me. And it's quite clear to me that Brian, himself, does not have the information you are looking for. I'm sorry."

And then, Bessie asks a question that she knows Andris is really not equipped to answer. Still, she stubbornly decides it's worth a try.

"What do you think we should do next to help Brian?"

"I am not a medical person, Mrs. Hildebrand, and so it is difficult for me to be authoritative medically or scientifically. I can only answer intuitively. And my intuitive response to your question would be that escape for Brian from his locked-in life might have to come from outside reality."

"Wait a minute," Ray interrupts. "What do you mean by outside reality? Virtual reality? Magic? Mysticism? Science fiction? What are you talking about? It sounds a bit surreal."

"It may be surreal, virtual, other-worldly. The truth is, I don't really know. All I can say for certain is that you should keep searching. If you can locate Millie and bring her here, maybe she will have the magical powers Brian thinks may help. And, finally, let me remind you that, perhaps, there is a clue in Brian's feeling that somehow, the solution to his various problems lies right here, under his nose, under all our noses, in this institution, in Woodgreen House. Maybe the magic he hopes for is right here."

48

Amos Persists

ANDRIS'S READING of my mucked-up mind having come to an end, Andris and Lina bid us all farewell and go back to Riga. I try not to think about what lies in wait for Lina as her not yet diagnosed, inoperable brain tumour progresses. Struggling with the mess in my own mind, I try not to feel guilty for being unable to help, even though I know that my helping would not have helped. So many helpings and so much helplessness. I seem to be cursed with unhelpful aphorisms.

We all miss the lovely Latvian couple almost immediately. Bessie and Ray talk about them endlessly and approvingly. Jefferson reminds us repeatedly what amazing people they were. In his enthusiasm, he has a way of drawing out the middle vowel in the word amazing, extending it. Amaaaazing!

Elissa says little. She just nods her head silently and grows teary eyed any time Andris and Lina are mentioned. There seems to be unlimited agreement in my limited social circle that Andris was helpful, but no one can pin down precisely how helpful. The best that can be said was that he extracted from me enough additional information to enable putting together in a more meaningful way the pieces of what was already learned. Now, everybody knows that Millie lives in Sedona, Arizona. But no one knows if she really exists and if she does, how to find her. We're not there yet, dammit. We've got a ways to go. Let's get on with it.

I am trying to deal with all this in a head still clotted with confusion. It's hard to think clearly when your head feels like it's plugged with peanut butter. I used to love peanut butter but now, I'm not sure. The only thing I'm sure of is that I don't care for it in my head. I fervently wish it would go away, the peanut butter, the confusion, the unhappiness, all of it. Away with it. Peanut butter, be gone.

Bessie and Ray are still hoping for more responses to the last Google ad, but no emails arrive. We're stalled. No one seems to know what our next move should be. For my part, I keep expecting, hoping, wishing, praying that, maybe, Millie will pop back into my head at any moment and I can tell her how to contact Bessie and Ray so they can bring her here as a visiting psychic along with her mom. And then, maybe we can make some headway. But so far, no word, no Millie. Besides, who knows if combining plan B with Plan C will happen. And if it happens, will it work? Millie is a big question mark. I'm so uncertain about her reality, her existence, her being able to return. Every time Millie leaves, I fear the worst. I worry that she will never come back. Despite all these negatives, I am obsessed with the notion that the maybe magical Millie will be able to communicate with me in some extraordinary way and pass on to my support group the information that only she can glean from a meaningful exchange between us, information that could somehow assist the rescue squad in extricating me from my limbo. I have absolutely no idea what that information might be, but I continue to worry and wonder and wait and hope for my salvation by a perhaps non-existent, perhaps magical, twelve-year-old school girl in Sedona, Arizona. I'm not being very logical. I don't know what's logical anymore. There's nothing logical about a head full of peanut butter. I'm sure of that.

What with my much-constrained state and a head full of peanut butter, I can't tell the days from the nights except that the nights are dark and scary and full of hideous monsters that I dream up or hallucinate in between my many non-activities. The monsters come through my door. I don't know where they're coming from or where they're going, but they seem to be using my room as a shortcut to get there. Like all monsters, they're frightening to observe but luckily for me, they don't threaten me or even look my way. I'm just another thing on their route to who knows where. I could be a lamppost or a letterbox as far as they're concerned. Well, at least, that beats being a phone booth or a parking meter, I suppose.

One night, no monsters this way come. Instead, I get a return visit from the wanderer. It's Amos, clad as always, in his ancient chenille dressing gown and worn slippers and clutching his plastic shopping bag filled with torn bits of paper that he explained on his last visit was the manuscript of his novel that he carries with him everywhere for fear of losing it.

"Hey, Brian. Brian's room. Right? See. I didn't forget. I can still find it."

"I'm glad you remembered."

"Actually, I think my memory has improved since I died. You know that I died?"

"I know. You told me last time."

"Oh, yeah. I did. I forgot."

"Well, at least, you didn't forget that your memory has improved."

"I'll try to remember that."

"What are you doing with yourself these days, Amos?"

"Oh, you know. The usual."

"You always do the usual?"

"Usually."

"Doesn't it get boring?"

"Sometimes. But I'm used to it. You been eating peanuts, Brian? I smell peanuts."

"It's peanut butter. I'd offer you some, but I can't get to it. It's in my head. My head is full of peanut butter."

"That's okay. I'm not nuts about peanuts, anyhow. How are things going?"

"Don't ask."

"Too late. I already asked. Sorry. You don't have to answer if you don't want to."

"It's okay. I'll answer. Is there an adjective for feces?"

"That would be shitty."

"That's how I'm doing."

"Maybe, it's all that peanut butter in your head."

"Why didn't I think of that?"

"Maybe, you're too plugged up to think."

"That's a thought. You spoke to G-O-D about m-e. Thank you."

"Yeah, I tried. But he has a very limited attention span."

"Still, he dropped in to talk to me."

"Was he any help?"

"Not to me. Said he didn't do help."

"Not to me, either. Said he wasn't a clothing store, didn't do wardrobe. So no new dressing gown and slippers."

"Oh. That reminds me, Amos. A rabbi came by, red haired, English accent. He was carrying a lovely gift box with new dressing gown and slippers for you. He'd come to the wrong room and was saddened to learn that you had died several months earlier. He said your mother had been a member of his congregation and she had asked him to take care of it."

"That's really odd. My mother isn't Jewish. She's Roman Catholic."

"He was very ecumenical. Maybe he was a Roman Catholic rabbi."

"I'll have to ask my mother."

"How's you mother doing?"

"Okay. She says, hi."

"Did she have any ideas for me?"

"We talked about you. I told her no lobotomy. In that case, she says your best bet is right under your nose, here in Woodgreen House. But she says to warn you to be careful you don't get trapped in the conspiracy."

"I had no idea there was a conspiracy here."

"She says it's all a conspiracy."

"I thought it was all peanut butter."

"She didn't mention peanut butter."

"Nobody mentions peanut butter. If my head wasn't full of it, I'd never mention it either."

"Gotta go. I'm on my way to meet my publisher."

"You have a publisher? How did you manage to get a publisher?"

"He died recently and plans to keep working. So we've been talking about my novel. He likes it and we're negotiating."

"Does your novel have a title?"

"It's called Torn Scraps of Paper in a Plastic Shopping Bag."

"Intriguing. That would make it social realism."

"I guess so. It's dedicated to my mother."

"I'm not surprised. Say hi to her for me. And good luck with your novel."

'Thanks. See you."

"Right. Don't be a stranger."

"Hey! Don't worry about it. I value our friendship."

49

Professor Kerb

I haven't discussed waste removal very much because, let's face it, it is the sort of unsavory subject that people tend to pooh-pooh. Still, I have to mention it now because I may be imagining it, but the last few days, the waste draining from me and going down the tubes through my life support system seems just a tad darker than usual. In my normally abnormal circumstances, this would not normally be a good omen. But since the traffic flow in and out of me is being closely monitored and calibrated and since no great hue and cry has been raised about the hue of my output, I can only assume that the slight colour shift doesn't indicate any life threatening changes in my body chemistry. So this is all to the good and one less thing for me to worry about. My worry list is way too long already.

Still, it gets me wondering if the colour change is the result of the peanut butter in my head finally working its way out of my body. Of course, I can't substantiate this any more than I can substantiate that peanut butter was what my head was full of in the first place. None of this would stand up in a scientific forum. But then, neither would I, even if I could.

In any case, I start to feel better and slowly begin to return to my standard state of brooding pre-hysteria. And, of course, I start to think more clearly again, relatively that is. Everything about me is relative to everything else all about me. That has a kind of rhetorical ring to it. The rhetorical device I have in mind is bound to have a name. I don't know what it is. I'm appalled by how little I know. If only I had known back then, how little I know now, I might have tried to stay in school and get to know more. Retroactive regret is the most useless kind. Maybe that's what makes it one of my favorites. I'm deeply into useless. Unlike tyrants and dictators and sociopaths who say they regret nothing, I regret everything, even things I had nothing to do with. My kind of regret may be a form of existential guilt. And, of course, I regret that, too.

Never mind. There's good news! Another psychic has responded to the Google ad, and we all get excited again not only because he seems to be a promising candidate but also because he's so conveniently located in a lovely, leafy, nearby Toronto neighbourhood and available almost immediately, no travel required, no timetables to juggle. His name is Angus Kerb. He's a psychology professor at York University and his field of expertise is PTSD. As you may have gathered from some of my previous slurs, having been wrongly labeled with the acronym, PVS, I am not keen on acronyms. I may even be hostile to acronyms. Besides, I don't know what PTSD is. There I go again, reminding myself, of how much I don't know. There seems to be more I don't know all the time. More and more, I know less and less. My lack of knowledge is expanding rapidly. And in all directions. I guess I'm not doing enough reading. I'm thinking of joining the public library, although I'm not sure how I would do that. In the meantime, what the hell is PTSD?

The ever-knowledgeable Jefferson explains to Bessie and Ray what PTSD is.

"It stands for post-traumatic stress disorder, an anxiety condition caused by a life-threatening traumatic event. PTSD can cause hallucinations, flashbacks, nightmares, and depression and has to be treated with special psychotherapy."

I realize with a shock that I'm an almost perfect match for the definition. In addition to my obvious affliction, I may also be afflicted with PTSD. But only I know this. No one in my cheering section makes this connection because they're unaware that I'm having hallucinations, flashbacks, nightmares, and depression. Is it just a coincidence that an expert in PTSD, unbeknownst to anyone including himself, has found me, and for a reason other than PTSD? I grow concerned but my concerns are swept away by Jefferson's ongoing dissertation. "The latest therapies for treating PTSD go by the clumsy handle of eye movement desensitization and reprocessing or EMDR."

Oh, no. Not another acronym. In the interests of science and the attempts to solve my locked in problem, I do my best to throttle my aversion to acronyms.

Kerb, it turns out, is a high-profile psychologist, with lots of learned papers and half a dozen books to his credit. His psychic capabilities, however, haven't been widely publicized. He's kept his telepathy pretty much to himself. I suppose you could describe it as his own private pastime, a sort of personal, recreational interest like, say, rock watching or bird climbing.

The professor knows how to make a good first impression, I'll say that for him. Instead of responding to the Google ad by email, Kerb unexpectedly phones Ray's unlisted phone number and demonstrates his formidable powers of extra sensory perception not only at a distance but also at length, reeling off what he intuits, sight unseen, about Ray's activities and secret philanthropies. That's reel one. A moment later, in reel two, he does the same with Bessie and concludes finally in reel three with what he has picked up about the object of the exercise, the patient patient, recently promoted to patient client, the never-say-die me. Simply put, whatever we know, he knows, not a hundred percent, mind you, but pretty darn close. To quote Jefferson, it's amazing!

Ray and Bessie are much impressed by Kerb's telephonic, telepathic performance and after discussing it with him, and agreeing that his fee will be donated to his favorite charity, a home for down on their luck, burnt-out country rock musicians, in Lubbock, Texas, they set a time the next day for Kerb to visit me at Woodgreen. But fate, as it so often does when you're looking the other way, intervenes. On the morning of the planned meeting with me, after a hearty, high-fiber breakfast topped with fresh organic blueberries and raspberries, Angus Kerb is viciously attacked by his sporadically troublesome gallbladder in what he later describes as the mother-in-law of all acute gallbladder attacks. An ambulance quickly summoned by the alarmed daughter of his mother-in-law quickly carts him off to the emergency ward of Sunnybrook Hospital where they wisely refuse to part with him until he parts with his unruly gallbladder and its malcontents. The almost immediate removal of the recalcitrant organ and its dissident, longtime resident gallstones is nimbly accomplished by laparoscopic surgery after the surgeons assure him that the procedure is not only quick but also largely painless. All going well, he could be free and clear of his gallbladder and back home the next day.

Three miniscule, band-aid covered, bodily punctures later, he's good to go but there's an unforeseen, no good to go cascade of debilitating complications: unwelcome inflammation, unrelenting infection, uncooperative antibiotics, you name it, his chart is full up and so, too, is he. And thus, though minus his gallbladder and missing it not at all, the professor stays in the hospital for a week to be subtly motivated into speedier recovery from his setback by the threat of ongoing healthy hospital food. This might qualify as persuasion by oxymoron. Mind you, it can't be more unappetizing than what they feed me. That would be whining about dining, I suppose.

And, so, the Kerb mind reading has to wait. And so do I. And the wait turns out to be longer than expected because of yet another complication. After a week in the hospital, the professor is set loose and sent home to finish recuperating in the comfort of his own surroundings only to be unpredictably afflicted with temporary paralysis of his lower limbs. Given time, he is assured by his healers, this chilling condition will melt away of its own accord. For the moment, however, Professor Kerb is confined to bed. He's not going anywhere. And that includes Brian's room.

It makes me want to scream. Is there no end to these complications? And then, it strikes me. Could this be the conspiracy that Amos's mother keeps harping about? I don't get time to ponder it because Professor Kerb is bound and determined not to be thwarted by conspiracies, real or imagined. He's keen on the Brian mind-reading project and wants to get on with it. In a phone call to Ray and Bessie, he explains how he proposes to read my mind from his bed. He will do it on the phone just as he did with Ray and Bessie when he replied to the Google ad.

"Distance has never been a problem for me. I can work quite well on the phone using a speakerphone for Brian to hear me. What I pick up is actually enhanced by hearing the voice of the person whose mind I am reading. I'm aware that Brian can't speak. But we can get around that with a recording of his voice prior to his accident, if it's available."

"I'd have to check," Bessie replies. "There may be something on my computer, an old video clip, maybe, of Brian saying something. But I can't be sure."

"Hold on. I have a thought," Ray offers. "How much of Brian talking would you need to make this work?"

"Not much," Kerb replies. "A few words would do it."

"Would two words work for you?" Ray asks.

"I think so," Kerb says. "We could simply repeat them, if we needed more."

"I know what you're thinking," Bessie says. "Hallelujah, brother!"

"Exactly. I'd better explain to Professor Kerb."

"No explanation necessary. Hallelujah, brother! That would do just fine. I gather that every so often, at random, without rhyme or reason, Brian blurts out two words, always the same two words, Hallelujah, brother! Why don't we set up a digital recorder near him so when he says, Hallelujah, brother! we record it, several times, if possible. That would do it. One more thing. The middle fingers of Brian's hands are erect and menacing. Is that correct?"

"They are. How did you know?"

"Once you hear the words, Hallelujah, brother, it's pretty obvious. You don't have to be a mind reader to know that."

Maybe not, but it would help.

50

Phoning It In

Bessie and Ray organize Brian's room for the telephone mind-reading session with Professor Kerb. The phone in my room is already equipped with a speakerphone function. Press the button with the speaker icon on it and incoming calls are broadcast to the entire room for everybody to hear. Just like talk radio, it strikes me, but without the nasty, argumentative, ill-informed opinions and the endless commercials. As for a digital voice recorder, Ray already owns several he doesn't use much any more. Before the advent of smart phones, he used to record verbal reminders to himself on his travels. He charges up the one with the longest battery life, sets it up on my bedside table, turns it on, grins at me and with a wave of his arm, makes a mock announcement.

"And now, for a few words from the star of today's show, Brian Hildebrand. You're on the air, Brian. Go for it."

Without giving it another thought, I spring into non-action. I think I've already established, several times, in fact, that there's no pushing this two-word monologue of mine. I'm not running the show here, or anywhere else, for that matter. Sometimes, it seems to me, that all the mindless things about me and my much-constricted life have minds of their own. My mind has no say whatsoever. I have no choice but to wait patiently for Hallelujah, brother! to erupt sporadically of its own volition, as it usually does, inconveniently, uncontrollably, several times a day. But wouldn't you know it, it's not happening today, dammit. Some days, it just doesn't happen. Other days, it just doesn't stop happening. Today, there is nothing. My lips are sealed. The next day, however, I hit the jackpot and manage to deliver, Hallelujah, brother! six times in half an hour. It's some kind of record. I'm so worn out from the concentrated exertion that I may not be able to run the marathon tonight. Talk about wishful running. But the good news is that the digital recorder faithfully captures all six of my explosive shout-outs of Hallelujah, brother! before the frequency diminishes to one every four or five hours.

So now, finally, we're all set up for Professor Kerb's telephonic, mind-reading session. The supporting cast, Bessie, Ray, Jefferson, and Elissa assemble in Brian's room and Ray telephones Kerb.

"Hi Professor. It's Ray Triggs. We're all organized and set to go at this end. We have a speakerphone. And we have Brian's voice, six Hallelujah, brothers, on a digital recorder. We're ready, if you are. Is this a good time for you?"

"Perfect. Let's review a few things before we start. Earlier today, I talked to Mrs. Hildebrand and I confirmed what you've been able to piece together with the help of other psychics. I hope to go beyond that, extending from what we already know, perhaps, into some totally new areas of information or insight."

"Sounds good," Ray replies. "Let's go for it."

"Are you okay," Bessie asks, "with four of us in the room as observers during your session with Brian?"

"No problem, Mrs. Hildebrand. The interactive effect of people close to Brian, both physically and emotionally, could prove helpful. In fact, I encourage anyone in the room to speak, ask questions, or make comments at any time during the procedure, with one proviso. Don't address Brian directly. We don't want to interfere with his focus. Talk only to me. To avoid ambiguity and confusion, I suggest addressing remarks to me by starting with my name, Angus, or Professor. When I ask you to play the recording of Brian's voice, please do so. I may do this at intervals during our session as I feel the need. We'll start with the recording. Please, play the recording of Brian's voice, now."

Ray presses the playback button on the recorder. My recorded voice comes through loud and clear, delivering my uncontrollable, meaningless mantra six times in succession.

"Hallelujah, brother! Hallelujah, brother! Hallelujah, brother! Hallelujah, brother! Hallelujah, brother! Hallelujah, brother!"

In my insider's view, I sound like the village idiot. Make that the Woodgreen idiot. This can't be a good way to start. Is this going to work? I wonder.

"Hallelujah, brother Brian," responds the professor. "I'm Brother Angus and with your help I'm going to read your mind. This will not be an internal conversation in your head that you may have experienced in the past and may be used to. I will not be a voice dropping into your mind talking to you in the privacy of your head. Instead, I will be making suggestions to you over the speakerphone for everybody to hear and I will be asking you to focus and aim your thoughts directly at me so that I can tele-pathically pick up what you're thinking. Then, I will repeat what you convey to me for everyone else to hear. Let's try it now as a test. Brian, summarize your condition for me."

There is a pause as I do as requested.

"That's good. I'll repeat it: I'm on life support after an accident, having been wrongly diagnosed as being in a persistent vegetative state but, in fact, I'm not vegetative. I'm conscious, cognitive, all my senses work but I can't move and I can't talk. I'm locked in, a prisoner in my body, a prisoner in my mind. Okay. That's Brian's summary of his condition. Now, please, play the recording."

"Hallelujah, brother! Hallelujah, brother! Hallelujah, brother! Hallelujah, brother! Hallelujah, brother! Hallelujah, brother!"

"Brian, I detect a sort of duality in your inner voice. There's a kind of duplication of your thoughts that you haven't shared with anyone else. What can you tell me about that?"

"Well it's only just recently that this has happened. It feels like there are two of me in my head. There are two internal voices and they're both mine. They're identical and say the same things, but they overlap so that one lags slightly behind the other. It's almost an echo. I suppose, you could compare it to double-vision. Only in this case, it's double thinking."

"Why do you think this is happening?"

"I'm not sure. It could be old brain damage. My head may be messed up from the accident in ways not noticed before, or from all these years on life support, or it could be from some of the treatments that have been tried on me."

"Does this duality in your head, this doubleness, threaten you in any way? Is it worrisome?"

"No, not really. I guess I've gotten used to it. It's puzzling. That's for sure. But it seems to be benign and isn't worrisome. What is worrisome, though, is that sometimes, suddenly, in inner moments of hysteria, I'm not sure I exist."

"When that happens, how does that make you feel?"

"In those inner moments, I feel as if I'm a figment of someone's imagination."

"Whose imagination do you think that might that be?"

"I don't know. With my ongoing rotten luck, it might be the imagination of someone who also doesn't exist. Which, of course, is absurd. That would make me a figment of a figment. But then, I get the notion, and this is even more absurd, that the imagination behind all this is my own imagination, that, maybe, I'm imagining myself. Maybe, I'm making myself up. Maybe, I'm a figment of my own imagination. But it doesn't make sense. How can that be?"

"Exactly. How can that be? That would be unlikely, don't you think?"

"I suppose so. Then, again, I could be dreaming, hallucinating, having visions. I have trouble telling them apart anymore. I've got nothing but time on my hands and my hyperactive mind desperately wants to keep busy. So one way or another, I may be filling the time by making up a lot of things."

"What kind of things?"

"Death, as a beautiful woman, for instance. She invites me to meet her for a drink and we talk about my prospects and I assure her that I am hanging in and no way ready to leave. It could be a dream or a vision or a hallucination. Still, she pays for my beer."

"Have you made up anybody else?"

"Amos, the Woodgreen wanderer, maybe. He was a patient here, but he died. He still comes to visit me. He likes to keep in touch. If he's real, he's a ghost. If he's not real, he's a hallucination. If he's not a hallucination, then, I must be making him up."

"Please play the recording."

"Hallelujah, brother! Hallelujah, brother! Hallelujah, brother! Hallelujah, brother! Hallelujah, brother! Hallelujah, brother!"

"What about Millie the school girl from Sedona, Arizona? Are you making her up, too?"

"I can't be sure. But sometimes, I think so. When she doesn't show up for long periods, I worry that she's not real. But then again, she may be a psychic of some sort who drops in and visits people in their heads. Strangely, I feel that I have a special connection to her, that she's somehow out of the ordinary, and I have the perhaps foolish notion that she's in some inexplicable way committed to me, which may be complete nonsense. Still, there's something unusual about her, something otherworldly, something magical, that I like to think might help me escape this prison of mine. If Millie's not real, maybe it's because she's an angel. At least, I hope so."

"Do you believe in angels, Brian?"

"I don't believe in very much of anything any more, but I need to believe in Millie. I could use the help of an angel right about now. Or some serious magic."

"Professor Kerb," Bessie interjects. "Is there some way Brian can give us more clues, so we can try to track down Millie in

Sedona? Then, maybe, we can get her to come up here and possibly be helpful to him."

"Can you help us locate Millie, Brian?" asks Kerb. "Is there anything that you haven't told us that might be useful?

"All I know is what she tells me, that she lives with her mother in Sedona, Arizona. That's if she's for real. I don't know her last name or her mother's. I don't have a street address or phone number. The best I can hope for is that Millie will drop in on me again soon and I can ask her for that information or better still, tell her to get in touch with Ray and Bessie. If Millie doesn't come back to visit or if she does and turns out to be nothing more than a figment of my imagination then, I just don't know how to help anybody help me. Of course, if Millie is magical or an angel that might solve all my problems."

"But Brian, hold on. I understand that you think the solution to your problems may be right under your nose in Woodgreen. How does Millie fit into that?"

"Well, I've been mulling that over and I can think of two possibilities. The first is that if she comes to visit me here, then, she'll be right under my nose. The second is that if there's a conspiracy here, it's already right under my nose and maybe Millie's part of the conspiracy."

"That's the first we've heard about a conspiracy. What's that all about?"

"I don't really know. Amos's mother says it's all a conspiracy and told him to warn me to be careful."

"How reliable is Amos's mother?'

"Not very, I'm afraid. She agreed to Amos's prefrontal lobotomy. How reliable is that? She's a bit of a crackpot. And, of

226

course, she's dead. They're both dead. That's how Amos is able to stay in touch with her. They talk almost every day, he tells me. The thing is, assuming that I'm not making all this up, your question should be, how reliable are the dead? I don't know the answer to that one."

"Oh, boy. Please, play the recording."

"Hallelujah, brother! Hallelujah, brother! Hallelujah, brother! Hallelujah, brother! Hallelujah, brother! Hallelujah, brother!"

"What makes you think that the solution to your problems may be right under your nose here in Woodgreen?"

"I honestly don't know. It's not rational. But I'm not always rational. Let's say, it's just something I sense."

"Brian, is it possible that you're a psychic like your mother?"

"I wish I were but I'm not. Mind you, since my accident, I've developed some pretty remarkable diagnostic skills. I'm able to look at people and know immediately what ails them. But that's all I can do. And that doesn't make me a psychic. I can't read minds. I can't predict the future. I don't know where the treasure is buried. Besides, as things stand, I'm unable to pass on what I do know. So I'm no help to myself or to anybody else. When you get right down to it, I could be described as useless."

"You're being too hard on yourself, Brian. I, for one, would not describe you as useless. You may be silent. You may be immobile. But you're not useless. You have a great deal to offer. There's a lot to be learned from you and there will be more as progress is made toward unlocking you and tapping into your newly acquired skills."

"I appreciate your positive attitude, Professor. You're very supportive. Ideally, that should inspire me to try harder to be helpful. But let's face it, I'm mercurial and I could suddenly and unapologetically change my mixed-up mind at any time. The fact is, I'm not only useless, I'm unreliable."

"Thank you for the heads up, Brian. But somehow, I don't get the feeling that you're unreliable. What I sense is that you're holding back, suppressing information that could help you."

"Well, if I am, I must be doing it subconsciously because I'm not aware of holding back anything."

"Can I persuade you to dig down deep into your mind and try to root out whatever you may have buried there?"

"I'll give it a try, but I can't promise..."

Suddenly, my mouth explodes into one Hallelujah, brother! after another. This is not Ray playing the recording. This is me, live, and counting the tortured, verbal explosions. One. Two. Three... I get to ten before I lose count. And then, as suddenly as they start, they stop, leaving me totally exhausted from the intense exertion, but with a puzzling thought that hadn't occurred to me before. Between the explosions of Hallelujah, brother! I seem to be experiencing a sudden intuitive leap of understanding that I simply don't understand. But that's contradictory. What am I supposed to make of it? Do I need another puzzle to plague me? For a moment, I'm lost in uncommunicative thought. Or maybe, I'm just lost period.

51

The Doorway

"Brian?" The professor sounds concerned. "You've gone silent on me. I'm not picking up anything from you. Are you all right?"

"I'm okay, but I'm exhausted. I don't think I'm going to be able to run in the marathon tonight."

"What marathon? What are you talking about?"

"You could call it a running gag, or a case of wishful running. I was just recycling one of my old jokes."

"You mean to say you make jokes?"

"Or recycle old ones. I do it all the time. Don't you?"

"I suppose I do. But only some of the time. I didn't know that someone in your dire circumstances could make jokes."

"No one knows. I've kept it to myself. Making jokes helps me preserve what little is left of my sanity. It's another one of my secrets."

"Well, there you are. You see, Brian, the learning I talked about has already started. Let's keep working on this. What else can we learn from you?"

"Well, between all the Hallelujah, brothers, a puzzling thought popped into my head."

"Tell me about it."

"The thought is: There are two sides to every doorway."

"There are two sides to every doorway. That seems obvious. Why is that puzzling?"

"I don't know what it means."

"It could be a metaphor."

"Metaphors make me uncomfortable. I try to avoid metaphors."

"Fine. But what do you think it means?"

"I don't know. Metaphors muck up meaning. That's the trouble with metaphors."

"Still, it has to mean something."

"Maybe. But I don't get it."

"Okay. Give it some thought, Brian. Just pretend you're answering a multiple-choice question. And if you don't know the answer, guess."

"All right. Well, where do I start? There are two sides to every doorway. Let me think. A doorway is a passageway, a portal, between what's on the two sides of the doorway, between two spaces, two environments, two worlds. I'm going to have to guess that on one side of the doorway is everyday reality and on the other side is another dimension, make-believe, illusion, fantasy, otherworldliness, whatever. Now, if my guess is correct, then just passing through the doorway could be life changing."

"Good. Now, apply that to yourself and your own circumstances."

"My own circumstances? Well, supposing I could pass through the doorway, maybe I could escape from my life on life support and return to my former life, the way I was before the accident. Wouldn't that be something? But how likely is that?"

"That would depend entirely on you, Brian. No one can answer that question for you. But first, you would have to find the doorway, pass through it, going in the right direction, and see what happens. And remember, don't take it too literally. It could be a metaphor."

"Here we go again with a metaphor. A metaphor for what? This is getting to feel more like a conspiracy all the time. I'm worn out. Sorry. But I'm going to have to stop. I don't think I can be any more help today."

"That's fine, Brian, I think we've done all we can for the moment. After I'm back on my feet, I'd like to come and see you for a face-to-face, follow-up, if that's okay with you."

"Talk to Bessie and Ray. They can decide. It's up to them."

"No problem, Professor," Bessie and Ray say, almost in unison. "Let us know when you're mobile again."

52

MY MISTAKE

Two days have gone by and I'm still in a foul mood, when who should suddenly pop into my head but Millie.

"Hi, Brian. It's Millie. I'm back."

"Finally," I reply, trying, unsuccessfully, not to sound grumpy.

"I'm sorry it took so long. I've been having some problems."

"Your mother still giving you a hard time? Is that it?"

"It's not mom. It's me. I'm having trouble getting to drop in on you. It's become really difficult to make it happen no matter how much homework I do. And that's not the only problem. Doing my algebra no longer helps me extend my visits. I don't know why any of this is happening. But it means I can't visit as often and, when I do, I can start drifting away at any moment. There's not much time to talk."

"Well, then, let me quickly tell you about a new plan for you to help me. Google an ad on the internet with the headline, Serious Psychic Sought. Got that? Serious Psychic Sought. It will put you in touch with my mother and father. They'll explain everything to you and your mom and pay all the expenses for both of you to come to Toronto. Serious Psychic Sought. Can you remember that headline?"

"Serious Psychic Sought. Don't worry. I won't forget it. I'll Google it and we'll contact your parents. Oh. Oh. I'm drifting."

"Wait. One more thing…"

"Sorry. There's nothing I can do. I …."

There is a sound like a sigh and then, silence. And she is gone. Here we go again. Why does this keep happening?

Millie's sudden departure in mid-discussion leaves me with more than the usual feeling of disappointment. It leaves me with a feeling of foreboding. Something is not right. I sense I've done something wrong. But what? In my harried mind, I replay the wording of the second Google ad:

"Serious Psychic Sought. Psychic wanted to telepathically read the mind of a locked-in accident victim currently on life support and unable to move or talk but conscious and cognitive. If you're the psychic we're looking for, you will contact us right now."

I grow uncomfortable as I slowly realize there may be a problem, a big problem. Like the first Google ad, the second ad, just as Bessie and Ray decided, contains no contact information, no name, no address, no phone number, no email address, nothing to make it clear to whom to reply or how. To be sure she would be able to make contact, I should have given Millie the missing information but there was no time, dammit. As it stands, the ad depends on the reader being a serious psychic with superior psychic powers. Unless Millie is a serious psychic – and that's up in the air; I've never really been sure – I may have just given

233

her useless information. When she Googles the ad, she still may not be able to get in touch with Bessie and Ray. And guess what? Here I am, stuck, again, left with no option but to wait for Millie to drop in on me. The trouble is, with Millie's latest problems, it could take a long time or maybe not happen at all.

I have to do something to sort this mess out. The question is what? Unhappy and worried, I review the situation and make some assumptions. Assuming that Millie can't psychically figure out who placed the ad, and so can't contact Bessie and Ray, and assuming that Millie may not be able to drop in on me for some length of time or maybe forever and assuming that she'll keep checking Google for more information, then the only way to deal with this is for Bessie and Ray to run a third ad with all the contact information in it and hope Millie sees it. Somehow, I have to convey this to Bessie and Ray. But how?

I agonize over this. And then, it occurs to me that the answer may be Professor Kerb. If he comes back to see me face to face after he is mobile again, as he has said he would, and does a follow-up session with me, I will pass the vital information onto him in the presence of Bessie and Ray that the Google ad has to be revised to include the contact information and run again so that Millie can respond to it. And that should do it. At least, I hope so. But there are no guarantees that Kerb will return to see me. Or that any of this will happen. I have to wait and hope that he will do as he said.

Wait and hope. That could be my motto. That's what I've been doing for almost six years. Wait and hope. It would make a great a bumper sticker. All I need is a bumper.

53

A LITTLE WHINING

TIME PASSES quickly for most people but then, as you may have gathered by now, I'm not most people. Come to think of it, I'm almost no people, at all, and I'm fretting about it at the moment because time feels like it's dragging its fat ass past my shrinking viewing platform. I'm annoyed and destroyed that I'm not hearing from anybody, dammit. Not from Millie. Not from Professor Kerb. Not from Dr. Roopa. Where the hell is everybody who's supposed to be getting back to me? I've always been of a progressive mindset and now, I'm getting progressively pissed off. Bessie and Ray, of course, are here loyally and lovingly and reliably and talking to me, telling me all the things they think I might want to hear but not necessarily what I think I want to hear. But I have no way of conveying my current concerns and my impatience to them. I have no intermediary, no telepathic, psychic, mind-reading advocate to relay my thoughts and make my case. All I can do on my own is croak out an occasional, meaningless Hallelujah, brother! And that's no response, what-soever, even on those rare occasions when completely by chance it immediately follows what is said to me. I do my best to compensate by making up bitter poems in self-defense, or maybe its self-abnegation, whatever that is.

> Am I living? Am I dying?
> Why do I persist in trying,
> If all I'm doing is lying to myself?
> Am I winning? Am I losing?
> It gets more and more confusing.
> Maybe I should be refusing to go on.
> Just push the button, yank the chain.
> Bye-bye world. Bye-bye brain.
> Off I go, down the drain.

They're truly dreadful poems, dreary doggerel and dishonest, as well, because I have no way of refusing to go on, no way of giving up, no way of pulling the plug on myself. And besides, the truth is, I don't really want to. I'm not ready to pack it in. I just want to whine a bit. So for the moment, at least, I'll spare you any more samples of my bad poetry and the associated angst, mine, yours, everybody's. It's viral. You wouldn't want to catch it.

Unbeknownst to my vast legion of fans and admirers, and as I've repeatedly and not always happily reported, there's too bloody much going on in this hyperactive noodle of mine. It may be making me even wackier than I already am. It's as if there's a multiplex in my head pulsing with images, dreams, hallucinations, visions, figments of my imagination, and fragments of conversations that I may be plucking out of the air or clawing off the virtual wall between me and the world out there or maybe inventing from scratch whenever I get the itch. Hey, I'm diabolically inventive, after all, no question about it. Hell, I may even have invented myself. What I can't understand is, if I invented myself, why didn't I invent me outside this prison of mine. Clearly, I wasn't thinking ahead at the time. Or maybe, come to think of it, I wasn't thinking, at all.

To be fair – I'm not sure to whom – I can't be certain any of this is happening. It may all be in my mucked-up mind that is getting to be a mini cesspool. That would make it a cesspuddle, I suppose. To make matters verse, or blankety-blank verse, if such a thing is possible, I, myself, may not exist except in the mind of someone else who also may not exist except in my mind. Is it possible that I'm the missing link in a sort of daisy chain of non-existence? Or am I just stalling for time, not ready to confront where this is going? Where is this going? How will it end? When will it end? What if it doesn't end but goes on and on ad infinitum? Or beyond? Wow! That's really far out. What will happen to me? I'm starting to whine again. I must stop.

54

YET ANOTHER FLASHBACK

As IF I don't already have an endless cavalcade of stuff dancing and prancing about in my nagging noggin, every so often there are more of the flashbacks, some of which I've already shared with you, a harrowingly accurate series of recollections of, or reconnections to, obscure past events in my life that suddenly flash into my mind like film clips. And there's nothing unreal or surreal about these flashbacks. They're not made up. They're coming out of my memory, and they're hyper real and almost eerie in their preciseness, in every instance, leaving me with the feeling that I've just learned something about myself that I'd either forgotten years earlier or somehow missed recognizing the first time around. In their unexpectedness and accuracy, these flashbacks are distressing.

Suddenly, without warning, no music, no credits, I'm back in the duplex on Churchill Street that Blaine and I lived in. Blaine and I have just gone to bed, but I can't get to sleep. I keep squirming and fidgeting. Something is bugging me, something dark and worrisome, but I don't know what it is. All I know for sure is that I'm keeping Blaine awake. Finally, she turns to me.

"What's wrong, babe?"

"I'm frightened."

"By what?"

"I don't know. But it's not anything good."

"You're just tired."

"It's more than that. Something's going to happen to me, something bad. I can feel it."

"Come on. Try to get some sleep. You'll be fine in the morning."

"But what if I don't make it through the night? What if I don't wake up in the morning? This could be our last night together." As I say this, I sound just like Woody Allen at his apprehensive worst which is usually his comedic best.

"In that case, I'd better hold you until you fall asleep."

It takes a while, but in Blaine's comforting embrace, I finally drift off to sleep. In the morning, I awake and I'm back to normal and no longer apprehensive. Over coffee, Blaine and I joke about my fears.

"Well, you didn't die during the night, I see."

"Are you sure?"

"Absolutely. Can't you tell?"

"I have to give it some thought. I hesitate to make hasty decisions about matters of life and death."

"Do you suppose it was the way I held onto you that saved your life?"

"I wouldn't be surprised. It seems to have worked. You'll have to save my life more often."

It's a snowy Sunday in late January. And I'm slated to have brunch that morning with Carey Shumaker, a visiting former teammate of mine from Cornell.

"You're going to brunch with Carey Shumaker today. It's snowing. It may be slippery. Drive carefully."

"No problem. I got the snow tires put on Thursday. And there's a hundred-pound sack of sand in the trunk."

There, as if clipped off in the editing room, the flashback comes to an abrupt end. And now, all these years later, it dawns on me that on that Sunday, the day after that unsettling, sleepless incident of years ago, my life changed. I was run over by my own car. What I experienced that distressing night before must have been a premonition of what was going to happen to me the following day. It never occurred to me till now that I was having a premonition. Only in hindsight was I able to make that connection. What, I wonder, if back then, I had recognized my premonition for what it was and cautiously decided not to drive my car to meet Carey that day? Is it possible that I might have avoided the accident and not be where I am today? I'll never know, will I?

55

THE TOUR

I CAN'T BELIEVE what's going on this morning. I'm not making this up. This is actually happening. Here I am, hanging about in my usual unmoving and uninspiring manner when Jefferson comes running in–literally–looking perplexed. What's his problem?

"I'm really sorry about this, dude. I don't know how this happened. But you've got company coming in, a whole bunch of company. And they don't speak English. I have no idea who they are or why they're here."

Well, I think, if they speak Latvian, I'm okay with that. I've already proven that I understand Latvian. But it turns out that they aren't speaking Latvian. Today's visitors are speaking Japanese and despite this unexpected, linguistic challenge, I seem, much to my surprise, to understand Japanese as well as I understood Latvian.

Don't ask. I don't know how I do it, either.

From all the excited talk flying about me, I learn that the excited talkers are a tour group from Osaka, Japan, no less. There are seventeen of them, young and old, men and women, led by an eighteenth, a middle-aged man in wire-rimmed glasses and white running shoes, smiling broadly and carrying a little green triangular flag on a telescoping metal rod that looks like a car antenna that he jiggles above his head at intervals to maintain the chattering group's attention, if not order itself.

They're a lively lot and seem to be having a good time. But Jefferson's repeated attempts to converse with them in English are met with noncomprehension, if not outright confusion. Even their flag-jiggling leader can only manage two words in English. The two words are "American Express." And he repeats at them at frequent intervals as if they explain everything.

American Express? What's going on? Who are these guys? Why are they here?

Although unable to engage them in conversation, I understand what they're saying in Japanese and thus learn that they're on a North American tour organized by American Express. Their extensive travel itinerary includes Los Angeles, Las Vegas, San Francisco, New Orleans, Miami, Nashville, Washington, D.C., New York City, and Brian's Room in Toronto. I'm a stop on their North American tour, for Pete's sake, the only stop in Canada. Is that weird or what? Who arranged this? How did I get on their itinerary? How did Brian's Room become a tour destination, let alone a tourist attraction? The Japanese love Country and Western music. Why wasn't Branson, Missouri, on their itinerary?

A dozen or so of my Japanese visitors carry masses of yellow daffodils, which they are persuaded by Jefferson not to deposit on the foot of my already overburdened bed. Instead, they unload the flowers onto him. He accepts armful after armful of

242

the yellow blossoms with some uncertainty, not knowing what he will do with this sudden burst of golden abundance. I can read the checklist on his face. It will take a lot of vases to deal with all these. Where will he get that many vases? And then, where will he put all the vases? He looks at me, shakes his head in disbelief but tosses off a reassurance.

"Never mind, dude. Enjoy your company. I'll go wrangle up some vases."

An hour goes by. The flower-laden Jefferson is still out rounding up vases and my visiting Japanese tourists are still here, discussing me and my suspended condition animatedly, all the while looking at me almost worshipfully. From the respectful buzz of all the conversations, I make out that in Japan, due to the intense media interest in my case, I have become some sort of celebrity. At home, I'm a nonentity. In Japan, I'm a hero. As they say in showbiz, I'm huge in Japan. While this is flattering, I'm not looking for recognition or respect. I'm looking for help.

Help, where are you? I need you.

Jefferson finally comes back with vase after vase of daffodils and after he fills the window sill with them, he brings in more vases of daffodils and for lack of other options, he puts them on the floor at the foot of my bed, slowly filling the space with them and reducing the standing room until the visitors urged on by their flag-jiggling leader are eased out the door and into the corridor and their visit to Brian's room is over and they are gone, leaving behind on the floor a host of golden daffodils. As I may have already mentioned, flowers are my favorite thing, and I'm pleased with the view, very pleased.

But missing Branson, Missouri? That really bugs me. How could they have left Branson, Missouri, off their itinerary?

56

OF MEN AND MICE

As PROMISED, I'm not going to inflict any more of my wretched poems on you, at least for the moment. I'll spare you the products of my impatience for a while. Instead, I'm giving the poems a pass and trying to ease my angst by taking a shot at dialogues, scenes, playlets, I'm not sure what to call them. They're based on random conversations in the corridor outside the door to my room that I overhear thanks to my acute hearing. Let's call them corridor dialogues. I'm never sure precisely who the players are or what their problems are. I assume they're Woodgreen residents. Or I suppose they could be staff members. Maybe it doesn't matter who they are. You can decide.

Here's a corridor dialogue between a couple of men. They'd be in their forties, I'd guess, judging by their voices.

"What about the doctors? What do they say?"

"They say there's no hope."

"No way. Come on. There's always hope."

"Nope. No hope. They say it's too far gone."

"But what about all those research breakthroughs we keep reading about?"

"What about them?"

"Well, what do the doctors say about them?"

"They say they work on mice."

"Well, that's a start, isn't it?"

"But I'm not a mouse. For humans, they say, a cure is maybe ten years away."

"And your problem is you're human, right?"

"Used to be. Lately, I'm not so sure."

"You're human. Trust me. I'll vouch for you."

"Thanks. But I'm running out of time."

"How much time do they give you?"

"About twenty minutes."

"When did they tell you that?"

"About two weeks ago."

"Well, so far you're ahead of the game."

"So far may not be far enough."

"You have a way with words. You're quick with a turn of phrase."

"I was going to be a writer."

"What happened?"

"Nothing. That's what happened."

"What did you say you were suffering from again?"

"There's no again. This is the first time."

"So what exactly is it?"

"That's what the doctors keep asking."

I relate strongly to this puzzled guy's plaint.

57

The Reality of Unreality

RIGHT NOW, I'm precisely nowhere. Never ever, even in the worst of times, did I expect to be nowhere, not even after the suddenness of my self-inflicted accident. The purgatorial status that I now find myself in did not come upon me suddenly. I was not an overnight success when I was succeeding, and I cannot claim to have been an overnight failure. It took me awhile to sink to my present level of nothingness. And only now, having descended to this level, am I beginning to make some sense out of all the absurdity caroming about in the constricted confines of my angry consciousness. I haven't been able to express it before, but all along, without realizing it, I've been groping for some sort of unifying thesis, that would fuse all the disparate strands, all the comings and goings, all the entrances and exits, in the bricabrac of my broken brain into a single, crystalline coherency and give a modicum of meaning to the madness of my circumstances.

Okay. That sounds a bit overblown, I admit. Still, there are times when a little hot air is unavoidable. In fact, in perpetrating the overblown, hot air may be preferable to cold air. It certainly seems to work that way for hot air balloons. In any case, now, at least, at long last, I've come up with a thesis that neatly ties together all of what's going on up here in the lack-of-control tower that I'm trapped in. I'm now ready to describe the frantic and confused activity between my ears as—a drumroll, please—the reality of unreality.

The reality of unreality. That's what I, Brian Hildebrand, am about. That's what Brian's room is about. That's what this book is about. The reality of unreality. It sounds vaguely philosophical, doesn't it? It may be going too far putting it that way. Still, it's concise, all-encompassing, and it makes you stop and think, right? It certainly makes me think, I can tell you that. Mind you, I don't have to stop in order to think. I'm thinking non-stop all the time. Thinking, after all, is all I do, twenty-four/seven. I'm a thinking machine, a one-man think tank, a thinkavore, a thinkie junkie, running in an endless thinkathon. I think I'm repeating myself. I think we should move on. I think that's what I think.

The reality of unreality. My insight into this unifying thesis of mine comes to me as Jefferson earnestly reads me an excerpt from a science article in the New York Times.

"We are not who we think we are," the article says. "We narrate our lives, shading every last detail, and even changing the script retrospectively, depending on the event, most of the time subconsciously. The storyteller never stops, except perhaps during deep sleep."

Clearly, Jefferson has something in mind and is trying it out on me. "How does that grab you, dude?"

How does that grab me? It grabs me by the head, that's how it grabs me, the very same head that's the site and the source of all this non-stop commotion. As suggested in the Times excerpt, my life is an unending tale, and I'm the unrelenting storyteller whose telling is never stopped in deep sleep because deep sleep eludes me. I'm not even sure of shallow sleep. As Jefferson reads to me, I see so clearly that my clinging-to-life tale, whatever else it may be, is the reality of unreality. But I'm unable to share this epiphany with Jefferson. At the moment, I can't even offer him a "Hallelujah, brother!" Maybe I'll spout it out later when he's least expecting it and when it'll be totally inappropriate. But I can't promise. Hell, that isn't all I can't promise. I can't promise anything. I seriously lack promise.

"I thought I'd use the quote as an epigraph for my novel," Jefferson explains, "when my literary agent finds me a publisher. She's been shopping the manuscript around, but I haven't heard from her for a couple of months. I wonder how she's making out. Maybe I'll email her for an update."

But, it turns out, he doesn't have to ask for an update because later that day, Jefferson receives an encouraging email from London that he excitedly shares with Bessie and Ray as well as with me.

"Good news from my agent. She thinks she has a British publisher interested. The manuscript is being passed around and so far it's been read by four of their editors. It looks promising, she says, but no offer has been made yet. So there's no guarantee. She advises me to be patient and isn't saying who the publisher is unless and until we have something in writing. Is that a progress report or what?"

"Sounds like progress to me, mate," Ray says. "Looks like you're about to connect. Good on you. I knew you could do it."

"I couldn't have done it without your help, Ray. I'll always be grateful for your advice."

"Oh, I'm sure you'd have figured it out on you own. Maybe I saved you a little time. But that's all."

"How exciting to have a soon to be published author among us," Bessie says. "We're rooting for you, Jefferson."

So am I. Jefferson deserves to succeed. I want him to make it as an author. But when he does, I lose him. I've known that all along, of course. But now, the imminent loss of my caregiver looms. And even before the fact, I experience a sense of loss. What will I do without Jefferson? Nothing. Nothing whatsoever. Just like I'm doing now. Still, he's been such a great support. What will happen to me without him? I've come to depend on him. Will my clinging-to-life tale go on? Will I continue to endure the reality of unreality?

"We are not who we think we are. We narrate our lives, shading every last detail, and even changing the script retrospectively, depending on the event, most of the time subconsciously. The storyteller never stops, except perhaps during deep sleep."

58

Surprise, Surprise

It's another not particularly exciting day here deep in the heart of Limboville. I'm in my characteristically pensive mode when Ray & Bessie come marching excitedly into my room arm in arm with an unexpected visitor. Well, look who's here, none other than the estimable Dr. Victor Roopa, my microwave guru on a surprise visit all the way from Baltimore, Maryland.

Smiling broadly, eyes gleaming, Roopa negotiates his way through the tangle of gear around me and embraces me.

"I haven't forgotten you mate," he says, giving me a few little encouraging punches on the arm.

He hasn't let go. He's still on my case. Hope springs. Pulse races. Excitement builds. Why is he here? Has he come bearing news? Can it be the news I'm hoping for? I can hardly wait to find out.

"My mate, Roopa, surprised us this morning by showing up out of the blue," Ray explains. "And we're delighted to see him. Best of all, he's onto something that he hopes may work for you, Brian."

"I'm very hopeful about a new possibility to help you, Brian," Roopa says, "so hopeful, in fact, that I decided to jump on a plane this morning and come up to Toronto and try it on you personally."

"How exciting," Bessie says. "We want to know more."

"Well, what I'm talking about is an unlikely discovery about a drug called zolpidem. It's a sleeping pill. Researchers gave it to a restless patient in a coma to try to help him sleep. Instead, it woke him up, out of his coma. That's how it started. By chance, they found that when zolpidem was given to brain-damaged patients on life support who had been believed to be in a persistent vegetative state or PVS, it woke some of them out of coma for short periods."

"How short is a short period?" Ray wants to know.

"Two or three hours. After that, they would regress back into coma. But then, when given zolpidem again, it would wake them again for another few hours."

"A sleeping pill does that? That's incredible," Bessie says.

"What's even more incredible is that with repeated use of the drug, some of the patients treated got progressively better. A few made close to a complete recovery. No one knows why zolpidem does this. It's a paradox."

A pox on paradox. My life is already a paradox. Do I really need another paradox? Yes, please. If it works for me, I guess I do.

"Recent research now indicates that forty percent of patients believed to be in a persistent vegetative state are not PVS, at all, but are actually in what is described as a minimally conscious state, aware, but locked in just like you are, Brian. The good news is that zolpidem works even better on minimally conscious patients. It not only wakes them but also increases awareness, sometimes profoundly. As I said, it doesn't work for everybody but when it does work, it can be of great benefit."

Paradox or not, I'm delighted with this information. But I wish I could point out to everyone that I'm already more than minimally conscious. In fact, I'm more aware than ever. But I have no way of making my case. Maybe I'll just go with the flow. Provided, of course, there is some flow. Please, let there be flow.

"So with all in favour, we're going to try zolpidem on you, Brian."

"All in favour," says Bessie.

"Go for it, mate," says Ray.

"Hallelujah, brother!" says Brian.

Just a coincidence, I swear. But for a change, the timing is perfect.

59

Let's Go With The Paradox

Preparing to proceed with the zolpidem test, Dr. Roopa announces that he is going to administer the sleep drug as an injection into my buttock. He chooses the right buttock as the injection site. Jefferson and Elissa crank me up and rotate me slightly to one side to make the selected buttock accessible and Elissa swabs the area with isopropyl alcohol to disinfect it. If there is a reason for choosing the right buttock over the left, Roopa does not say and none of my entourage questions the choice. Still, as I briefly hover rotisserie-like, grateful there are no red-hot coals beneath me, I find myself pointlessly wondering about the choice of right buttock over left. The whole world seems to be moving to the right. Ouch! I say to myself in response to my private pain when the needle goes in. You may recall my mentioning earlier that my sense of touch is intact and acute and I can feel pain. Well, the jab in my right buttock reminds me to remind you.

"Reaction times vary," Roopa explains to his small but attentive audience. "It might take as little as fifteen minutes to see any results but then, again, we might have to wait an hour or more. And, of course, it may not work, at all. We just have to wait and hope."

Wait and hope. There it is again, my bumper sticker. And still, no bumper.

The room is quiet. No one is saying very much. Everyone is waiting expectantly for me to respond in some way, any way, just so I respond. But I'm not cooperating. I'm taking my time, not rushing into this. Easing in, I begin to feel totally relaxed. But I'm not asleep. I'm floating somewhere, up near the ceiling, looking down on myself, though not in a condescending manner, hearing again fragments of what Jefferson read me from the New York Times as his hoped-for epigraph for his book.

"We are not who we think we are. We narrate our lives, shading every last detail, and even changing the script retrospectively, depending on the event, most of the time subconsciously. The storyteller never stops, except perhaps during deep sleep."

And once again, I am the relentless, non-stop storyteller and I'm not in deep sleep, but I may be in a side effect of the zolpidem, a kind of drug induced trance, and I'm looking at a box and telling a story about it. Now, why on earth would I be blathering on about a box? Wait. Maybe it's not a box. Maybe it's a hallucination. Or maybe it's a clue. But how can that be? I'm clueless.

60

THE BOX

THE BOX I'm contemplating is not your average box. Among the things that make this box different is the fact that there are people living in it. No one knows for sure who these people are. And the people in the box don't say. They are not an outgoing bunch. They never go out. Decidedly inward looking is what they are. They keep to themselves mostly and don't talk much to outsiders. Inevitably, this leads to endless speculation by the curious and gossipy as to whom the people in the box might be. They might be a family, some suggest, an extended family most likely, since they appear to be numerous. Or is it possible, wonder others, that they're a tribal group of some kind? Or a racial group, perhaps? What about an ethnic group? Or why not a religious group? A cult, say? Let's hope not. Then again, they might be an interest group, bridge players, for example, or bridge builders or quilters. Not that anyone ever sees any quilts come out of the box. Or any bridges, either. Come to think of it, they could even be an internet group, though they don't seem all that digitally inclined. But who's to say what the digitally inclined seem like? The speculation grows, feeds on itself, proliferates, turns small talk into big talk and wears out the gossips. And still, no one knows for sure who the people in the box are.

Despite the words "This Side Up" clearly printed on one of the flaps, the box lies on its side. This makes it possible, not only to read the words without having to fly over the box in a helicopter, but also for the insiders to open the flaps on those rare occasions when it is necessary to confer with outsiders. During such exchanges, the outsiders are never invited in but remain outside, while residents of the box stay cautiously just inside the open flaps, never venturing beyond them, never stepping outside the confines of the box itself. Immediately upon the conclusion of these brief encounters, the flaps are quickly closed again.

And of course, there is the question that pervades the entire phenomenon: What on earth possesses these people to live in a box? Outsiders puzzle over this. The box people are no help whatsoever, never answering questions, except with other questions, never explaining anything. There doesn't seem to be any way of getting to the bottom of it. All that is certain is that the group is totally committed to living in the box, from which they never emerge. And once again, outsiders can only guess at what their reasons might be: custom, culture, belief system, tradition, habit, history, longtime practice, inertia, blah, blah, blah. The list goes on and on. And so does the puzzle. Everything about the box is a puzzle, many puzzles, a series of puzzles.

Take the construction of the box. No one knows for sure what the box is made of. It appears to be corrugated and the colour of cardboard, but it plainly isn't corrugated cardboard. It is something considerably sturdier, something clearly impervious to assault by the elements and perhaps, even to assault by man. It is hard to say precisely what that considerably sturdier something is. That may explain why no one says what it is.

From every angle, the box has a sort of fortress-like aspect to it. A moat around it would not have been out of place. That's not to say that the box is a gated community. There are no security features that anyone can discern. There is no gate, no gatehouse, no entrance, no lobby, no concierge. In fact, except for the box flaps, there are no openings in the box of any kind, no doors, no windows, no skylights, no clerestory. It is a wonder any light gets into the box. And people do, in fact, wonder if any light gets in, without ever finding out if it does or doesn't.

And of course, there is the matter of its size. To characterize the box as enormous would be an understatement. In fact, it is the size of a city block, or larger. Or even larger than larger. It may be extra large or giant or jumbo or super-size. No one knows for sure. The only information on the box is the bar code printed on one of the flaps and the words "This Side Up." Nowhere is there any indication of size. Even those who live in it don't appear to know how big the box is, and they don't really seem to care. All they seem to care about is being in the box and staying in the box, no matter what goes on outside. Not that all that much goes on outside. Still, just having the "in or out" option is what should matter. But apparently it doesn't.

Nobody knows how the box got where it is or where it came from. According to the history of the area, one day the neighbours get up to go to work and the box is just sitting there. As for the box people, they behave as if it has always been there and has always been their home, their community, their environment.

They are born in it, live in it, and die in it. That is all that matters to them, all they need to know. Whatever their roots are, assuming they have any, they show no signs of wanting to go digging them up. Genealogy does not appear to interest them. Their history is a mystery. And as far as they are concerned it can stay that way. Maybe they just like the rhyme.

The name of the group in the box is Jacques and each and every member of the group, all the men, women and children, also go by that name. Each is called Jacques, which though confusing to outsiders, does not seem so to the many Jacques. They differentiate between the various Jacques with shifts in pitch and a series of vocal inflections of the name, none of which are at all apparent to the uninitiated.

As for how the many, many Jacques occupy themselves in the box, all that can be ascertained is that they spend their days thinking. Or thinking of thinking. Although it involves no physical activity, thinking is their principal activity and their only pursuit, their only occupation. The purpose or point of all this thinking is not known even to the thinkers. Staying inside and thinking is what they have always done. It is all they know. For many years the people living outside the box live with this mystery in their midst. Then, one day, the manager of the neighbourhood supermarket thinks he might have a way of solving the mystery and he calls on the mayor.

"I have an idea," he tells the mayor, "that might solve the mystery of the box. But I'll need your help."

"Fine," says the mayor. "The mystery has gone on far too long. How can I help?"

And so, one evening when the streets are empty and no one is about, a fire truck as arranged by the mayor, with a cherrypicker at the ready and sirens off, slips silently over and cherrypicks the box, while a firefighter with a portable bar code reader in hand reads the bar code on the flap. Then, firetruck, firefighter, and bar code reader quickly come away with a read-out and the following information:

This seems to be the copyright page of the book, you may recall, that I promised at the very beginning this was going to be. If I may quote myself, I described it as "a rousing saga of a thousand and one sentences, beginning with the life sentence that I'm serving as a prisoner in my own mind. After that, this convulsive and compulsive chronicle of mine takes off daringly and unsparingly in all directions with a thousand other sentences that it will likely take to tell my unlikely story."

When it comes to unlikely tales, could any tale be more unlikely than the tale of this box? Well, you never know. There are still several hundred sentences to go in this cavalcade of sentences to make it to a thousand and one. I might yet surprise us all with something even more unlikely. Please, don't give up on me. Persevere.

61

Fade Out / Fade In

The unlikely box tale fades away and the box and the bar code information fade with it and Brian's room comes glaring into my staring eyes and, for a brief moment, I am overcome with alarm as I become aware of all the anxious faces intently peering into my face as my mouth moves with unexpected ease, and I'm able to speak to all the assembled and, for a change, what emerges from my mouth is not the tortured and tiresome "Hallelujah, brother!" but speech, actual speech! And omigod! I'm awake! Awake and talking! I can't believe my ears. I already can't believe the rest of me.

"He's talking," Bessie says. "At long last, Brian is talking."

"The zolpidem is working," Roopa says. "Brian's waking up."

"But why can't I make out what's he saying?" Ray wants to know.

By this point, I'm wide awake and talking a blue streak. But there's a hitch. I'm talking in one of my recently and inexplicably acquired languages. And no matter how hard I try, I'm unable to switch back into English. I try and try but I seem to be stuck. It makes no sense.

Bessie agrees with me. "I can't make any sense of it. What's going on?"

Elissa comes to the rescue. "It's Latvian," she explains to Bessie. "Brian is talking Latvian."

"Latvian? How can he be talking Latvian? Brian, you don't speak Latvian. Talk to us in English," Bessie says.

I tell Bessie I can't. But I have to tell her in Latvian. That's no help to either of us. This is a lose/lose situation, the one not recommended by management consultants.

"You understand Latvian, Elissa. What's he saying?"

"Brian is saying he is trying not to talk Latvian. But he cannot switch over to English."

"Talk slowly, Brian," Bessie says. "Elissa will tell us what you're saying."

I talk slowly in Latvian. Elissa listens carefully and translates.

"This is a dream come true. I can't tell you how it feels to be awake and to be able to talk to you. And in case I don't stay awake very long, Bessie and Ray, the first thing I want to make sure, is that you revise the serious psychic Google ad and include all your contact information. I've had another visit from Millie and told her to Google the serious psychic ad to get in touch with you. But I had no time to give her any other information and now, I worry that Millie may not be a serious psychic and will need to know more to be able to contact you so you can arrange to bring Millie and her mother to Toronto to visit me. All this, of course, assumes that Millie is real, that she exists, and is not just something I made up. At the moment, I'm just not sure what's real any more."

"Not to worry, Brian," says Ray. "We'll revise the Google ad straightaway. And when we get a reply, we'll organize the trip for Millie and her mother."

"I'm grateful to all of you for your ongoing support and you especially, Dr. Roopa. I can't tell you how much this means to me. I also can't explain why I'm speaking Latvian. It started when Andris was here. For the moment, I'm stuck in Latvian. If I can stay awake long enough, I hope maybe this will change. In the meantime, thank you Elissa for translating."

"Brian, can you describe how you feel physically right now?" Roopa asks.

"Well, obviously, I'm wide awake and can talk. But physically, except for my mouth and lips, I can't move anything. And just as they've become during my coma, all of my senses are not only working but they're hyper-acute."

"It's cool to hear your voice, dude, even in Latvian, "Jefferson says. "I can't wait to hear you speak English."

"I will, as soon as I can, if I don't run out of time," I reply. "But I can already feel myself slowing drifting out of wakefulness and I may be going back into …"

Suddenly, I'm speaking English again but it's too late. It's happening in my head and, once again, I'm talking to myself. I'm back into coma and not at all happy about it but unable to complain to anybody else, in either English or Latvian.

"He's gone back into coma," Roopa says. "I'm going to give him another shot of zolpidem and up the dosage and see if we can wake him up and keep him awake longer. Let's try the left buttock this time."

62

ONE MOTHER OF A METAPHOR

JEFFERSON AND ELISSA crank me up, again, rotate me slightly to access the left buttock, which Elissa swabs with isopropyl alcohol. Now, the whole world seems to be moving to the left. Ouch! There's that needle again. And, of course, I can guess where all this is going to go on second try. I'll wake up in half an hour or so, still unable to move and talking my head off, not in Latvian this time but in Japanese. Or maybe in Urdu or Uzbek or some other obscure tongue I've never heard of. And then, of course, there will be a mad scramble to try and find someone in Woodgreen who understands the language I'm talking. And it will turn out to be someone in accounting or receiving. Or the building superintendent. Somehow, this feels more like a computer game than reality. But there's not a computer anywhere in sight. Maybe it's a board game. Or maybe it's just a mind game. Yes. That could be it. I'm prone to mind games. Prone? I'm prone period. Hell, I may be a mind game. Now, there's a thought. Wouldn't that be something? I'm a mind game. That's right up there with Amos's mother's conspiracy thing. What complicated lives we lead.

So once again, the waiting begins and, once again, I'm off somewhere. I'm always off somewhere. And somewhere is nowhere in particular, an indescribable vastness, an endless plane of sand, dotted with twelve-foot-tall flowering cacti and cluttered with a throng of giant film screens all vying for my attention so that I don't know which one to look at first, or even second, and echoing with the deafening clamor of endless voices, none of which I can make out, all talking at me simultaneously.

I don't know how I can be imagining all this because the din and the chaos are unimaginable, and yet I must be. Or otherwise it wouldn't be there. And then, through this circus of sights and sounds, a blurry moving dot in the distance morphs into an elderly woman in a babushka walking slowly towards me, getting closer and closer and, finally, when she is directly in front of me, coming into sharp focus. It is vaguely reminiscent of the opening shot in the film, Lawrence of Arabia, but minus the camel. The woman in the babushka stops and addresses herself to me.

"I am in Brian's room, yes?"

"You are in Brian's room, yes."

"And I am talking to Brian Hildebrand, yes?"

"Absolutely. Accept no substitutes. And he is talking to you. Yes."

"Then, listen, Brian, why you are hanging there like a leg of lamb? All these people in your room, they are barbecuing you, yes?"

"No. They're not. They're here to support me and cheer me up."

"It is some kind of celebration, yes?"

"Not yet. I'm hoping it will get to be, if I'm lucky. So far, it's only a drug test."

"Drug test? You are doing drugs, yes?"

"No. Doctors are doing drugs on me."

"Doctors? I don't like to talk about doctors."

"Okay. No doctors. What would you like to talk about?"

"My son."

"Your son?"

"My son, he came to see you. He say to me you are looking for help, yes? He does not do helpful."

"Does not do helpful? As I recall, that would be your son, the metaphor. And you would be the mother of the metaphor. Is that correct?"

"No. Is not correct. My son would not be metaphor. My son would be Amos. And I would be mother of Amos."

"Ah, the mother of Amos, my friend, Amos. And how is Amos doing these days?"

"Amos is not one hundred percent."

"What percent is he?"

"Maybe fifty percent?"

"What's wrong with Amos?"

"He is not eating."

"Why not? "

"Eating give him heartburn."

"Has he tried antacids?"

"They are not available in his area."

"What is his area?"

"Twelve square feet, maybe. Don't ask me metric. I don't know metric."

"So you think you can help me without metric?"

"Help you? No one can help you. You have to help yourself."

"Is that what you came to tell me?"

"No. I came to remind you to watch out for the conspiracy."

"There is still a conspiracy?"

"Still, yes. It does not stop. It is all a conspiracy."

"All? That's a lot of conspiracy. What would you do in my place?"

"As much as possible. What else?"

"That sounds reasonable but it's probably improbable."

"My advice is watch your ess, Brian."

"Watch my ess? How will I do that?"

"Look over your shoulder."

"I'm not in a position to do that right now."

"You will find a way. Maybe you will meet a tall, dark stranger, yes."

"How will that help?"

"Who knows? It was in a fortune cookie. I must go. It is supper time. I am making polenta."

"Polenta? I used to love polenta. Thanks for coming. Give my best to Amos."

"I will try. But it may be too late."

She turns, walks away and slowly goes out of focus, diminishing into a speck in the distance. And then, she is gone. And once again, minus the camel.

63

SIDE EFFECTS

In Amos's mother's place and space, there now appears a face and it is the face of the esteemed Dr. Roopa in extreme close-up. At close range, the impressive tribal markings on his visage are particularly striking, startling even. But I'm not quite awake and still too lightheaded to be startled even.

"Are you awake, mate?" Roopa asks.

"That depends," I reply. "Amos is not eating. And the conspiracy is still on. And maybe I will meet a tall, dark stranger. And I have to watch my ess."

Roopa looks puzzled. He doesn't seem to understand what I'm saying. This is not surprising since I don't seem to understand it myself.

"Brian's waking up again. He's become quite the linguist. This time, he's talking Japanese. Anybody here speak Japanese?"

"I am sorry, "Elissa says. "I do not speak Japanese."

"There must be someone around who speaks Japanese," Ray says.

268

"Jefferson, is there anyone in Woodgreen House who speaks Japanese?" asks Bessie.

"I think there's someone in the front office," Jefferson says. "I'll try to find her, if she hasn't already gone out to lunch."

Out to lunch seems to be the dominant theme here at the moment. Or maybe, it's the common denominator. We're all of us out to lunch, it seems to me, including me, especially me. Even so, I'm excited by my second reawakening, and I keep jabbering away in Japanese with no one knowing what the hell I'm saying. Half an hour passes and I'm still talking a mile a minute in Japanese when Jefferson returns with a Japanese woman.

"Sorry, to be so long. This is Carol Okata from accounting. I had to go down the street to find her. She was having a sandwich in Starbuck's at the corner. I wish I'd thought of Carol when that Japanese tour group was here. But I was too busy looking for vases for all those daffodils. I never saw such a host of golden flowers."

"Hi Carol," Bessie says. "Thanks for helping us out. Can you tell us what Brian is saying? He's been going on, non-stop, in Japanese for half an hour. Brian, start from the beginning and talk slowly."

Well, here we go again. At Bessie's request, I slow down and start again. Carol translates my Japanese into English. Now, here's the oddest thing. After being incommunicado and whining about it to myself all these years, I find I don't really have all that much to say that matters to anybody but me. It must be pretty obvious that I'm self-absorbed. That makes me sound like a paper towel. But that's what I am, no question about it. I've talked to myself so much about myself that I may have to learn to talk to others all over again. I know that I talk a lot to myself, but the fact is, when you get right down to it, I don't say very much. And the worst of it is, I keep repeating myself over and over about things that bug me. It strikes me that behavior of that kind is a lot like prayer. Not that I know much about prayer. I'm not really into in plea bargaining with supreme beings. Mind you, I tried it years ago, in three desperate days, one cruel May, and it didn't work for me. So I decided enough of that. Anyhow, if I'm going to be awake and able to talk, I have to be careful that I don't keep repeating myself and turn into a crank. Or a one-way street going the wrong way. And I also have to be careful that what I talk about doesn't become a rant. I may be hard pressed to manage it.

Carol Okata faithfully passes on what I have to say about my unhappy condition and how I'm desperately eager to escape it, but you've heard it all already, so I won't inflict it on you again, at least not right now. Maybe later. She also translates my thoughts about our unfeeling unfairness to aboriginal peoples, our heartlessness toward the homeless and the poor, and our willingness to spend vast sums of money punishing lawbreakers but not on compensating their victims. Carol also transmits my allegations about the lack of true separation of church and state, about the widespread hypocrisy of ideologues of all stripes, and about how greed has corrupted our economics and our culture.

"Wow!" Jefferson says. "I'm going to want to hear all that again, dude, not in translation but in the original, when you're speaking English."

Roopa, however, shakes his head disapprovingly and takes me on.

"You're either a frigging radical, mate. Or a bleeding-heart liberal. Which is it?"

"Neither," I respond through Carol. "I'm not an activist. I'm just a finger pointer. Even if I were in a position to change things, I wouldn't do a single fucking thing."

"Why not?"

"Because basically, I'm a hypocrite just like everybody else."

Silence follows this sally. I'm trying my best to start an argument. But no one takes the bait.

I've been awake for maybe two hours at this point and talked myself silly, but not said a whole hell of a lot. And now, my response to the zolpidem is wearing off and my time awake is dwindling and I'm on my way back into limbo and once again talking to myself, in English, of course. As I simultaneously drift into outer silence and inner chaos, I hear Roopa talking about my ranting to my support group.

"I should explain that although I fenced with him about it, Brian's rant is not politically motivated. It's actually one of the side effects of the drug. Zolpidem makes some patients fractious."

"Fractious?" Ray says nodding.

He likes the word. And so do I. I never thought I could be fractious.

"Side effects?" Bessie says. She sounds annoyed, if not betrayed. "We didn't talk about side effects."

"All pharmaceuticals have side effects," Roopa reassures her. "They vary by dosage and by patient. We don't always know what they're going to be."

"Does zolpidem have other side effects besides fractious that we have to worry about?" asks Ray.

"There's a whole list of side effects. But truly, there's no need to worry about them, mate."

"Truly? Okay. But a whole list? Better tell us," insists Bessie.

"Well, the most common but least problematic side effects of zolpidem are diarrhea, dizziness, drowsiness, dry mouth, headache, nausea, nose or throat irritation, sluggishness, upset stomach, fatigue, and weakness."

Bessie doesn't say a word. She stifles a groan. I groan, too. But I don't have to stifle mine. My groans come pre-stifled.

"That's quite a list, mate," Ray offers. "Are you sure we don't have to worry about any of it?"

"I wouldn't concern myself," says Roopa. "Most of it is minor stuff."

"Besides," interjects Jefferson, "working with Brian day to day, I can tell you that, even without the zolpidem, he already experiences many symptoms like those on the list. And it doesn't seem to faze him. Elissa and I cope with it, no problem."

Actually, it's one hell of a problem. Mind you that's the view of the ultimate insider. The fact is, life support has its side effects, too, and they're no piece of cake, bowl of cherries, or walk in the park. Or insert your own favorite cliché. Still, there's not much I can do about it except be grateful to Jefferson and Elissa for their help.

"Thank you, Jefferson. That's reassuring," Bessie says. But she doesn't sound reassured.

"All good," Roopa says. "But in the interest of full disclosure, you should be aware that with zolpidem there are also less common and more worrisome side effects."

"Oh, no. This isn't going to be another list, is it, mate?"

"Actually, it is. But no worries. None of this affects Brian. I'll explain why in a minute."

"All right. Let's have the list, then."

"Well, the really nasty stuff includes severe allergic reactions like rash, hives, itching, difficulty breathing, tightness in the chest, swelling of the hands, legs, mouth, face, lips, eyes, throat, or tongue, throat closing, unusual hoarseness."

That's pretty ugly stuff. And Roopa's only part way through his list. Does that mean I could be even worse off than I already am? It doesn't seem possible, I try to reassure myself but, like Bessie, I'm not reassured and Roopa presses on.

"Also on the nasty list are abnormal thinking, behavioral changes, chest pain, confusion, decreased coordination, difficulty swallowing or breathing, fainting, fast or irregular heartbeat."

At this point, I'd like to say, "Oy vey!" But I don't speak Yiddish. So far, besides English, I only speak Latvian and Japanese. And not on a regular basis.

"And while I'm at it," continues Roopa, "I should also mention hallucinations, memory problems, mental or mood changes such as aggression, agitation, anxiety, depression, shortness of breath, suicidal thoughts or actions, and vision changes."

This elicits a group groan.

"But fortunately," Roopa goes on, "we don't have to worry about any of those."

Really? That's easy for him to say. He's not the one getting the needle in the butt.

"That's one hell of a lot of worrisome stuff not to have to worry about, mate."

"I'm going to explain, in a minute, why we don't have to worry about any of it. But before I do, let me add that this is not a complete list of all side effects that may occur. Having said that, I want to quickly reassure you that most of the side effects that do occur are the minor ones and they mostly occur when zolpidem is administered by pill. When zolpidem is administered by nasal spray, side effects occur somewhat less frequently. To further minimize the risk of side effects, I've had the drug specially formulated into an injectable solution. Administered this way, zolpidem is a bit of a pain in the butt for Brian and, as you have just seen, makes him rant a bit but that's about it. We avoid all the other possible side effects."

Oh goody. More pain in the butt.

"Well, now, that we've avoided all that, where do we go from here?" Bessie asks. She sounds worn out.

"Let's give Brian a little rest," suggests Roopa. "Say about half an hour. And then, we'll inject him and wake him up again and see how long he stays awake. And if we decide he's making progress and had enough for one day, then we'll go at it again tomorrow."

It's strange being talked about this way. I haven't been consulted. I haven't been asked for my opinion about any of this. It makes me feel like a guinea pig. Once upon a long while ago, I was a party animal. But this ain't no party, baby. Right now, I'm a lab animal! Maybe I need help from the animal rights people.

64

Timeout

ALL RIGHT. So I'm having a timeout after the first two doses of zolpidem and doing my own personal review of where I stand, even though I don't stand. The drug seems to be working, waking me, and enabling me to talk. And best of all, my time awake after the second injection was longer than after the first. The question now, is will the third injection give me even more time awake? And what language will I be speaking next time? Will it be English or yet another language I never knew I spoke?

Where, I wonder, will Roopa jab me with the next needle and the third dose of zolpidem? Which of my limited number of buttocks will be stabbed this time? With only two to choose from, options are limited. It's either right or left. And then, I run out of buttocks or, for that matter, any other places with meat on them that will be a suitable injection site. As I've already indicated, I'm extremely gaunt, almost skeletal, in fact. There's not much meat on me and the little there is extra lean. Well, at least, it isn't minced. For the moment, at least.

As I regress back into limbo, I'm immediately aware that the usual incessant din in my brain, the cacophony that I have lived with for so long, has shut down. Can this be another side effect of zolpidem? Or more logically, chronologically, can this be an after effect? Roopa didn't mention after effects. Maybe I'll ask him about after effects when I'm awake again. I can't believe how silent my head is, now that the circus has left town. This would probably be an ideal time for a startling flashback or a harrowing hallucination or an overblown 3D movie or a prophetic vision or a scary dream or some other highly implausible and inexplicable event, but strangely, nothing is going on in the theatre of my mind. The stage is dark, at the moment. And lulled by the darkness, I'm in a state that I can only describe as almost relaxed. For me, almost relaxed is as good as it gets and it's too good to last. And sure enough, it doesn't. A voice I don't know breaks into the untypical stillness in my head. Damn!

"Hey, Brian."

"Hey, yourself, "I respond curtly. I'm not really in the mood for talk.

"This isn't much of a conversation, is it? You angry or something?"

"Well, it's hard to have a conversation when I don't know who I'm talking to."

"Oh, come on, Brian. Don't be that way. It's Jacques."

"Jacques who? Do I know you?"

"Of course, you do. I'm one of your people."

"My people? That's too Hollywood for me, or too tribal. My people are the human race. Please, identify yourself."

"I'm Jacques, one of your box people."

"But you people don't normally leave the box."

"Yeah. But this is a special situation. I was chosen to find you and talk to you."

"Besides, there are thousands of Jacques in the box. How am I supposed to know which one you are?"

"Well, yeah. That's true. But that was your dumb idea, Brian, not ours. The box was your baby, your concept. You invented the box with all that copyright crap in the bar code to try and promote the book you're hoping this will be. Fine. You put people in the box. Fine. You decided to make it thousands of people. Fine. But then, you blithely named everybody Jacques, which has to be the stupidest idea I've ever heard of. And now, you have the gall to tell me you don't know which one I am. Give us all a break, Brian, and stop being a prick."

"Look, Jacques. I don't mean to shrug you off. But right now, as we speak, I'm in the middle of treatment in a medical trial and I really don't have time to apologize or explain. So, make it quick. What's your special situation? Why are you here? What do you want? And please, be brief. I'm about to get another injection. And when I wake up, if I wake up, I may not be speaking English."

"Okay. Look. I'm sorry I barged in on you at a bad time. But here's the thing. All the Jacques in the box had a meeting and the long and short of it is we're worried about what's going to happen to the box and to all of us, now that you're about to escape from the coma you're in. I was sent to talk to you about it and find out."

"Now, hold on a minute. All you Jacques in the box are jumping the gun. My escape is still very much up in the air, a huge question mark. At the moment, this is all still research, a medical trial. I don't know how it's going to end up. Neither do the researchers. All previous attempts to help me went nowhere, and this one may go nowhere, too. Until I know for certain the outcome of this test, I don't know what to tell you about the box. For now, all I can suggest is that you hang in, just like I'm doing. I'll get back to you as soon as I know what my future looks like."

"That sounds to me like you're passing the box, Brian. Isn't there something promising you can tell me to take back to the other Jacques in the box?"

"Something promising? Okay, Jacques. Tell you what. I promise that no matter what happens to me, even if I'm still in a coma after all this that the box and the box people will be in the book and be treated favorably. In fact, I'll see to it that a picture of the box is on the back cover."

"Really? On the back cover? Wow! All the Jacques in the box will be thrilled. I'm going to go back right now and tell them. Thank you, Brian. And good luck with your injection."

"Good luck with my injection. Right. Thank you, Jacques. I'll be in touch."

65

Third Time Lucky?

After Jacques leaves and goes back to the box to share his news with all the other box people, the silence returns. It's as silent as the night before Christmas. I try to enjoy it while I can, hoping that for a while, at least, there will be no more interruptions. And there aren't. Except for my own. After rummaging around in my cluttered archive of unanswered, and often unanswerable, questions, I interrupt my internal silence by asking them. This is not new behaviour.

Will the zolpidem help restore me to my former self? Isn't that going backward in order to go forward, like a car stuck in a rut? Could this be the subject of a learned medical paper—Treating Coma as Life in a Rut? Will I ever be able to get out of this rut and live a normal life again? What if the restoration is only partial and I make a comeback as a vegetarian or a vegan? That beats a feeding tube every time, but will I be able to put weight back on and be the beautiful boy I once was? (Sometimes, I sound just like Bessie. She used to call me that.) What if, in the end – pardon the pun – the zolpidem injections don't

279

ultimately have any lasting benefit and leave me with no hope and nothing but a sore ass to show for all this? Who will I show it to? Who wants to look at a sore ass?

Trepidation, apprehension, foreboding, lurk behind all my questions. The fact is, I'm worried about the zolpidem, worried about where this diligent effort on my behalf is going, worried if it's going anywhere. Everybody is trying so hard to help me. Why am I being so ungrateful? Is it because I'm selfish and shallow and afraid of failure? Or am I experiencing more side effects, after effects, miscellaneous effects of the zolpidem? When things don't work out and there's no one around to blame, who do I blame? God? How do I blame god, if he's not available? There's has to be somebody I can blame. We can't all be blameless, can we? Why doesn't someone step forward, please, and take the blame?

There's a beat for emphasis, or maybe it's for suspense, and someone steps forward. But he doesn't take the blame. He takes the needle because that's his job de jour and he gets ready to jab me with it. It's Dr. Roopa. No surprise there. Were you expecting Dr. Frankenstein? Hey! I may not be much to look at but I'm no monster.

"Okay, mate. Recess is over. This will be injection number three. All right, team," Roopa says to Jefferson and Elissa. "Let's rock and roll. We'll have another go at the left buttock."

Jefferson and Elissa quickly facilitate access to the site. I'm hoisted, rotated, swabbed and – Ouch! – the deed is done. The bloody needle seems to hurt more every time. But maybe it's all in my mind just like all the other things that bug me. If I may embroider and exploit the much-quoted Descartes, I think, therefore, I am troubled.

Maybe it's because I'm troubled, that the third injection of zolpidem strikes me as different, somehow, from the first two. Maybe not. It's hard to be categorical. Mind you, some people don't find it difficult, and they're categorical most of the time. Avoid them, if you can. Do not linger in their poisonous presence.

Once again, we wait for the drug to kick in, to take effect, to have its way with me. Half an hour goes by and the watched paint is not drying. The well-wishing watchers grow restless. I know half an hour has passed because Ray says so to Roopa.

"That's half an hour, mate," the usually patient Ray advises Roopa.

"Not to worry," Roopa says. "Zolpidem kick-in times can vary widely. They're all over the map. Sometimes, it can take a couple of hours.

"Sure enough, a couple of hours go by but still nothing is happening. My head is silent as the tomb and so, in fact, is Brian's room. I hope it won't be here I meet my doom. And then, the rigid and menacing middle fingers of both my hands tingle ever so slightly. Now, what? I wonder. The middles tingle a little more and then, there's a slight, almost indiscernible, pop in each. But my hyper-acute ears nonetheless hear the pop–pop almost but not quite in unison, and both my middle fingers go limp just like my other fingers and, it now occurs to me, just like the rest of me.

Engrossed in the fresh coffee Jefferson has just brought in and engaged with Inez's latest cookie triumph, flourless mango and ginger chocolate wedges dusted with pomegranate seeds, no one has noticed my sudden, two middle finger turnaround. The onlookers stop looking, silently sip the coffee, munch the goodies, and glance at my face only at intervals, waiting for me to wake up and talk, perhaps in a language I don't normally speak and they're unlikely to understand.

And suddenly, though not awake, my mouth moves uncomfortably and I talk, vigorously spitting out, "Hallelujah! Hallelujah! Hallelujah!" My unwanted mantra, gone silent during the zolpidem injections and I hoped perhaps, gone for good, is now, back, dammit, albeit brotherless! Well, isn't that a crock of bad lock? I seem to be chock-a-block with crock. And what, I wonder, happened to brother?

Startled by the unexpected recurrence, Dr. Roopa looks me over and checks me out and discovers the change in my middle fingers. He shakes his head.

"This doesn't look promising," he announces. "For some reason, the zolpidem has not performed predictably this time out but done something else. Every case is different. We may be out of luck. But to be sure, I suggest, we give Brian one more try with the zolpidem and if that doesn't work, we'll give it up."

Another needle? I'll be a bloody pincushion before they're through with me. Still, maybe there's a chance that this time the zolpidem will work. Okay, g-o-d. I've made light of you. How about shining some of that light on me? Let's see how forgiving you are. And be prepared. I'll blame you, even if you're not available.

66

The Fourth Try

AFTER the fourth injection, we seem to wait forever for the zolpidem to kick in. Forever is an infinitely long time. We wait and wait and wait and nothing happens. Infinitely long is too long. Forever becomes never. On this fourth try, the zolpidem simply doesn't do what it did on the three previous tests. Disappointment abounds. Darkness descends. Roopa shuts the project down.

"Sorry, Brian. The zolpidem isn't working any more. But not to worry. We're not about to give up on you. My team in Baltimore will keep working on ways to try to help you to escape the prison you're in. At this very moment, there is another promising drug in the pipeline. And when it's ready for testing, I'll be back. It could be a matter of weeks."

This may be so, or it may just be a Roopa pep-talk to keep my spirits up. Lord knows, nothing else is up. The fans in the bleachers look glum. They hate to lose. Bessie fixes her eyes on me and sighs deeply. Ray gives her a hug of encouragement. She leans her head on his.

"Onward!" she says.

"Right on," Ray says. "Ever onward."

During all of the above, I haven't looked at my window but finding myself without a needle in my butt and no other personal project to engage my attention, I do so, now. And who should be looking back at me over his busy squeegee but my little dangling man, the window washer? He gazes at me sadly, shakes his head in what appears to be sympathy, and flashes me an encouraging V for victory sign. Then, he hoists himself up on his dangling rope and out of sight above my window, headed for the roof, I suppose, or maybe even for heaven. Well, why not heaven? He could be a heavenly messenger, for all I know. But I'm disappointed that he's sharing no cryptic messages with me today. Never mind. I'll just have to be my own counsel. But a possible, though not very probable, option presents itself, when out of the cerulean, an unexpected but vaguely familiar voice speaks to me. It takes me a moment to place the voice, but then, I nail it. It's g-o-d. Now, what on e-a-r-t-h does he want?

"Remember me, Brian?"

"How can I not remember you? You're the metaphor who doesn't do helpful."

"You got it. And that hasn't changed. And don't get your hopes up about blame, either. I'm not here to take the blame."

"But it just can't go on this way. Somebody has to take the blame."

"Well, it won't be me, kiddo. Taking the blame qualifies as helpful. And I don't do helpful. We went through all that last time."

"Then, what are you here for this time?"

"To pick a bone with you for putting that loopy mother of Amos's onto me. She drives me crazy, that woman. She tells me she talked to you. Says no one can help you but would I like to try anyway? I tell her, no way. But she won't leave. She's persistent. Wants me to come for supper. She's making polenta. I tell her I don't do carbs. I'm on the Atkins diet. She's never heard of it. Gets annoyed. Says I'm trying to make a fool of her. I tell her its too late. It's an old joke. Still, she goes away in a huff. Some people just can't take an old joke. You'd think old jokes would be easier to take than new ones. Old jokes are really just clichés. Everybody uses them. Everybody gets them. No one laughs any more. No one takes offense. But she gets pissed off. But Brian, let's get back to you. What prompted you to put that wacky woman onto me?"

"I didn't put her onto you. I swear. She came to see me unexpectedly, for no good reason. Told me no one could help me, told me I had to help myself and only mentioned the polenta as she was leaving. But at no time, did you come up in the conversation. I never spoke your name to her. I never speak your name to anybody. The fact is, I wrote you off after our first unhelpful meeting."

"Thanks a lot. Then, how do you explain your wanting me to shine some of my light on you?"

"I was on drugs. That was just a little prayerful wordplay between medical tests. I know better than to expect you to act on it. But, like it or not, if things don't work out for me, I do expect to put the blame on you."

"Now, why would you do a thing like that?"

285

"Well, somebody has to take the blame and who else is there?"

"What about the pharmaceutical company?"

"Oh, come on. I always thought you were in league with those guys."

"Not me, kiddo. I'm in a league of my own."

"You certainly are. And not helpful to a single soul."

"Well, a little symbolic icon shtick. But that's about it."

"Don't you ever feel guilty about never doing helpful?"

"Of course, I do. I'm obsessed with guilt. Guilt is all I ever feel about anything. I actually have feelings of guilt about things I've never done, never heard of, and know nothing about. In fact, I'm very forward looking and I feel guilt over things that haven't even happened yet and may never happen."

"That's really odd. I have feelings of guilt about the very same things."

"Well, that makes us kindred spirits, doesn't it?'

"Does that mean I can start to do icon shtick, too?"

"It's not that simple. You have to die first. Maybe we can talk about it then."

"Forget it. I'm not about to die. I'm not ready to die. That's too high a price. It's just not worth it."

"I'll be honest with you. I often feel that way myself. But I'm in too deep. There's no turning back now."

"Look. Since I've got you here and since we seem to be kindred spirits, is there anything you can tell me that will stand me in good stead? You'll notice I haven't used the word helpful. I'm not asking you to do helpful."

"What are you asking for?"

"Advice. Wise counsel. A user name and password to something useful. Pragmatism."

"That's very cunningly contrived and consequently very complex. I'll have to go away and ponder your request and get back to you."

"Yeah. I'll bet. I'll probably never hear from you again."

"Don't be so untrusting. I'll be back. You have my word."

"You're a metaphor. How good is the word of a metaphor? Metaphors muck up meaning. I've never trusted metaphors."

"Hey. I'm not your average, run-of-the-mill metaphor. Trust me."

"All right. Let's find out. Just this one time, I'll take a chance. Can I expect to hear from you soon?"

"You got it, kiddo. I'll be back in a flash."

"Okay. But no burning bush. None of that show biz stuff. This ain't Las Vegas."

"Did anyone ever tell you you're a nag?"

"No."

"Well, I'm telling you."

67

The Diva of Darkness Returns

I'VE BEEN in and out of my head this morning. I knew right off it was going to be one of those days. Jefferson must have known it, too. He was less voluble than usual and grinning mischievously as he left my room.

"Chin up, dude," he said. "Don't roll over. Be resolute."

He had something up his sleeve. Maybe up both his sleeves. Sure enough, a mere heartbeat later, larger than life, who should arrive but the Right Honorable Lady MacDeath.

The diva of darkness was back on my case and in my face, sleek and slick and dangerous as ever. Attaché case in well-manicured hand, she marched briskly into my room and hovered untotteringly on her six-inch heels at the foot of my bed, her high fashion all-black outfit and her modishly cut, jet black hair set off by the startlingly blue makeup around her icy slate grey eyes and brought further to the fore by the dazzling whiteness of her teeth that emerged at intervals from between the striking scarlet lipstick of her lips when she smiled. And she smiled often. Perhaps, too often. It was fascinating and blinding and achingly painful.

"Well, now, old friend," she said with a little wave of her attaché case.

"I wasn't expecting you," I said rather redundantly, not quite sure what to expect.

"No pressure," she said. "I just happened to be visiting one of the other residents who is, sad to say, in advanced departure mode and thought I'd look in on you."

"Well, I'm definitely not in departure mode. But I do thank you for thinking of me."

"My pleasure. All part of the job description. How have you been making out?"

"I'm still in ongoing clinical trials and we've had some short-term successes. We're trending to long-term results. I could be out of the woods any day now."

"Well, I'm certainly rooting for you. I love a good success story and, besides, I'm in no rush to do business with you. Life is short enough without my having to push you over the edge. Sooner or later, we'll do business together. And later is soon enough for me and gives you the least grief. And that's what this is all about."

"Considering your calling, I can't get over your generosity of spirit."

"It's not generosity, Brian. It's pragmatism. In dealing with the inevitable, there's nothing as pragmatic as finality. I just wait for it and go with it."

And then she went with it and was gone.

68

Kerb Calls

No word from Millie. I still don't know if she has Googled the Serious Psychic Sought ad. All I know is that, so far, she hasn't responded to Ray and Bessie and she hasn't popped in on me. In the meantime, our own conveniently located, serious psychic psychology professor has resurfaced and is back in the game, if it is a game. Maybe it's not a game. Maybe it's just a book. Or a film. Or a DVD.

Now recovered from his string of medical setbacks and mobile again, Angus Kerb, as promised when we last heard from him, calls Ray, to organize a face-to-face follow-up with me. Eager that I have as many opportunities to communicate as possible, Bessie and Ray are delighted to have the professor back for a personal visit.

As usual, of course, nobody asks for my opinion. That's no surprise. In any case, and especially in this case, I'm not sure I have an opinion. I teeter-totter on the fence. On the one hand, I should be keen to communicate and make myself heard through the intermediary services of the remarkably psychic Professor

Kerb. On the other hand, I find it intimidating, when he pushes me to venture outside my comfort zone. I'm not sure what my comfort zone is. I can't explain what it is but I know it when it starts bugging me.

Not unexpectedly, Kerb arrives already knowing all about zolpidem and my adventures with it and expressing his sympathy that the drug didn't help me.

"Great shame, the zolpidem didn't work for Brian," he tells Bessie and Ray. "I gather some people have had surprising success with the stuff. That's the thing about pharmaceuticals. They're not only iffy, they're chancey. They help some people and miss out on others. And, of course, even when they work for you, there are always hordes of side effects to be concerned about. In any case, don't despair. There's a lot of promising research going on. Science is always out there searching, and science is bound to come up with something for you, Brian. Mark my words. You just have to be available when science calls."

I respond and Kerb repeats to the faithful what he telepathically picks up from me.

"No problem. I'm always available. I'm a stay-put kind of guy. But I have to tell you, I'm tired of being locked in, tired of being a guinea pig."

"That's quite understandable, Brian. After all, you've been through a heck of a lot. But you've shown that you're very determined and that you always carry on and deal with it."

"I'm not sure I deal with it. But I certainly live with it. I have no option. Still, at times, the ups and downs feel like a roller coaster. It's very stressful and I worry that it's making me a little weird."

"A little weird? In what way?"

"Well, for one thing, I worry that I may be losing my grip on reality. I've talked about this with you before. There's so much going on in my mind that, often, I can't distinguish between the real and the surreal. It's a colossal mash-up. I'm seeing things and hearing things and experiencing things that may not be real. They may not exist. Hell, I, myself, may not exist."

"Now, hold on, Brian. That's an old refrain of yours. Just stop and think about it. You're talking to me at this very moment. Ergo you do exist."

"That's all very well. But what if ergo is only in someone else's mind? What if ergo someone is making me up, inventing me?"

"How likely is that? I'm right here with you. Your mother and father are here with you."

"But what if someone else is making all of us up?"

"Who would that someone else be? And why would they bother?"

"I don't know who that someone else would be. And I don't know why they would bother, except to say, that maybe inventing people is not such a bother. Maybe, it's no bother at all. Maybe anybody can do it."

"All right. Let's agree to agree that the stress of your ups and downs may be making you, as you describe it, a little weird. So why don't we try an experiment? Slow down, go with the flow for a while and let's see what happens. Hopefully, the stress will diminish. And then, maybe the weirdness you feel will disappear."

"OK. Let's say, I stop feeling a little weird. But what about my anger?"

"What are you angry about?"

"Well, every time, just as I think I'm about to get some serious help, something goes wrong. This has happened to me repeatedly. I sometimes get the feeling I'm being picked on, victimized. Now, I'm beginning to wonder more and more if maybe Amos's mother is right and there is a conspiracy."

"But Brian, you've already told us you don't consider Amos's mother reliable."

"Yeah, that's true. I did. Maybe I'm just so desperate for answers that I'm willing to believe anything."

"Besides, why would anyone want to conspire against you? For what reason?"

"That's an interesting question. I can think of two responses. To begin with, no reason would be necessary for a conspiracy against me if I was paranoid. I would be my own reason. But I don't think I'm paranoid. I already have enough on my pate. And that's not a typo. And second, if there is an actual conspiracy, maybe the conspiracy isn't about me or against me. Maybe, it's just happening all around me and I'm trapped in it just by virtue of where I am, by virtue of my location. Maybe my problem is proximity, proximity, proximity."

"But this is all speculation on your part. You can't really prove that there is a conspiracy going on here, can you?"

"I guess not. When you get right down to it, there's nothing I can prove. I can't prove a single bloody thing. I can't even prove I exist. I'm not only unimprovable, but I'm also unprovable."

"We've already covered that, Brian. Let's move on. When we last spoke, I sensed you had a deep-seated secret that you were withholding from me. When I pressed you on it, you grew reluctant and backed off. Do you feel like talking about it today?"

"I do and I don't."

"You're going to have to explain."

"All right. Yes. I do have a deep-seated secret. And no, I'm not going to share it with you because I'm unable to share it with myself. I know it's there, deep down under all the silt, under all the detritus, but I can't dig it out, I can't access it. Right now, as things stand, I'm aware that I have a secret, but I have no idea what the secret is. It's a mystery to me, too."

"Do you find that troubling?"

"Not at this point. Somehow, I've managed to put the mystery on hold. It's just one more item on a list of personal concerns that's even longer than the list of side effects of the zolpidem that just failed me. Besides, it doesn't hurt to have a little mystery in my crazy quilt life. It gives me something to ponder and to puzzle over."

"I'm puzzled, too, Brian. You're not alone."

"Oh, yes, I am, Professor, Oh, yes I am."

69

The Return of the Metaphor

"Brian?"

Well. Well. It's g-o-d, the metaphor, back just as promised. Maybe he is trustworthy, after all.

"Are you here?"

"Of course, I'm here. Where else would I be?"

"Don't have a snit. The question is rhetorical."

"So is my answer. I rarely leave the premises."

"I'm aware. I didn't really expect you to be anywhere else."

"Even if I could have been somewhere else, I wouldn't have budged, not till I heard back from you."

"Well, here I am, kiddo. You're about to hear back from me. Are you up for this?"

"Absolutely. I've been looking forward to it. After our last get together, you went off to ponder, in heavenly solitude, I presume, what you described as my very cunningly contrived and, consequently, very complex request, and now you're back with a response. Am I correct?"

"You got it. But let me reiterate, I don't do helpful. I'm simply responding to your request, and I quote, for advice, wise counsel, a user name, and password to something useful, pragmatism."

"My words precisely. You may not do helpful, but you do a good quote. This is beginning to sound promising."

"Promising is not a good word choice. I'm not promising anything. I'm simply responding to your request item by item. First of all, let's talk about advice."

"Fine. Advice, it is."

"My advice to you is: Don't trust a word I say. Never. Ever. Under no circumstances ever take my advice. And I mean that sincerely."

"You're saying, never trust a metaphor. Old news. I knew that and do that. What about wise counsel?"

"My wise counsel is precise and concise. Don't step on the cracks."

"More old news. I already observe that caution, albeit not by intention but by circumstance. Can you, perhaps, offer wise counsel on wise cracks?"

"I wouldn't step on those either, if I were you. Timing is everything. You'll have to watch your timing."

"How can I watch my timing when I don't have any?"

"That's a good question but rhetorical. I will, therefore, press on. Your user name is brianh and your password is hallelujahbrother. All lower case, no punctuation, no spaces. Having them ready when you're asked for them, which could happen at any time, could prove useful."

"Who's going to ask for them?"

"I'm not about to tell you. Even if I were to tell you, you couldn't count on it. All I'll say is you'll be surprised. But, of course, you can't count on that either. So either way, you'll be surprised, no matter what."

"And you say that the user name and password, will, in fact, lead to something useful?"

"I didn't say that. I said could prove useful. Let me add that what's useful to me may not be useful to you. So at the appropriate time, you'll have to judge for yourself what's useful."

"What's the appropriate time?"

"You'll have to judge that for yourself, too."

"I don't get to do much judging. That might be interesting. Pragmatism. What about pragmatism?"

"Ah, yes. Pragmatism. I've encapsulated this for you in an aphorism. Now, note this carefully: Never forget that the flapping you hear is not the wings of an angel but laundry drying on the line."

"Just what I need, an aphorism delivered by a metaphor. What am I supposed to make of that?"

"Make of it as much as you can, as much as it takes, as much as you can get away with. Stop thinking 'angel'. Start thinking 'laundry.'"

"That's not very …"

"Hold on! Don't say helpful. We've been there. I don't do helpful. You know that. That's not what we agreed on. That's not what you asked for."

"You're such a needle nose. Spending time with you is no fun at all."

"It's not a barrel of laughs for me, either, kiddo. I do the best I can within the constraints of tradition. This is not a fun job. If you were in my sandals, you'd hate it."

"I hate it now, even without sandals. No offence."

70

London Calling

JEFFERSON has just heard from his literary agent in London and is sharing his news with Bessie and Ray and, of course, with his silent sidekick, immobile me. Jefferson looks disappointed.

"Well, I've finally had word back from my agent, and it's not what I was hoping to hear."

"That doesn't sound promising," Ray says.

"What does she say?" asks Bessie.

"She says there's a problem. A bump in the road, my agent calls it."

"Oh. Oh." Bessie and Ray say, almost in unison. That's what happens, I suppose, when you spend a lot of time together. Or if both of you have great minds that think ... well, you know.

"The long and short of it is that the publisher that's been considering my novel all this time is prepared to publish it. But there's a but."

"But what?" asks Bessie.

"What's the but?"

"But only if I rewrite the ending."

"What's wrong with the ending?" Bessie wants to know.

"Nothing, as far as I'm concerned. I slaved over that ending. I'm really pleased with it. But the publisher's people, the editors, don't like it. It's too meta in their opinion."

"Too what?" asks Ray.

"Too meta," Jefferson repeats.

"Too meta? What's meta?" Ray wants to know.

"Metafiction," Bessie explains.

Librarians know all this literary stuff. Architects, not so much. Coma patients on life support, hardly any. Still, I keep listening and learning.

"All right," Ray persists. "In that case, what's metafiction?"

"Well," says Jefferson, "metafiction is fiction that emphasizes the nature of fiction, explores the techniques and conventions used to write it, and analyzes the role of the author. That's according to Google. According to Jefferson Baines, metafiction is fiction that is self-reflexive. It circles around itself, examines itself, studies itself, and has discussions with the author as the story is told. Does that help?"

"Sort of," says Ray.

"He's teasing," Bessie says. "That explains it very well, Jefferson. Right, Ray?"

"Right. You look so pissed off, Jefferson, I thought a little levity might help. But seriously, what about rewriting the ending? Is that an option?"

"Not in this case because it would change the intended nature of the novel. I wrote it to be metafiction and I don't want to turn it into a potboiler."

"Where is your agent on all this?" Bessie asks.

"She agrees with me that the ending should not be rewritten. She's already looking for another publisher. I wonder how long it's going to take this time."

"That certainly is a bump in the road," says Bessie. "But you'll drive through it."

"Patience. Patience. Just hang in, mate. You'll outsmart the buggers. It will happen."

But in the meantime, until it happens, Jefferson is not divulging the title of the book or any information about the story. There are times when life seems to be one delay after another. This must be one of those times. We're, all of us, it seems, being delayed. And there's more delay to come. Wait for it. And when it comes, wait some more.

71

SATCHIMOTOMONKEYMAN

It's morning, afternoon, evening. Who knows? Who cares? I've lost track. I'm tired of keeping track. There is no track, alas, alack. But never mind. I'm not going to get into a bind. Right now, I'm trying to descend into silence and serenity. But it is not to be. In my head, a voice suddenly intrudes. It's not a voice I know.

"Brian?"

"Yes."

"May I come in?"

Polite. Well spoken. Who the hell is this?

"You are in, dammit. What do you want? I'm trying to meditate."

"Sorry. I had no idea you were into meditation."

"I'm trying to get into meditation."

"I totally approve. Meditation beats medication."

"That's all very well. But your unannounced, unanticipated arrival results in meditatus interruptus."

"I apologize for my bad timing. If you prefer, I can come back when it's more convenient."

"It's never more convenient. It's never convenient period."

"Never?"

"Never. It's always frantic in here and space is limited."

"That must be very stressful for you."

"I have no choice. I live with it. If I could walk, I'd have to watch my step."

"I'm sorry to hear that."

"You're in my head, you know. This is private property. You're trespassing. How did you get in here? Did someone lower the drawbridge? Did you swim the moat? Did you bribe the concierge?"

"None of the above."

"Who let you in?"

"Nobody let me in. I was referred."

"Referred? By who?"

"Whom."

"I don't follow you."

"Grammar. By whom?"

"Oh. Right. By whom were you referred?"

"By Milagra."

"Milagra?"

"You know her as Millie."

"Millie. Okay. What's your name?'

"Satchimotomonkeyman."

"Odd name."

"It is meant to be an appellation of endearment."

"Sounds Japanese. Are you Japanese?"

"No. I am Irish."

"What's your connection to Millie?"

"I am her Soft-coated Wheaten Terrier."

"You're a dog? Millie's dog?"

"Millie's deceased dog. I died three years ago. I was run over by a car."

"What an odd coincidence. So was I. And it was my own car."

"I was run over by someone else's car. I never owned a car. Millie has been telling me all about you."

"You talk to Millie?"

"From time to time. We stay in touch. I'm in dog heaven, now. Doghalla, we canines call it."

"I've never met a talking dog before, Satchimotomonkeyman."

"Call me Satch. It saves time. I am not really a talking dog. I communicate telepathically. I couldn't do this before I died. Once you're dead, of course, it becomes quite simple, especially with others who are deceased, comatose, or severely disabled."

"You must be communicating with me for a reason."

"Of course. All communication must have a reason. But this is a delicate matter. How shall I put this?"

But the delicate matter never gets put. Jefferson comes in to change my diaper and turn me to prevent bedsores.

"Never mind," Satch says, as he abandons the premises. "I will try to come back when you are not so busy."

"Wait," I say. But I'm talking to myself. Satch is gone.

"Hey, dude! What've you been up to?"

Well, what I've been up to is a delicate matter. But I don't know what the delicate matter is. Just as Satch was about to reveal the nature of the delicate matter, your arrival scared him off. Now, I may never find out what the delicate matter is.

Jefferson doesn't hear a word I say. He never listens. Nothing new there. And, of course, it's just one more delay. Somehow, I feel conspired against. Or manipulated. Or both, maybe. Is it possible to be both conspired against and manipulated? And if so, by who? Correction: by whom?

72

Farewell Hallelujah

You may recall that after my buttock-puncturing encounter with Dr. Roopa and the drug, zolpidem, my startling, two-word shout-out "Hallelujah, brother!" was abruptly reduced to a one-word "Hallelujah!" I'm guessing that the sudden dropping of one word, the word, brother, from my already limited vocabulary may have been an after-effect of the drug.

The late breaking news is that now, I seem to have lost my Hallelujah! as well. Or maybe I misplaced it. There's no sign of it around anywhere. In any case, Hallelujah! has disappeared, leaving me once again wordless and completely silent. I didn't notice it at the time, but in retrospect, I realize that my Hallelujah! outbursts were getting less and less frequent and then, before I knew it, the decreasing Hallelujah! frequency turned into absolutely no frequency whatsoever, which suits me just fine. Hallelujah! has taken wing and is gone. And for good, I fervently hope. I say, Hallelujah! to that. What does this loss mean to me? Not much. How am I affected by it? Not at all. Do I have any other questions about this phenomenon? Not really. But now, anyone who wants to have a word or two with me is out of luck. Unless, of course, they're seriously psychic, tremendously telepathic, or dead as a doornail.

No one has remarked on my diminished verbal status. I thought that Jefferson might have picked up on it and made a comment, but the change seems to have slipped by him unnoticed. He appears preoccupied lately with concerns of his own. At first, I assume they're about his novel having to go the rounds of publishers again. But it turns out I'm wrong. His preoccupation is actually with brain damage. It's become an interest area for him, and he's been reviewing an archive of recent research papers on brain damage and has discovered some amazing findings. Or as he likes to say, ama-a-a-zing!

"You may not believe this, dude. But I've been checking out some of the recent the literature on brain damage, and I've come across some information that you may find helpful. The gist of it is that in rare cases, cases like yours, brain damage can actually be beneficial. That's unheard of. It's never come up before. What that means is that inside that beaten-up head of yours, unbeknownst to medicine, unbeknownst to the world, you may have become a genius, with special gifts you never had before your accident. Can you believe it?"

Shock! Alarm! Joy! Of course, I can believe it. It explains so much. I am overcome with an overwhelming feeling of usefulness. What Jefferson is telling me would explain my remarkable diagnostic capabilities and also the incredible acuteness of all my senses. And it would also explain my sudden language fluency in Latvian and Japanese. Proof, at last, that I'm not just a diminished, depleted being, clinging precariously to a leaking life-raft in a stormy sea.

Need I say that I am transfixed and transformed by Jefferson's news and I briefly experience something I can only describe as rapture. Despite my debilitating condition, I feel superhuman. Within the inert figure, within the wreckage of the man I once was, I am a source of power, a serious resource capable of helping humanity, poised like a superhero atop a skyscraper, ready to save the world. But first, obviously, I have to save myself. Am I capable of saving myself and figuring out how to communicate all this in order to save others? It's a good question. I wish I could answer it.

"According to what I've been reading, dude, brilliance may actually have been bestowed on you by permanent brain injury," Jefferson says. "You may be what the shrinks call an acquired savant. That's somebody with extraordinary talent who wasn't born with it and didn't acquire it from outside sources later. It all came from within. These added abilities were already buried deep in the convolutions of the still intact part of your brain and the accident had simply unlocked them."

Now, if I could just unlock myself as well from the prison I'm in, I could get out there, be a superhero, do super good without being supercilious.

"This is really amazing information, dude. Listen to this. When the brain is injured, it tries to repair itself in a three-step process. First, it recruits still-intact cortical tissue. Then, it rewires brain signals through that intact tissue. And finally, it releases dormant potential within that area of the brain. In other words, savants may be unlocking parts of the brain that the rest of us with undamaged brains simply don't have access to. Sounds like science fiction, but the thing is that research has documented all this stuff. This isn't speculation. I'm going to have a talk with Bessie and Ray about all this and then, maybe they'll want to get Roopa involved. This could be exciting."

Yes, it could. Very Exciting. Unlike the metaphor, Jefferson does helpful. And hopeful.

73

WEDDING BELLS

THE DELAYS I've been sounding off about continue. Not a day goes by without a delay of one sort or another. The latest example of this is Jefferson's delay in sharing with Bessie and Ray what he has learned about the acquired savant syndrome that may have made me a secret savant. Jefferson is not to blame for the delay. It's the result of the decision by Bessie and Ray to get married.

After much discussion of the pros and cons, the risks and benefits, Bessie and Ray have finally decided to commit themselves to the institution of marriage and make an honest son of me. They're so full of wedding thoughts and plans that, as Jefferson discovers, it's difficult to get their attention long enough to talk to them about anything else.

The happy couple agree that it will not be a church wedding. Though not as irreverent as Bessie – who is? – Ray is only too happy to chicken out of church.

"I've been churched a few times in the past but now that, at long last, I've finally been reunited with my one true love, that's all that matters. That's all I care about. I wouldn't want to go through all that splashy stuff again. I'm not about to march down an aisle."

'There's no aisle in city hall," Jefferson offers. "It's a quick, no-frills ceremony but it's legal, dignified, and an accepted credential. That's how Inez and I got married. It works. Our parents were upset. My preacher father was particularly annoyed. He would've liked to marry us. It took a while, but he got over it."

"At our age and stage," Bessie says, "city hall would work for us, too. And, of course, we no longer have parents to please. But the thing is, we want our kid to be with us at our wedding. And, as we've discovered, moving Brian from his room is a huge hassle and has to be hard on him. So we've resolved not to do that to him again. Instead, we've decided, that we're going to tie the knot in the heart of Greenwood, right here in Brian's room."

Bowled over by this diabolically simple plan, Jefferson can't hide his glee.

"Wow!" he says. "You guys are brilliant."

"It was Bessie's idea," Ray says. "I can't take any credit for it."

Elissa has just come in and she grins broadly at the wedding news but then gets all teary eyed. Ever committed to protocol, she has a question.

"Who will officiate?" she queries Bessie quietly.

"We'll probably bring in a judge or a justice of the peace," Bessie says.

"Wouldn't you rather have a preacher?" asks Jefferson mischievously. "One of those roaming preachers who wander in and out of Greenwood could do it, no sweat."

"No way," Bessie says. "I'm not having any of those clowns at our wedding. This event will be singularly secular and one hundred percent preacher-free."

"I'll say amen to that," says Ray. "Now, all we have to do, is find someone who is not a servant of god but a servant of people and legally licensed to marry them."

"Exactly," Bessie says.

"How would you feel about being married by a magistrate?"

"A magistrate would be fine. Can we find one that makes Greenwood House calls?"

"No worries. We have a magistrate right here on the Greenwood board of directors."

"I wasn't aware of that."

"Not only that, he's the chief magistrate."

"You're talking about the mayor, Ray."

"Yes, I am. He's on the board."

"The mayor's not going to marry us, Ray."

"You might be surprised. I'll ask him."

Ray asks the mayor if he will marry them as a special favor. It will only take a few minutes, he assures the mayor and he doesn't have to stay for any of the follow-up festivities, if he doesn't want to. Ray is hard to resist. The mayor agrees. A date is set. It's in one month. No one asks me if the date works for me. All dates work for me. And I just happen to be there anyhow.

"It will be a small affair," Ray assures us.

"Absolutely," Bessie agrees. "No big hoo-ha. Just a few friends who know Brian. I'll make a little list."

The little list includes Jefferson Baines and his wife, the renowned cookie maker and X-ray technician, Inez Baines;

Elissa, the world's most taciturn caregiver; former street person and born-again student, Aurora; Latvia's loveliest couple, Andris and Lina Lapsa; medicine's boy wonder, Victor Roopa, and his filmmaker wife, Derrine; and serious psychic, ProfessorAngus Kerb, and his historian wife, Prue.

The list does not include Millie and her mother, Amos and his mother, Jacques of the many Jacques in the box, Lady MacDeath, g-o-d the metaphor, the window washer, Satchimotomonkeyman, assorted clergy in a variety of colours, sizes and persuasions, the eighteen-member Japanese tour group, or nameless and numberless, the hallucinatory monsters.

"Maybe, if we hear back from Millie and her mother in time, we could ask them to join us," Bessie muses.

But so much time has elapsed since we had any word from Millie, that I wonder if we'll ever hear back from Millie and her mother again.

74

WHERE DO WE GO FROM HERE?

THE WEDDING list is made up, but Millie and her mother are not on it, despite Bessie's thoughts of them, because, until they get back to us, we don't know where to contact them.

Before the invitations are sent out, serious psychic Angus Kerb replies:

"Thank you for your invitation. No need to send an email. We were already planning to come. And don't worry, we won't bring anything."

Then, email invitations go out saying: Bessie and Ray are getting married in Brian's room in Woodgreen House, a month from now on June 15 at 2:00 p.m. It will mean a lot to the three of us if you can come and be with us for this special occasion. No gifts, please. Your presence will be our presents.

There is almost immediate acceptance from everybody on the list except Andris and Lina who decline because, as Andris puts it, Lina is not well and cannot travel. He does not explain further. But sad to say, I already know what Lina's illness is.

Several replies are accompanied by the age-old query, what can I bring? Among the suggestions: champagne, finger food, hors d'oeuvres, smoked salmon, shrimp balls, Maryland crabcakes.

Bessie responds to the offers: "Thank you for your generous suggestions. But everything is taken care of. Please, come empty handed. Bring nothing. There will be guards at the door. Those carrying parcels will not be admitted."

Bessie and Ray review this message and giggle to each other. Guards at the door? They're having a good time.

As the wedding plans fall into place, Bessie and Ray become more accessible and Jefferson finally gets to talk to them about his brain damage findings.

"This sounds like science fiction, I know. But it's not. It's real science. There are clues that Brian may be an acquired savant and a genius. And I think you should maybe pass this along to Dr. Roopa and see if knowing about this possibility can be of some benefit in getting Brian somehow restored and operational."

"This is above and beyond the call of duty, mate. Very thoughtful of you. And very helpful. I agree, we should get Roopa involved. What do you think, Bessie?"

"I think it's a good idea. And I have another idea, as well. We should talk to Professor Kerb about working with Brian again to specifically try to find out more about Brian's possible savant status. If we have a secret genius on our hands, we should know about it and somehow try to exploit it to help him."

"I think you're really onto something with Kerb," Jefferson agrees. "I puzzled over Brian's sudden ability to speak Latvian and Japanese. I didn't know what to make of it. But in Kerb's interview with Brian, when Brian revealed he had acquired special diagnostic powers, the penny dropped. That's what finally sent me looking into the research on possible positive results of brain damage."

"Great detective work. Good on you, mate."

"Jefferson, thank you so much for this. Where would we be without you? You are a treasure."

"My pleasure."

"Ever the poet," Ray says.

"Or maybe just a rhymester," Jefferson replies. "Or a once-upon-a-timester."

75

Not Again

I'm conflicted. There's nothing new about this. When have I not been conflicted about one thing or another? Right now, I'm conflicted over all the recent information that I'm having trouble processing.

On the one hand, it appears certain that I am a so-called acquired savant with enhanced cognitive powers in at least two areas, medical diagnostics and foreign languages. And, in that case, who knows? There may be more areas of enhanced cognition and more languages lurking about in the still-intact cortical tissue of my battered brain that neither I nor my support group are yet aware of. Nonetheless, these cognitive enhancements may just be waiting to emerge and make me some sort of phenomenon. Or a freak, maybe.

On the other hand, I'm not at all certain about my mental status. It's true that I've been saying this off and on all along, too, but now, it seems to have come to a crunch with what I believed was the actual visit of Millie and her mother who then, turned out to be my daughter and Rivalda respectively. Was it all in my head? Was I making it up? Hallucinating? Dreaming? It was so real, so plausible. It dovetailed so well with my personal history. Rivalda could easily have been pregnant with Millie when, with good cause, she angrily walked out on me years ago.

But how can I be certain Millie and Rivalda were actually just here, when no one else seems to be aware of their visit? No one mentions it. No one talks about meeting Millie and her mom. It's as if they were never here, as if it never happened. Bessie and Ray are still talking about hoping to hear back from Millie, so they can organize the trip here for Millie and her mom. Bessie and Ray are still back in yesterday and I'm ahead in tomorrow that may not have happened.

Where does that leave me? Here I go again. I'm repeating myself. Were Millie and her mother actually here? Did it really happen? Was it a dream? A hallucination? Am I making it up? Is somebody else making it up? The truth is, I've been disappointedly trying not to deal with it, trying my best not to think about it, trying to put it behind me, and trying, instead, to go back to waiting and hoping like everyone else, to hear from Millie. I'm not sure I'm doing the right thing. It seems like pretty lame behaviour for an acquired savant, not to be able to deal with this. And even if I could do so, I still wouldn't know which way to turn. It's a dilemma. And I'm stuck in it. And now, suddenly, mid my dilemma, I am confronted with another dilemma, a bigger one.

It's the top of the morning. Jefferson is working on me, getting me set up for the day's inactivities, when Bessie and Ray come rushing excitedly into my room. Needless to say, we're surprised to see them at this hour. Noon is their usual expected time of arrival. They have come early today with news.

Cut! Just a minute. This doesn't feel right. It's like a movie that I've seen before. What's going on?

"Well, it's finally happened," Bessie says. "Millie and her mom have responded to our Serious Psychic Sought Google ad. We've been up half the night emailing back and forth. And they've accepted our invitation and agreed to come to Toronto."

Cut! Why is this repeating? It makes no sense. Is this a summer re-run or what?

"Wow!" Jefferson says.

"It's all arranged," Ray adds. "Plane tickets, hotel, driver, everything."

Ray looks at his watch and then, delivers the knockout punch line.

"They're in the air, right now. They'll be here this afternoon at 2:15."

Cut! Hold on. Is my mind playing tricks on me? Haven't we been through all this already? Of course, we have. I just don't get it. And it doesn't stop. It goes on.

"Awesome!" says Jefferson. "You guys are amazing." He draws the word out in his own Jeffersonian way. "Am-a-a-a-zing."

"This is exciting for all of us," Ray says grinning.

"Millie wanted to drop in on you, Brian," Bessie says, "and tell you herself that they were coming, but she's been having trouble getting to visit. Doing homework isn't working lately. She asked me to tell you."

Cut! This is definitely déjà vu. Very déjà vu. Déjà vu all over again, like the old joke. This simply can't be happening again. But it is. How do you fight déjà vu?

My room is buzzing with expectation. Everyone seems to be talking at once. No one is leaving to meet the plane. The limo driver arranged by Ray is picking up Millie and her mother at the airport and bringing them directly to Woodgreen. It looks like everybody's going to hang in till they get here. I certainly am.

Jefferson finishes getting me organized and brings coffee but there are none of Inez's cookies today. Inez is away at a radiology conference in Cleveland.

Cut! Why does it keep repeating? Who's in charge here?

"It will be 3:00 p.m., at least, maybe 4:00, before Millie and her mom get here from the airport," Jefferson says. "You'll be starving. Have you had breakfast? I can organize something."

"No need," Bessie says. "We're fine. We managed to have a little something between emails. I think we'll just sit tight for now. What do you say, Ray?"

"All good by me. Let's decide about lunch closer to noon. We can always run out and grab something, if hunger strikes. Right now, I'm too excited to think about it."

Bessie takes Ray's hand. "So am I," she says.

Cut! Not again. Stop!

Mom and dad. It feels like a scene in a bad play. I'd snicker, if I could. Still, I can't help being touched by their devotion to each other and to me, their baby boy, their big, helpless baby boy. On further reflection, maybe I wouldn't snicker. Maybe, I'd whimper. Or sob.

Cut! But all of this has already happened. I can't go through it all over again. But I'm trapped on some sort of film loop and it's making me loopier by the minute.

We wait. And then, we wait some more. The coffee keeps coming. The time keeps passing. Noon comes. Noon goes. The afternoon arrives. The afternoon departs. No one budges. No one mentions food. No one looks hungry. Elissa shows up for her shift. She is quietly excited by what's happening. Jefferson's shift is ending. He doesn't want it to end. He makes a decision. He's not leaving.

"I'm not about to miss this," he announces. "This could be a singular event, a magic moment. I want to be here for it."

"We'd like you to be here, too, mate," says Ray.

"Absolutely," Bessie says.

As for me, it feels like I'm in the middle of a family get-to-gether. Am I turning into a cornball? Or maybe it's a nutbar?

Cut! Is this re-run for real or is the film loop in my nutbar head?

"It's almost 4:00," Bessie says. "Where are they?"

"Patience. Patience." Ray says. It's his favorite piece of advice. He says it often. "Not to worry, they'll get here when they arrive."

"I just checked plane arrivals," says Jefferson. "The flight was right on time. They're probably hung up in traffic. You know what airport traffic is like."

"Hell, yes," Bessie says. "We've been there."

Finally, uncertain footsteps down the hall. They come our way and stop just outside the door to my room. Inside, the room goes silent in anticipation. No one speaks. No one moves. We are frozen in an expectant tableau. I don't want to brag but no one is more frozen than me.

Cut! Whoa! Wait a minute. What's going on? This is not the same. This is different. There's no sign of Millie. Where is Millie? Has she been edited out? Has she wound up on the cutting room floor?

Millie's mom enters alone, takes one look at me, freezes in her tracks, starts to cry, grows hysterical, and proceeds to unravel. And this isn't just post-travel unravel. This is high-up upset.

"Oh, God! Brian! Oh, God! I hoped it wouldn't be you. I prayed that it would be another Brian Hildebrand. Oh, Brian! Brian! What have you done to yourself?"

At this point,there are a lot of upset people in my room, including me. Among the most upset is Bessie who is trying to understand what's going on.

"What's wrong? Tell me."

I, of course, know what's wrong but can't tell anybody. Millie's mother manages to pull herself together and still sobbing makes her way over to my bedside where she stuns everybody in the room but me by what she says.

"Brian Hildebrand is Millie's father."

Then, she breaks into tears and then, despite all the daunting hardware surrounding me, she manages, somehow, to throw herself on me and cling to me, while continuing to cry. I am crying, too. Secretly. Privately. Painfully.

By now, it must be obvious to all that Millie's mom is my lost, long ago love, Rivalda Santiago, the light of my Cornell life that flickered and faded.

"But where is Millie?" Bessie asks.

Rivalda stops crying, gets off my bed and turns to Bessie.

"Millie, I'm sorry to say, died three years ago. She was out walking our dog, Satchimotomonkeyman. And they were hit by a car and both of them were killed."

Bessie is stunned. She finally manages to say, "I am so sorry."

And so am I. There goes my hope, my magic, my angel. Bye-bye, Millie. I can't tell you how much I will miss you.

Either by unlikely coincidence or by the unseemly manipulative machinations of some unknown but controlling intelligence, events have conspired to come full circle. Can this be the conspiracy Amos's mother keeps warning about? I wish I knew. Conspiracy or no, lo, Rivalda is back in my life, my not too lively, locked-in life.

It all feels so programmed, so automated. Is there a sneaky, hidden algorithm clicking away around here somewhere? Click and I'm a father. Click and Bessie is a grandmother. Click and my daughter and Bessie's granddaughter is dead and gone. Click and the hoped for, but possibly delusional, expectation of my restoration to wholeness and normality through the powers of otherworldly magic is gone. Click and I'm a man with no prospects and without a lifeline. Click and it's all a crock. And you don't want to know what it's full of.

And then, it's lunchtime and Bessie arrives as per usual with sandwich and coffee in hand and greets Jefferson and me.

"Still no word from Millie," Bessie says. "I wonder if she ever found our Google ad."

Now, I have two scenarios to contend with. In one, Millie is alive. In the other, Millie is dead. They can't both be real.

Which one is real? Which is a figment? What if both are figments? Where does that leave me? Nowhere. That's where I've been all along. But that was before Jefferson figured out I was an acquired savant. And now that I'm an acquired savant, nowhere is no place to be. Nowhere doesn't happen overnight. Nowhere is, after all, an acquired taste. It takes years.

76

WHATEVER

BILLED AS SMALL, or as Bessie calls it, a micro-event, the wedding, is, nonetheless, a huge success. Gregor Spitalnick, the mayor who officiates as a favor to Ray is, as noted, on the Woodgreen House board of directors, where he and Ray are friendly. The mayor is a short, skinny guy with exopthalmic eyes, a gleaming bald head, a large protruding adam's apple and a deep rumbling voice. He calls everybody folks. The media call him the no-nonsense mayor. They could just as accurately call him the non-stop mayor. He is a non-dithering, decision-making dynamo. He lists the choices, pinpoints the options, quickly decides what to do and does it. If he had a bumper sticker, it would say, Gregor gets things done, including, as it transpires, this wedding ceremony.

"This will be painless and it will be over quickly," he assures Bessie and Ray as they stand before him. "You folks want to get married. Is that correct?"

"Yes," say both in unison.

"Ray and Bessie, I now pronounce you man and wife. That's it, folks. You're done. Here's your wedding certificate. Four copies. You can sign all that legal stuff later. Who wants to propose a toast to the couple?"

Jefferson steps forward and raises a glass of champagne. "Here's to Bessie and Ray. We wish you much happiness."

Everyone in the room raises a glass except Aurora and me. She's a recovering alcoholic on the wagon. And I, at least so far, am a non-recovering coma victim on life support. How I would love a glass of champagne. Never mind. The room is filled with the chatter of best wishes and compliments and many clumsy attempts to applaud the happy couple with one free hand and one hand clutching a champagne flute. I do not have this problem, of course. I have my usual problem.

In the midst of all this happy chatter, at the peak of the party noise, the door to my room opens and in walk two visitors I hadn't expected. The din drops and then stops as all eyes turn inquiringly to the two tardy arrivals.

"Sorry we're late. The plane was held up."

The din rises again as Bessie and Ray greet the latecomers.

"Well, finally, you made it. Good on you. We're so happy to see you."

"Did we miss the ceremony?"

"There wasn't much to miss."

"It was bogglingly brief, serviceable rather than scintillating."

"Not to worry. The fun is just starting."

"Brian will be thrilled you're here. We kept it a secret, as a surprise for him."

Whoa! I'm taking all this in, of course, and it's a huge head-ful, I can tell you. The new arrivals, obviously, are Millie and her mother, who once again turns out to be Rivalda, my old flame who looks like a young flame. She doesn't seem to have aged. It's uncanny. She's just as I remember her from years ago. If I could breathe unaided, it would take my breath away. Not having had a heads-up from Bessie and Ray to expect Mille and her mom at the wedding, I am truly surprised and thrilled that they're here. I must say that Bessie and Ray took me in completely. They never let on that they had heard back from Millie and her mom just a few days before the wedding or that Millie and Rivalda were, in fact, planning to attend.

After hearing the name, Hildebrand, and having been filled in by Bessie and Ray on my unhappy circumstances, Rivalda quickly figured out who I was and what was going on and was able in turn to explain it all to Millie. Thus prepared, meeting me now, in person is no shock for either of them, no surprise. As it turns out, I'm the only one surprised but enjoying it nonetheless.

"Let's go talk to your dad," Rivalda says to Millie.

They come over to my bedside.

"Hi, Brian," says Millie. "It's me. I'm back."

"Brian's your father, sweetheart. It's okay to call him dad."

"Hi, dad," Millie says, taking my hand. "It's me. I'm back."

"Hi, Brian," says Rivalda. "It's me. I'm back, too."

She tries to suppress it but I see a little tear in one eye.

I'm glad you're here, I say in my head, expecting Millie to pick it up and repeat it to her mother. But Millie's not respond-ing. I'm not getting through to her. It may mean she can't read me face to face, that her psychic powers, such as they are, work only from afar, from Sedona, and lately, maybe not even from there. I seem to be out of luck as far as direct conversation with Millie is concerned. I am extremely disappointed by this turn of events. I shouldn't have counted on it.

Now, my hoped for, but possibly delusional, expectation of restoration to wholesome wholeness and normality through the powers of otherworldly magic, or who knows what, may be gone, may not exist, may not, in fact, have ever existed. Suddenly, my agent of hope is at hand, but my hope is not being fulfilled. Suddenly, unexpectedly, I'm a family man with no prospects and without a lifeline. I've been repeating that dismal concern almost word for word, lately, but continuing to hope it isn't true.

Bessie has been keeping an eye on me and my little family reunion and senses that there is a problem. She looks inquiringly at Rivalda who shakes her head.

"It's not happening," she says to Bessie. "Brian isn't getting through to Millie. She can't read him."

Ray comes to the rescue. "Let's get Kerb to talk to Brian. Maybe he can be the intermediary just as he was before."

"Brilliant," Bessie says. "We'll ask him right, now."

Bessie and Ray approach Kerb but before they can utter a word, he agrees to use his psychic and telepathic skills to be the intermediary between Millie and me.

"Happy to help," Kerb says. "We can do it right now, if you like."

"Are you okay with all these people here?" Ray asks.

"Oh, sure. Everybody's chatting away, having a good time, and we'll just chat away too. They'll hardly notice and it doesn't matter if they do. It won't get in the way."

"Brian will talk telepathically to Professor Kerb who will then repeat what Brian tells him, so you can have a conversation," Bessie explains to Millie and her mother.

"Hi Brian, I'm back," Kerb says to me.

Seems like everybody's back, I reply, showing off my powers of pattern recognition.

"Seems like everybody's back," he repeats to our little family group who look uncertain about what significance this has, if any.

"Brian. Tell me what you want to say to Millie."

Okay, I say. Anytime you're ready.

"Okay," he repeats. "Anytime you're ready."

"Millie, I'm glad you and your mom are finally here."

"Thank you, Brian. Sorry. I'm so used to calling you Brian. I mean, thank you, dad. I'm happy that mom and I were finally able to come and visit you."

"We talked about it for a long time, Millie. I really looked forward to you're being here. Before I found out that I was your father, I always thought of you as maybe having – I don't know – a gift of some sort, special powers, and I had this notion that you could speak on my behalf and somehow help me get restored to the way I was before the accident."

"I'd like to help you any way I can, dad."

"I was hoping for some kind of magical intervention. But now that you're here, you're wonderful but you don't seem magical."

"I'm not. I'm just your average, puzzling pre-adolescent. But maybe Albert can help. He's sort of magical."

"Albert? Who is Albert?"

"He's the window washer I sent to see you."

"I wondered who he was. Where did you find Albert?"

"I was doing my algebra homework and I just popped into his head. Has he talked to you?"

"No. He just hangs there outside my window. Sometimes, he writes stuff on a chalkboard. But I can't figure out what it means."

"You have to be patient with Albert. He's studying you."

"Why?"

"Well, you see, he's not really a window washer. That's a kind of disguise he puts on so he can look into people's windows without alarming them. Albert is actually a Zuni shaman from New Mexico and he has special powers, healing powers. He helps people. Maybe, he can help you."

"I'm not so sure," Rivalda says. "I wouldn't count on it."

Dr. Roopa has been listening to all this with interest. "An aboriginal shaman, you never know," he says. "Maybe he can pull it off. They sometimes do surprising things."

"Da," agrees Elissa, nodding silently.

"But I'm the only one who sees Albert," I protest. "No one else sees him. Maybe I'm making him up. Are you certain he's here?"

"If you see him, dad, he's here. The thing is he makes himself invisible to everybody but the person he's studying. Zuni shamans can do all that weird stuff."

"Right on," says Roopa. "Once in a while shamans can be quite amazing."

"And you really think Albert can help me?"

"There's no guarantee, dad. He said he would check you out and see. He never promises anything. After he finishes studying you, he'll tell you if he thinks he can help or not. If he can't help, he'll say so and just go away. Sometimes, when he's uncertain if he can help or not, he goes away for awhile and comes back."

"Why does he do that?"

"There's some kind of Zuni spirit mountain in New Mexico that he goes to for a second opinion."

"A second opinion from a mountain?"

"That's what he calls it. I think he goes up the mountain and meditates and maybe the second opinion is really his own second opinion."

"Well, then, I'll look forward to Albert getting off his rope and coming inside and talking to me."

The afternoon dwindles away, the din diminishes, the champagne runs out and the celebration loses its momentum. The party's over. I'm worn out, depleted of psychic energy. It's time to call it a day and ask Kerb if he can continue to help me communicate with my visitors over the weekend. Bessie is about to do so but before she can, Kerb volunteers to be available as an intermediary between Millie and Rivalda and me for the next couple of days while the two are in Toronto. Bessie and Ray invite all the guests to a midday brunch the next day at the Four Seasons hotel where Millie and her mom are staying. In the meantime, they troop off, taking the Sedona visitors on a tour of the city to be followed by dinner. Brian's room empties, and I am left to my own devices which, as I've said many times before, are ugly and unfriendly looking but life supporting.

Jefferson is the last to leave. "We're both fathers now, dude. If you prefer to be called, dad, instead of dude, I'll understand. Just let me know."

77

WHERE IS ALBERT?

AFTER LEARNING from Millie that Albert, the window washer, is, in fact, a Zuni shaman possessed of special healing powers and that he might, maybe, have the magic to help me escape from my coma, I watch my window with foolish ferocity and almost religious regularity, hoping to see Albert on the other side of the glass, squeegie at the ready. But there's no sign of the little, dangling man out there. Now, that Millie's hoped-for magical possibilities seem to have been little more than a product of my fevered imagination, I hang my head, so to speak, in disappointment and my hopes on something else; and at the moment, Albert, Millie's recommendation, is the only something else I have. Needless to say, I'm eager for him to appear again, and tell me what my prospects are, if any, for help from him. But no such luck. He hasn't been around for several days.

In the meantime, I have visiting family to think about and to be with. Having school and work commitments back home in Sedona, Millie and Rivalda can only stay until Monday. My reunion with them continues over the weekend, facilitated by the helpful Professor Kerb who comes every day as promised to enable communication. Mostly, Rivalda and I talk about the past, about what was, about Ithaca, about Cornell, about hockey, about our stormy relationship, about our painful breakup, about her pregnancy with Millie, and how she managed to deal with it while staying in school and finishing up her degree. Some of it is very painful for both of us and at times, as Millie listens intently, for all three of us. Every so often, there are tears but since I'm dry of eye and tearless, tears come only from two of us. Still, two out of three isn't to be snuffled at.

"Oh, Brian, you were such a self-indulgent schmuck and I was such a young, foolish, infatuated girl and desperately in love with you. I guess I never really got over it, never dated, never hooked up, never co-habited, never married, stayed single, and rebuilt my life around Millie and my work. But back then, when we were together in Ithaca, I watched you deteriorate and I became absolutely certain you were going to be a bum. I was terrified you were going to drag me down the drain with you. So I bailed. But as it turned out, I was wrong. You got your act together, turned yourself around, and became successful, only to be cut down in your prime by your accident. It's so unfair."

"Well, life isn't always fair and it's rarely free of risk. Random events can turn into disasters. In many ways, just being alive can be a crapshoot. Besides, I mindlessly brought the accident on myself. How brilliant was that? If I'd run over somebody else, I might have gone to prison. But having done it to myself, I became my own prison. Just thinking about it, gives you pause. It certainly gave me pause, permanent pause."

Millie clings to me and joins in the conversation at intervals. She's slowly getting used to calling me dad. Father and daughter compare notes about what it's like growing up without a dad and then later finding him, an experience we've both been through.

"Growing up with mom and without a father, I learned to be resourceful and independent just like mom. We had no time to feel sorry for ourselves. We were always too busy doing stuff, going places. Something was always happening. School was huge. I loved school. I loved books. I loved knowing stuff. Everybody said I was precocious. But I never thought of myself that way. I thought of myself as focused."

"Well, Millie, being focused at an early age, is, in fact, precocious. I, myself, was never focused or precocious. When I was growing up without a father, I was your basic jock. Sports were my thing. I ran. I swam. I worked out. And I was a nut for hockey. Bessie wasn't just a non-stop mother and father, she was also a rink-side hockey coach and manager. Life with Bessie was like a long-running sitcom. We talked endlessly, clowned around constantly. It was an absolute romp. I didn't really know I was missing a father until recently and retrospectively when Ray found us and I realized how much he meant to me, how much I loved the guy."

"That's exactly how I feel about finding you, too, dad. I missed not loving you. But I love you now."

"And I love you, too, Millie. Both of us got our long missing fathers back. But I got Ray, the wonderful. And you got Brian, the useless. You were short changed. I wish there was some way that I could make it up to you."

"You don't have to make it up to me, dad. I'm thrilled I found you, no matter what. Just do the best you can and maybe Albert will be able to help."

"My little smarty-pants says it better than I can," Rivalda assures me. "We'll be thinking of you all the time, Brian, and keeping our fingers crossed for you."

"And for Albert," Millie adds.

"And for Albert," Rivalda agrees.

"And we'll stay in touch and be back to see you again, next school break."

And then, they're gone, my one true love and my precocious child, back to Sedona. I feel a great emptiness, an emptiness even greater than my usual emptiness. I try to keep it to myself, but it's hard to keep anything from the all-knowing Professor Kerb who tries to comfort me.

"I know how you feel, Brian. But they'll be back and you may have good news for them by then."

"What good news? Do you know something? Please, tell me."

"That's really all I know at the moment. Maybe, if I met Albert, I'd know more. Chances are, you'll meet Albert before I do, and you'll find out what you want to know without my assistance. Still, I'll be glad to help, if you need me."

78

Unfinished Business

"My agent called last night," Jefferson tells Bessie and Ray when they visit today. "She has another publisher interested in my book."

"Well, that didn't take too long, did it?" Bessie says.

"To tell you the truth, I was surprised by the speed of the turnaround."

"Sounds to me like your agent knows what she's doing, mate."

"Oh, I'm sure she does. But, of course, now, we go through the whole exercise again. The manuscript gets passed around at the publisher's and read by who knows how many editors and then they have an editorial meeting, discuss the book, exchange opinions, and decide if they like the book enough to make an offer and, if they do, what the offer will be. This takes time. And all the while, we wait to hear from them. My agent is very hopeful, but she counsels patience."

"Sounds just like Ray," Bessie says impishly. "Ray is big on patience. You haven't been talking to Jefferson's agent, by any chance, have you Ray?"

The teasing begets laughter all around from everyone but me, of course. Which is kind of a shame because patience is all I have going for me. Or maybe it's not patience. Maybe it's just the lack of options.

"Never you mind, my love, patience got me where I am today," protests Ray.

Bessie can't resist. "Really. And where are you, today, my sweet?"

"Right here, precious. By your side and in your loving arms."

That stops Bessie's teasing but elicits Jefferson's.

"Would you two like to be alone?"

"Not right now," says Bessie, trying to keep a straight face.

"Maybe later," suggests Ray.

"Oh, come on, Ray, let's stop this nonsense. We're letting Jefferson off the hook. We must get him to tell us more about his book."

"Quite right. How about it, mate?"

"No way. Not yet. As I've already said, I'm not going public until I have the publisher's signed offer clutched in my hot little hand. That still goes. In the meantime, like certain others I know, I counsel patience."

There is more laughter all around. It's a giggly group.

"You are a rascal, mate."

"A charming rascal."

"Hey! That might look good as a quote on the jacket of my book."

79

THE SHAMAN SHOWS

"GOOD AFTERNOON, Brian," says a strangely quiet voice in my head. It's not a voice I recognize.

"I wouldn't call it good," I respond tentatively, not abandoning the edge I reserve for unknown visitors.

"How would you describe it?"

"I'd be inclined to call it a normal afternoon, which is to say, depressing."

"Depressing doesn't equate with normal, from my perspective."

"You may be onto something. It's all a matter of perspective, isn't it?"

"It certainly seems that way. Perhaps, I should introduce myself."

"That would be helpful, from my perspective."

"I am Albert Tusa. I have been watching you for some time while washing your window."

Albert's voice is not what I would have expected from the tough looking little guy dangling outside my window.

"I assume Millie has told you about me."

"Yes. Millie has told me about you. You're a Zuni shaman. And you've been known to help people. You were a great help on my window, by the way. It became very clear. But I haven't seen you hanging out there lately. In fact, I don't see you out there, right now."

"That phase of my investigation, the observational phase, the study phase, is now over. Having hung about to study you at length, from without, I have retired my squeegie, coiled my rope, and come in from the cold and the wet, so to speak, and am now in your head and studying you from within."

"I've been expecting you. I'm very pleased you're here. And I hope you're going to be able to help me."

"It is too soon to say at this point. In cases like yours, there are rarely any certainties and never any guarantees. We will talk. We will think. We will see."

"But you do understand my problem?"

"Of course. You are in a coma as a result of an accident and are conscious but locked in and unable to communicate. Your cognitive powers are not only intact but have actually been enhanced by the trauma, and you would like to be unlocked and returned to your original self, ideally, I assume, along with your enhanced powers."

"That sums it up."

"But now, there is an addendum. Your powers are not merely enhanced. You, Brian, are an acquired savant. Acquired savants are extremely rare. This is the first time I have the honour and opportunity to engage with an acquired savant. And to ready myself, I have thoroughly researched the phenomenon and learned a few things about acquired savants. Because they have been through a grievous ordeal and have been deeply marked and moved by it, acquired savants tend to be more empathetic, more compassionate, and more understanding of the human condition than the rest of us and thus are capable of making valuable contributions to their fellow man, especially their suffering fellow man."

"I would very much like to be able to do precisely that for my fellow man, if only I can get myself unlocked."

"Your unlocking could well prove to be of benefit to others, and perhaps, a boon to humanity. However, let me underline, that unlocking you is not without its challenges, among them, how to deal with your extremely troubled state of mind. Brian, tell me about your state of mind. Be frank or even brutal, if necessary."

"My state of mind. Well, let me put it this way. I'm depressed and dejected much of the time, but I'm stubborn as hell as well and determined not to give in. That's why I'm still around. That's why I cling obstinately to my difficult existence. It's not easy. It's an overflowing crock. And that's on good days."

"That must be very taxing for you. Tell me, are you rested? Are you relaxed? Do you sleep?"

"Rested? No. Relaxed? Definitely not. Do I sleep? I'd like to think I sleep some of the time but I'm not really sure. No one on my support team knows for sure, either. It's quite possible that I never sleep. I may be awake all the time."

"How do you spend all that time?"

"Thinking. That's all I do. That's all I'm able to do. It's my fulltime occupation. But since I'm not paid for it, maybe I should call it a hobby. Except a hobby is supposed to be a leisure pursuit engaged in for pleasure and relaxation during spare time. But I have no spare time. I have only full time. My time is full time. And besides, thinking doesn't provide me with pleasure or relaxation. So let's not call it a hobby. Let's say I'm a thwarted thinker fulltime."

"A thwarted thinker. Well put. And would you say that because you think full time, therefore, you are full time?"

"I recognize what you're paraphrasing but I'm not sure that I understand the question."

"Let me approach it another way. Do you believe that because thinking is all you do that this confirms that you actually exist?"

"I think, therefore I am? I've never looked at it quite that way. I think because I can. I think because I have no other options. I think because it's all I can do. So I'm not sure whether my thinking confirms that I exist or not."

"Brian, in this endlessly thoughtful but tentative and constricted state of yours, do you ever question whether you really exist?"

"Yes, I do, dammit. I do. I question it, often. And lately, more than ever. But the answer to the question always eludes me. The few clues I get are fleeting. I've never been able to pin down anything that helps me definitively make sense of my circumstances. And then, when I grow angry and corner myself, I get the creepy feeling that I may be nothing more than an idea in someone's head."

"Whose head might that be?"

"I don't have a clue. Sometimes, I wonder if it's my own head. And that's really weird. Is it possible I'm making myself up? How can I be making myself up?"

"There may not be an answer. Your circumstances are complex, Brian, and perhaps, even circular."

"I'm not sure what you mean by circular."

"By circular, I mean that your life, at present, appears to be a loop of some sort, a puzzle within a puzzle that I must ponder further. Perhaps, clarity will come to me."

"I hope it will. Circular. I haven't heard that one before."

"Setting aside your state of mind, for the moment, all I can say with certainty so far is that in studying you, I am confronted with two principal problems. One is the coma you are trapped in. This may very well turn out to be the lesser problem. The second is the problem of your existence. This problem may be much more difficult to solve. Even at this preliminary stage, it appears there is a serious and growingly uncomfortable possibility that you may not exist. That might account for the circularity I spoke of. Need I add that if you do not exist, it may be difficult for me to help you, perhaps, even impossible?"

"If I do not exist, it will be unnecessary to help me. If I do not exist, who am I? Where am I? What's going on? What's this all about? How do we resolve this?"

"I have yet to make that determination. There may be perfectly good reasons for you not to exist. Perhaps, you can shed some light on this. Can you think of any reasons for you not to exist?"

"Maybe it's part of the conspiracy, I keep being warned to be wary of."

"What is the nature of the conspiracy?"

"I don't really know. I've never been told."

"Who are the conspirators?"

"I don't know that either."

"From whom is the warning coming?"

"From the deceased mother of another patient, now also deceased."

"This would be classified as dead-end data and is not very helpful."

"She says it's all a conspiracy."

"All? All is far too encompassing for my limited powers. I can only deal with some."

"Truth to tell, I'm not sure there are any reasons for me not to exist. Having said that, I'm not sure there are any reasons for me to exist, either."

"You are fast becoming a conundrum, Brian. I will need to consider this at some length. Perhaps, it is wisest for me to retreat to the mountain for a second opinion."

"But that means while you're away, I'll once again be left in uncertainty. It will be an uncomfortable time for me."

"True. But take comfort in the fact that I will return with my findings. And then, perhaps, we can decide what to do next, if anything. Till then, remain resolute. Remain calm. Do not use the elevator."

"The elevator? I'm on the main floor. I would never use the elevator, even if I could."

"Just a little departure joke, a feeble attempt on my part to depart on a lighter note."

"My mother, who is a great one for jokes and understands what jokes really mean, says departure jokes are a sign of uncertainty."

"I am only too aware of this and for that reason make departure jokes only on rare occasions."

"And is this one of those rare occasions?"

"Perhaps. I am not really certain."

"Do I need to worry about your uncertainty?"

"Not yet. Perhaps, later. For now, I take my leave and we will talk again when I return. Till then, I bid you, good afternoon."

That's all very well for him. But I'd still call it a normal afternoon. Albert leaves. There are no departure sound effects. After Albert goes and I'm left to unhappily mull over his cautious comments, I'm overcome with the uncomfortable feeling that maybe, after all this, after all that's happened to me, after all I've been through, I really and truly and actually don't exist. Really and truly and actually? That's a bit much. What am I saying? I really and truly and actually am beginning to babble.

What if, on the other hand, I do exist, really and truly and actually, but I'm not me? That makes no sense. If I'm not me, who the hell am I? And who are all these loyal, caring, devoted people around me doing their damnedest to keep me going? To keep me going where? I have to stop deluding myself. I'm going nowhere. I'm getting nowhere. I am nowhere. I'm in stasis, stuck, stalled, or worst-case scenario, stalling. Stalling? Why would I be stalling? What am I avoiding? What am I afraid of? Question marks. Where would I be without question marks?

80

New Duds

LATE LAST NIGHT, unsung, unheralded, unbridled, unlikely, who should come breezing into my room but my old buddy, the late, lamented, now departed Amos, the Woodgreen wanderer. And to my great surprise, this is not the gray, shuffling, bedraggled Amos of old but a whole new Amos, a shining faced Amos, an Amos, resplendent in a dazzling new designer dressing gown of billowing scarlet silk with gold trim and – are you ready for this? – golden slippers. For a moment, I think he's about to break into a song and dance. Oh, dem golden slippers. Oh, dem golden slippers. They look so neat to walk the golden street. But he doesn't. Dispensing not only with a possible vaudeville turn, but also with the usual tentative greeting and rambling preamble that I've come to expect from him, Amos stands before me, strikes an open-armed, theatrical pose, follows it with a pirouette showing off the billowing twirlability of his spectacular new dressing gown and ends with a deep bow, a very deep bow. Notably inflexible myself, I am very impressed by his flexibility.

In fact, for a deceased person, his flexibilty is nothing short of remarkable.

"You like it?" he beams at me.

"Wow! I'm almost speechless with delight."

"I knew you'd like it."

"Amos, you are something else. What a transfiguration. I almost didn't recognize you."

"Who did you almost think I was?"

"I almost thought you were Yul Brynner."

"Who is Yul Brynner?"

"You should know Yul Brynner. He's dead, too. He was the king in the King and I."

"Oh, yeah. That Yul Brynner. Funny coincidence. My mother said I looked like a king in my new duds."

"So she liked the new look?"

"Well, she wondered if it was maybe a little over the top. But she was happy that I finally got a new dressing gown and slippers."

"I can't believe g-o-d broke down and got you a new dressing gown and slippers."

"Oh, the new duds didn't come from g-o-d."

"Then, how came you by such finery, milord?"

"From the red-haired rabbi with the English accent that you told me about, the one who came carrying a gift box and looking for me but got the wrong room."

"So the rabbi finally found you?"

"Well, actually, I found the rabbi."

"You found the rabbi? How did you manage that?"

"It wasn't that difficult. You see, he passed away recently. And our paths crossed in the hereafter."

"Hey, keep an eye out for Yul Brynner. You may cross paths with him, too."

"Good idea. With that shiny dome, he should be easy to recognize."

"Right on. You'll be able to compare dressing gowns."

"That might be fun."

"Shame about the rabbi's passing. He was still a young man."

"Yeah, well, young, old, there's no telling who's going to pack it in next. Like my mother says, it's all a crapshoot."

"I thought she said it was all a conspiracy."

"That too. These things are not mutually exclusive."

"True. Exclusive, maybe. But not necessarily mutually."

"Anyhow, there he was, the rabbi, still toting that beautifully wrapped gift box."

"And you recognized each other?"

"Not at first. But the gift box rang a bell. So I introduced myself. Amos, here, I said. And he said, Armani, one size fits all, and handed me the box. That's when I knew for sure, that he was the same rabbi."

"And did you ever find out if your Roman Catholic mother was a member of the rabbi's congregation?"

"I asked her about that and she said that she never heard of the rabbi and had never talked to him about getting me a new dressing gown and slippers. The only one she had talked to about the new dressing gown and slippers was g-o-d and he told her he wasn't a clothing store, didn't do wardrobe, and to get lost."

"Well, that is a conundrum, then, isn't it?"

"Maybe, g-o-d told the rabbi about the dressing gown and slippers."

"That would be another conundrum."

"That would make it two conundrums."

"Not to change the subject but I notice with some surprise, that you're not carrying the shopping bag with the manuscript of your novel."

"Oh, yeah. Right. It's gone to the publisher. I have a publishing deal. The book will be out in April."

"Congratulations. April 1, right?"

"Right. How did you know?"

"Just a foolish guess. That makes it three conundrums."

"I stopped counting."

"Maybe it's just as well."

"Gotta go. I'm giving a reading at a writer's workshop."

"That'll be four conundrums. Thanks for sharing your new duds with me. And, of course, your conundrums."

"My pleasure. What are friends for? I'll invite you to my book launch."

"Sounds like fun. Wish I was mobile. Love to go."

"Oh yeah. I forgot about that. Maybe we could have the book launch right here in Brian's room."

"Why not? It's already a travel destination. And we just had a wedding here. Hey! Brian's room is turning into an events venue. Why not a book launch?"

"I'll suggest it to my publisher. Anyway, I'm off."

"Maybe, we both are."

81

Patchwork

Throughout all of the foregoing, the remarkable and relentless Dr. Roopa stays on my case and, every so often, trots out a treatment plan he hopes will pry me from my prison. His latest hoped-for breakthrough is an experimental drug still in clinical trials. It's called Resurrex. A cleverly suggestive name for a pharmaceutical, I think to myself, only later recognizing its cunning ambiguity.

"Resurrex is another one of those drugs with an unprepossessing provenance," Roopa explains. "It came out of a clogged sink drain in a Pittsburgh hospital. Despite what was believed to be scrupulous sanitation, hospital inpatients were somehow being infected with hitherto unknown bacteria that they had not brought into the hospital with them. These mystery bacteria appeared to be coming from somewhere inside the hospital but for an alarming length of time, the precise point of origin eluded the bacteria trackers. Finally, in a concerted effort dubbed Sink Drain Week, the drains in all the hospital sinks were meticulously inspected and all but one was cleared of clogs and suspicion. The single suspicious drain had an odd clot of sludge in it that was retrieved and sent to the lab for analysis. And sure enough, the sludge harbored a colony of hitherto unknown bacteria capable of causing respiratory infections that could be life threatening to the very young, the very old, and the frail.

"Fortunately, when the pitts bacteria, as they were called, were treated with a recently developed antibiotic, they quickly expired well before their due date. But in expiring, they exuded a strange, green, viscous liquid. This green liquid exhibited a few peculiar characteristics. It never dried, never evaporated, becoming instead fluorescent. Tested extensively in the lab on mice in induced coma, it woke them for long periods, often for as long as four weeks. Given the name Resurrex, it was then tested in clinical trials on humans in PVS, and it also woke them for equally long periods. In males, however, there was an unanticipated side effect."

"Now, hold on, mate," interrupts Ray. "We're not going to have to worry about another long list of side effects, are we?"

"No. No long list this time. There's just one side effect. It's puzzling but I wouldn't call it problematic."

"Let's have it," interjects Bessie.

"Besides," continues Roopa, "Resurrex is easy to use. No painful injections in the butt this time. It's applied with a skin patch on the abdomen and it stays on as long as it's effective. Four weeks is the best time so far."

"Stop stalling, mate. What's the side effect? Out with it." Ray insists.

"Well, the side effect, only in males, mind, is …" he hesitates.

"Is what?"

"Is an erection."

"An erection? Is that all? Well, that's no big deal."

"Actually, it is a big deal, in a way. It's a rather large erection."

"Next thing you're going to tell us is that Resurrex grows hair on billiard balls and can also be used to treat erectile dysfunction in kangaroos," says Ray laughing.

"Well, no, I'm not," Roopa laughs back.

"All right, then," Bessie says. "You've had your little laugh. Let's have the rest of the story."

"The rest of the story is that it's long-term."

"You already told us that, mate. The patient is awake for up to four weeks."

"I'm talking about the erection. It lasts all the time the skin patch is on."

"Four weeks?"

"As much as four weeks. Right."

"That's a bit much, isn't it?"

"It depends on whom you're talking to. Some lads would be delighted."

"We're talking about my kid," Bessie says. "He's no lad. He hasn't been a lad for years."

"And he can't talk back, mate. We have to protect him from embarrassment."

"I agree with Ray. It doesn't seem right, somehow, doing this to him in his present circumstances."

"Now, hold on, both of you. Brian might be okay with it."

"All right. Ray, why don't we get Professor Kerb to come in and work with Brian, so we can get Brian's take on this?"

"Good idea. I'll call him."

"You may not have to. He may call us."

At that very moment, Ray's cell phone rings. And, of course, it's Professor Kerb.

"Long-term erection?" Kerb says and Ray repeats. "That's a new area for me. I'll be there to talk to Brian later this afternoon, about three, if that works for you."

Bessie nods to Ray in agreement.

"Three is good. Let's go for it," says Ray.

Roopa has been thinking. "There's just one more thing," he says.

"Don't tell me. Not another side effect?" groans Ray.

"Not really. It's part of the same side effect."

"Well, come on. Let's get it over with, mate."

"The large, long-term erection is accompanied by fluorescence."

"Fluorescence?" Bessie repeats. "What does that mean?" She doesn't sound pleased.

"It's a sort of blue glow just like the Resurrex itself."

"A blue glow? Wait a minute." Bessie and Ray say in unison.

"Not too worry. It has no effect on the patient and goes away when the patch is removed."

"But while the patch is on, Brian will be all lit up and pointing at the sky like the CN Tower," Bessie says. "I'm not sure he's going to like that."

"Let's not decide for him," Ray suggests. "We'll find out what Brian thinks when Kerb gets here."

'Wait a minute," Jefferson suddenly says. "We're forgetting something. The catheter. What about the catheter?"

"We haven't forgotten it. All the patients in the trial so far have had catheters."

"And they stayed in place during the trial?"

"Right."

"No discomfort, no pain?"

"None. The catheter continues to work normally. The only difference is that it fluoresces blue like the erection itself. But that's it."

Ray clears his throat uncomfortably but says nothing.

"Oh, dear," Bessie says

"I'm sorry I asked," Jefferson says.

"Not to worry," Roopa says. "It hasn't been a problem."

Waiting for Kerb to arrive, I'm of two hands about this looming luminescent possibility that will protrude from my loins. On the one hand, wearing the Resurrex skin patch, I could be awake and talking my head off for four weeks, having lots of animated conversations with Bessie and Ray, explaining myself, sharing my thoughts, speaking on the phone with Millie and Rivalda, fencing verbally with Jefferson, feeling useful, maybe even helpful. That would be an exciting change for me and I would like that. On the other hand, four weeks of talk, talk, talk, with a large, blue, fluorescent erection sticking out of me, I don't know about that. I could look even weirder than I look already, sort of like an installation in an art gallery. Not to blow this out of proportion but if due diligence is not exercised, Brian's room could morph from the event venue it already threatens to become into a satellite of the Museum of Modern Art. I'm not sure I'm ready to be a modern art object. I'm not sure I'm ready to be admiringly gazed upon by hordes of modern art lovers. Or more likely, in this case, by hordes of modern art gawkers. Besides, even if we manage to steer clear of the possible artscapades that the Resurrex side effect might bring forth, a long-lasting, large, blue, fluorescent erection could be seriously distracting not just for me personally but also for all my caregivers who would have to work around it in performing their daily duties.

Any way you look at it, having a kind of light fixture illuminating my otherwise diminished and no longer used or useful loins, verges on the problematical and perhaps even the grotesque. As you may have noticed, I have not previously discussed my loins at any length, intending my tale to be suitable for reading by the whole family. I hope, therefore, that you will be forgiving of the editorial need to bring the matter of my possibly lit-up loins to the forefront at this point. The fact is, I'm not sure I'm up to the Resurrex skin patch treatment and its bizarre side effect. Still, for the sake of argument, let's say that I decide to stick my loins and my neck out and agree to wear the Resurrex skin patch and to co-exist with the startling side effect. Fine. And then, Albert comes back, returns from the Zuni mountain of second opinion and in that quiet voice of his earnestly informs me, "I'm sorry, Brian but you don't actually exist." Then what?

As I've declared, perhaps, too frequently, I'm already nowhere. And now, if Albert tells me that I'm not only nowhere, I'm also nobody, where exactly does that leave me? And then, another question arises: If I don't exist, what becomes of my large, blue, fluorescent erection? The question is right up there with the classic query: Where does the light go when you turn it off? In my case, where does the large, blue, fluorescent erection go when you turn me off?

I am pensively pondering all this possibly pending impenetrability when Professor Kerb arrives as agreed upon. Bessie and Ray and Jefferson and Elissa and Roopa instantly perk up and look expectant. This is immediately followed by an excited but redundant exchange of information with Kerb who, as we should be aware from previous encounters with him, has already telepathically divined all he needs to know. As we've discovered, though not always remembered, he usually seems to know what we know, sometimes, even before we know it ourselves. Nonetheless, he listens attentively.

"We'd like to try the Resurrex treatment on Brian to see if it will wake him from his coma for an extended period as it has done for others in clinical tests," Roopa explains to Professor Kerb.

Kerb nods thoughtfully. "So I gather," he says. He's very polite, courtly, in fact.

"But," Ray explains, "we don't want to do it against Brian's wishes. If he's unhappy or embarrassed by having to put up with a large, blue, fluorescent erection for maybe four weeks, we simply won't do it."

"Absolutely not, "agrees Bessie.

"So I gather," Kerb says, continuing to nod thoughtfully.

"We'd like Brian to tell us what he thinks, to let us know how he feels about it. We'd like him to say, yay or nay," Bessie says. "It's his life, after all, his body, his…" she searches for the right word… "his privates. His privates should be his call."

"So I gather," Kerb says, still nodding thoughtfully. If he sees any humour in this unnecessary briefing, he remains straight-faced and doesn't let on.

Am I alone in finding all this amusing? No one else seems to be amused. Everyone seems to be super serious about what the next move should be. But wait. In Jefferson's face I detect the slightest hint of what appears to be a suppressed grin. He and I seem to be in amused but silent cahoots on this. And it occurs to me that if I agree to the Resurrex skin patch and its highly conspicuous side effect, Jefferson's amusement is likely to know no bounds and to continue accompanied by his teasing me with all sorts of smartass comments. I can hear them already.

"That's a strange place for a nightlight. Mind you, that's a strange nightlight."

"Do you keep each other up at night, dude?"

"If Roopa gets you walking, you'll have to be careful you don't trip over it."

"I'm trying to get you into Guinness Book of Records, dude. But they wouldn't take my word for it. They're coming over to measure it for themselves."

My pal, Jefferson. He'll have a field day with my side effect.

At the same time, if I'm awake for four weeks, I'll be able to respond in kind, won't I? I haven't been able to do that for some time. A bit of banter, some snarky, sparky repartee, an exchange of punch lines wouldn't hurt. It might even heal. I could rebut Jefferson with a few zingers.

"Look to your own loins, knave."

"Don't be jealous, Jefferson. Maybe I can get Roopa to put a skin patch on you, too."

"We both agree it's awesome. But you just can't keep saying awesome every time you walk in here. How about anomalous?"

What the hell! The more I think about it, the more I think it might be fun to go the Resurrex route. Maybe I'll go for the skin patch and live with the consequences and also take my chances with Albert on his return. I may not get another opportunity to be this daring, this brave, this reckless, again. True, my bravado might do me in. Then, again, it might do me a world of good. I'm going to gamble it and keep my fingers crossed and my thighs apart.

"Well, Brian," says Professor Kerb, cutting to the case, "You've been listening to all this talk. How do you feel about it? What do you want to do? Are you game to go with the Resurrex skin patch and the possibility of being awake for four weeks? Or are you so concerned about the spectacular side effect that you would prefer not to participate in the Resurrex trial?"

I share my thoughts with my telepathic intermediary, and he passes them on.

"I've been thinking about it and trying to decide what to do. There seems to be agreement from all of you that it's my call. Fair enough. But, since all of you have invested so much time and love in keeping me going, I'd like to get an honest opinion from each of you about what you think I should do in light of the Resurrex side effect. And then, I'll make my final decision. Including you, Professor Kerb, there are six opinions here. What does each of you say? How do you vote?"

Bessie is the first to speak. "Brian, I have reservations about the Resurrex patch and its side effect. Having to endure a large, blue, fluorescent erection for as much as four weeks could prove to be an embarrassment for you and make you a possible source of ridicule. I worry that you could have all of Woodgreen troop-

357

ing in here to ogle you, and you might find it unbearable. I'm not sure you should put yourself through all that. Call this a mother's bias, but with qualms about the Resurrex side effect, I vote no."

Then Ray has his say. "This may be a male chauvinist point of view, but I don't consider erections of any kind, small, medium, large, very large, long lasting, blue, fluorescent, whatever, as embarrassing or detrimental to males. Erections, after all, arise only in the male. Erections are what males are all about. Erections are connections, the conduit to the future, the hope for tomorrow. And for you, Brian, trapped in a coma, you need all the hope for tomorrow possible. I vote yes for the Resurrex patch."

Jefferson is grinning broadly now. "I've voted in all sorts of elections in the past, but I have never before voted in an erection election. And let's face it, ladies and gentlemen of the jury, a long lasting, large, blue, fluorescent erection is not your standard, everyday domestic device. It's a standout, a once-in-a-lifetime phenomenon. It's eye-catching, it's mind bending, it's hair-raising and, above all, it's highly hilarious. And since it's my firm belief that humour heals, I vote, yes, for the Resurrex treatment."

Elissa looks very uncomfortable but carries on bravely albeit in a low voice. "In my country, an election like this would not be allowed. But I am not in my country, and I can vote what I feel. I have much sympathy for Brian, and I feel that in the long run the side effect of the Resurrex patch may be more benefit to Brian than the medication itself. My vote is yes."

"I'm not going to make a speech," Roopa says. "You know where I stand. Science must move on. Progress is not always comfortable but it's inevitable. If the patch helps Brian, the side effect will soon become little more than an amusing anecdote. Obviously, my vote is yes."

Professor Kerb is the last to vote. "Brian, I know you've already made up your mind to go for the Resurrex patch and to take your chances with the side effect. I commend you for your bravery and spirit, and I go along with you. I vote, yes."

Having already largely decided on my own and then, been bolstered by the majority vote, I announce my final decision.

"Thank you all for voting. I'm going to go for the Resurrex patch treatment and its side effect and hope for a happy outcome."

"We all hope for a happy outcome," Jefferson says. "There's nothing as happy as a happy outcome. That's either a quote or a cliché. I'm not sure which."

"Maybe both," Ray says. "But no worries. It's appropriate in the circumstances."

Bessie, clearly not happy with the circumstances, has that concerned look of hers but remains silent.

Roopa goes about his business. With a marker, he writes the date and time on the back of the Resurrex patch. The patch is skin-coloured, round, and about the size of a toonie, Canada's two-dollar coin. Roopa peels off the protective cover exposing the fluorescent blue Resurrex gel in the centre and the adhesive border around it and fastens the patch to the right side of my abdomen about six inches west of my navel. I have not spoken of my navel before, but this seems an opportune time to do so since there may not be another opportunity. No one talks much about navels these days. How times change. In any case, the

Resurrex gel feels cold and my skin tingles faintly. And I wonder if it's going to do more for me than make me tingle.

"That's it," Roopa says to the assembled around me. "That's all there is to it. And when the patch stops working, we simply take it off."

"And then what?" Bessie wants to know.

"And then, if we feel it's appropriate, we replace it with another patch. We can decide at that time, depending on overall results."

"But aren't we getting ahead of ourselves?" Ray wonders. "The patch hasn't even started working yet. How long does that take?"

"Not long. No more than a few minutes usually."

But actually, it has already started working. With no overture, no fanfare, I'm awake. I can speak. And I proceed to do so with great gusto. Or maybe, it's with unbridled brio.

"Hey, listen up, everybody! It's working. The patch is working," I say without the help of my telepathic intermediary who already knows what I'm going to say but doesn't get a chance to pass it along because I say it before he does.

Jubilation erupts amongst the voters, hugs, high fives, handshakes, back slaps, a burst of verbal approval, a blast of excited body language, everything but dancing. Even the worried Bessie loosens up and joins in.

"My kid," she says to me with a smile. "How nice to hear from you again."

"Mom," I reply. "You are still a hoot."

"You called me mom. I don't believe it."

"It was slip of the tongue, Bessie. I apologize. I'm not myself today."

"I hear you. That's all that matters."

"I'm so happy to be able to talk to you."

"I'm so happy to be talked to."

Chit for chat, the banter is contagious.

"Hey, dude." Jefferson joins in. "You sound like you've been talking for years."

"I have been. To myself."

"What about the side effect, Brian?" Ray wants to know. "Anything happening?"

"Not that I can tell," I reply.

"Would you like me to check?" Jefferson asks.

"Don't bother," Roopa interrupts. "The side effect takes a little longer, maybe a day or two. And trust me, you won't have to check. It will be pretty obvious when it happens."

Questions about the pending side effect quickly get pushed aside in the eagerness of everyone to talk to me and have me talk to them. And, of course, I'm as eager to talk as they are. In no time at all, Brian's room is buzzing like a busy restaurant. The sound seeps out into the corridor where the Woodgreen grapevine picks up the noise and the news and soon, staff from all over the hospital come wandering in for a look and a talk with the newly talkative Brian: physiotherapists, lab techs, nurses, cleaners and even some of the mobile inmates, both walking and wheeling. All want to talk to me and listen to me talk to them. I experience a strange exhilaration, a sort of rock star concert aftershock without the rock star or the concert.

I talk, talk, talk the afternoon away. My enthusiastic visitors grow weary and start to drift off. As the room quiets down, I remind myself that I want to share my latest news with Millie and Rivalda. I ask Ray to call Sedona for me. He calls and turns on the speaker phone, so I can talk unannounced and surprise whoever picks up the phone in Sedona. It's Rivalda.

"Hello," she says.

"Surprise," I say. "Guess who?"

"Omigod! Brian! Is that you? You're talking!"

"I am. Long distance. Sparing no expense."

"I don't believe it. I recognized your voice right off. It hasn't changed."

"It sounds like the old me to me, too. But I'm not the old me, and the talking won't last. I'm in an experimental drug trial with Dr. Roopa."

"What a surprise, being able to talk to you on the phone."

"I should be able to talk for maybe four weeks and then we'll see where we go from there. I'll try to talk to you and Millie every day while I can."

"Millie is just coming in from school. She'll want to hear your news. Hold on. Millie, pick up the other phone, sweetheart. You'll never guess who's calling."

"Hello."

"Hi, Millie."

"Dad! Wow! You're talking. It's so cool to hear your voice."

"I'm in a clinical trial. They're testing a new drug on me. I'm going to try and call you and your mom every day and keep you posted on what's happening to me."

"Oh wow, Dad, that will be great."

"Brian, thank you for calling and sharing your news with us. It's exciting to hear from you and learn that you're starting to make some progress towards recovery. "

"Well, I've got a long way to go."

"We're rooting for you all the way, Brian."

"Go for it, Dad. We love you."

"And I love you guys, too. I'm so happy I found you. I'm going to say bye for now. I'll call you tomorrow."

Promises. Promises. The next day, there are more developments, some expected, some not, and I don't get to make the promised phone call.

82

Out of the Darkness

WHATEVER ELSE our lives may be, they're always a jumble of variables and constants. Every life has its own jumble and every jumble has its own formula. The proportions vary, of course, life by life. In my so-called life, to take the example I know best, the variables are few and far too infrequent. The constants, on the other hand, the dismal, unrelenting constants, are countless, and they hang heavily on me around the clock. Obviously, my coma is the most constant of all the constants I endure and the most arresting. Literally. It locks my body in its iron grip and imprisons me in my own mind. And without fail, ever since my self-inflicted accident, my coma is always there for me (wrong! make that, always there against me). And my coma's constraints persist even during the occasional brief window like the current wakeup-and-talk breakthrough with the Resurrex patch for which I am indebted to Dr. Roopa and his latest medical intervention.

Other constants that bedevil me are the uncertainties that I have already at length lamented (all right! make that, whined about) like not knowing if I really exist, like not knowing if I'm imagining all this, like not knowing if I ever sleep, like not knowing if I'll ever escape this prison of mine. And I'm surrounded by more constants: the room that never changes, the devices in my life support system that are in me and on me and around me and never leave me, the tubes in, the tubes out, the whirring, the buzzing, the clicking, the darkness after nightfall that is the darkest darkness of all darknesses in which I now lie, a limp lump, only lately talkative, playing with the newest variable, my temporary ability to speak, by reciting aloud, in the best declamatory mode that I'm able to muster, fragments of verse and ancient shards of other writings memorized in my childhood or remembered from my youth and now randomly recalled for no good reason other than to listen to myself talk. Oh, how I like the sound of my voice. I missed it for so long. But finally, after an hour or two of talking out loud to myself in the darkness, I am reduced to utterances in which hodge is closely followed by podge:

"Mary had a little lamb and thought it overcooked. Little lamb who made thee? Was it the same maker who overcooked Mary's lamb? Only someone who sleeps around would lie down with lions rather than imitate the action of the tiger, tiger burning bright in the forests of the night. That's not a mural, that's my last duchess painted on the wall looking as if she were alive. The time has come the walrus said to talk of many things. That's what comes of hanging out with funny looking animals. Stone walls do not a prison make nor iron bars a cage. You should try to get out more often. Half a league, half a league, half a league onward. These distances are approximate. When all at once I saw a crowd, a host of golden daffodils. What were they doing half a league onward?"

Having recited my excited self into a mash-up, I'm worn out, weary of all the loud talk, my own loud talk, and slowly succumb to silence and self-contemplation. I think this is as close to sleep as I ever get but I'm never really sure. My eyes don't close, my mind doesn't drift off but stays in place, treading water or maybe air, and I continue my fixed stare into the darkness, seeing nothing but vaguely sensing something. What is it? I wonder. And then, so suddenly that even bad puns slip by, glow and behold, blue light emanates from the fork in the road about eight inches south of my umbilicus and slowly drives the darkness away from me as my bed bluelights up and up and up. And now, that I'm on the up and up, I know what's up. It's me. Oh, my! Oh, me! This cannot be!

Despite being newly able to talk, I'm speechless. What is there to say? Shall I allude to the lightsaber of Obi-Wan Kenobi in Star Wars? I don't mean to make comparisons since they are invidious even to those unfamiliar with the word. But as light would have it, the lightsaber of Obi-Wan Kenobi springs to mind. In any case, as I lie here in a pool of blue light, marveling at my new role as a fluorescent blue phenomenon, I think I detect another presence in my room in addition to my own and that of my newly lit lighting rod.

This presence is confirmed when from somewhere in the shadows beyond my patch of green light a quiet, vaguely familiar voice addresses me.

"Good morning, Brian."

"It's too early to be sure," I reply. I tend to be grumpy this time of the morning. Who the hell is visiting at this ungodly hour? What am I thinking? Aren't all hours ungodly? Existence, itself, is ungodly. Of course, if anything god comes of it, a retraction will appear on page two bottom right.

The unexpected visitor comes towards me and moves into the blue glow around my bed. It gives his face a somewhat blueish cast. Still, I recognize the wiry little guy in the faded blue windbreaker with a scraggly black beard, one raised eyebrow, and squinty gray eyes. It's Albert, my window washer cum shaman. He's back from that Zuni mountain of his with a second opinion and - wouldn't you know it - right smack in the middle of my clinical trial. I hate being overbooked. Too many things are happening to me all at once. Somehow, I feel as if I'm on a collision course and I'm not behind the wheel – there is no wheel - and there's no way I can steer myself out of it. It's an uncomfortable feeling. If I want to vocalize my discomfort, I'm in a position, at least temporarily, to rant, scream, growl, make ugly noises, but I decide, instead, to bite my newly loosened tongue and wait until I learn more about what's coming at me. Maybe later, I will vent. Good tantrums, after all, should be planned, thought through, rehearsed, otherwise they're just boring behaviour or bad manners. It varies.

"I have returned as promised," Albert says. "And since you are conscious and talking, at least for the moment, it seemed appropriate to present myself in person and speak to you face to face rather than as another voice popping into your head as I did on my previous visit."

"I'm glad you're finally back. But I must say you chose a strange hour to arrive."

"This was intentional. I did so in order to protect your privacy. No one is likely to interrupt our conversation at this early hour."

"Would it matter if someone did?"

"It might well. You see, Brian, at the moment, far too much is happening in your life. I thought it wisest not to introduce another complicating element."

"Permit me to offer you a bumper sticker of my own creation from my growing collection: Let us now eschew complicating elements."

"Well put. Sadly, I have no bumper on which to affix it. Unfortunately, I have never owned an automobile."

"Unfortunately, I have. But I was at fault."

"You speak like an insurance adjuster. But all that is backstory. How have you fared in my absence?"

"It's been complicated. I have not been able to live according to the bumper sticker. I'm currently in clinical trials of a new drug called Resurrex which has awakened me from my coma and enabled me to talk."

"I am aware of that. But what are we to make of this large fluorescent erectile phenomenon that appears to have taken you over? How did this come about?"

"This fluorescent phenomenon is a side effect of the Resurrex patch I'm wearing."

"An impressive side effect, to be sure. If it were to be bruited about, you are certain to be the envy of your peers and to be looked on with longing, as well, by members of the opposite gender. But to what purpose?"

"As far as I can tell, like most side effects, it has no redeeming purpose. Only I can give it purpose but clearly, I'm in no position to do so at the present time. And perhaps, never will be. Still, it may be a beacon of some sort meant to herald something. Maybe, it's meant to herald your final determination of whether I exist or not, based on the second opinion you've brought back about the reality or otherwise of my existence."

"An interesting speculation, Brian, and timely for, as previously promised, I am about to share my conclusions with you, if you are ready to hear them."

"I'm more than ready. I'm eager and hoping for something promising."

"Please, recall, that in promising to report back to you, I cautioned that I was making no promises other than to return. I could not promise anything promising, I said. I made a point of telling you that we – both of us – would have to wait and see."

"Well, we've waited, I've waited. And now, I'd like to see."

"Very well. Brian, I have pondered the mystery of your history and the severity of your circumstances at considerable length and with the utmost rigor in an extremely high place, a place so high I scarce could breathe and between bouts of semi-consciousness, it became painfully clear to me that you, Brian Hildebrand, are not real. You do not exist."

"That's not what I was hoping to hear."

"I am aware of that. But hear me out. You do not exist in this world. But you may, perhaps, exist in another world, a world of your own making."

"By a world of my own making, are you saying that I'm making myself up?"

"Not necessarily. Someone else may be making you up but not without your help. As they say in courts of law, you may be aiding and abetting."

"What am I supposed to make of that? I get the feeling that you're not telling me the whole story."

"I am unable to tell you the whole story, Brian. I do not have the whole story. It is still going on, still unfolding, still being told."

"But how will it end? What will become of me? Do I die? Do I disappear? Do I fade away? What?"

"Despite the intensity of my analysis, I cannot answer any of those questions at this time."

"That leaves me in limbo again. What am I supposed to do?"

"You are supposed to do what you are already doing - wait."

"Wait? Wait for what?

"Wait for a resolution."

"Albert, I don't mean to raise my voice to you. But you're not helping me."

"That is incorrect. In fact, Brian, though you do not realize it yet, I am helping you by encouraging you to do the one thing in particular that you have become accustomed to, and that is to wait. Simply wait. Then, as you will shortly discover, the world will turn, the oceans will rise, circumstances will shift, and you will be able to move on. Wait. That is my advice and my final word. And that, Brian, concludes my efforts on your behalf. And now, I must bid you a final farewell. Bon chance."

"Albert, wait."

"No, Brian, you wait."

And then, without another word, he backs out of my patch of blueness and into the darkness and is gone. Bon chance? Fat chance.

83

META LATE THAN NEVER

IN RESPONSE to Bessie's stubborn insistence that the bizarre side effect of the Resurrex treatment not be permitted to turn me into a sideshow, my support group commits to sealed-lip silence and closes ranks around me, in effect turning Brian's room from what almost became a gallery of modern art into a gated community. A hulking, hurly burly security guard in a menacing Kevlar vest jangling with handcuffs and assorted metal rings is posted outside the door to my room around the clock. Nobody uninvited, nobody outside my inner circle, gets by this large, obstructive person. No pushy press, no nosy media, no roaming religionists, no goofy gawkers, no tourists are allowed in to see Brian and view the fluorescent erectile phenomenon. My hardworking caregivers mull the matter and go a step further, shifting into reverse public relations. No tweets on the internet. No coy leaks. No raving press releases. No intimate, one-on-one interviews. Rumors are quickly run down, run over, and squelched. Just like my head. I'm still on my rack of life support, of course, but off the radar. It occurs to me that I'm not only headed toward possible non-existence, I'm already invisible in media terms. This is a conundrum too difficult to parse. So I'll be parsimonious and won't.

Despite all of the foregoing, I'm grateful for this strange state of affairs because, even though I'm still talking non-stop to those around me and also to Rivalda and Millie in Sedona, I've let myself become unhappy with Albert's dispiriting comments about my non-existence and grown impatient with the need to wait, wait, wait, for who knows what, what, what, if anything. Determined to keep talking as long as I'm able but not to reveal my dark thoughts to anybody, I'm careful not to rant or give voice to my complaints. Fortunately, for me, my facial expression and body language don't give me away because they don't exist, just like me. Don't exist? Just like me? What am I saying? Am I losing it? Or maybe it's losing me.

I may be going down the tubes, but my support system is intact. Jefferson seems to sense my mental state and takes it easy on the teasing while continuing to talk to me in his normally supportive manner. In my uncertain state, I'm enormously grateful to him for this.

For six days, I talk, talk, talk, and wait, wait, wait. But I'm not sure what I'm waiting for. Whatever it is, it doesn't happen. If I'm to believe Albert, I'm supposed to be waiting for a resolution. A resolution to what? What resolution? What does that mean? I have no idea but I'm getting pretty pissed off. I'm even more pissed off when on day seven I hear a low, insistent thrumming in my head, and I slowly stop talking, slip into silence, descend back into coma, and land up locked in once more in my battered head where I start talking again but only to myself. Been there.

Done that. But how can I be talking to myself if I don't exist? How can this be? Do I exist or not?

To Roopa, I still exist. He looks me over, checks me out, shakes his head in frustration. "I'm afraid Resurrex is not working for Brian. I'm terribly sorry."

He removes the Resurrex patch from my abdomen. The large, green fluorescent erection wavers weekly, slowly deconstructs, dwindling down into the wizened weenie that it once was, and the blue fluorescence winks weakly a few times and turns off.

Everybody, it seems, turns off. It's sad in a way, the end of an aura. There is a widespread lack of cheer among my loyal band of cheerleaders. Jefferson is silent, says nothing, but is clearly distraught. He's really hurting for me and looks as if he's about to cry. What a good guy. What a dedicated friend. I can't help but wish him all the success he hopes for and deserves, even if it comes at my expense which seems inevitable, since once he publishes, even if I don't lose my existence, I will likely lose Jefferson to literature or meta fiction as he has called it in trying to explain it to Bessie and Ray.

AND THEN, one morning, meta fiction arrives in a manuscript box, that a smiling Jefferson deposits without comment on the windowsill. His eyes are gleaming. He must be the bearer of good tidings. But he's not yet the sharer of those tidings and, once again, I'm in no position to ask. He keeps looking at his watch. He's waiting for noon when Bessie and Ray are slated to arrive. He's excited and eager to share the news with them and with me at the same time. Bessie and Ray show up right at noon.

This is one of their days to have lunch together. Jefferson can hardly contain his excitement at their arrival. Bessie twigs right away.

"You've gone and sold your book, haven't you Jefferson? I can tell. Congratulations, you lucky fellow.""

But wait a minute. I haven't told you anything yet. Are you reading my mind?"

"She doesn't have to, mate. It's written all over your face. Well done."

"That's wonderful news, Jefferson. We're thrilled for you. Now, you must tell us the whole story."

"Well, my agent in London called late last night. She has sold the book to Canongate Books, a UK publisher known world-wide for publishing only work of literary excellence. We have a contract, no cuts, no changes. Excuse the bragging."

"You've earned the right. Good on you, mate."

"You must be delighted."

"Delighted isn't the half of it. I'm almost hysterical with delight."

"We're so happy for you. Now, finally, you must tell us all about the book."

"Right. No more stalling. You've kept it from us long enough. Out with it. What's the title?"

Jefferson hesitates, looks at me contemplatively for a moment. Then, he looks at Ray and Bessie, takes a deep breath, and speaks.

"The NeverMind of Brian Hildebrand," he says a little too quietly.

"I don't understand," Bessie says.

"That's the title of the book. THE NEVERMIND OF BRIAN HILDEBRAND."

Suddenly, the air goes out of Brian's room only to be replaced by silence that hangs like a cloud over Bessie and Ray as they look uncomfortably at each other in what appears to be a mixture of suspicion and alarm. They don't like what they're hearing. I, however, have no problem at all with what I'm hearing. But no one is asking for my opinion.

"Then, your book is about our Brian," Bessie says rather curtly out of a stern face. "Is that it?"

"Well, no, not exactly. It's a novel. It was inspired by Brian. But it's about a fictional Brian. I made him up."

"Now, hold on. You call it The NeverMind of Brian Hildebrand," insists Ray. "And here we are in Brian's room. What are we to make of that? It has to be about Brian. Isn't that so?"

"Well, yes and no. I used Brian as a model, but the details are fiction, dreamed up in my imagination. I did my best to make them sound as if they came out of Brian's head but, in fact, they all came out of my head."

"Oh, Jefferson, you know we love you dearly," Bessie says, softening. "And you've been such an enormous support for Brian. But I have a serious concern that your novel, Ther NeverMind of Brian Hildebrand, may be exploiting our son's misfortune. We can't have that. He's our kid. We have to protect him from the harsh realities of a cruel world."

"Believe me, Mrs. Hildebrand, I love the dude as if he were my own brother. I would never exploit him."

"I believe you, Jefferson. But I must say, the title is a bit of a shock. It wasn't what I was expecting."

"Now, listen, mate. You've become like family to us and we trust you to do the right thing by our Brian."

"And when you read the book, I'm sure you'll agree that I've done the right thing by our Brian. He's my Brian, too. In the meantime, I think you should hold off and suspend judgment. For now, let me underline again that the book is a work of fiction based on my real-life experience with Brian in which I conjure up what I think must be going on in Brian's locked-in mind as he desperately wants to tell his own story but can't. So I make up the story and tell it for him in his voice which I also make up. It becomes a fictional first-person autobiography and a sort of salute to Brian. In actual fact, I'm not exploiting Brian. I'm exploring him. And in exploring him, I'm honoring him."

"Honoring my kid? Oh, Jefferson. What am I to do with you? You're so clever with words, so convincing."

"Being convincing doesn't make me a con man, Mrs. H. I'd prefer to be called passionate."

"OK. You win. Passionate it is. And I prefer to be called Bessie."

"I must say you make a compelling case, mate."

"The story is imagined but it's based on research I did on coma patients in PVS. The idea for the book came from several articles about new findings by cognitive scientists studying coma patients believed to be in PVS but actually conscious. The term the coma specialists use is minimally conscious. Brian is more than minimally conscious. He's fully conscious but locked in. In dealing with this subject, I don't mean to claim nobility of purpose, but the point of all this is that the conscious world simply can't write off the mind in coma and pull the plug. There can be a heck of a lot going on in there."

"Well, obviously, we totally agree with that, Jefferson."

"All right, then. Let's move on and read the book. Support the author, I say, just as you've been doing all along."

"We've been looking forward to reading it for some time, mate."

"Look no further. A hard cover is months away. But I've brought you a copy of the manuscript. You can start to read right away."

"Really. That's very thoughtful of you, Jefferson."

"It's the least I could do. After all, you two are the ones who have been really thoughtful. And you also helped me get published. I couldn't have done it without your encouragement and advice. Here you go. It's all in here in this tidy package, 383 pages, 90,751 words. I entrust it to your tender mercies and, I hope, wise judgments."

Bessie accepts the manuscript box that Jefferson takes from the windowsill and hands to her. She holds it before her for a moment, almost reverently, puts it on her lap, takes a deep anticipatory breath, and lifts the lid to look at the title page that she then reads aloud.

"THE NEVERMIND OF BRIAN HILDEBRAND by Brian Hildebrand."

Another silence. Another look of alarm passes between Bessie and Ray.

"What's going on here, Jefferson? You're the author. Why isn't your name on the title page?"

"What if I were to tell you that Brian actually wrote THE NEVERMIND OF BRIAN HILDEBRAND himself? What if I were to tell you he's the author and he channeled the book to me?"

"But how can that be? You just told us…"

"Wait. That's an option. There are more options. What if I were to tell you that I actually wrote the book but I'm using Brian's name as a pen name?"

"Why would you need a pen name? This is some kind of literary game, isn't it?"

"Maybe. Or maybe it's a meta-fiction game. And there's a third option. What if I were to tell you that Brian is positioned as the celebrity author and I'm the behind-the-scenes ghost writer?"

"Ghost writer? Come on, mate. What's going on here?"

"That's for you to decide. You have three choices. You can pick one. Or come up with one of your own."

"I don't know what to say," Ray says.

As the so-called celebrity author, I don't know what to say either and couldn't say it, even if I did know. But three choices? I love it. We're a great writing team, Jefferson and me. What a way to end to my circumscribed life.

"Jefferson, why are you doing this to us?"

"Maybe, I'm not doing this to you. Maybe, Brian is doing it to you. Maybe, you will have to read the book and then decide."

"You think readers will put up with this kind of trickery?"

"Well, I didn't intend it as trickery. It's fiction. Besides, right now, you two are the readers. Let's see if you think it's trickery after you've read it."

84

Closing Remarks

I don't want to get melodramatic at this point, but we seem to be running out of story. This really saddens me. I hate to see all this come to an end. For one thing, it's not the end I was hoping for. Still, I'm quite buoyed by it insofar as a non-existent person can be buoyed. I mean, after all, if I'm not going to exist, this is a hell of a good way not to exist and to be gone.

I'll take a few questions, now. You sir, in the toque, in the front row.

Do I have any regrets?

Yes, I do. I regret having to leave the people who, unlike me, actually do exist and who invested a lot of themselves to keep me going. I'm grateful to them and will miss them. Next question?

Do I have any plans for the future?

Well, I have to face the uncomfortable fact that I may have no future. When you don't exist, it's pretty hard to have a future. I'm not even certain that I have a past. I may hire a lawyer to see if there's some way to get my past back. If that works out, I might go back to school and study dentistry. I was always fascinated by root canals. I'm just joking. I thought a little levity might brighten up my departure.

We have time for one more question.

If THE NEVERMIND OF BRIAN HILDEBRAND is a success, will I write another book?

We'll see. I don't know if I have another book in me without Jefferson. He'll have to decide.

Excuse me. I seem to have a visitor.

"Hey, Brian. You're still here. I'm glad I caught you."

"Amos? What are you doing here? I'm on my way out. I'm about to be gone."

"Yeah, I know. I came to see you off and say goodbye."

"That's very thoughtful of you, Amos. Thank you."

"I'm going to miss my visits with you, old buddy."

"I'm going to miss you, too Amos."

"We had a special relationship, didn't we?"

"We certainly did. It frequently transcended logic."

"And time and space, as well. Let's not forget time and space."

"I would never forget time and space, especially when transcending."

"Right. And we had some great conversations."

"I think it's fair to say we learned a lot from each other."

"And you got your book published."

"We both got our books published."

"Well, not exactly. My publisher has just backed off, says the book is too long. He wants cuts made."

"Really, Amos. I'm sorry to hear that. What are you going to do?"

"My mother says it's all part of the same conspiracy, not to put up with any of it. So I'm looking for another publisher."

"That shouldn't be a problem. There must be lots of publishers where you are. They're dying all the time."

"I'm gonna check it out. My mother said to wish you a fond farewell. Give a fond farewell to Brian. That's her actual wording."

"Isn't that nice? How's she doing, your mother?"

"Oh, you know. Into polenta, makes it daily. Told me to remind you she was right about it all being a conspiracy. Don't rub it in, she said. Just remind Brian I recognized it first. She didn't want you to leave thinking she was just a crazy dead lady."

"Maybe she was smarter than all of us. What do you hear from g-o-d?"

"Not a peep. Silent as a lamb."

"Not even a bah bah?"

"Not even. Never comes around."

"That's really weird. Maybe he's been transferred."

"Yeah. By who?"

"By whom. But a good point."

"My mother says he's part of it."

"Part of what?"

"The conspiracy."

"Right. It's pretty all encompassing, isn't it?"

"It would have to be."

"I guess you and I won't be seeing each other again."

"Doesn't look too promising. Who's going to get your room, Brian?"

"No idea."

"Brian's room. Shame. It was a nice room."

"Yeah. It had a certain quiet cachet."

"And I could always find it."

"Right. Anyhow, Amos, be well."

"You, too."

Well, that's it except for brief closing remarks. Bessie and Ray, you've been everything to me. I love you dearly and will miss you. And Rivalda and Millie, that goes for you, too. It's hard to have found you only to lose you again. As for you, Jefferson, thank you, man. What can I say that you won't say better?

This is where the rope ends.

About the Author

MARTIN MYERS is the author of five novels, *The Assignment, Frigate, Izzy Manheim's Reunion, The Secret Viking,* and *The NeverMind of Brian Hildebrand.* His writing has been glowingly reviewed in the U.S., Canada and Britain, and praised by literary critic Stanley Fogel for "…its Barth-like interplay of traditional narrative and unsettling authorial intervention, its Joycean play with form, its catalogue reminiscent of Barththelme's experiments, its Nabokovian word play and its Borgesian awareness that reality is a construct."